BRATVA'S REVENGE

BRATVA'S REVENGE

TOM SLOAN

Copyright © 2024 Tom Sloan.

All rights reserved. No part of this book may be used or reproduced by any means, graphic, electronic, or mechanical, including photocopying, recording, taping or by any information storage retrieval system without the written permission of the author except in the case of brief quotations embodied in critical articles and reviews.

Archway Publishing books may be ordered through booksellers or by contacting:

Archway Publishing
1663 Liberty Drive
Bloomington, IN 47403
www.archwaypublishing.com
844-669-3957

Because of the dynamic nature of the Internet, any web addresses or links contained in this book may have changed since publication and may no longer be valid. The views expressed in this work are solely those of the author and do not necessarily reflect the views of the publisher, and the publisher hereby disclaims any responsibility for them.

Any people depicted in stock imagery provided by Getty Images are models, and such images are being used for illustrative purposes only. Certain stock imagery © Getty Images.

ISBN: 978-1-6657-5872-7 (sc)
ISBN: 978-1-6657-5873-4 (e)

Library of Congress Control Number: 2024906774

Printed in the United States of America.

Archway Publishing rev. date: 12/13/2024

TESTIMONIALS

Bratva's Revenge, the second installment of Tom Sloan's Russian Organized Crime saga, hits hard and keeps the punches coming. Sloan delivers a story wrought with intrigue, violence, and cut-throat strategy as though he were inside the Bratva trenches himself. A fast-paced plot and a plethora of dynamic characters delivers a story that will keep looking over your shoulder for a long time! *TJ O'Connor*, thriller and mystery author, *The Hemingway Deception*.

Enjoyed the new work. Fun read with tons of insider insights that any reader would enjoy. Also enjoyed local color references and the parallels I could draw between the characters and people we've known from our past (in the Secret Service). Having read the *Bratva Rose Tattoo* it was easy for me as a reader to jump right into the character/ plot flow…*Bob Degen*

"This thrilling adventure will capture the reader from the first page. The sequel provides a seamless transition from *Bratva's Rose Tattoo* where you will enjoy connecting with the same characters. Sloan's experience and knowledge gained from many years as a secret service agent leads to fascinating insights into how different agencies work together to solve crimes. A must read!!!" *Tom Farrell*

I don't read often and when I do I have trouble staying interested long enough to finish books. I picked up the book last night at page 60 and couldn't put it down. Just finished it. Loved it. And loved the local references as well…Best of luck with book. Frank DiTullio.

This book was so enthralling, I read it by flashlight when the power was out during hurricane Ian! *Sherry Ann Long*

I saved reading *Bratvas Revenge* for the flight over and back from Ireland. I couldn't put it down… Great job, I thoroughly enjoyed it. Thanks for my role at the Embassy in Guatemala. Truth be known I'm glad it was fiction. I also enjoyed the Cranford references. Well done!!!!! *Bob Cozzolina*

I thoroughly enjoyed your action-packed thriller! Right from the start, I was able to formulate a picture of the characters' images and the interactions they had with one another. I especially enjoyed your plot development as I couldn't wait to find out what was going to happen next. I couldn't wait for the Bratva mob guys to meet their fate! — Susan Catanzaro

DEDICATION

"Ryan Larkin loved being a Navy SEAL. He loved the teams," his dad, Frank, said of his son. "He achieved personal accomplishments beyond comprehension." As a SEAL Ryan knew he could make a difference, an idea born out of his visit to Ground Zero a few weeks after 9/11. Ryan convinced his dad to take him to the devastated site in order to walk through the killing field's evil destruction. He was fourteen years old. The walk cemented his fate. Ryan told his dad, "I am going to be part of the solution."

Frank was promoted to a new White House Secret Service position, and returned his family back to the familiar Annapolis, Maryland, where they lived years earlier. Ryan graduated high school in 2005 and within the ensuing year surprised his folks with a decision to enlist in the Navy. He wanted to be a SEAL like his dad had been. His mom, Jill, now pissed at her husband, thinking he was behind it, acquiesced. Jill knew Ryan. Following basic training in 2006, he attended Basic Underwater Demolition SEAL training (BUD/s), and in 2008 became a special warrior. Eight years as a SEAL exposed him to an abundance of "blast over-pressure" events. These occurred during training, as well as his multiple deployments to Iraq and Afghanistan.

The multiple blast exposures had serious consequences. During the spring of 2015, Ryan sought help for insomnia. He suffered, like so many of our nation's warriors suffer, from increased anxiety, memory loss, headaches, loss of coordination, vision problems, all of which progressively erode mental and physical health. Ryan was honorably discharged from the Navy in 2016. Tragically, the damage to his brain was done.

Ryan died April 23, 2017, "from combat injuries suffered in service to our nation, he just didn't die the right way," his dad lamented. "Ryan, like so many who have served us these past twenty plus years, was taken down by the insidious nature of invisible wounds…we lose twenty-two of these brave men and women a day." The prescient warrior instructed his parents to donate his brain to "Brain injury/Breacher's Syndrome Research," in the event he should die. At the time of his death, Ryan was dressed in his SEAL Team-7 T-shirt, wore red-white-blue board shorts and had illuminated a shadow box beside him with all his medals, insignias and other symbolic memorabilia. This book is dedicated to Ryan Larkin. Rest in Peace.

ACKNOWLEDGEMENTS

I AM FORTUNATE to have friends and family who generously provided their time to review my work as it progressed through the difficult, but needed, editing process. Foremost, is my fellow Secret Service (retired) colleague, and forever friend, Dennis Lynch. Dennis was not bashful about pointing out flaws in my early narrative. If they still exist, it is my fault and no one else's. Dennis was a partner helping me to produce my first novel, *Bratva's Rose Tattoo*, and the historical pictorial that celebrated the U.S. Secret Service's 150th anniversary, *Guardians of Democracy*. Others to whom I am grateful: Tom Farrell, Mike Cavalla, Bob Cozzolina, Sherry Ann Long, Frank DiTullio, Bob Degen, Susan Catanzaro, Mary Davidson, and author, TJ O'Connor.

With the publication of this novel, I seek to support another Secret Service (retired) colleague, Frank Larkin. The death of Frank's son, Ryan, inspired me to commit to use the book as a vehicle to raise awareness for veterans who suffer from military related injuries. We must, as a nation, continue to support our veterans who suffer, mentally and physically, long after a war's end. My own dad, Francis J. Sloan, suffered WWII battle fatigue, but survived. He gave his monthly disability money back to the government. More must be done to mitigate traumatic brain injury due to blasts ("TBIb") and nurture our warriors away from the notion of suicide as an answer. I completed this novel for them. I don't get a dime. Rest in peace Ryan Larkin. You didn't die in vain.

CAST OF CHARACTERS

- Arvydas Belov, former Bratva chieftain
- Alexei, Belov's right hand man
- Vladimir Emmanuel Belov, son of slain Bratva Chieftain
- Maksim Vladimirovich Dostoevsky aka: Max Bratva super hacker and mixed martial artist
- Frank Larkin, slain Secret Service agent.
- Will Strain, US Coast Guard Intelligence Commander/Captain
- Carly James Strain, US Secret Service cyber sleuth/SAIC Miami Field Office
- Vadim Kostenko, aide to young Belov
- Boris Makov, aide to young Belov
- Larry Cassell, former Director of the US Secret Service
  - Rosemary Cassell, wife
  - Dorothy Cassell, daughter and GW student participant in Guatemalan archeological dig
  - Bobby Cassell, son and US Naval Academy plebe
- Professor Michael Bligh, GW University in charge of Guatemalan archeological dig
  - Bernie McGovern, GW student participant in Guatemalan archeological dig
  - Sid Rosenberg, GW student participant in Guatemalan archeological dig

- ○ Tom "Chubbie" McCarthy, GW student participant in Guatemalan archeological dig
- ○ Bill Berthrong, GW student participant in Guatemalan archeological dig
- ○ Stephanie Zirgulis, GW student participant in Guatemalan archeological dig
- Evangeline Bozzuto, Guatemalan State Prosecutor
- Juan Villacorta, Guatemalan Justice Minister
- Gail Fitzpatrick, United States Ambassador to Guatemala
- James Solarski, United States Department of State Regional Security Officer (RSO)
- William "Bill" Davies, Baltimore City Police Department Criminal Scene Investigator
- Captain Luis Otero, Guatemalan State Police
- Mary Logue, USSS (retired) Office of Training
- Lou Granda, USSS Special Agent in Charge, Office of Training
- Jim Davidson, Mary Logue's husband, USSS Office of Training
- George Hamilton, SAIC-USSS Newark Field Office
- Lieutenant Savannah Riera, USCG Communications Officer
- James F. Keegan, USCG, Assistant Commandant for Intelligence
- Curtis Culin, USCG Commandant
- Mr. Garcia, Keegan's USCG aide-de-camp
- Jorge Christo, witness to the La Antigua massacre
- Sergeant Pedro Martinez, Guatemalan State Police Investigator
- Eli Polack, former Israeli Special Warrior
- Torre, Max's Pit Bull Terrier
- Tatiana, KGB operative
- Anton Abdulov, Annapolis Bratva operative
- Leonoid Baranov, Annapolis Bratva operative

- Pavel Agapov, Annapolis Bratva operative
- Admiral Donny Merz, Director of National Intelligence
- Colonel James "Holt" Bishop, Florida Civil Air Patrol
- Shorty, Max's best friend
- Ivan, Max's NHL hockey player dad
- Ekaterina "Kate" Petrov, Max's mom
- Charlie Gergich, NCIS Investigator
- Josephine "JoJo" Smith, NCIS Investigator
- Harper Rose, NCIS Investigator
- Shane Ryan, NCIS Investigator
- Raymond Schwartz, Navy SEAL
- Sergio Lopez, Navy SEAL Chief Warrant Officer
- Major Dallas Pope, Maryland State Police
- Rip Cleary, NCIS special agent
- Jim Brown, Chief, Annapolis Police Department
- William "Bill" Golden, Night Stalkers
- Michael "Mike" Durant, Night Stalkers
- Pam and Chris O'Toole, parents of the bride
- Emma and Matthew, the married couple
- Paul Swallow, Scotland Yard Intelligence
- Gina, USSS Miami Field Office receptionist
- Richie Deschak, USSS duty desk manager
- Rosa, salon employee who witnesses Carly James' abduction.
- James Thrift, Miami Field Office Deputy
- Jim Murray, current Secret Service Director
- Joe Savage, young USSS agent driver
- William Peters, GW University President
- Bob Cozzolina, DEA - Attaché to Guatemalan Embassy
- Officer Phillip Lomonaco, PAPD Officer (Uncle NJSP Phil Lomonaco)

- Ryan Greco, Chief - Cranford (NJ) Police Department
- Mike Cavalla, DEA agent
- Frances Larkin, first female USSS Counter Sniper
- Tom Fenney, Sergeant - Cranford (NJ) Police Department

PREQUEL

Literature is rife with descriptions of the Russian mob's romance with preying on the vulnerable through a vast criminal enterprise. Since the end of the cold war, Bratva has been the fastest growing criminal enterprise in the world. Historically, the mob was well integrated into Russian culture, even during the brutal Stalin era. Even he couldn't control the thugs, not on the streets, and not in the jails. The underground economy was too strong for any authority to control. Parents handed down the corrupt culture to their children to form today's Bratva. Their actions may suggest a lack of organizational discipline, but the international gang remains as cohesive now as ever. This is not surprising. It has recruited heavily from the dismantled KGB intelligence agency in the early nineties. This included from the former USSR satellite countries. Members of this red mafia hailed from all the 'Stan' countries: Kazakhstan, Uzbekistan and the like. They were educated, sophisticated and deadly. Some were Russian Jewish immigrants who relocated first to Israel after the end of the world war, and then on to Brighton Beach. It became generational. Jail was no threat to them. They were descended from an older generation who served time in Russian prison camps. They were tough and ruthless. Bratva's current generation seeks greater profit from all that is illegal and illicit. The Bratva is prolific; it proffers entire military arsenals through various international black markets. It manages international car theft rings and conducts human trafficking in an efficient operational experience. They don't just kill, they do it with malevolent glee, carving the human torso into sections, tearing organs out to feed to animals, cutting heads off and impaling them on relatives' fence posts as an expression of dissatisfaction.

PROLOGUE

The Saint Patrick's Day Parade had concluded, and the day had morphed into a remarkably warm, spring-like Thursday. Manhattan taverns were overflowing with Irish faithful. It did not matter; many were anything but Irish. On this day everyone was considered an honorary Irish son or daughter, and that included the Russian mob. Long ago, Arvydas Belov had adopted the day as his own. It was one of the rare times he allowed himself to loosen up with a few glasses of Guinness.

Belov celebrated his recent return from Aktau on a high note with Irish cheer. Ireland had been one of his favorite countries from which to identify and nurture KGB recruits, primarily harvested from the IRA, and a great place for someone with a thirst for liberal amounts of beer.

"Time to get back," he told himself. It was late afternoon, and he had dinner planned back in Brighton Beach. Belov thought the New York City subway system was the best way to travel throughout the city and could not understand why Americans didn't appreciate the system they had. "Shit," he told his friends, "If Americans knew what the underground transportation was like in Moscow, they would never complain about their own. This is a fucking Cadillac compared to our Moscow clunker."

He squeezed his way through the throngs inside the Irish tavern and clambered up the steps and out onto John Street, walking briskly to catch the Number Four subway off William Street. It departed lower Manhattan before changing to the B line, which dropped him off at the elevated platform onto Brighton's Sixth Street and Brighton Beach Avenue. He could do this blind.

He decided to head down toward the ocean for a walk on the boardwalk to smoke one of his Cuban Trinidad Robustos. Belov only smoked Cubans. He savored their subtle flavor and aroma. He never smoked anything that didn't have great girth and length. "Size matters," he often joked to his fellow Bratva members. He lit up, puffing slowly to stoke the cigar.

Belov, the previous mob chieftain, used to say, "If the fuckers want a submarine, we will get them one." He was speaking of the Colombia terrorist, turned drug organization, FARC (Revolutionary Armed Forces of Colombia).

Under a false Robin Hood-like narrative, the Bratva controls the Russian diaspora who live in the Brighton Beach section of Brooklyn, New York. The Bratva gives some of their ill-gotten monies back to the diaspora community in exchange for their loyalty. It is bribery, don't talk about what we do. And if that doesn't work, the mob silences those that speak openly about their corrupt business with a swift and grisly response.

"If you don't like the money, the Bratva will simply butcher you," Belov promoted. His message was not to fuck with the Bratva. The Brighton mob continues to control crime around the globe.

Biting down firmly on the Cuban, he crossed Sixth Street, not even glancing in either direction. Let others watch out for the Bratva chieftain. He walked over to Fourth Street and turned left, walking past the Miramar apartment building where he lived. He entered the ramp at the end of Fourth Street leading up to the Riegelmann Boardwalk and passed his favorite eatery, the Café Restaurant Volva.

He was slated for an early dinner with his sidekick, Alexei, but first he would take time to savor his Cuban and appreciate the unusually mild March Day. Belov thoroughly enjoyed these opportunities to be alone. By nature, he was a loner. The quiet afternoon also gave him time to evaluate the recent events in Kazakhstan. At dinner, he would share his thoughts with his cronies and then begin to outline the mob's future initiatives.

Belov had every reason to be confident about his future. He was extremely gratified with what he perceived to be a brilliantly choreographed abduction of the Air Force plane and the successful Kazakhstan exchange. "I beat the U.S. government at its own game," he said to himself, beaming with pride. "The money I agreed to pay in reparations was chump change. I would have agreed to pay more if they had pushed it. How great is this? An old Cold War operative can outwit the former enemy and continue a good life in the lion's den. Ha!"

Belov's thoughts shifted quickly to Max, whom he had not seen since Kazakhstan. The brotherhood had him sequestered in the Caribbean, giving him time to get his head together, but mostly, to keep him out of the grasp of U.S. federal investigators. Belov had arranged for Max to go to an exotic location at St. Martin Island.

Young Russian mothers pushed their baby strollers along the boardwalk, finding the mild afternoon as tempting as did Belov. Today they escaped the boredom of their bleak apartments to share local gossip while their lily-white faces absorbed the early rays of the year. Belov weaved his way through the maze of strollers, keeping as close to the boardwalk handrail as he could in order to avoid them. Nevertheless, the stare of one of the young women caught his eye. He demurred, and she quickly lowered her gaze out of both respect and fear for the Russian Godfather, as he was known throughout the enclave. They all knew not to approach him on the boardwalk unless there was an established relationship. Violating his personal zone risked provoking his wrath. His stroll was personal time, his time to think, and his way of fleshing out his schemes before presenting them to the mob leadership.

In fact, it was here he carefully developed the Kazakhstan exchange scenario - it took him only a few hours of pacing along the boardwalk to formulate the plan. Max's public arraignment in federal court for hacking activities gave Belov the impetus he needed to piece the plan together. Quickly, he notified the Bratva's lady operatives long imbedded at Ramstein Air Base to execute his abduction plan. It worked so effectively that he knew the United States would never want to let it be made public.

"Ah, better head to the restaurant."

Belov timed his arrival at the restaurant so he could savor the Trinidad cigar's dying moments. He picked up his pace. Stepping off the boardwalk at Second Street, he headed to Brightwater Court where he made a right, one block away from the Café Restaurant Volva, which was located directly across from the Benderskiy Motel. He had never liked that place; it made him uneasy. He saw Alexei waiting for him across the street, not far from the wooden ramp that led to the front of the Café Volva. He would soon follow up the cigar with his daily dose of a sixteen-year-old, single malt, Lagavulin whiskey.

"Today, Alexei pays," laughed Belov, under his breath, "He never picks up the fucking tab, the little bastard. But today he will."

He took a final puff from the remnants of the cigar before throwing it onto the street and aggressively twisting it under his shoe, flattening the remainder to a pulp then kicking the debris into the roadway. He straightened his tie, dusted the ash from his sports jacket lapels, and entered the pedestrian crosswalk at the intersection of Fourth and Brightwater Court, just fifteen feet from Alexei. Belov looked up at him and smirked. Alexei said something, but Belov never heard it. "Alexei is headless," was Belov's final thought. The top of Alexei's head flew off completely; the bottom seemed to dangle down around his neck. It all happened in a second. There was nothing left; no brain matter, no cranium, nothing. The bullet did its job. The thug was gone. His body fell limp to the concrete; the weight of the corpse hitting the ground pinched Alexei's wallet from his rear pants pocket. It bounced a foot away from the corpse.

Peering through a Leupold Vari-X-dot riflescope, the gunman took a full, deep breath, then released half of it before slowly squeezing the trigger a second time. Both reports were suppressed to reduce the noise and muzzle flash typically associated with the discharge of a powerful weapon. The shots were fired two seconds apart, and each bullet took less than a second to reach its intended mark. The second bullet struck Belov's head, leaving him similarly decapitated. His blood flowed liberally from the exposed carotid artery onto the street pavement. The streaming blood began to be absorbed by Belov's cigar ashes in a macabre euphemism: a revenge death has no dignity, except for the avenged.

The sniper had been perched in shadow at the Benderskiy Motel's third floor window, located a short distance across from the Café. The motel had always made Belov uncomfortable.

The weapon, an MK-11 Mod Sniper Weapon System was a standard Navy SEAL tool often used by experienced snipers. The 7.62 caliber round was well known for its devastating effect on soft targets. The bullet was launched through a simple, but explosive process that delivered its destructive load through the barrel's finely honed lands and grooves. From the distance between the crosswalk and the window, the bullet had expended a small fraction of its potent energy before striking, leaving an obliterated, unrecognizable victim.

The sniper efficiently disengaged and retrieved his spent casings. He didn't take time to gloat. He placed the weapon in its beige carry bag before he exited the room, headed quietly down the back stairwell, and made his way out to Brighton Beach Avenue.

CHAPTER 1

EARLIER IN THE year, the former Bratva chieftain and his lackey lay slain on a blood-soaked Brighton Beach side street, in the late afternoon sun. A local Brighton Beach crowd emerged, displaying little respect, as it encroached on the scene, attempting to observe as many of the headless corpses as they could before the NYPD units arrived. Several took to snapping the graphic scene with their iPhones. They were recording evidence of an event that would send a shock wave throughout the corrupt Bratva organization.

When word reached Vladimir Belov, the son cried for hours in a fit of uncontrollable, dark emotion. He had last seen his father in Saudi Arabia at a formerly secret U.S. airbase. There, less than two months earlier, his father's plan to force down an American Air Force cargo plane containing U.S. government personnel and military assets had been brilliantly executed. The cargo plane, on its way to support a presidential visit in Kuwait, became Belov's asset. He used it to force the United States to liberate a jailed Bratva protégée, super hacker Maksim Vladimirovich Dostoevsky.

Maksim Vladimirovich Dostoevsky was known to his friends as Max. The handsome brawler with the blue eyes, blonde hair, and a chiseled body was barely in his mid-twenties. He thrilled in the drama of violent physical competition, man against man, just like the father he never knew who came to the U.S. from the Soviet Union in 1990 to become a National Hockey League standout. Max inherited his father's intense focus. He was a physical and cerebral standout, in and out of the ring.

Max, global hacker extraordinaire, enjoyed gaining covert entry into closed network systems, and not only for entertainment, but to make money. The endgame for cyber criminals, according to law enforcement sources, is to take full control of a computer system and use it to help carry out on-line thefts and scams. This was true for most hackers, but for Max the cyber experience was much more. His included forays into secure systems – credit card processors, on-line banks, e-businesses, and less lucrative but very seductive government systems. The Russian hacking sites were known to be the best; the most sophisticated hackers relied on them. These were portal sites or carding sites that openly advertised their services. Max knew them all. Displayed on these portals were thousands of openly posted announcements offering to buy or sell stolen credit card data or credit card tracking data for white plastic cards used simply to exploit the stolen data still resident on an active credit card.

While at the Saudi airport, the Bratva chieftain embraced his son, Vladimir, with a tight, emphatic hug, kissing him on both cheeks before congratulating him on the deadly decision to take out Secret Service Agent Frank Larkin while the American cargo plane was being emptied. Larkin, a trained counter assault agent, was shot as he exited the plane by Belov's son, who took Larkin out with one shot.

"Immanuel," his father said using the son's formal name, "the agent made a fatal decision to challenge our takeover. It was his doing; you performed admirably, my son, and I am proud of you. Your decision only strengthens my belief that you will soon take control of our Bratva and lead it to an even greater global footprint."

Arvydas Belov's biological son knew his father had a great affection for an adopted son. It was Max, whom Belov often referred to as "the son of Bratva." Max, as a young man under Belov's paternalistic nurturing, morphed into a savant hacker and a distinguished, feared mixed martial arts champion. He may not have been "blood," but he had been cherished by the deceased Bratva chieftain. Max knew the fondness Belov had for him and had respected Belov until he learned the dark history of what happened to his parents. Belov did not know that Max became aware that it was Belov who had his dad brutally murdered. Max learned about the truth from Coast Guard Commander Will Strain, a United States Intelligence operative. Strain led the U.S. effort to successfully negotiate the liberation of the cargo plane's passengers, which included the Commander's wife, Carly Strain.

"Max," Strain had told him, "There is a deep, dark Bratva secret your Belov does not want you to know. Belov ordered the murders of your parents when you were an infant." Max's dad had been an upcoming, talented Russian hockey player who courageously refused to "throw" NHL games for the Bratva. Max's dad was an emigre from Russia playing professionally for the New York Rangers. He wore the honor of playing for the NHL with unmitigated pride, not to be disgraced. Commander Strain's comments only confirmed what Max had always suspected. During the ensuing weeks, Max elected to keep a low profile within the cabal to assess his future with it. This kept him off Vladimir's radar and allowed him to enhance his new relationship with Will Strain. He liked the guy.

CHAPTER 2

UNLIKE THE ITALIAN Costra Nostra, the Bratva is not a top-down command and control organization. The Bratva built a highly complex human structure so that it can survive the loss of a leader. When Belov was assassinated the Bratva engaged in a search for its new leader. What may have looked chaotic was, in fact, an orderly process of elimination to identify the strongest chieftain. Belov's son, Vladimir, emerged as that man.

"Tell the community, I am now the authority to all the citizens of Brighton Beach. That is all they need to know. I am their new normal. If they want to survive, then support me and do not ever challenge us," Vladimir told his loyal lieutenants. He emerged from the competition by being the most brutal. His ruthlessness ensured his control.

"I want these bastards that killed my father," he growled. "I want them dead. I want it to be painful and the more gruesome the better, and I want fucking photos to look at."

"The death of my father will not go unanswered, I promise you that," Vladimir lamented in a private thought as he sat in his Brighton Beach residence, mourning his father's death. Every shade in the well-furnished, but poorly lit room, had been pulled tautly closed. The new Bratva chieftain, also known as Immanuel or *Иммануил* in Russian, sat in his darkened living room that masked the tears trickling down his rose-colored cheeks. Only his father called him Immanuel; to everyone else it was Vladimir. Others didn't dare use that name and risk the son's wrath.

His thoughts kept drifting back to the previous Saint Patrick's Day, when his father, Arvydas Belov, the former Bratva chieftain, took a final puff from a Cuban cigar while strolling on the Brighton Beach boardwalk. There was nothing left; no brain matter, no cranium, nothing. The sniper's bullet did its job. Belov was not just dead; his body was headless. This remained a constant irritant for Vladimir. It enraged him.

"We will track down my father's assassins and we will kill them all," he growled to himself, spraying the seemingly unstoppable tear flow down his cheeks about the room as his animated head swung from side to side in anger.

Vadim Kostenko entered the room and stood silent in Vladimir's apartment as the grieving son continued to spew his angry rhetoric. "I want the bastards who did this to my father not just dead, but grossly disfigured. We will use every barbaric act to achieve this. I should have killed them at the Saudi airport. Unfortunately, my father's instructions that day permitted me only to shoot and kill the Secret Service agent. If I had known then that my father would have made a deal with this devil, this Larry Cassell guy, perhaps I could have argued against it. For some reason, my father calculated that exchanging the cargo contents and personnel was in the Bratva's best interest. All to get this fucking cyber whiz kid, Max, back. I hate that kid too, the asshole. I don't care if he's a champion fighter; I'll hit him over the head with a baseball bat if I find out he's not a Bratva player. Vadim, pay attention, here's what we know. Cassell and his people killed my father. And worse, shot him in such a manner that deprives me from kissing him goodbye. These bastards blew his head off," Vladimir screamed in anguish.

"Vadim, I want to know where Cassell lives, what he wears, where he works, what he eats, how many children he has, is he married, does he have any vulnerabilities, like other women or young boys, whatever there is for us to exploit, to get to him and destroy, not just him, but everything he treasures, like his family, particularly his family. And this fucking Coast Guard guy, whoever he is, needs to be sliced up and his wife fucked."

"Here we go," thought Kostenko, "I've seen him like this many times, and when he's on a mission, when he's focused, there's no diversion, no way to stop him, or slow him down. Whoever this Cassell guy is, he is a dead man, and so is the Coast Guard guy."

Kostenko knew it was far better for him to be within Vladimir's inner circle than outside it. He observed the son's maniacal quest to carry on his father's reign over the Bratva. Vladimir sent out a personal message that he, and no one else, would inherit the mob's leadership position. The message was not veiled, but rather a well-produced dictum that those who challenged his leadership would be dealt a mortal blow. As a result, an increasing number of Bratva senior leadership fell in line behind Vladimir. It would eventually endow him with the sustainable influence he would require in order to lead the effective and brutal global enterprise for a generation to come.

"Vladimir, you've had a pissy three days. You need sleep. We can complete the remaining arrangements for your father's funeral," advised his aide, Vadim Kostenko. "Go get some rest."

"I will go when I feel compelled," he snarled back without looking at the sycophant. "I don't need to be told what to do."

"Yes, Vladimir, when you are ready," Kostenko countered meekly.

CHAPTER 3

THE UNITED STATES Naval Academy is an undergraduate college that attracts a special breed of young men and women. Bobby Cassell wanted to attend the historic school since he was ten. His dad was eager to support the boy's dream. "After all," he teased his son, "it will save me a ton of money, money that I will have to spend on your sister's college." Bobby's older sister was matriculating as a junior at George Washington University, which costs a lot of money, even factoring in her scholarship money the school granted.

The mid-July day soon came for Larry and Rosemary to drive Bobby to the Academy to begin the grueling Plebe Summer. Bobby packed lightly, knowing he would not require a lot of clothing for the near future. Cassell placed Rosemary's bag in the back of her new Lexus along with his hang-up bag. The three of them departed their New Jersey home in time to get to the Westin Hotel near Parole, Maryland, which was a stone's throw from the Naval Academy. Getting to the hotel by six would permit them to have their last dinner together before Bobby was expected to report to the Academy. Cassell was emotional but didn't want to betray himself in front of Rosemary. He knew it would not take much for her to break down in tears. He hoped the three-hour ride would be a joyous one, and he would do his best to steer the conversation toward pleasant family memories while driving. Much of the talk centered about their daughter Dorothy's anticipated trip to

Guatemala for an archeological project. "Just think, Bobby, as you attend the Army-Navy game in November your sister will be getting her hands dirty every day in Guatemala, looking for historical artifacts," the proud dad joked.

"Well, perhaps we can change places; she endures the anticipated hazing we will receive daily, and I could use a shovel to look for dinosaurs," Bobby chuckled back.

"Do you know what you are going to expect this summer, Bobby," asked a respectful dad.

"Yes, I do. I think you are more nervous about it than I am. I will be okay, dad. Trust me. I got this."

His mom, near tears, sat in the rear seat of the Lexus. She had let Bobby sit in the right front seat. He was a young man changing in front of her eyes. He now deserved the honor to sit next to his dad. She did not like Larry's last question but understood why he asked it. He was nervous for his boy. She tried to block out the anticipated answer. It didn't work. She listened intently.

"Well dad, the official reason for experiencing Plebe Summer is to ensure we get properly indoctrinated and rid the class of those that don't really yearn for the program. I get the purpose of it, and I am not intimidated by it. I will be the best team player I can be. I will make it."

Cassell smiled. "This kid is the total package. The Navy is getting a great plebe," he said as he looked over to Rosemary. He could not be prouder of his once little boy, who was now a man. His thought raced through the four years and the thought of his boy as a young ensign. He began to well up.

"Okay, Admiral," with his voice betraying his sadness. "Keep your mom and me informed of your progress as you go through the summer if you can. Furthermore, Bobby, if you find out this is not for you, please know mom and I will still be there for you, grateful that you gave it your best effort."

Bobby was never just a cute kid. From the day he was born he was "damn handsome," as proud dad would tell anyone who would listen. As the Director of the Secret Service, that was just about everyone. His older sister, Dorothy, was equally blessed with model good looks. Both had infectiously inviting smiles, symmetrically agreeable eyes, high cheek bones, and what they saw in the mirror was the image others saw. Bobby's good looks, along with an equal dose of self-confidence, were displayed on the athletic field, as well in the classroom. If ever there was an aspirant to one of the military academies whose resume was validated by a first impression it was Bobby.

The family arrived at the United States Naval Academy displaying a special pass issued prior by the academy that allowed the parents on the grounds to drop off the plebes. Bobby had a small bag with personal items, mostly toiletries. He would not need more. If he failed in the early months, he would go home in the clothes he wore. That was not to happen to Bobby. Larry's wife watched as he got the first hug; a tight, close, lingering hug. Larry did not want to let go. His wife was eager to intercede. Rosemary wanted her boy in her grip, and as tears welled up, her lips quivered.

Bobby understood his mom's emotion and reacted quickly by picking her up inches off the ground. "Love you, mom." He gently put her down and picked up his small bag. "Love you guys, too much!"

It was a quiet ride home to Westfield, New Jersey.

CHAPTER 4

"BY THE TIME you're a junior in college, you need to have a passion for this stuff. Some kids know what they want to do at an early age. I did," Professor Michael Bligh shared with a prideful grin. "I knew what I wanted to do when I was thirteen. Like most kids growing up, it was either police investigative work, or something perhaps from the A&E channel, that featured some global archaeological dig. Do you remember Spielberg's *Raiders of the Lost Ark*? Well, that did it for me. I just wanted to dig after that," Bligh continued.

The George Washington University's program was consistent with other major universities' listings of their archeology programs as a subfield of Anthropology. "Through excavation and research, each of the undergrads will discover key lifestyles and cultures of ancient civilizations or, at least, centuries old living," read their brochure. The description reads, "Students focus on past cultures." Professor Bligh employed a standard commentary when students and parents came by his department for orientation. "Welcome to GW's Columbian College and its Department of Anthropology." After some interpersonal marketing of the program, Professor Bligh usually gave out a cautionary message: "Some students who matriculate in our program are more passionate than others. Some are in it because they think it's an easy grade. Oops, that lasts about a semester until they realize it requires a lot of reading, a lot of dedication. Our program is an interesting mixture of fieldwork, lab work, and research. Oh, and lest one forgets, we require a second language be taken for two years. I hope I haven't scared anyone," as he flashed a warm smile. "Bottom line is our kids have a great time, and the program prepares them for a variety of post-graduate opportunities in the private or public sectors."

Once back for the George Washington University's fall semester, Professor Bligh hosted an orientation for all six students who were to travel to Guatemala, to give them an opportunity to meet and talk briefly about themselves.

"I want all of you to feel comfortable with each other. So to begin, let's introduce ourselves," Bligh began. "I'll go first. I received my Doctorate in Anthropology from the University of Michigan. I have been at George Washington University for the past ten years. Many of those years have been in field research in various parts of Latin and South America. I did some classroom teaching during my time at Stanford University while pursuing my master's degree. I speak fluent Spanish, AND, I love to watch college basketball.

Dorothy, how about you," asked Professor Bligh. The Dorothy to whom Professor Bligh was referring was Dorothy Cassell. Larry and Rosemary Cassell had been married ten years before their first child, Dorothy, was born. Rosemary Cassell nee Chen was born in California. She was half Caucasian, half Chinese. Dorothy's mixed ethnicity produced a stunningly adorable baby. Her beauty was the proud talk of the mixed family.

"You should put her into modeling," said one family member.

"The last thing I am going to do to my daughter is place pressure on her to demonstrate, or let me say perform, in front of a camera. I want her to have a kid's life," Larry Cassell said respectfully, mildly admonishing the relative. "Rosemary and I will have her play sports, go to school, join scouts, play with dolls and toys, and not be adversely affected by eccentric differential experiences."

"Differential experiences," asked the relative. "I am not messing around with anyone who says that." Everyone laughed. "I wish your daughter only the best in life, but let me hasten to add, with her good looks, life could be easier than it has been for you!" the relative chuckled, as did those around them.

Dorothy grew up to be a statuesque, confident woman. When she arrived at the George Washington University campus, her presence commanded attention. She didn't flaunt it; she exuded confidence. Her countenance didn't intimidate, it invited. "In high school, she didn't try to aggregate large numbers of friends; friends migrated toward her. She is honest, direct, and unafraid," one of her references wrote to the university on her behalf in support of her college application.

"George Washington is lucky to get you," her dad told her when she had been accepted.

"I know, dad, and the scholarship money they're giving me has to make you happy. I know it is not a full ride, but after four years it may be enough for you to buy that Porsche, you've always wanted," Dorothy joked. "And you can give it to me once I graduate."

Dorothy spoke to the group. "Well, I am the older of the two Cassell children. My brother, Bobby, just entered the United States Naval Academy, located not far from here in Annapolis, Maryland. So, hopefully I'll be able to see him now and again during his time there. My dad retired from the Secret Service as the Director while I was a freshman in high school. I thought of going into law enforcement as a career, but I've been turned off with all the vitriol directed towards the profession. I just don't have the patience or the wit to be looked upon with such disdain. I know it is sad to say, but the political events have driven a wedge into the profession, unfairly, I believe, but it is there. So, the next best thing to wet my investigative appetite seemed to be archeology," Dorothy ended with a slight giggle. As she looked at McCarthy, he took the queue.

"I'm Tommy McCarthy from Massachusetts. My first choice of colleges was nearby Providence College, but then my buddies and I had an opportunity to visit DC during the summer before our senior year in high school, and we saw what GW had to offer. It had all the elements of college I was searching for: bars, good-looking girls, and close to the White House where I expect to hang one day. Oh, and I love good practical jokes, so during our semester away, beware!"

The young man to McCarthy's left took the next opportunity. "My name is Bernie McGovern, from the Bronx. If you think my accent is funny, you should hear my dad's. He emigrated from Ireland and spoke with a strong brogue; most who hear him probably need an interpreter. In fact, his accent can be so humorous I used to let friends listen in on my calls home. I look forward to our trip to Guatemala. I don't speak an ounce of Spanish, so I'll be relying on the Professor to get me through."

"Thanks for that tidbit, Bernie," responded Bligh. "How about you Sid?"

"Yes, I am Sid Rosenberg, and I come from Boca Raton, Florida. My close friends know me to be a crazed sports fan. They think I'm an encyclopedia on sports. I just love sport stats and digest them daily. I pretty much follow every sport out there, all year. Personally, I wanted to go to Villanova University, but I couldn't get in. Just kidding, but it would've been a blast to have been there these last couple of years to watch their basketball teams win national championships. I also have to say that my friends tell me that sometimes my mouth can't keep up with my mind. You'll learn that in La Antigua. I'm also a physical fitness nut, so I hope there are some gyms down there. And by the way, I don't drink."

Sid looked to his left, prompting Stephanie, a tall, slim Dutch exchange student to speak up. "Hello everyone, my name is Stephanie Zirgulis; I hail from Amsterdam, Netherlands. My dad is American, and my mom is Dutch. I have one sister who says that I am direct and snarky, but in a funny way, and I have a dark side, so be careful while sleeping. Just kidding. I look forward to getting to know each of you. And, Tom McCarthy, I will try to avoid standing next to you." The group chuckled and waited for McCarthy to respond.

"You didn't hurt my feelings. You won't be standing if we ever get that close, sweetie," quipped McCarthy. He retorted quickly, and with a franchised Irish grin. He didn't disappoint the group.

"Mr. McCarthy, I guess you haven't been paying attention to the #*me too* movement," joked Bligh. "Bill, you're the last to speak; tell us a little about yourself, please."

"Thank you, Professor; yes, I am Bill Berthrong. I'm kind of a hybrid here at GW. I am a student and belong to the University's Navy ROTC program, so hopefully, I will be commissioned an Ensign upon graduation. My dad and brother went to the Naval Academy at Annapolis, Maryland. So, Dorothy, I am familiar with the school. By nature, I am an adventurer, inquisitive, but somewhat stoic. I do have a dry sense of humor, at least that's what my friends say. Because of the way my parents raised me, I try to always be polite. The current political environment makes that sometimes difficult," explained Berthrong with his lips pressed slightly.

"Why didn't you go to the Naval Academy, Bill," asked Dorothy. "My kid brother, Bobby, always wanted to go there. He loves it."

"Well, all I can say is, while I like the disciplined life, I am not totally comfortable giving up all my time to a military academy. ROTC is not as all-consuming as the Naval Academy can be. I think for me, personally, I will have more to offer the Navy having experienced a different perspective of the real world. I think going to La Antigua on the dig will surely add to that experience."

"Well, I've got to tell you guys in earnest: you're not only going to appreciate your junior year by participating in this adventure. Your entire GW educational experience will be fondly remembered, and this opportunity to do a dig in Guatemala will be at the forefront. I am thrilled that each of you will be with me; you will make it special for me. You should be aware that the University will be featuring this extra-territorial adventure on various social media platforms," Bligh concluded. "It will help our department recruit interested students for next year's dig in Peru."

CHAPTER 5

THE GROUP SAT together on the flight down in two three-seat rows, row 28 just behind the window exits. Their mentor, Mike Bligh, a young George Washington University professor, sat in an aisle seat in row 29, within earshot of them all. It was 10:00am when the plane landed in Guatemala. The plane took the entire runway to land, decelerate and come to a slow turn at the runway's end, and then began to taxi to the terminal when Bligh spoke up.

"Hey guys, as a reminder, we will be heading to the Intercontinental Hotel soon after clearing immigration. It'll take less than a half-hour to get there. Once we get checked in, I want you to take time to get squared away with your rooms and contact your families or friends. We will meet in the hotel lobby at 2:00pm to go over some travel logistics for our bus trip to La Antigua early tomorrow morning, and perhaps talk about dinner tonight."

"How early will we be getting up in the morning?" McCarthy asked.

"6:30"

"Okay, we'll just stay up all night," McCarthy joked.

"Me, too," Bligh deadpanned. McCarthy wasn't sure he was kidding.

Nineteen hundred miles from their Washington, DC campus, the small, quirky group of George Washington University students arrived at the Guatemala La Aurora International Airport. The airport is located about four miles from the city's center, and fifteen miles from

La Antigua, their eventual destination. The group would first spend an overnight in the capital city before navigating the next day on a difficult hour-long trek taking them through the country's mountainous terrain. It would be a slow trip to the ancient city.

Flying in and out of the Central American capital was not considered an easy task, but the Guatemalan government's ongoing modernization and expansion project at the airport was almost completed. For many personnel assigned to the local US Embassy who transit through it frequently, the completion could not come soon enough. For the George Washington University students, the international trip was their first, and their excitement tempered any annoyance with the inevitable chaos of airport construction. The Guatemalan government was steadfast in its commitment to renovate the airport terminals. The older airport structure had been demolished long before the students' arrival. They wouldn't have any appreciation for the transition, but Professor Bligh knew from previous visits to the country.

Bligh expressed his delight, "When I was here, less than five years ago, the old terminal was in disarray. The improvements to this international terminal are phenomenal." The small group were among the first to enjoy the modern glass-enclosed concourse. "Unlike the old terminal, this one provides an abundance of ambient light."

"Professor Bligh, maybe you ought to audition as the local docent for the daily gaggle of newly arrived travelers," McCarthy blurted. Bligh looked about, but wasn't sure who the newly minted jokester was, so he ignored the crack. He would have guessed McCarthy but didn't think McCarthy would have known what the word docent meant.

"If nothing else, it'll brighten up your immigration experience," Bligh continued as they joined the visitors' immigration line.

"Hey Professor, it looks like it may be easier to enter our southern border than through here," McCarthy quipped. Bligh continued to ignore him yet as the immigration line formed, and the international passengers shuffled toward passport control, Bligh noted that the Guatemalan line, once as lengthy as theirs, dissipated much faster. "Some things never change," he thought. The Guatemalan immigration agents manning their posts were known not to take the complaints of international travelers sympathetically. Sometimes the process took less than an hour, sometimes more.

Bligh looked back to ensure his six young protégés were still in tow. "Maybe the immigration officers' interpersonal skills will catch up to the enhanced ambiance of the new terminal, and we get through this quicker," he joked.

"No Professor, Dulles airport can be just as bad," said Dorothy Cassell, one of his more serious students. "It's that situational power thing that these agents all seem to have in common," she frowned. "When my dad was a Secret Service agent, my mom and I would tease him for having it, as well. I think it is just a self-preservation technique they use to avoid having to be chatty."

The group eventually made it to baggage claim and customs control without a glitch. Their arranged hotel transport was waiting at the appointed location. "Sweet," Bligh thought.

Bligh, and his six neophyte archeologists boarded a small bus arranged through the Intercontinental Hotel to take them to the hotel. Bligh noticed a number of brochures inside the pocket in front of his seat. The one that struck his eye was entitled, *La Antigua*.

"Hey guys, here's how the hotel brochure describes our intended dig site, 'Antigua is quite the contrast from modern day Guatemala City. It was founded in 1543 and for more than two hundred years served as the residence of the military governor. It is in the central highlands and features Spanish Baroque influenced architecture, now evidenced by the old colonial church ruins. The city was the robust epicenter of

Guatemalan life until 1717, when an earthquake destroyed over three thousand structures, and most of the city's architecture was ruined."

Bligh, who spoke fluent Spanish, had organized the modest expedition to Guatemala the previous semester. He found the idea of a La Antigua experience most compelling. The old city would serve as a target rich dig site for the six eager university archeologically trained students from George Washington University. All except McGovern spoke Spanish, as well. Bligh believed the students would find La Antigua a refreshing contrast to their campus. Situated in one of the most famous cities of the world, George Washington University was a mere three blocks from the White House. Its buildings and dormitories formed a western flank to the President's home. The Secret Service designated the George Washington University Hospital for Presidential medical emergencies within the Nation's capital.

CHAPTER 6

"JUST OVER AN inch in diameter, or about the size of a half-dollar coin, an Apple AirTag is a pocket-sized tracking device. They're so small that when slipped into a purse or jacket pocket, they're hardly noticeable. Air Tags use Bluetooth and ultra- wideband technology to transmit location data so you won't lose track of any essential accessories like keys, headphones, wallets, or backpacks. An AirTag works by sending out a signal to the iCloud which is picked up by Apple devices in the "Find My" network. These include devices iPhones, Mac devices, and iPads. If you have a knack for losing things, you can open Apple's Find My app to see where your AirTag is located, or ask it to sound a "ping," using built-in speakers."

The six students awoke as the hotel bus entered the apron to the front door at 11:00 am. Like zombies, they exited the bus with their personal items as the bellhops gathered their luggage from the bus's belly. Bligh wondered, "Did these kids sleep the night before we left for Guatemala, or stay up partying?" He answered the question himself, "They're college kids."

"Okay guys, I will grab the room keys from the front desk and pass them out. Just hang in the lobby for a few minutes; then you can go to your rooms for a couple of hours," Bligh informed them. "This will be the only opportunity you will have to enjoy individual rooms; when we get to La Antigua you double up. I will say more about that later. Once again, let's be back here in the lobby at 2:00pm for more detailed brief on tomorrow's trip to La Antigua."

Within minutes the group trudged to their separate rooms.

"Hi daddy, I just got up from a quick nap. I miss you and mom. We are here in Guatemala City at the Intercontinental Hotel. It is really nice. Tomorrow, we head to the old city, La Antigua, to begin our digging. How's Bobby doing at the Naval Academy?"

"Sweetie, Bobby is already a big man on campus, or I should say the 'Yard.' He seems to like it a lot. Not sure I understand how standing twenty-four-hour duty is an enjoyable experience, but you probably know your little brother better than I do," responded Larry Cassell. "He's got that guard duty coming up in a few days. Standing post outside is something I've done many times, but not like he will be doing it. At least it is early October, and the weather won't be too bad."

"Daddy, Bobby is a disciplined guy. Like you, he thrives in that environment. Now that he's through the summer grind, and into his first semester, he'll have learned how to pace himself. I am a bit more progressive; I could never survive that military stuff. Tell Bobby I love him too much when you talk to him next."

"Dorothy, let me know when you get to the hotel in La Antigua. I don't want to be an alarmist, but you really need to keep a low profile. Stay with the group," cautioned a concerned Cassell. "And make sure you and your friends keep their tracking devices on their persons." Cassell had agreed to let Dorothy travel with the George Washington University group if she promised to wear a simple GPS tracking device, and have it on her person at all times, or at least attached to the "fanny pack" which she always wore on her hip.

"Dad, no worries, we all have your silly tracking devices," Dorothy joked.

"When I convinced your professor that it would be a good idea for all of you to carry one, he didn't object. In fact, he really liked the idea. When I told him I would pay for them, he jumped at the idea," Cassell joked back.

"The group thinks you guys just want to spy on us," Dorothy retorted.

"Just have it with you, please," Cassell petitioned. "And remember to relax."

"I'm on it dad, and I'm breathing like you taught me. I've got to go to the lobby shortly and meet with the Professor and my fellow students for a travel briefing. I will stay in touch; love you guys." Dorothy held back choking on her words as she said good-bye.

At the afternoon lobby meeting, Bligh gathered the group and had them sit together on some lobby sofas. "After spending the first night here at the Intercontinental Hotel, we will bust a move tomorrow morning. It'll be an early departure. So, make sure you're all packed and ready to go by 6:30am. The new hotel won't be as fancy as this one, and you will double up, but you will appreciate the ambiance," Bligh gleefully promoted. "In the morning, I will check everyone out of this hotel. Your assignment will be to ensure you double check your rooms and leave nothing behind. Check your safes too, please. And make sure that you have all your belongings, particularly your passports. You'll need them to register at the next hotel. Any questions?"

"Can you tell us a bit more what the next hotel is like," asked Dorothy.

"It is a small boutique hotel, called Hotel Casa del Parquet," he responded. It's located only three blocks from the dig site. After we check in later today, we will informally visit the dig site to get oriented. Then, you will have the rest of the day off. Tomorrow morning, we will walk over to the site with our equipment and begin our work."

CHAPTER 7

A NEWLY MINTED twenty-four seat bus was positioned on the street directly in front of the Intercontinental Hotel's sliding glass doors. The students managed to stuff their individual suitcases in the rear of bus. Additionally, each had similar looking waterproof rucksacks loosely hung over their shoulders. Within each bag were the dig tools they would employ to get "down and dirty" at the excavation site. Most of the students were gingerly carrying a cup of the Intercontinental Hotel's courtesy coffee, along with a handful of the small sugar cookies that had been pre-positioned beside the coffee canisters. Numerous cookies were wrapped in paper napkins for the hour-long ride to La Antigua. One by one, the six students and the professor boarded the bus to head to La Antigua and their new hotel where they intended to reside for the duration of their dig.

"Hey chubby, if this is what we have got to look forward to for breakfast each morning, we are going to lose a lot of weight. Your family won't recognize you." Rosenberg joked. McCarthy ignored him.

"When we return, will we be the same likeable students we were when we left?" asked Dorothy Cassell with a grin. "My dad has me practicing a breathing technique to keep me on an even keel. He said he learned it in Secret Service training." She was referring to her dad, Larry Cassell, former Director of the United States Service, and now one of the elite corporate chief security officers, or CSO, in the private sector.

"I'm sure it's a great technique, and I am sure it'll get you through the dig, and yes, Dorothy, you'll return to GW as a normal person," responded Bligh.

"Professor Bligh, we've heard of the dangers here in Guatemala, but La Antigua seems to be a protected place. Is that still your thought, too?" asked Dorothy.

"This is a beautiful country, but the threat of violence does exist in certain parts of it. You don't want to be in the wrong place at the wrong time. However, La Antigua is a special place. Guatemala invests a lot of assets to protect the population and the thousands of tourists who attach value to this great place."

"Well, hopefully nothing happens to us while traveling to La Antigua," Dorothy answered.

"No worries, Dorothy, we will be in La Antigua soon enough; it is rather quaint and safe there," Bligh assured her.

As the bus departed the city, the distant mountains to which they were headed became visible in the early morning sunrise. Conversations between the students began to percolate as their excitement grew.

"Have you read all this shit about what you girls can, and can't do," asked McCarthy with an ear-to-ear grin. The group knew what was coming next, a full-blown joke ignited by whoever responded first to his comment. By now, each of them knew better, but someone always answered just to give license to his humor. "The recommendations suggest that the two of you girls will have to mind your manners. Now listen up, you should avoid discussing sex-related topics when men are present."

McCarthy's statement piqued Professor Bligh's attention. This guy, he thought, could make a joke out of anything, but this was a serious topic in Guatemala, and these girls need to take the recommendations to heart. He didn't want to trivialize them.

"Hey Professor, I know you can't dress Dorothy and Stephanie in traditional Mayan attire, but it may be safer for them to dress that way in La Antigua."

"Mr. McCarthy, the ladies won't have much to worry about as long as they remain in proximity to you. The Guatemalans' attention will always be focused on the talisman," retorted Bligh.

McCarthy didn't fully appreciate, or understand, Bligh's response and kept prodding. "Well, if we get invited to a local home, the recommendations say they should wear a skirt and dressy blouse. Well, that blows it for us. All they got are jeans and t-shirts."

"We brought proper dress, chubby," chimed in Stephanie. "And, if we were to get invited we would dress accordingly. Our only concern would be you setting international relations back one hundred years because no one here gets your humor. Oh, and since shaking hands is customary here, they'll know, in short order, that there are only five of us in the group. Your handshake will go missing."

McCarthy wasn't sure if that was a shot at him, or not. "I'm only trying to keep you girls out of harm's way. This is male chauvinism central, where the men look at foreign women as promiscuous. Of course, you're not, at least as far as I know. So I agree with the Professor; you need to remain close to me at all times."

"Only if you shower, chubby," chuckled Dorothy.

"Why do you two keep calling me chubby"? McCarthy asked.

"Because we noticed that the extra weight you've put on," Stephanie replied with a deadpanned face. "It looks good on you."

"Professor Bligh, do you believe I have to put up with this. They tease me and I'm only trying to help them understand that the way they dress may have dire consequences for them. I am now recommending that they both wear Burkas."

They all laughed and knew to signal a truce for a short period, or at least until McCarthy felt compelled to make another joke.

It didn't take long. The affable Irish kid had a reputation for bursts of disconnected thoughts.

"Hey, who knows what the local currency is called," asked McCarthy.

"It's named after a bird, but I'm not sure which one," chirped Professor Bligh. "A quetzal, I believe."

"Correct, Professor Bligh, it's their national bird," responded McCarthy. "Do you know the exchange rate?"

"Interesting questions coming from you, chubby, since you still have your First Holy Communion money in the bank," Sid Rosenberg teased.

"How does a Jew know what we get for First Holy Communion," asked McCarthy.

"Be careful, chubby, should you mention Jew in a certain tone, it can get you branded as a Nazi," Sid said with a wink toward Dorothy. He was hoping to stoke McCarthy. "Then you'd never be able to get back to the United States. You keep that anti-Semitic stuff up, we may have to arrange to send your little Irish ass back to Ireland. As a leprechaun, you'd certainly fit in nicely."

"Let me tell you something, *Sidney*, Ireland is a great place to live, and we don't have to worry about those pesky little Arab bombs flying into our backyards," a chagrined McCarthy retorted.

"Hmm, interesting," said Sid. "Guess you forgot it wasn't too long ago you had those damn bombs detonating in parts of Northern Ireland, and the Protestants were hunting your asses down."

"Listen, twerp, get your history correct. It was the IRA kicking their asses before they decided to stay on their side of the street," McCarthy quickly countered, thinking it was checkmate.

"Okay boys, that's enough of that chatter; I don't want to see this escalate into an international dust-up. We all have to live together for another month," Dorothy interjected. She was quickly establishing herself as one of the adults in the group.

"Hey, anybody got an iPhone I could use to call back to the States?" Bernie McGovern asked.

"You don't have a phone?" asked McCarthy.

"I do. I was just asking for you. Since you have short arms and deep pockets, I didn't think you wanted to use your own money to call mommy. I know for sure you didn't sign up for any global plan to make it cheaper," Bernie added.

"What's with you guys today? You're piling up on me for no good reason, making me sound like a cheap asshole," McCarthy said.

"Nope, just trying to see how far we can go before you squirm, get pissed, and beat us all up. Besides, you make it way too easy," McGovern added. "Now look at Bill Berthrong. Neither Sid nor I would think twice about busting Bill's balls. Why? Because he just sits there quietly, stone-faced. Not a care in the world. If we start busting him, he may be the kind of guy that would take it out on us while we slept and cut us all up. We don't need to piss him off. Understand, chubby?"

"You guys are sick bastards," McCarthy responded.

"We still love you, chubby," Sid said.

Bernie and Sid were morphing into a team. It was going to be a tough time for McCarthy, and he knew it. He sat quietly for the rest of the trip.

The bus stopped right in front of the Hotel Casa del Parque. "Okay guys, we've arrived. We will first check in to the hotel. Hopefully, they will let us into our rooms. If not, we can stow our luggage in a storage area; just make sure you hang onto your personal stuff, particularly wallets and passports," Bligh announced as he stood up in the bus to address his students. The hotel was not fancy. It didn't come with Internet or cable, nor did it have a refrigerator stuffed with sodas, beer, or candies like the Intercontinental Hotel; but it was clean.

"I hope you guys have already considered who you're pairing up with because it is two to a room again. The rooms will be a little smaller, so do your best to just suck it up without complaining too much. We've got eight weeks of digging before we return back home to Washington, so you've got to be physically and mentally tough," Bligh advised.

CHAPTER 8

"ROSEMARY, IF I calculate this correctly, Dorothy has arrived at La Antigua. The group should begin their digging activity, if that's what it is called, by tomorrow. According to the *AirTag* tracker they have arrived at the Intercontinental Hotel," Larry Cassell reported to his wife.

"I don't know why, Larry, perhaps a mother's intuition, but I am worried for Dorothy," Rosemary replied. "I am glad you have her tagged with that tracking device."

"George Washington University conducts these international trips all over the globe. They are well briefed by the U.S. State Department with current country threat profiles. If the university thought for one minute it would be problematic to have its students in Guatemala, I don't believe it would have permitted the excursion," Larry advised.

"I will defer to your judgement, Larry. I always have, at least on security issues," Rosemary winked. "Now, with both our children away at college, I guess we will be having more discussions over concerns about the kids," she added. "Hope I don't burn you out with worry."

"You won't; I worry as much as you. I just don't display it."

CHAPTER 9

THREE MALE SUPERVISORY Secret Service agents sat across an expansive, solid oak table in the field office's conference room, preparing to interview applicants for the special agent position. The first was Carly James. Forget that she was attractive; these journeymen interviewed a lot of attractive applicants wanting to be part of Secret Service lore. But, beyond being attractive, James exuded confidence in the way she walked into the room and sat at the table. Perfect posture," thought the most senior of agents. James' resume preceded her, and the interviewers knew beforehand that she was as genuine a prospect for the agent position as they would ever encounter. She had been an attorney in a previous career, but had grown bored with personal injury cases, and working the municipal and county court circuits. She was eager to find something more adventurous than her legal career. She was encouraged to apply during a serendipitous meeting with one of her clients, whose son was a Secret Service agent.

"Bravo to you," said one of the three interviewers, in an unusually rare utterance of approval from the panel. "It is not often that applicants finesse their way through this." The prior question had to do with Carly observing another agent stealing cash from an evidence vault. "If the agent has the balls to steal in front of me, then he better have the balls to defend himself because I would kick the shit out of him for thinking he could put me in that position."

Carly James was almost six feet tall, and without an ounce of "butter" on her. She wore her dark brown hair in a ponytail, except when she went out on the town and then she let it flow freely. It was said she could wear a low-cut dress better than a Wall Street broker's wife. She could cause a stir when she wanted to, and sometimes even when she didn't intend to do so. James had always been more than just an academic standout. She played lacrosse at Villanova University and was considered an outstanding player. Some of her teammates said she could have played for the men's team. She was that fast, that powerful, and that determined, and she knew how to score goals.

When agents conducting her background investigation asked her college lacrosse coach for his assessment of her, he was effusive in his praise. "Carly put more lacrosse opponents on their butts than they did to her. She had her share of bruises, but she never complained. I really admire her composure, strength, and courage."

"Mom? I just received a call from the Secret Service. They offered me a position as a special agent. I'm going to take it. I love you, Mom." James left the message on her mom's voicemail. She looked forward to a new chapter in her life.

CHAPTER 10

"MARY, YOU'VE BEEN assigned as class coordinator for 228," advised Lou Granda, special agent in charge of the Secret Service's training facility located in Beltsville, Maryland. Mary Logue, with a dozen years on the job, had recently transferred to the Beltsville training facility from the Presidential Protective Division. Her five years assigned to protection of the president, in addition to her previous seven years in the Los Angeles Field Office as a seasoned criminal investigator, gave her strong credentials for the training assignment.

"I know you have two classes under your belt as a deputy class coordinator, so we believe you can handle a new class as class coordinator. Let me just add this, Mary, the class will feature fifty percent women. They'll need a mentor like you to help them understand this agency," Granda added.

"Thank you, sir I am thrilled, and look forward to it," responded a chipper Logue. "Is there a list of attendees I could look at to prep myself for them?"

"Of course, I will get a complete list with pedigree information to you by noon. Also, Jim Davidson will be assigned as your deputy."

Davidson had been recently assigned to the office of training as well. He was a former National Football League (NFL) player, and a tremendous athlete. Mary knew she had scored a touchdown as she envisioned introducing the training team to class 228 on its first day.

"Again, thank you sir for your confidence in me. I will start to prepare lesson plans now and get them to you as soon as possible," Mary offered.

As Mary digested the class roster and the attached briefing materials, one attendee in particular caught her eye. A young attorney, Carly James, had received glowing performance reviews at the previous academy held for criminal investigators at Glynco, Georgia. Later in the day when she ran into the Training Division's Special Agent in Charge, (SAIC), Lou Granda, she said, "Boss, this is a great class, I am happy for the agency to have so many quality women entering law enforcement."

"Mary, no doubt you will become a mentor to many of the young ladies in this class. This is what generational law enforcement is all about these days. We pass this wisdom that we received from those who came before us to those who follow us," said Granda. "It's our duty to our organization. Hopefully, we pass on the good stuff."

"Sir, that sounded like a commercial" Mary chuckled. "But I know you are right.

"Okay, Mary, time for you to get to work." Granda shot back, "besides anyone who has the moniker "Lock 'em up Logue" must have a lot to be passed on. How did you get tagged with that one anyway?"

"When I began my career with the Secret Service I was perceived to be an aggressive investigator, having made a half-dozen counterfeiting arrests before I even went to Glynco," Mary replied with pride.

"Well earned Mary. Furthermore, anyone who spends five years protecting the President of the United States can manage a class of twenty-four recruits. They'll be lucky to have you."

Mary blushed at the compliment.

CHAPTER 11

CARLY JAMES ARRIVED for her first day of training at the James J Rowley Training Facility (JJRTF), with her twenty-three fellow students. They were directed by the guards at the front gate to aggregate in front of the facility's administrative building where they would be greeted by their class coordinator.

"Ladies and gentlemen, I want to welcome you to the finest training facility in law enforcement. Here you will learn how to shoot, fight, swim, and further hone your investigative skills in bank fraud, cybercrime, counterfeiting, protective intelligence, and specialized protective skills. This is a five-hundred-acre compound that serves to provide tailored curricula to Secret Service employees. You will soon observe that this compound features an airport tarmac used for defensive driving, a small city used to conduct practical attack-on-the-principal ("AOPs") scenarios, a live shoot house for specialized counter-assault tactical training, retired fuselages of an Air Force One airplane and a Marine One helicopter, and an Olympic-sized swimming pool where you will spend much time learning water rescue and survival skills. You will become intimately familiar with sophisticated gun ranges where you will spend so much time that you will go to sleep at night dreaming about the various weapons the Service uses.

"My name is Mary Logue. I am your course director, and this is my deputy, Jim Davidson. We will be living with you for the next five months. You will get to know us and we will get to know you. Eventually, you will graduate, and the chances of us working together one day in the near future is very real. That is why we want you to learn our trade to perfection, so that when you practice it in the real world, your performance will be seamless. We will get on these buses now and tour the compound before we break for lunch and some required administrative chores, Any questions? None? Okay, let's load up."

All the students were attired in a similar fashion: khaki pants, dark running shoes and a dark golf shirt bearing the Secret Service star on the left breast, inscribed with the word ***Trainee*** below it. Each attendee received five sets of pants and shirts. The students would be responsible for cleaning and maintaining their own clothing.

Mary climbed onto the first bus and after ensuring all twenty-four students were on board, took a seat behind the driver and next to one of the female students.

Mary turned to the student on her left and broke the ice. "Hi, we will be issuing name tags later today, but in the meantime, I want to welcome you personally. May I ask what your name is?"

"Yes ma'am, I am Carly James from the Newark Field Office. I live in New Jersey now, but I actually grew up in the Annapolis area."

"Oh, you're the attorney who graduated from Villanova University and Seton Hall University, two great Big East schools," Mary blurted.

"Yes, thank you for knowing that about me."

"I actually know you played lacrosse while at Villanova," replied Mary. "You shouldn't have much difficulty with the physical requirements here."

"Well, I am afraid I am not much of a swimmer," Carly admitted.

"Neither was I, but you will be when you graduate. Don't fear it, you will just develop confidence during the weeks you spend here. We are not here to expel you; you have already proven your worth. Our job is to mold you and give you the tools to do the job successfully. I think you'll enjoy it. And, I am so glad we have a rich number of female students. Some of them will become your lifelong friends," Mary noted.

"Thank you for that, ma'am," Carly said.

"You can call me Mary. I will be advising everyone to do so shortly."

CHAPTER 12

"MARY, I WANT to tell you how much I appreciated our initial conversation the first day I showed up for training. You made me, and the entire class, feel special and welcomed in the Secret Service. I did not expect that level of empathy. If I become half the agent you have been, I feel I will have succeeded in this organization."

Thank you, Carly, Class 228, is for me, a pleasure to manage.

Both women grew close during the five-month training program, often engaging in off-the-record conversations. "I hope after graduation you won't mind it if I contact you during my career for advice," Carly asked. "It's such a tremendous responsibility we all share now as we are charged with fulfilling our duties and responsibilities, but you make it seem like a family value. I will never, ever forget the tribute you paid to your mom and dad in our many conversations. While your dad might have wanted you be a tomboy, you are model for this job as a competent and beautiful woman."

Mary reached out and embraced her. "Thank you, Carly. Please stay in touch. You have a great career ahead of you and I look forward to watching it develop." Mary backed off, looked and smiled before another graduate stepped forward to engage Mary.

The following Monday after graduation, James reported back to the Secret Service's Newark Field Office. As was customary for new agents, she was assigned to a fraud squad and presented with a score of investigative leads to "run out". She excelled at credit card fraud investigations, particularly West African fraud, that is, financial crimes committed by multi-national groups from Nigeria, Cameroon, and Benin. She knew them to be the most intelligent fraudsters the agency encountered. They were seldom, if ever, violent, but they were wily and given the chance, might run. Unfortunately for them, James could outrun and outthink most of them.

She loved the adrenaline of executing warrants and relished the moment when the fraudster knew she outsmarted, outguessed, and outmaneuvered him. Her success as a field investigator proved ephemeral. Headquarters loves winners; her time to transition to a protection assignment had arrived. As a young agent she had hungered for the opportunity to protect the president close up. Nevertheless, after five years in the field with so much investigative success, she had second thoughts about leaving for a protection assignment.

"Too bad," puffed her field office supervisor, George Hamilton. The no-nonsense Newark field office agent in charge hardly looked at her. "PPD doesn't want slugs on the detail, Agent James. Fortunately for you, your reputation precedes you. Headquarters called; you're going to the White House Detail." The White House Detail was Hamilton's alternate reference to the prestigious Presidential Protective Division.

Hamilton had given the pep talk countless times, but it was a much different talk than the one he was accustomed to giving to agents who were picked for the less desired family details. In these circumstances, he tried his best to make the smaller detail assignment at least sound palatable, but his efforts generally fell short. Younger agents tended to go for the smaller detail because it fit their family needs or perhaps, they wanted to attend graduate school, but it would never match the experience of the White House Detail.

"You dress well, and you work hard. You shouldn't be surprised you got picked up for the 'Show' assignment."

Hamilton's Secret Service career spanned a generation. He was "old school." Anyone who pissed off the boss, or didn't perform field office chores to his satisfaction, went into career oblivion. This was how Hamilton managed his agents. Privately, he was proud to send his agents to the President's detail. He took similar enjoyment in sending those he had no use for to the boredom of a small detail. In the world of the Secret Service, the Special Agent in Charge, or "SAIC," controlled an agent's personal life.

"Look James, I expect you to do well in Washington. The Secret Service has changed in the generation I've been here. You 'girls' are now part of the team, I get it."

James nodded respectfully, recognizing Hamilton's clumsy admission was as close as it would be to him appreciating females working successfully in the Secret Service.

"The way I see it if we get enough females like you as the new standard, the Service will have a good chance at remaining an elite organization. I like your spunk, your drive, and the way you carry yourself."

During her first year with the presidential assignment, she performed her duties with pride. Protecting the most powerful person on Earth was the thrill of a lifetime. James allowed herself to privately gloat. Standing along the white-walled colonnade between the West Wing and the White House residence, she glanced past the Rose Garden toward the Ellipse and savored a brief private thought, which she shared later with her family.

When she called her mom at home, James boasted how special it was to work on the Presidential 'detail.' "How lucky am I to work in such a historic setting? Mom, the President of the United States walks by me, nods hello, and continues to the Oval Office, and in a way that makes me feel like I belong here. He makes me feel that what I do here, standing my post, is important." A slight smile graced her face.

Over the next two years James moved up the protective detail experience ladder, and by her third year, was assigned one of the most coveted roles on the detail short of a promotion: lead advance agent. It was during one of her Presidential advance assignments to a U.S. Coast Guard graduation ceremony located at the Academy in Connecticut where she met Coast Guard Commander Will Strain. At the time, Strain was assigned to the Coast Guard Headquarters' Intelligence Directorate, but tapped temporarily to assist the Coast Guard Commandant's arrival at the same graduation ceremony the President would attend.

It was love at first sight. Meeting Carly James didn't change Strain's appetite for an extraterritorial assignment, but it changed his stance against marriage. After a short courtship, James wore an engagement ring, followed swiftly by a small, private wedding ceremony. There would be time for a reception later—too much career work to get done first. "Honey, our early years will be rife with separations, and it'll be tough on a marriage, but I want to do it if you'll have me," proposed a love-struck Will Strain. "Will, yes, of course. I look so forward to a life together," she replied, embracing him.

Will's assignment was designed to prepare him for an elite overseas posting in the Middle East. His deployment was to last for two years, operating out of the United States Embassy in Kuwait City. Soon, he deployed to Kuwait.

"We talk all the time on the Internet," the now Carly Strain told her mom. "But when he's away from the Embassy, there are periods when he's out-of-pocket in Kuwait and we don't get to talk. That's when I miss him the most. I'll be moving from the Presidential detail soon to accept a promotion in the New York Field Office. What do you think of that, mom?"

Her mom answered, "Honey, you have a gift for making the decisions that are best for you. If you are comfortable with the idea, then I say go for it."

"It is time to move on, Mom. With Will's deployment to Kuwait City, the new assignment will keep me focused on something new. And it comes with a promotion. I will be taking over the office's elite Cyber-Crime Squad." What she didn't tell her mom was she needed the new assignment to keep her loneliness at bay. She tired of the heavy travel requirements on the Presidential Detail; living out of a suitcase two weeks out of each month became oppressive.

"Honey, that's terrific and you will be closer to family. I know it is hard on you and Will, but it will pay dividends," her mom quipped.

She missed her husband. She didn't like being lonely. "I think the transfer will help a lot, Mom. I will give you more details soon. I Love you!"

Little did the Strains know that one day soon, the Russian mob, Bratva, would come to affect both their careers and serve to bring them closer than they would ever have imagined. Carly's computer science studies while in college prepared her for a Secret Service management position as cyber-crime squad leader in the New York Field Office, following her successful presidential protection assignment, the transfer came with a promotion. She was now Assistant Special Agent in Charge or "ASAIC."

Several months into her new assignment Carly called Will to share some exciting news. "Will, my squad just arrested a Russian super hacker from Brighton Beach. It's a big deal. He'll be remanded to the Metropolitan Correction Center for a while and not likely to make bail. But here's the good news, I've been asked to travel to Kuwait to support a presidential visit. I will be in charge of a seventy person jump team, flying in an Air Force C-5."

"Carly, what a great opportunity. I will be working on the visit, as well. We will have a great week together. There are so many things to show you here. The first order of business will be to introduce you to a lonely Coast Guard Commander," Will teased.

The visit ended up more classified than it began, and little is known about it by the public. A great deal of money was spent to help keep it a classified event with some degree of success, but the lives of some of the passengers aboard the ill-fated Air Force transport plane were forever changed. That is another story. The truth remains that a C-5 was abducted in a masterful Bratva operation. A brave Secret Service agent was killed, and many more were taken hostage. Carly excelled in keeping the remaining contingent of agents alive. The Bratva chieftain, Arvydas Belov, got his hacker protégée back in exchange for the valuable human and material cargo aboard the C-5.

Will Strain didn't take kindly to Bratva, abducting his bride. His actions following the exchange were known by few. They were deadly to the Bratva mob.

CHAPTER 13

COMMANDER STRAIN SAT alone at his desk in a windowless office located in the basement of the Coast Guard Headquarters when the duty operations desk called. Strain had recently returned from a two-year assignment in Kuwait. The basement office was a temporary location while his new office was being renovated.

"This is Strain."

"Sir, this is Lieutenant Savannah Riera, I have Assistant Commandant James F. Keegan on the phone for you. May I connect you?"

"Yes, Lieutenant, thank you."

"Will, this is Jim Keegan, how are you?"

"Well sir, if I was any better, I'd be in Heaven. Thanks for asking."

"Ha, that's a good one. You might want to take the rest of the day off and have a celebratory glass of wine with your bride," Keegan offered, "because I am letting you know the Commandant has just approved your promotion to Captain, Atlantic Command, Miami Sector – Intelligence, effective immediately, immediately come on home."

"Well, I didn't expect this call today. Sir, thank you for all that you have done for me. You have been more than supportive of my career.

"Come on upstairs and I will give you more details about your new assignment," Keegan said.

"Roger that." Strain hung up the phone and quietly relished his new opportunity before leaving his office to meet Keegan.

"Go ahead sir, the Assistant Commandant is expecting you," Garcia, Keegan's assistant, told the newly minted Captain.

"Thanks," Strain entered an open door to find Keegan on the phone. Keegan motioned for Strain to have a seat in front of his desk. Strain complied.

While on the phone, Keegan handed Strain a document that detailed a new organizational structure for Strain to review:

> *Maritime Intelligence Fusion Centers (MIFCs) serve as the central hub for fusion, analysis, and dissemination of maritime intelligence and information at the operational and tactical level.*
>
> *District Intelligence advises the District Commander on all intelligence matters and enables the integration of intelligence into USCG operations/activities at the District and below level.*
>
> *Sector Intelligence advises the Sector Commander on all intelligence matters and ensures integration of intelligence into all USCG Sector missions.*

When Keegan terminated the call, he stood up and reached his hand out to Strain to congratulate him on his promotion. "Captain, please have a seat."

Strain accepted the invitation. "Sir, thank you for having me."

"Will, you'll have a full plate with your new commands. Wonder if you will have enough time to take Carly out to dinner before you go operational," Keegan joked. "Anyway Captain, here are your new commands. The Commandant wants you to look at all three of them and determine how more efficiencies, if any, can be developed. He also wants to give you more authority to develop our Latin America and South America intelligence relationships, to include Cuba. You not only have the skill sets, but the Commandant thinks you are the guy that can take the Coast Guard to another level within the Intelligence Directorates. He wants you to manage all aspects of intelligence activities within the Miami sector to achieve maximum support for the Coast Guard mission. Will, the last imperative is right out of our Coast Guard mission statement for a reason. It's what we believe will improve our performance," said a now more sober Keegan.

"Will, me, as a civilian here at Coast Guard headquarters, I can tell you how impressive the organization is: like its publications describe it as a preeminent military, multi-mission, maritime, uniformed service of the United States Department of Homeland Security and one of the nations' six armed services. You've helped build that reputation. I believe that you, Will, embody it more than anyone I know. Your promotion validates this belief and I congratulate you on your new role."

"Sir, I will do the best I can," Strain replied.

CHAPTER 14

AS WILL PERUSED yet another incident report, the phone rang. He put down the document, rubbed his eyes, and answered the phone.

"Honey, I hope you are sitting down," said an unusually exuberant Carly Strain.

"Of course, what do you have to tell me? Because I have something to share with you as well, and I hope you are seated."

"I've been selected as the next Special Agent in Charge of the Miami Field Office. The Secret Service gives us four months to tolerate, but quite honestly, I am ready to get there tomorrow," Carly said exuberantly.

"Strain blurted with equal excitement. This doesn't get any more synchronistic. Guess what? I've been selected as the new Captain of the Miami Sector for Intelligence and Investigations. I will have oversight over all of Latin and South America. Time for us to learn Spanish!"

"Ha, ha, Will, you always try to outdo me. When I get off the phone with you, I need to let mom know about the promotion and our new location. I look forward to her coming to visit us in our new Florida home. She deserves the best. I only wish my dad were still alive to enjoy the opportunity, too. Damn that ALS."

"Not trying to outdo you honey, just trying to keep up with you. Where are you thinking of us living? In my new assignment I will have to visit Key West frequently. Will that be in your district, too?" Will asked.

"I think Key Largo offers the most practical locale, particularly if we decide to retire to this area. Former President Nixon used to frequent the Ocean Reef community when he would visit his best friend, Bebe Rebozo. The Miami Field Office knows the community well, having conducted multiple site advance work for the former President's visits. In fact, a former Miami SAIC lived there and commuted to the field office, so there is precedent, honey. That may be a good place to start to look."

"Whoa, girl, let's get our sea legs first. Southern Florida is chock full of great properties. By the way, where are you getting the money for such a place," Will countered, a tongue-in-cheek.

"Oh, hush up Will. I got to go, love you too much," Carly said.

"Love you, too."

CHAPTER 15

"HI MOM, I'VE got great news to tell you," said an obviously excited Carly.

You're pregnant?" her mom quickly responded.

No. Sorry, mom, not that kind of news. I've just been advised that I will assume the Senior Executive Service (SES) SAIC role in the Miami Field Office. This puts Will and me in the same geography for the first time in our married lives."

"I had a hunch that would happen when you told me he was being considered for different commands," Mrs. James replied. "The Miami posting seems very practical. Now I will have a place to go during the winter."

"Will and I are talking about possibly getting a home in Ocean Reef, a gated community, not far from Key Largo. It provides easy access to the Florida Keys, and north to Miami. Our field office is actually off of Route 75 and not in the city proper," Carly said.

"Honey, I am thrilled for you both, and I am sorry I teased you about having a baby." Mrs. James didn't want to caution Carly about her biological clock, but it did worry her.

"Mom, don't worry, it is something we can talk about, as well." Carly was aware of her mother's age. If she were to make her mom a grandmother, and have her enjoy that role, it had to happen soon, she thought.

CHAPTER 16

AN EARLY CALL from Larry Cassell interrupted Will Strain's morning routine.

"Captain Strain, this Larry Cassell. I am calling to congratulate you on your recent promotion and new command in Florida. I also heard that Carly has been named the Special Agent in Charge of the Secret Service's Miami Field Office."

"Sir, as always, it is an honor to receive your call. Carly and I are blessed. We have fast forwarded plans to move to Florida and have purchased a home in the Key Largo area, specifically, Ocean Reef. We can't be more excited that our careers have allowed us to move forward in tandem," Strain respectfully replied.

"What's ironic, Will, is the fact that when I was a baby Secret Service agent, I was assigned to former President Richard Nixon. I made numerous trips to the Ocean Reef community when Mr. Nixon visited his good friend, Bebe Rebozo. That is a great place to live. I can see you'll both be retiring sooner rather than later now that you are living in the lap of luxury," joked Cassell.

"Well, the homes in Ocean Reef don't come cheap, so I suspect I will be working for quite some time to come. Carly and I were just talking about you, and how wonderful it is to learn that your children are doing so well. We understand that your son is attending the Naval Academy."

"Thank you Will, that's another reason I am calling you. My son, Bobby, is a plebe at the academy, and so far has not been rejected, nor has he rejected the difficult challenge. It's something he's wanted for a long time, so Rosemary and I are happy for him. My daughter, Dorothy, is a sophomore at George Washington University. She leaves tomorrow for Guatemala. She and her fellow classmates will be participating in an archeological dig for the semester, or at least most of it, in the La Antigua area of the capital. I wanted to let you know, particularly now that the country is in your sphere of influence. You, more than most, would know the area well and share with me any problematic issues that may exist there, now, or in the immediate future," Cassell said in a concerned parental voice.

"Sir, if you give me her dates in country, I will make sure the responsible folks in the embassy, and some other friends the intelligence community, have their antennas up, and remain sensitive to her temporary residency in La Antigua," Strain offered.

"Will, she and her classmates are due to arrive in Guatemala City on or about September 30, spend a night in the city, at the Intercontinental Hotel before traveling to La Antigua on October 1st, they then travel to La Antigua to register in a hotel in close proximity to the dig site. I believe they begin their dig the next day, on the 2nd. They are projecting to spend at least five or six weeks in the country," Cassell added.

"Great, I will get on it. The weather should accommodate a dig at this time of the year. Hurricane season is pretty much over," Strain said.

"Will, she's my little girl. I am never comfortable with letting her outside my grasp. With her in Guatemala, I've lost my grasp. So, I personally thank you for your helping hand," Cassell responded, slightly choking up.

Strain detected the father's concern in the voice. "Sir, let me work on developing the connections. Thanks again for your call. I will get back to you soon with some contact information to help raise your comfort level."

CHAPTER 17

"MINISTER VILLACORTA, I urge you to call the American Embassy," petitioned Evangeline Bozzuto, the anxious Guatemalan State Prosecutor. "They will expect a heads-up on something like this. Otherwise, they will be all over us for not notifying them. Trust me; we don't need that crap right now. The U.S. Embassy has a new ambassador to Guatemala, Gail Fitzpatrick. We don't want our President's relationship with the new ambassador to start out on the wrong foot because of a lack of communication."

"Okay, I can handle that," Juan Villacorta, Guatemalan Justice Minister, calmly answered. He knew what to do, and he knew who to call.

"Minister, if they offer crime scene forensic support, I'd advise us to take it," Sergeant Pedro Martinez said, "it is a difficult crime scene to process and with international implications, we could certainly use their cooperation and expertise.

Within minutes, the Justice Minister reviewed his iPhone contact list. He knew most of the important embassy folks, even Fitzpatrick, the new American ambassador, but it wasn't the Ambassador who could achieve the desired result. He wasn't quite sure what technical capability a call could elicit on such short notice but had no choice except to reach out to his contact.

"Hello, this is Jim Solarski," answered the seasoned Regional Security Officer, often referred to as the United States Embassy's "RSO." He had been assigned by the State Department to the embassy in Guatemala City for the past two years. The U.S. Marines, assigned to defend the embassy, reported directly to him. As a former Marine himself, he quickly bonded with the security detail, and they with him.

"Hello Jim," Villacorta quickly responded. "I am sorry to report that we have a horrific, deadly event playing out in La Antigua as I speak. It appears to involve some American college students, and unfortunately, I must report to you that the victims have been brutally murdered at an archeological dig site there. We've only been on-site for two hours. Our forensic specialists arrived in the past hour. However, due to the complexity of the crime scene, we believe American expertise may be helpful. It is not just bloody mayhem, but also our folks on the ground think there may have been a kidnapping. Also, there has been some peculiar interest by some influential Guatemala potentates. I can explain that notion later. One thing is certain, friend, this will soon be the focus of an intense international media," Villacorta explained.

"I understand, Minister Villacorta. If these victims are indeed American students, the pressure to process the crime scene meticulously will be enormous for you. We will, of course, do whatever we can to assist you, in keeping with the highest forensic standards," replied Solarski.

"Yes, Jim, an American standard."

"Well, as luck would have it, we have a regional Transnational Crime Seminar going on here at the Westin International Hotel. One of the speakers today is Bill Davies from the Baltimore City Police Department. The kid gave a presentation today to the attendees about the nuances of crime scene forensic techniques. I attended it myself and can tell you he has participated in the forensic analysis of many macabre crime scenes, perhaps more than anyone should have to be exposed to in their lifetime. I believe he's still at the Westin; let me attempt to reach him. If I do, does your office have transportation that could ferry us up to the mountains?"

"That will not be a problem," Villacorta responded. "I will arrange for a military helicopter to take you up to the crime scene."

CHAPTER 18

"MADAM AMBASSADOR, I regret to inform you that the Guatemalan Justice Ministry has reported to me within the last few minutes that their State Police have uncovered a gruesome crime scene in La Antigua with murdered victims who appear to be American students. I am working with Minister Villacorta to respond to the scene with a US forensic expert. My office is alerting the U.S. State Department's Operations Center at this time," advised Solarski.

"Jim, this is sad news to receive. Is there any other information that you can provide me? I anticipate a barrage of calls once this becomes known."

"Madam Ambassador, we know from the Guatemalan State Police that six people are dead. The victims appear to be from George Washington University, located in Washington, D.C. They were found on a parcel of property where they had been engaged in an archeological excavation. Captain Luis Otero is on the scene and has requested assistance from the U.S. Government. As luck would have it, we have forensic crime scene investigator from the Baltimore Police Department here in Guatemala. He was brought down by the U.S. State Department to conduct a class on crime scene investigative best practices for the local police. I am on my way to his hotel. We will then be transported to the crime scene to assist. I will absolutely update you on any new details as they emerge."

"Jim, I will make myself available to you the rest of the night to receive updates. You have my cell number; please use it when you have additional information," Fitzpatrick advised.

"Thank you, Madam Ambassador, I know this is one of those difficult events that we pray never happens. I appreciate that you will be receiving a plethora of inquiries from the States in short order. I will do my best to ensure you have the latest information," Solarski concluded.

CHAPTER 19

SOLARSKI FOUND DAVIES at the Westin Hotel bar munching on some chicken wings. A cold Coors Light draft sat next to the wings. It hadn't been touched. The Westin was only a short distance from the Intercontinental Hotel. Both hotels were part of an enclave of such hotels where most foreigners stayed. The area was relatively safe by U.S. standards.

"Hey, Bill, I am glad to have found you," said Solarski as he approached the crime scene savant.

"Hello Jimmy, can I buy you a beer?" Davies offered.

"Well, I would love one, but not at the moment. I am sorry to say my reason for being here is to request your assistance in a pressing embassy matter involving multiple homicides. I am afraid it means now."

Davies put the stripped chicken wing on his plate and wiped his hands with the napkin from his lap. "Sure, how can I help?"

"From what I know from the Guatemalan officials thus far, there's been an unimaginable slaughter of American college kids at La Antigua. The crime scene has been secured and the Guatemalan police have their forensic team up on the mountain now scouring the mayhem. The Justice Minister has asked for American support. I heard your presentation today at the conference and believe your participation could be invaluable.

"Well, I am sorry to hear about the victims. Let's go," said the eager Baltimore City police crime scene investigator. "I am assuming my role will be solely to review the process the locals are using and consult where I think appropriate?

"You will have the freedom to guide them as you think necessary," Solarski replied. "We have technical equipment at the Embassy. Just tell me what you may need, and we will get it," Solarski said.

"You'll buy me a beer when we get back?" asked Davies with a grin.

"After we visit the scene, we may need more than one," the dead panned RSO responded.

"The Justice Ministry has a helicopter inbound now. It should arrive in minutes, and land in a field two blocks away."

CHAPTER 20

SOLARSKI LED DAVIES out the Westin Hotel's front lobby door to a police vehicle waiting for them under the hotel's canopy. Soon, the RSO and the commandeered Baltimore City crime scene investigator arrived at a landing zone the Guatemalan police had hastily established in a nearby park.

The flight took less than twenty minutes, and the helicopter set down less than one-half mile from the crime scene.

"Wheels down," Solarski yelled. With the helicopter's rotors still rotating, the two Americans hopped off the helicopter onto the makeshift landing zone. One of the pilots led them to a waiting police vehicle that then drove them the short distance to the crime scene. Davies could see the perimeter tape reflecting off the powerful emergency lighting the Guatemalan police had put into place by Captain Otero's men to illuminate the carnage. "This is like a Hollywood movie," Davies thought.

As Davies exited the police vehicle, he looked at the RSO and said, "Jim, this place has an odious smell. When we get there, tread carefully, and let's see what they've got before we go forward into the mass of corpses."

Solarski stared at him in appreciation, as he witnessed Davies kick into a CSI mode. "I love this guy," Solarski thought.

Captain Otero saw Solarski and Davies approach and moved quickly to intercept them twenty feet from the taped off crime scene. His facial countenance projected a seriousness Solarski knew and understood. Otero extended his right hand to greet Solarski.

"Hola, mi amigo mio," said Otero. Although the two have known each other less than two years, they had become fast friends. In fact, a few months earlier Solarski escorted Otero to Washington, D.C. for a State Department conference. He showed Otero the town. Breaking into perfect English, Otero said, "I am grateful that you brought Mr. Davies. Otero held out his hand to Davies and grasped his tightly. He didn't let go while staring Davies straight in the eyes for what seemed like minutes but was only a moment. "I am deeply grateful to have you here, Mr. Davies. With a tragedy like this it is imperative we get it right. The Americans are brothers to us."

Davies replied with a deferential tone, "It is my honor to meet you Captain Otero, even in this circumstance. I hope I can be of service. May I approach your crime scene?" Davies knew the captain had control and custody of the grisly site. He was in charge. Davies intentionally presented himself as deferential to him.

"Claro, of course, follow me," Otero offered.

Davies deftly withdrew his iPhone from his left pant pocket and began to photograph his approach to the crime scene's outer perimeter. This was his practice at all crime scenes he surveyed while working and responding to the raging crime in Baltimore City, Maryland.

As he moved closer, he changed the camera's video selection to 'pan' to capture the totality of the gruesome site. He was on autopilot running through his mental checklist of a crime scene investigator's "to do list" before he would begin to analyze, and then catalog, a crime scene. Soon, the smell and other physical anomalies came into focus. He knew the message: death. He had seen it over a hundred times.

"I count six bodies," he said softly to Solarski. The human frames, with their heads awkwardly disjointed, lay eerily still. "Let's stop here for a moment. I want to scan the inner perimeter for any signs that may suggest how the crime was committed, and more importantly, what might be missing." He also wanted to determine if Captain Otero and his men had made any mistakes. This concern he would not want to verbalize. They stood in silence until Davies moved forward.

"I will remain outside the tape boundary," advised Solarski. He read body language which suggested to him that Davies wanted to limit the number of persons inside the boundaries of the crime scene.

"Yes, we don't want to contaminate the scene." Davies answered in earshot of Captain Otero.

"Captain Otero," Davies asked, "Have you determined from what direction the victims may have entered the dig site?"

'Yes, we believe they entered the park from the east. They were all registered at the Hotel Casa del Parques, and walked the short distance from there to here," answered Otero. "The site is virtually invisible to any pedestrians walking contiguous to the location. It's off the beaten path, as they say."

The dig site was located three blocks from their new hotel located between 3a Calle Oriente and 4a Calle Oriente. The small hotel was one of several small hotels available in the area that served a growing tourism appetite. Compared to the Intercontinental Hotel, however, the del Parque had been disappointing to the students.

Now, it didn't matter. They were dead.

"Captain Otero, at what time were the authorities notified about the massacre, and how long before the police arrived?" asked Davies.

"We have no witnesses to the murders, but a pedestrian later stumbled upon the scene. He apparently needed to take a pee. He was frightened by what he saw and notified the local police at about 4:45pm," Otero reported. "The police arrived and secured the scene within minutes. They contacted my office around 5:00pm."

"Taking into consideration the exposure to the day's pleasant weather, the bodies' temperatures may not shed an accurate measure of time of death for us. Rigor mortis has set in, and inasmuch as they are reported to have arrived at the dig in the early morning, yields a pretty good estimate that they were murdered four to six hours ago, perhaps late morning or early afternoon, Davies observed.

"Jim, as you may know there are four postmortem stages of death. Science teaches us that once death occurs the body changes in an orderly and timely way. Analyzing the body visually, we can determine the time of death. The body at first remains flaccid, but within one to two hours, the muscles stiffen. A state of rigor mortis, considered the second stage, sets in, and provides us with predictable timeline," Davies continued to talk as he moved about within earshot of Solarski.

"It doesn't help that they have all been partially decapitated," Solarski added.

"The bodies are pale because of the tremendous loss of blood, but you may notice each of their facial expressions are frozen in fear. They knew they were about to die a horrific death. There doesn't appear to be any inappropriate rigor mortis. Sometimes, when we find bodies we note that a body was moved after the rigor sets in, probably by scavengers moving the deceased looking to take their valuables," Davies related. "Considering the scene is off the beaten path, the person who reported could have violated each of them for whatever money and jewelry they had, but he didn't. His name is Jorge Christo. Mr. Christo didn't engage in that, good for him."

"Captain Otero, there appears to be blood splatter evidence in proximity to the bodies that indicates something was removed. The uncanny outline of a human torso and arm are defined by blood stains," Davies commented as he continued to survey the bloodied scene.

"Mr. Davies, my Sergeant Martinez made the same observation just a short time ago. I told him I was amazed what they taught in the police academy these days. But now that you have confirmed his observation, are we now talking about someone who may have survived?" Otero queried.

"Perhaps," responded Davies as he looked over at Solarski. The three of them sensed the importance of the discovery. "This may have evolved into an abduction."

"With the time that has elapsed, and the many directions of egress from here to anywhere, we may need a lucky break to move forward with an effective surveillance," Otero advised. "We don't have many video surveillance cameras in proximity to this location, I am afraid. Regardless, I have put out orders to have the location surveyed in order to determine if any cameras caught images of any vehicles or persons departing the immediate area."

CHAPTER 21

"CARLY, THIS IS Mary Logue, how the hell are you, girl?"

"Mary, I am fine and so glad to hear from you," Carly replied. "I've been meaning to reach out for you to catch up on all that has been happening to me."

"Carly, I am so proud to hear that you have been selected to be the new Special Agent in Charge of the Miami Field Office. Your time in the New York Field Office and before that, on the president's detail, will serve you well."

"Wow, news travels fast," Carly replied. "Well, I am going to need some advice and counsel from time to time, and I hope you'll let me lean on you and learn from your time as Special Agent in Charge of the Boston Field Office," Carly said. "In fact, looks like your days as my mentor will never end, even in your retirement."

"I accept, but only if you invite me to visit you in Miami during the winter," quipped Mary. "There will always be a room for you," Carly uttered excitedly. "As soon as Will and I get to go house hunting, that is."

CHAPTER 22

WILLIAM STRAIN, "WILL" to his buddies, graduated from the United States Coast Guard Academy in 2003. He majored in international affairs, with a minor in Russian.

His first posting upon graduation was at the Pensacola Naval Air Station for aviation training, where he completed helicopter flight school within the normal 12-month period. He was subsequently assigned to the U.S. Coast Guard's Helicopter Interdiction Tactical Squadron, known as HITRON, at Cecil Field in Jacksonville, Florida. Cecil Field was home to the Squadron's 10 MH65C helicopters, used to intercept fast-moving powerboats bound for the U.S. mainland with illegal drugs and other contraband from the Caribbean. His many flight hours often took him close to Cuba. He knew its coastline well.

When his father asked him what his future duties might entail, he responded, "I will be tasked with tracking down go-fast boats from the Americas that are illegally transporting cocaine and other contraband. This may also include identifying and tracking human trafficking, coming out of there too."

"That sounds more like fun than anything else," replied the elder.

"Dad, everything the Coast Guard does is fun."

"Well, they certainly have you brainwashed, son," his father chuckled.

This Coast Guard unit was authorized to fire upon suspicious boats. Even the U.S. Navy didn't have that authority. The boat of many a smuggler turned out to be easy fodder for the tactical team's weapons.

He shaved his head of the blond locks that had attracted many a young woman and developed a distinct swagger that seemed appropriate for the elite Coast Guard assignment.

The young ensign loved to maneuver his helicopters' M240 machine gun into position, aiming his shots just ahead of a suspect go-fast boat's bow. He enjoyed the action-packed days and looked forward to repeating them. Strain relished his assignment, especially the excitement of the "gentlemen's war" against the drug smugglers, but he yearned to expand his Coast Guard profile. After completing this assignment, he became aware of a new Coast Guard initiative that piqued his interest. The newly installed Assistant Commandant for Intelligence and Criminal Investigation, civilian James F. Keegan, was interested in developing a SEAL-like program, specifically designed to enhance the capabilities of Coast Guard commands operating at the direction of the Department of Homeland Security. Keegan secured the cooperation of the United States Navy to permit qualified Coast Guard personnel to train for the coveted SEAL Trident with one caveat - that they serve for one year side-by-side with a SEAL team. The Navy wanted to ensure that the new operatives' capabilities were representative of the difficult training their own SEALS went through. Keegan agreed. Eventually, he believed, SEAL-qualified Coast Guard trainers would pave the way for the Coast Guard to have its own elite Special Warrior group. The Navy never looked at the Coast Guard as a threat, but rather, perceived the smaller maritime agency as its little brother with a lot of intestinal fortitude.

Strain jumped at the opportunity to get into one of the initial classes. He had had done enough flying for the time being. His desire to take on a new challenge within the Coast Guard organization, and to test himself, both physically and intellectually, was overwhelmingly potent.

Lieutenant Strain went to Basic Underwater Demolition School ("BUDS") training accompanied by a dozen of his colleagues, mostly young, athletic enlisted men. The USCG screened the applicants for mental and physical stamina and athletic prowess. They wanted to ensure that as many of them successfully got through the grueling BUDS training as possible to avoid inter-agency embarrassment. More importantly, the Coast Guard was determined to develop their own core of trained operatives as quickly as possible.

In his earlier days at the Coast Guard Academy, Strain excelled at baseball. He was a golden glove fielder by anyone's standards, and a pretty good hitter too. He always kept himself in top physical condition. By BUD's standards, he may have been considered an old man at twenty-six, and a bit of an oddity as a Coast Guard officer, but he was as fit as the proverbial fiddle, and disciplined in his physical regimen. Maintaining top physical condition was a lifelong habit he had begun to nurture as a youth.

Strain would have had a successful Coast Guard career without SEAL training, but he understood that by expanding his professional profile he could create greater opportunity and develop more career options.

With Strain's experience as a Navy SEAL behind him, he was ready and eager to come back home to his beloved Coast Guard and engage in a more academic mission. He wanted to do something that would let him capitalize on his knowledge and skills - international studies, his harrowing helicopter feats, and the operational capabilities he developed as a SEAL.

He didn't want to be just a trainer. He wanted something more vibrant. Then he received the fortuitous phone call from his future boss, Assistant Commandant James F. Keegan.

CHAPTER 23

"HELLO, ELI, HOW are you today?" asked Solarski. "I need to ask you a favor. Are you in a position to pick up Captain Will Strain at the airport and bring him to the Hotel Reforma for lunch? I am stuck in a meeting with the Ambassador this morning. Besides it would be a great opportunity for the two of you to meet. He is arriving from Miami at 1050 am via American Airlines. I can meet you at Hotel Reforma by noon."

"Absolutely mano, I will take care of that. I will call you when I have him in my car," Eli responded. Eli Pollack was an Israeli ex-pat, a foreigner living in another country, operating in Guatemala as a security consultant. Solarski liked him.

Strain arrived on an American Airline flight from Miami. His wife, Carly, had given him a hug and kiss from the departing Miami jetport less than three hours earlier. TSA always accommodated their fellow agency personnel with intimate departure opportunities. He would see her again in less than twenty-four hours.

"I can't wait to see you again," he whispered before walking to the waiting plane.

It was 11:30am when Eli Polack greeted the newly minted Coast Guard Captain as he walked out of the new International Arrivals Terminal.

Strain was on his way to seed some new friendships in Latin America. This was his first trip to Guatemala. He would rely on Jim Solarski to introduce him to people like former Israeli special warrior, Eli Polack. What Solarski didn't know was Strain already knew Eli Polack from previous classified assignments in different parts of the globe.

"Mano," Eli Polack blurted with a wide, toothy grin, as he grabbed Strain's hand with the gusto of an old high school buddy. Strain's grip was no less firm. The two had worked on several special operations around the world's most troubled global ports since the early 2000's.

"Eli, it is a pleasure to see you. I trust you are enjoying your civilian life, working here in Guatemala. How's the money transfer business," asked Strain.

"Not good; the Ambassador let me go last month. I now work freelance. The Ambassador uses a fresh cadre of former Shin Bet," said Polack. "He always thought of me as Shin Bet, believing my background was more closely associated with what Americans would think of as a mixture of your FBI and Secret Service," quipped Polack.

"How did he become aware of your real background," asked Strain.

"Not sure, but I guess he thought that I remained too close to my special forces group, the *Sayeed Matkal*, and I wouldn't be flexible enough to be read into some of the more sinister dealings he wanted to perform here in Guatemala. I was perhaps, for him, too polished; I intimated him. He would know I would not tolerate the corruption I would have seen. He also knew I would not kill for him, but I could kill him."

"Eli, you have a great way of explaining things," Strain chuckled.

"Some knowledgeable Israeli diplomat who knows the differences between the various Israel intelligence services must have told him, and he grew anxious that I could do him more harm than good. While he enjoys the diplomatic benefits with Israel, he remains deeply entwined with the Russian Bratva, and other global criminal enterprises. It's my guess he thought I was either not equipped to handle his personal security group, all thirty-five of his dedicated locally recruited brutes, or I was in position to take him down. These local recruits of his, they survive on his personal whims, occasional generosity, but more often intimidation. He hires mostly from the corrupt Guatemalan military, particularly those senior military who can run his money transfer business. When he says to them, attack his enemy, they use their rusted, weather-beaten shotguns. That's all they possess. They do it for him because the money is better than anywhere else, they could work. I tried to give his security detail some order, some discipline, but it was not to be. The new group of Shin Bet guys will learn quickly. Nonetheless, Mano, I will function here in Guatemala just fine without him," Polack grinned. "It is a reservoir of intelligence. In fact, there are so many dangerous Middle Eastern types migrating through here, it is a treasure trove of information. And guess where they are headed? Your southern border, it is more vulnerable now than ever."

"Well, I am pleased you have time for me," responded Strain. "I am happy that you can have lunch with Solarski and me today. He doesn't know our history, and that probably should remain."

"Mano, understood. I've known Solarski since he was assigned to the Embassy. He's like you, a good man. I have information to share with both of you. I don't understand all of it, but it needs to be shared quickly. It doesn't sound good for someone named Larry Cassell." Strain didn't flinch when he heard Cassell's name. The two walked to Polack's car, located in a nearby parking area, less than a football field from the La Antigua International's Airport's entrance.

"Mano, we are to meet Solarski at the Hotel Residencial Reforma next to the American Embassy. It's a good place to talk, but everyone will hear, so choose your words carefully." Polack winked, and then directed Strain to his Toyota 4 Runner.

"Eli, when's the last time you had this beast washed," Strain asked jokingly. "I hope it drives better than it looks."

"Captain Strain, don't be so snarky; perhaps you can walk. The Hotel Residencial Reforma Hotel is only three miles away."

Before the meeting, Polack returned from the nearby San Pedro Volcano located to the west of the city. It was a family outing. The terrain to get there lacked macadam roadways for most of the trip. "Or, Captain, you can wash my car when we get there," jested Polack.

"I withdraw my comment, friend," Strain said.

"Let me make a quick call to Jim, and let him know we are departing the airport," Eli said.

Polack accelerated quickly out of the airport parking lot en route the Avenue La Reforma north towards 14 Calle, an area offering a gaggle of American hotels. The U.S. Embassy is located about a mile from a hotel enclave, featuring a number of major western hotel chains. The Westin, Holiday Inn and Intercontinental were usually the places of choice for visiting Americans, rather than the small boutique hotels. There was more night action, and there area was relatively safe from Guatemalan street crime.

Polack parked his vehicle just beyond the hotel's brick and mortar entrance and wasted no time after exiting to wave away the approaching bell man. "I will park the car myself," Polack yelled. His brusque manner made it clear to the bellman. The car needed no attention and don't fuck with it. Strain walked behind the hustling Israeli, amused with the macho behavior. Once inside the lobby, Polack looked back to the trailing, cautious, Strain. "Let's go to the lounge in the rear, mano. Solarski will be inside. This time of day it is quiet, and while the lounge is small, the menu is good."

"Okay by me, Eli," responded Strain.

The Hotel Residencial Reforma, located adjacent to the United States Embassy along a busy Avenida Reforma, was right out of Hollywood's central casting. A small courtyard defended a white alabaster facade, two story Alamo-like designed building from the street. In the middle of the courtyard a large circular flower bed sat as a sentry, a lone concrete shaped winged bird, loyally surveilling the cars and pedestrians who breeched the hotel's compound. It is a typical boutique hotel, clean and affordable for any embassy visitor wishing to remain overnight. From a "gringo" perspective, the hotel could be found in any number of Latin American countries. It had a distinctly Spanish ambiance.

Inside the hotel, there was an array of clandestine venues. But it was the small lounge bar, surrounded by eight wooden bar stools, and facing a well-stocked shelf of spirits and house wines, that attracted most patrons. The bar's menu, featuring the local Guatemalan cuisine, often shocked most American visitors, who realized that the specialty of the house featured some form of grilled Iguana. An old cathode-ray television, which sat on top of a platform protruding from the wall to the left of the bar stools, a throwback to the past, didn't work. The hotel had not upgraded to any flat screen televisions; residents and visitors did not watch the local Guatemala *futbol* team in high density. No matter, people didn't go to this lounge to watch TV. Most went to discuss, petition, or negotiate with the Americans. Some knew, but some didn't, that their quiet meetings were monitored by the Guatemalans. The Guatemalans, in turn, didn't know that the Americans monitored their equipment, having conducted counter surveillance sweeps to detect electronic spy bugs within the hotel and bar lounge. The Americans knew listening devices were secreted in everyday products located in the hotel: smoke alarms, light fixtures, and even USB chargers. Solarski often carried an anti-bug detector with him; these days they are cheap. When having a lunch meeting, the Americans simply disabled the hidden listening devices electronically for the duration of a meeting. The Embassy didn't remove them, because they, too, were tapping into the various radio frequency. or RF. signals.

"Jimmy," said Eli, as he saw the RSO sitting in the lounge. "I've got a special visitor for you."

"Let me guess, Prime Minister Netanyahu," Solarski grinned.

"Fuck you, mano, I said a special guest," Eli quickly stuttered.

"Captain, I am glad you made it, and I thank Eli for getting you. I got stuck in a morning meeting with our Ambassador; it just went on and on," Solarski apologized.

"Absolutely no concerns on my part, Jim. I am just eager to share lunch with both of you. I am not sure Eli will let us get a word in though," Strain added, tongue in cheek.

"Fuck you, too, Commander," Eli chirped.

"He's a Captain, Eli," Solarski advised.

"Not if he busts my chops. I will demote him," he laughed.

The three sat at a lone table, away from the bar. It was 12:00pm, and the three talked freely, made easy as there were no others in the lounge. Yet they all knew their conversation would always have to be cryptic. Their waiter presented them with water, and asked if they wanted drinks. Polack instructed the waiter to bring some local red wine. "We will need a few minutes to look over the menu," he advised the waiter. Just bring the wine, please." Polack wanted a few minutes for the new Captain to digest the menu. He and Solarski knew it by heart.

Eli Polack enlisted in the Israeli Defense Force (IDF), as a young eighteen-year-old. Basic training was easy for him. He possessed nerves of steel, a high pain tolerance, and the courage of a lion. When he was presented the opportunity to qualify for the *Sayeret Matkel*, Israel's ultra-secret Special Force's unit, he was all in. He was hand-picked. Eli Polack was as confident as he was physically tough. His father was an original member of the revered Mossad, and nepotism served him well. The *Sayeret Matkel* loved familial connections. It served to strengthen the bonds among its members. Even so, Eli had to endure a 'notoriously grueling selection process' to gain access to the top-secret group. It lasted a demanding eighteen months. His training was not dissimilar from that which Will Strain went through as a provisional Navy SEAL: 'small arms, martial arts, navigation, camouflage, reconnaissance and other survival skills.' Eli couldn't get enough of it. He once told Will that when he completed the final test, "I won my red beret by carrying a fifty-pound knapsack on a seventy-five-mile march to nowhere, and I fucking did it." Eli laughed, "It was piece of cake, though I did ache a bit after finished the physical challenge."

Strain had the greatest respect for Eli. His broken English, magnified by a stutter, made Eli that much more interesting. He had more than physical adversity to conquer. English wasn't his native language, nor was Spanish, but he learned to speak both, albeit with a strong facial twitch, and a slight stutter. His altered countenance was most likely a consequence of one of his many violent encounters with Hamas, or another Iranian surrogate.

"Hey Eli, why is it you guys never wear a *Sayeret Matkel* insignia on your IDF uniforms," inquired Strain.

"We are a classified unit, mano," answered Polack.

"So, if everyone else in the IDF has an insignia, and you guys don't, can't it lead to the assumption that you are a special operator?" poked a playful Strain.

"Mano, our actions will speak louder than any insignia. I don't need to wear a fuckin" insignia to prove who I am, and besides we have the biggest cocks," responded a jovial Polack.

Strain laughed out loud, and Solarski raised his eyebrows as he sipped his wine.

CHAPTER 24

"JIM, I NEED to swing by the Embassy and share some information with you," Eli Polack stated over his iPhone.

"Of course, I am available right now if you want to come. I will notify the front gate," Solarski replied.

"I'll be there in fifteen minutes," Eli said.

Solarski greeted Eli as he arrived on foot, having parked his car in the Reforma's lot. Solarski's presence at the Embassy gate superseded the need for Eli to be further screened. "Eli, come on in." Solarski took him to a nearby interview room.

Without preliminaries, Pollack began, "We have recently acquired information that elements of the Bratva seek to avenge the loss of their deceased leader. They think a guy named Larry Cassell orchestrated the death of Arvydas Belov. They believe Cassell and some other American operatives were involved in his assassination, and from what I have heard, it was pretty gruesome," Eli said. "It is my understanding that Cassell is a former director of your Secret Service."

"That's right. He is retired, and now works in New York City as a private citizen," Solarski responded. "Trust me, Director Cassell would not kill anyone, unless it was in the performance of his duty, or to save a life. I know him and he's not someone who would have a dog in any fight that would have him stoop to the level of an assassin."

"Understood mano, but he comes up on our radar. What we know is the Bratva's planning has been extensive. They are preparing to conduct two operations on me. One at an unidentified military installation in Maryland, and another maybe here in Guatemala. Sources suggest that the Bratva's plans have been underway for some weeks now and that the new Bratva chief, who happens to be Belov's son, is about to give the green light," Polack authoritatively explained to Solarski. "We don't know what the plans are for Guatemala."

"Do the Israelis have a mole inside the Bratva that can be trusted?" asked Solarski.

"More than one," Polack declared. "More than one. They answer to Israel, not to the Bratva. But right now they are not close enough to understand and report his plans."

"Eli, Belov was a bad person. He was ruthless, cunning and ran a well-oiled global criminal enterprise. The Bratva's tentacles reach everywhere, and can touch everyone, including the U.S. President. They are corrupt with money, drugs, and human trafficking; if all else fails, they always, always resort to violence. Not long ago, the Secret Service arrested a young, internationally known Russian hacker. In response, Bratva put together a scheme to get the hacker back by hijacking a US Air Force cargo plane containing equipment and manpower to provide security support for a presidential visit to Kuwait. That happened earlier this year. Solarski explained the history to Polack, "In fact, listen to this. Captain Strain's wife, Carly, was on that plane. Mr. Cassell, in his private security role, was asked by the U.S. government to act as an intermediary in to resolve the issue with the Bratva. Captain Strain, then a Coast Guard Commander, and working in the U.S. Embassy located in Kuwait as a military attaché was asked to support Mr. Cassell. Eventually, there was an agreed upon transfer. Bratva got its hacking protégé back; the United States got its valuable cargo and manifested personnel back.

Unfortunately, a member of the elite Secret Service counter assault team was killed while trying to defend the plane. His name was Frank Larkin," Solarski said as he explained the history.

"I heard about this operation. I didn't know the Strain connection. It's also impressive that there's been no mention in the press or social media," Polack praised. "Having said that, mano, your President has the destructive habit of giving up way too much shit for public consumption. Not good for those of us who have to operate under the radar."

"The Bratva paid reparations to those abducted from our C-5 and to the murdered agent's family. It helped to keep the incident suppressed," replied Solarski.

"Mano, I heard that Belov the father, and another Bratva thug, had their heads blown away, each with a single shot. You know anything about that?" Polack inquired with a jaundiced eye, an insinuation that the U.S. government may have been involved.

Solarski stared directly in Polack's eyes without flinching. "I know nothing about who may have killed them. Listen, I'll pass your Cassell information on to the appropriate intelligence directorate after lunch and ensure you get proper attribution. I'm sure a small monetary token of appreciation will be provided. Besides you'll need it to pay for our next lunch," Solarski added.

"This is a small world, mano; our friend Captain Strain has his footprints everywhere. Somewhat strange for a Coast Guard guy, don't you think," Eli asked.

"We both know Strain; he's not just a Coast Guard guy, Eli."

Eli thought for a moment, "I understand, mano."

CHAPTER 25

"I HAVE NO knowledge who was responsible for the assassination of Belov," Cassell shared with Assistant Commandant Keegan. Larry Cassell was more concerned for his family's welfare, and that of Captain Strain, than his own. "My God, if anyone had a plethora of enemies it was Belov. It wouldn't be a surprise to me if it were someone from within his own enterprise."

After serving as a Saint Louis, Missouri, police detective, the desire for a federal position bit Cassell. He applied for the Secret Service and served with distinction: investigations, protection and intelligence. A previous U.S. President had described Cassell as "the most adept agent on the personal protective detail."

Cassell became the first African American to assume the coveted role of Special Agent in Charge of the Presidential Protective Division (PPD). Once talent met opportunity, his career took off. He later became the first black Director of the Secret Service. His appointment was based upon competence, not politics.

After he served honorably for several years, the word he was retiring quickly spread. "It's time to make some money, and get the kids through college," he said. Corporate recruiters' antennas went up and they lined up to get Cassell's attention. Cassell didn't relish the idea of being a CEO bodyguard. Soon, he found the right position, as the CSO, chief security officer, for a major global credit card processor and money transfer business. It was a perfect fit from day one. The salary and bonus offered were substantial enough to get his oldest kid through an expensive university and indulge his loyal bride. "Honey," Cassell said to his wife, "you've put up with me transferring from state to state for the last thirty years. It is now time, and my honor, to give something back to you." He handed her keys to a brand-new Lexus 470.

"Is it gassed up?" she asked with a grin, then threw her arms around him and hugged him tightly. "You didn't have to do that. I would have been happy with a mink stole," she laughed. He also hit pay dirt when his son was selected for the U.S. Naval Academy. "When you're ready, Bobby, I will buy you a car, too. That is, when the Navy allows you to have one," he said enthusiastically to his son.

On his first day as a civilian, and now a corporate CSO, Cassell gathered his new staff for an introduction. Always a strategic thinker, he trained his entire career to think in terms of prevention. "Here's my simple philosophy, if we don't plan every day to render crisis management unnecessary, then we are not doing our job. It is not that I don't believe in crisis and consequence management as component parts and critical to protecting our enterprise. I just believe that we ought to focus our efforts on prevention first. There's an adage that it is better to prevent than to cure."

CHAPTER 26

"HELLO, THIS IS Vadim."

Vadim, it's Vladimir, how are you? Hey, listen up, I need you to do something for me. I know this kid, Max, is a savant when it comes to manipulating the Internet. My father was fond of him. Personally, I couldn't give a crap about him. But, if he's that good, then we ought to use him to develop some social media background information to target the Cassell family. Make contact with him and have him collect some background shit we can use. I want to understand where they are, what they do, and how they move around so I can track their asses down and kill them. I need it now," directed Belov.

"I'll get on it, boss," Kostenko said.

"Dead, dead, dead," he added. "The more gruesome, the better." He chuckled mischievously over the phone as he relished his own idea. "I want Bratvas' revenge." He covered the phone's mouthpiece and began to weep uncontrollably.

"Okay, boss. Lately, the kid operates out of his condo and remains pretty low-key, almost reclusive. I'll shake his ass up and have him earn some of that monthly stipend he's been getting, courtesy of your father," Vadim responded.

A composed Vladimir replied. "Good, I want to know how many kids Cassell has, how old they are, and where they go to school. It can't be too hard. Cassell is community property. By that I mean he's a government asshole. His footprints are all over the Internet map. People like him tend to be featured on-line. Get a hold of the kid and have him do the research. If he balks, shoot him."

"I'm on it." Vadim hung up the phone and left his kitchen table seat to retrieve his apartment keys before walking the several blocks to the condo where Max resided. He hadn't seen him in a few months, but his boys kept tabs on his activities around the Brighton Beach community. He knew Max's reputation as a fighter, but it didn't cause him concern. "One good whack over the head with a baseball bat is the same as a black belt," he thought.

CHAPTER 27

VADIM HUSTLED THE short distance from his residence to Max's condo. He knew when Vladimir asked for something the answer was expected yesterday. "I don't need an ass chewing," he thought. "Particularly now with Vladimir being so depressed. This kid, Max, better have some answers."

Vadim stopped in front of Max's place on Brighton Second Street, just behind the Brighton Laundry mat, to survey the area. Then pushing past a small, unhinged gate at a sidewalk entrance to a small cement courtyard, he proceeded up to the outer door. As was his habit he continuously looked left to right as he climbed the single step to the front door. With a final, additional look behind him, and an unrestrained facial twitch, he rang the doorbell and then aggressively knocked on the door frame.

"Who is it?" came a shout.

"It's Vadim. I need to talk to you," he yelled.

"I don't know anyone called Vadim."

An irritated, impatient Kostenko knocked even harder and shouted, "My name is Vadim Kostenko and I represent Vladimir Belov. I need to talk to you on his behalf now, so open up the fuckin door."

The door opened, exposing a figure that dominated the door frame. He wore only a white T-shirt emblazoned with *UFT Champion*, a long-+legged pair of gym pants with white stripes on each outer leg, a pair of flip flops, and a gold chain with a Crucifix dangling outside the T-shirt.

"What do you want," Max retorted, connecting eye-to-eye with the smaller Kostenko as his nervous tick grew more prominent.

"Vladimir needs you to do some work for the organization," Kostenko shot back. "I'm here to tell you what it is."

"Do I somehow work for you or Vladimir? You got the balls to come knocking on my door like a crazed man and ask me to do you a favor? I don't know you and I don't have a relationship with Vladimir," Max said.

"Listen smartass, I don't know much about you. I am not here asking for a favor; I am here to tell you that Vladimir needs information about some mutt who killed his father and expects your ass to help him. Tell me you're not interested and that'll be it. I'll leave, but you won't like the results, tough guy," Kostenko replied.

Max smirked. "Okay, come inside little man, no need to be threatening. I certainly don't want you to have to come back and kick my ass. So, tell me, what does the young Belov need?"

Kostenko's contorted face projected his displeasure with Max's characterization of Vladimir. He carefully walked inside the condo, suspiciously looking side to side, the twitch not abating. He noticed a pit bull in the living room, not making a move, but clearly attentive to his presence, and not wagging his tail.

"What's your dog's name," Vadim asked.

"That's Torre. She only bites assholes, so be careful."

"They're the kind of dogs I like to kill," replied Kostenko.

"Not today, little man. So what is it your Vladimir Belov wants of me?"

"Well, we know you still get money from the brotherhood. Belov's father put the stipend in place when you were a baby, soon after your parents were murdered. My message to you from Vladimir is this: from now on, you start to earn it. Now that his father is gone, he is rethinking that stipend. To keep it, he wants you to begin to contribute, and here's your first work assignment." Kostenko handed Max a piece of paper. "Here's a name and some personal information for you to use to dive into social media and help us understand where the person lives, where his families live, what they do, where they do it, and any information that will give us an understanding of their fucking existence, their way of life, We need it like yesterday. For Vladimir, this is a priority."

"What is it you'll do with the information?" Max asked.

"It is none of your fucking business, cyber sissy."

"Ha, little man, you come off as pretty pissy yourself. It is amusing to me that you feel so empowered, but I will say this, little man, don't push it. Tomorrow I will have what you're looking for. I will notify you when ready."

CHAPTER 28

"VADIM, I HAVE completed an Internet deep dive on Larry Cassell. Come get it." Max left the voicemail on Kostenko's phone.

Kostenko played the message and grew annoyed. "This piece of shit is toying with me." He headed back to Max's condo. When he arrived, he banged on the door, ignoring the doorbell.

Max opened the door and passed a manila envelope to Kostenko. "Here's your background information; have a nice day," then he shut the door.

"Fuck you, piss ass," Kostenko said. As he walked away he opened the envelope and began to review the content. Cassell lived in Westfield, New Jersey. He worked at a financial services firm in New York City. His son, Bobby, was a plebe currently attending the United States Naval Academy's summer orientation. His daughter, Dorothy, was a student at George Washington University. The rest of the report was entirely open-source material providing phone numbers, addresses, relatives, and next door neighbors. "What the fuck," he thought. "I could have put this together, too sterile." He brought the information back to Belov with his concerns.

"Vladimir, this report sucks," Kostenko explained. "I don't know if he's dissing you, but he clearly didn't pick up on the request." Kostenko knew he couldn't tell Belov that he had previously told Max the reason for the requested information.

"Okay," Belov responded. "I will take care of Max later. Let me see what he provided. It may be enough for me to move forward with my plans."

Belov used the limited information to pass to a private investigator, when investigation indicated Bobby Cassell's presence at the Naval Academy, Dorothy's attendance at the George Washington University, and her intention to travel to Guatemala for an archeological dig in the near semester. The Bratva had the information it needed to move forward with multiple plans to simultaneously attack the Cassell family in the fall. Max was not privy to these plans.

CHAPTER 29

"VADIM, GO AHEAD and sign a sixty-day lease, and use a local bank cashier's check. Give them whatever security deposit they request, in cash if necessary. I want you to stay there to monitor the situation. Keep me informed as your plans develop and unfold. I want the most efficient deployment onto the Academy grounds as can possible. You will have some of our best guys to help you. If this thing fails, it could be a blood bath. Belov continued, "Let me know if you think sending in one of our girls would make the tenancy look more normal. We can send Tatiana; she's here in the States." Tatiana was a longtime Bratva loyalist who normally operated out of Germany, KGB trained, good-looking even in her fifties, and deadly, if needed.

"Boss, having Tatiana here would be more of a nuisance. I don't need horny guys in the house sniffing at her, so with all due respect I don't need her," Kostenko petitioned.

"Okay, I agree." Below hung up the phone without any further discussion.

The next day Kostenko reported back. "Vladimir, we have secured a rental property located at the end of Severn Avenue that dead ends on the water in Eastport's Spa Creek. It is a great vantage point from where to observe the Naval Academy, probably less than two-tenths of a mile by dinghy to the rocks that surround the Academy's perimeter. We've already begun to take notes of the nightly Academy police's patrol routine, and other activity performed by Navy personnel after the midnight hour. It hasn't taken long to establish their patrol protocols," Kostenko reported Belov. "They tend to sleep. We could use a dinghy to paddle over with the element of surprise."

"That's good, Vadim. Studying the geography, it looks like you and your men could approach the perimeter rocks, a short distance from the house you are renting, and that the young man's quarters located not far, from open athletic field," Belov commented. "But a dinghy? You're thinking of using a dinghy?" he asked jokingly. "You might want to explore other options."

Vadim ignored the ridicule. "Yes, it is surprisingly close. Our sources indicate the kid will soon have midnight watch duty. We should be able to get the exact day from an inside source, and I will let you know," Kostenko proffered.

"That's great stuff you've developed. You'd make a terrific intelligence operative for the United States. Better be careful they don't recruit you. Anyway, we will need to observe the Academy grounds for a few more weeks, no doubt. Can our guys survive in the neighborhood, keeping a low profile, that is, without being compromised?" Belov inquired.

"Yes, as long as they maintain a low-key posture. The Eastport area has plenty of places to eat, where they can alternate dinner locations and avoid the same place every night. The Annapolis downtown has less of a bar crowd due to the new development of bars and restaurants in nearby Parole. However, having said that, the upcoming boat shows will make it a lively place, and our guys should be able to blend in without consequence. The boat shows attract a large international crowd," Kostenko replied.

"Great, Vadim, you can buy me a thirty-foot Boston Whaler while you're on surveillance," Belov chirped back.

"That will depend on how much you pay me for abducting this kid," Kostenko replied, thinking the young Bratva chieftain would find it humorous. He didn't.

"I don't care what you do with the fucking kid. I just want to break his father's spirit, and then I can cut his throat. If the kid puts up a struggle, kill him." Belov turned hostile, and Vadim sensed it.

"Got it, boss."

"During those shows there will be many boats moored a short distance from the Naval Academy perimeter. Will this be a problem in your mind?"

"No boss, on the contrary, I think the little city harbor will be infested with similar dinghies coming and going back to their moored boats. That will give us good cover and prevent us from being noticed. Most of those boaters will be drunk and loud," a more measured Kostenko replied.

"Hmm," Belov sighed, his thoughts collapsing into place. When Belov allowed himself to grieve his father's death, his body would begin to shake as he seethed. He obsessed over the idea of abducting Larry Cassell's young boy. "If my operatives are successful, and their early morning plans are executed effectively, I will own this bastard, Cassell, and ensure his total capitulation. I will have his little bitch daughter, his son, and haven't even thought of his wife. In fact, if I get the opportunity, I will travel down to Guatemala, and screw the little bitch daughter myself before I put a bullet in her head."

CHAPTER 30

"BOSS, AS I previously advised you, we've acquired a single-family home at the end of Severn Avenue, in Eastport," advised Kostenko. "I know you've got a lot on your plate with Bratva's global business."

"Where the hell is the Eastport rental again?" asked Belov.

"Boss, I believe I told you it is directly opposite the Naval Academy," Kostenko said. "It sits prominently about eight feet off the ground level. It enjoys an almost one-hundred-and-eighty-degree view of the Annapolis Spa Creek harbor. That piece of land is called Sycamore Point by the locals. It gives us direct observation of the Academy grounds and Ego Alley, that is, the Annapolis' pier area."

"Ah, you did tell me. I am sorry for not remembering. But you sound like a fuckin' realtor, Vadim," teased Belov. "It's important to me that you keep me informed, but I am under a lot of strain these days. Cut me a break," Belov lamented.

Kostenko's choice of residence suited the Bratva's abduction plan well. A narrow roadway behind the house provided discreet parking for the snooping participants. From Sixth Street along Severn Avenue north heading toward the bay, the locale featured a half-dozen restaurant bars and grills. There was no need for patrons to frequent the area in close proximity to the surveillance house on a dead-end street, unless, of course, a lusty couple sought privacy for an encounter. There, they would find a lone bench to engage in kissing and petting. The same bench offered the Bratva operators a place to escape Kostenko and the confines of the residence during the day. They took turns venturing outside, having a cup of coffee and ostensibly reading a newspaper while studying the Academy's vehicular traffic patterns.

A slightly frayed American flag draped atop the flagpole in front of the house occasionally flapped in the early autumn breeze. Kostenko wondered how long it would last before it became so worn as to be a disrespectful eyesore. "In such a hyper-patriotic community as this," he thought, "it would be helpful to replace it before causing community angst. I could live here," he continued to ponder. "It is so vibrant during this time of year; this Annapolis remains a well-kept secret. I must remember to tell Vladimir on my next call.

"Vladimir, there are two separate boat shows that take place during the first weeks of October. The first will be the power boat, followed by the sailboat. The town explodes with people getting foolishly drunk in the bars down by Ego Alley," Kostenko advised.

"That's the second time you used the term, Ego Alley. Tell me what that means," asked Belov.

"It is a small inlet leading directly into the heart of the city. Absent the boat shows, boaters tend to slowly move their way into the inlet and back out as onlookers ogle their silent procession. The boat shows are different, more ostentatious. They're showing off," Kostenko advised.

"Well, what an interesting word, Vadim. You must be reading more. Anyway, the more useful idiots around, the better to obscure what you need to accomplish. But I suspect that with all the boats on display in the inlet and in such static positions will mean other smaller dinghy type boats belonging to the partiers will be coming and going all night, right? Won't that present a problem?"

"It's called Spa Creek. At 3:00 am, these fuckers, hundreds of them will be drunk and sleeping things off, or better yet, screwing each other inside their anchored boats, if they can get it up. Our motion in the water won't be detected as unusual by anyone, especially the academy cops on patrol," Kostenko confidently replied. I believe the large number of visitors attending the shows will be good cover for us."

After the call Kostenko went out onto the newly rented Eastport house deck and sat with the three Bratva operators Belov sent him. It was a week before the planned abduction, and he continually rehearsed in his mind how his Bratva team would engage the Academy grounds and successfully carry out the operation. Kostenko sat back casually and looked around from his chair at the deck table. His team, Anton, Leonid, and Pavel were already seated and enjoying the mild temperature and late September evening, each drinking a beer. Kostenko saw that they had taken the binoculars he had purchased and were checking out the display of stars in the sky over Annapolis. The binoculars, on an otherwise starless night, amplified the sky, magnifying an otherwise dark night.

"Shit, boss, there are thousands of stars up there," said Leonid.

"No, you dumb ass, there are millions," Kostenko responded. "Pass me a Stella."

"Well, boss, there are actually billions," Anton chimed in.

"Just shut the fuck up, Einstein," Kostenko retorted. He had enough. "Give me your binoculars so I can see."

"I hope these guys stay as focused on the job as they are on these stars," Kostenko thought. He then raised the binoculars toward the Academy. He could see the large rock formation paralleling Turner Joy Road and spotted the exact location where they intended to secure their craft.

Though there would be ample ambient light for the attackers to traverse the yard, Kostenko also purchased four Pulsar Edge GS 1x20 nighttime vision goggles. Unlike the binoculars, these goggles would be positioned on their heads and, if necessary, used for enhanced visibility.

He thought tonight would be a good time for him to hand them out and let the men play with them.

"Boys, let me go get the gifts I got you today," Kostenko alerted. He came back and handed each one a box containing the goggles. Pavel placed his goggles on first and grinned, "these light up the sky better than the night vision binoculars."

"They better," Kostenko said, "they cost ten times as much. Go ahead and walk around the house. They are easy to adjust to."

Leonid and Anton followed Pavel's lead, and soon all three were walking around the deck and down to the yard, almost out to Severn Avenue, the bordering street.

"These guys are like little kids," Kostenko thought.

"Do we get to keep these?" Leonid asked.

"Only if you guys successfully get the little bitch off the Academy grounds and get his ass up to Belov," Kostenko replied sternly.

"I have worked with nighttime vision glasses before, but these goggles are really great," Pavel declared. Anton nodded in agreement. Leonid didn't say anything, while still engaged in looking up at the sky.

CHAPTER 31

ASSISTANT COMMANDANT KEEGAN arrived back in the United States the night of October 1st. He and his wife, Cindy, were picked up at the Baltimore Washington International Airport by his loyal Coast Guard aide-de-camp, Garcia. Garcia waited until his boss stowed their baggage in the rear of the SUV and the couple entered the vehicle before advising him that Larry Cassell had just called on the vehicle's cell phone.

"Thank you, Garcia, I'll call him back in a few minutes. As you know, we will be making a quick trip to New Jersey in the morning to meet with Director Cassell." "We will be eating lunch at the Cranford Hotel. It is a pleasant little restaurant. In fact, it's where I had my first scotch and soda when I was twenty-one. It is just so ironic that Director Cassell ended up living in my hometown, Cranford, New Jersey, after his retirement from the Secret Service."

"I had my first drink when I was sixteen, sir, but there wasn't a whole lot of soda and man did I get sick. It was pure Southern Comfort," replied Garcia, "and, I never drank it again."

"Ha, ha, ha…"

"Tomorrow, I will be picking you up at your residence at 0800 to leave out of Joint Base Andrews," Garcia continued. "I understand it to be a fairly quick turnaround up there, unless you have some more business that I am not aware of."

"My parents are buried in a local cemetery not far from where I will be meeting Director Cassell. I may elect to visit there briefly to pay my respects," added Keegan.

"Always good to honor thy mother and father," Garcia said.

"Yes, it is," Keegan agreed.

Garcia arrived the Keegan's residence at exactly 7:30 the next morning and backed his government vehicle into the sloping driveway. Two large 7-11 cups of black coffee were inserted in the middle console. Keegan elected not to have his two-person Coast Guard security detail travel out to Annapolis, or to New Jersey.

"Garcia, I see you brought us coffee, but did you bring your Sig Sauer? You will be the only security asset today," Keegan chuckled.

"Sir, the detail was happy to hear they got spared the trip to New Jersey. Just kidding. Yes, I have my weapon," Garcia teased back.

"I understand we will be landing at the Morris County Airport. It is about a half-hour drive to the Cranford lunch location. If we have time, as I told you yesterday, I may elect to visit my folks' gravesite, located about a mile away in nearby Westfield. If time is short, I will just do it after my meeting with Director Cassell. We can play it by ear," Keegan advised.

"I'm prepared either way, sir," Garcia responded. "I've advised our New Jersey 'Coasties' about a possible diversion to the cemetery."

"Thank you," Keegan replied.

CHAPTER 32

THE U.S. COAST Guard C-37A is the military version of the civilian Gulfstream V executive jet. As it vectored its way to Morris County Airport in northern New Jersey, Keegan was on the phone, briefing the Coast Guard Commandant, Curtis "Grubbs" Culin, regarding the threat against the Cassell family from the Russian mob, the Bratva.

"Sir, it appears that Bratva is bent on avenging the death of its previous chieftain. Our British colleagues have provided electronic data indicating that certain elements out of Brighton Beach, New York, have been planning several events to harm Larry Cassell and his family. The Bratva have been surprisingly and effectively cryptic in their communication, but there is sufficient information to put Cassell on alert and even suggest that he and his family take preventative measures. I will be briefing Cassell shortly and can let you know his thoughts on this matter after that," Keegan informed.

"Jim, thanks for staying on top of this. As you know, I am a big admirer of former Director Cassell, and I support whatever resources the Coast Guard can muster to assist him and his family, even if his son elected to go to the Naval Academy rather than the Coast Guard Academy," Commandant Culin replied, tongue-in-cheek.

"I will pass your sentiments on to Larry when I see him," Keegan replied, "Talk soon."

As Keegan cradled the phone, Garcia stood before him. "Sir, we should be wheels down in fifteen minutes. Looks like there's plenty of time to go to the Fairview Cemetery before the Cranford location," Garcia interjected. "Your call, sir!"

"Let's do it. How did you know the name of the cemetery?" asked Keegan.

"Sir, you make me blush, and for a Latino that's difficult to do," Garcia chuckled. "There aren't that many cemeteries in Westfield, and none with such important dignitaries as your mom and dad. I understand Whitney Houston and her daughter are less than one hundred yards from your parents' plot. That's pretty good company for her," Garcia offered.

"Garcia, something tells me you've been working the Internet," Keegan responded.

The C-37A's landing gear lowered as the Coast Guard pilots began their approach, and they made a smooth landing at the private, suburban airport. Keegan grinned to himself, a small gesture of appreciation for the pilots' professionalism. He would express that gratitude personally as he disembarked from the aircraft. "Great landing, men," he winked as he poked his head into the cockpit. "Only you guys have what it takes to alleviate my ridiculous and irrational fear of flying."

Keegan's secure vehicle package entered the Westfield, N.J., Fairview Cemetery's entrance, directly across from the Holy Trinity Greek Orthodox Church, off Gallows Road. A short distance from the entrance, the vehicles moved at a slow clip toward his parents' plot. Keegan noted many headstones featuring names he knew, families and friends whose sons and daughters, mothers and fathers, he grew up with: Wilde, Haney, Kenney, O'Brien, Deschak, Waterson, and now, Whitney Houston and her young daughter, Bobbie Kristina, both buried less than fifty yards from his mom and dad.

"Garcia, I have always felt it was my duty to pay respects to my deceased relatives and friends. Don't know exactly how I got wired that way, but I'm glad I am," Keegan shared as he exited the car.

Garcia sensed his boss's emotion. He remained a respectful distance back with the running vehicle, accepting that the solemnity of the visit didn't involve him.

Keegan saw a bouquet of flowers had been placed at the headstone. As he advanced closer, he observed the inscription on the small card attached to the multi-colored array of flowers: "Mom and dad, if it weren't for your love, your support, your encouragement, I would not have ever been the person you made me, I love and miss you so." Keegan began to tear up, looked away from the flowers for a second, and then turned to Garcia.

Keegan, in a slow, deliberate manner said, "You are too much, Garcia. You just wanted to see me cry. Well shame on you, you did, brother. I appreciate the sensitive gesture."

"Boss, I wasn't trying to make you cry. I wanted to help you express your continued appreciation for those who have meant so much to you. I am wired the same way," Garcia replied as they fist pumped.

"Garcia, I could visit a dozen sites here, but won't. However, there is one more to visit up the hill. It's where my former police chief, Matthew Haney, is interred. If it weren't for him, I never would be in the position that I am in right now."

Garcia thought to himself, "Is this guy for real? He's the type of guy the rest of us would follow into hell for a heavenly cause, just a genuine human being. We are lucky enough to have our own Don Quixote."

"No problem boss, but don't look for any flowers there. I didn't have that intelligence, or the money either," Garcia chuckled to lighten the mood.

The SUV worked its way along the narrow, serpentine roadway to the Chief's gravesite. Keegan and Garcia exited the car. "It's a good thing you didn't work for Chief Haney. He'd be annoyed that you didn't see fit to have flowers here, too," Keegan chuckled, as he walked to the front of the Haney's headstone and bent over to retrieve two challenge coins that he had placed there.

"It is amazing to me, Garcia, that these Secret Service and Coast Guard challenge coins have remained on his gravesite memorial all this time. The worst that happens is when the landscapers knock them off the headstone base with their weed whackers."

"It's a nice touch to place them there, and it's just as nice that the workers leave them here, boss."

"Let's get to the restaurant, Garcia. You and the driver will eat lunch on me; get whatever you want from the menu."

"Roger that, sir. We will be there in five," Garcia advised. "We have an advance person now securing the tables." Keegan grinned, thinking to himself, "He is so efficient."

Keegan's car pulled up in front of the Cranford Hotel where the advance "Coastie" directed the driver to pull into a dedicated space. Then, the advance Coastie hustled ahead up the stairs in to the restaurant, took a quick scan of the premises and stood by the reserved table. Larry Cassell watched the young Coastie enter as he passed him, unaware that Cassell was the person Keegan was to meet. He had done it hundreds of times himself as a young Secret Service agent. As he walked into the restaurant he locked eyes with Director Cassell, standing inside the entrance.

"Jim, it's so good to see you," Cassell said as he extended his hand.

"Larry, it's always a pleasure to see you, too," Keegan replied. Keegan spotted the young Coastie by an unoccupied high-top table near the fireplace and took it as a queue as to where the two friends were to be seated.

Garcia soon motioned to the advance Coastie to come to him. "You sit with me and have lunch while the Assistant Commandant has his meeting," Garcia said politely. "I will order a sandwich for our driver and have it brought out to him."

"Thank you, sir. I can take it out to him."

Cassell intuitively knew Keegan's visit was not to be an opportunity to share family stories; he was a bit ill-at-ease, sensing something was awry. Further, he sensed anxiety,"

"Jim, this is one of my wife's favorite places to come on any given night of the week. The Hotel has been known for its cheddar burger since the 1970s. Though there is no music, both the lower level and upper-level bars hum each night," Cassell said.

A cache of assorted Scotch whisky sat well-protected behind the Hotel's thirty-foot-long bar crafted from dark Brazilian wood. A large mirror behind the shelves gave the illusion that there were more bottles than there were. Three-inch plaques nailed tightly to the curved rim bar bore the names of the most devoted customers, past and present. Clean crystal wine glasses hung over the copper veneered bar top, like silent sentinels.

"This is my kind of pub, Larry," commented Keegan with a slight grin, "and, it is not the first time I've been here. I grew up in Cranford, N.J., though I haven't lived here since 1977. My parents are buried in the cemetery not far from here. Our meeting today gave me an opportunity to visit their gravesite. I was delighted to hear that you purchased your home here in Cranford. Great school system, easy access to New York City, direct train to mid-town. I am guessing that's how you get to work these days. Does your wife, Rosemary, work?" asked Keegan.

"She is currently working here in Cranford at a small gift store, mostly to keep busy," Cassell responded. "We live not far from here, in a delightful condo on Prospect Avenue, English Village. It's a five-minute walk to the train station, and the gift store is up the street. There are plenty of parks and fields to jog or walk around. It is the kind of town where one hopes their kids eventually live with their kids. Hopefully, we become devoted grandparents one day, and get to dote over them. I am afraid I am a few years away from that opportunity. In addition, it's an incredibly safe town; the police department is top shelf."

Keegan nodded in agreement. "Larry, I am glad to have you free for the afternoon. I am here, however, for a more serious reason," Keegan said.

"I figured that, Jim," Cassell replied.

"Yes, I guess we could have predicted the threat the Bratva would pose in the aftermath of the Kazakhstan exchange. What we didn't predict because of your successful negotiation that event was an emerging threat directed specifically toward you and your family. An undeserved threat, I hasten to add."

Cassell looked at Keegan quizzically. "You mean you have intelligence that suggests my family is in harm's way because of my previous negotiations with Belov, the Bratva chief? My family is spread out. I have one kid at the Naval Academy and the other in Guatemala."

Keegan paused, took a deep breath, and responded.

"After Belov was killed earlier in the year, his son, Vladimir, successfully and brutally fought off all mob competitors. He assumed global control of the billion-dollar enterprise. He now has a vise-like grip on the Bratva's global criminal endeavors."

"Jim, with regard to this Vladimir, would I know him, or have I ever been in close proximity to him or his son?"

"You know of him, but you never met him personally. Belov's son, Vladimir, was the Bratva sniper that took out Secret Service Agent Frank Larkin Jr. on the Saudi airport tarmac. Larkin attempted to thwart the Bratva's abduction of the C-5 and paid for it with his life. The Bratva sniper took him out as he exited the plane.

When Belov was shot dead in Brighton Beach last March, there was a sense of relief in the intelligence community that the Bratva would morph into something less lethal and potent around the world. We aren't sure who killed Belov. It could have been one of his own thugs looking for a leadership change. We were just glad it happened. What his son can't shake is a nagging vengefulness toward those he perceives are responsible for his father's death. Our intelligence suggests that he thinks it is you."

"I don't disagree with your assessment. He deserved what he got, but I am not responsible for his demise, and now it appears I am in jeopardy because the Bratva mob thinks I did it?" Cassell sighed.

"Yes, Vladimir thinks the death of his father was something you orchestrated. Furthermore, we've received information from the Brits and the Israelis, to support that notion. According to them, Vladimir has put forward directives to kill you. Exactly how, and when, remains an open question. Do you carry a concealed weapon?"

"I do." Cassell replied. "I'm not worried about me. I don't want my family in jeopardy."

"Larry, we are prepared to assign protection for your family, and you, at least portal to portal," Keegan said.

"Well, I appreciate it, but I'm not looking for that. I think my kids are okay in the short-term. My daughter will be in Guatemala in a few days as part of a planned university project, and my son is a Plebe at the United States Naval Academy. A safe place, don't you think? Jim, I am not sure I want to alarm anyone in the family at this point. So unless there is more intelligence to present a clear and present danger, I don't believe I will do things overtly different to alter our lives with one exception - I am not averse to having my home discreetly protected by your operatives."

"Done deal, Larry."

CHAPTER 33

AMBASSADOR PETER COHEN was a powerful broker throughout Guatemala. His money transfer business routinely conducted illegal money transfers throughout Mexico and Central America, laundering drug money via what was ostensibly a legit global money transfer business. Cohen owned and operated a large franchise which was so profitable that the U.S. based company looked the other way.

Belov held a lot of markers that Cohen was obliged to honor. The Drug Enforcement Administration (DEA) had become aware of Ambassador Cohen's association with the Bratva back in 2002. The seventeen U.S. intelligence directorates knew of Cohen's vulnerability, particularly the Coast Guard which frequently worked with the DEA and the State Department to interdict Bratva operatives on the water transporting drugs to and from the Americas.

"Hello, Vladimir, how are you? It has been a long time since we spoke. I want to express my deepest sympathy to you and your family for the terrible loss you have suffered. Your father was one of my favorite people in this world," Cohen said in ambassador-like speak.

"Listen, Ambassador Cohen, enough with the bullshit, my father may have liked you, but I don't. I know for a fact you didn't like him, so fuck you and listen up," Vladimir responded crisply.

"I am sorry that you have taken offense to my comment. I apologize. How can I be of assistance to you," Cohen, now shaking, asked.

"We need some of your boys to do a job. I will be sending my right-hand man, Yuriy Khovasov, tomorrow to meet with you. Yuriy will explain what we need assistance with, understood?" Vladimir growled.

The Ambassador knew he could not say no but wanted to do so. After all, he was an Ambassador to Israel. "I should no longer feel obliged to the son," he thought. "His father was with whom I had the relationship. Why do I need him further? I have my own army down here, for Christ's sake." Yet in his heart he knew the Bratva owned him, and that it was time to pay the marker.

"Vladimir, I am sure that whatever your needs are, we can accommodate them," Cohen replied in compliance. Vladimir hung up the phone.

Cohen did not know the breadth of the forthcoming request. "If I do not comply, my family and I can kiss our wealth and stature here in Guatemala good-bye."

The Yuriy Khovasov demand might be the biggest test of his life. He grew nervous.

CHAPTER 34

AMERICAN AIRLINES FLIGHT 1603, out of Miami, arrived in Guatemala at 12:56pm. The direct flight was an indicator that Guatemala was emerging as a significant Latin American destination. Yuriy Khovasov disembarked without haste, blending in with the other passengers, mostly Guatemalans. He proceeded to the immigration checkpoint where he was intercepted by a local arranger whose job was to expedite the process. The arranger led him to a private lounge, where Ambassador Cohen was waiting.

"Hello, Mr. Khovasov, welcome to Guatemala. I am Ambassador Cohen."

"Nice to meet you," Khovasov responded.

"Please provide the arranger with your passport and he will ensure you proceed through immigration and customs without difficulty. We can stay here and chat over a glass of wine if that is okay with you?" Cohen said with an almost obsequious tone.

"I don't drink wine. How about a glass of scotch?" Khovasov replied tersely.

Cohen looked at the hostess and nodded. She brought a glass of Johnny Walker Blue with ice on the side for the cranky Russian, and a glass of red wine for the cautious Ambassador.

"I assume you would like to wait until we get to my office before discussing the business at hand," suggested Cohen.

"No shit," Khovasov blurted. "You think I want talk here? In fact, I want to go to your residence, not your office, and we can talk in your personal bedroom. I am sure you won't be compromised there with any monitoring devices. How does that sound, Ambassador?"

"Well, that certainly can be accomplished," answered Cohen, as he sipped from his glass.

Khovasov took a gulp of the scotch and asked, "Actually, I am assuming you have a large bathroom adjacent to your bedroom, so let's talk there. No way is anyone monitoring that place, unless your wife is suspicious of you."

Cohen looked puzzled. "Wherever you wish, Yuriy."

The arranger walked in with a freshly stamped passport and customs clearance.

"Ah, thank you for these," Cohen said as he stood and slipped the arranger a neatly folded twenty-dollar U.S. bill.

Yuriy glared at the Ambassador and realized they were about to leave, so he took a longer gulp to empty his glass. "Great drink," he said to the server. "Thanks. Let's go."

The arranger led them to the exit. "Just follow me to my car, Yuriy; it's a short walk to the VIP lot."

As Khovasov came closer to the ambassador's car, a Lexus 450, he noticed that the car had an escort vehicle tailing it. He instinctively knew it to contain his bodyguards. Strange he thought, "They all look Israeli."

"Hop in the rear with me," Cohen said. Once in the car, Yuriy took out his iPhone and dialed up Vladimir. "I'm in the car with the ambassador. We are headed to his residence. I will brief him on our logistics and let you know how we are doing after that, boss."

"Great, Yuriy. Let him know the importance of this and that he better not fuck it up. Let him know we have not previously used his enterprise, so he owes us," Vladimir advised.

"I'm all over that, boss." Vladimir hung up.

"I am assuming that was your boss," said Cohen. "We will be at my home in ten minutes."

"Yes, that was Vladimir, Ambassador Cohen. He has me here to brief you on an upcoming event for which he requires your support," Khovasov responded.

"Fine, go ahead with your information," Cohen urged.

"Like I said, in your bathroom," Khovasov insisted, and he said no more.

CHAPTER 35

"MR. KHOVASOV, FOLLOW me to the master bedroom," Cohen directed.

As Khovasov entered the bedroom he looked about in amazement at its size, a thought short-lived as he entered the bathroom. "Holy shit, Ambassador, this is the biggest fucking bathroom I have ever seen. Are those fixtures made of gold?"

"No, just gold plated," Cohen acknowledged stoically.

"First time I have ever seen two independent showers in one bathroom. Not bad, the money transfer business must be serving you well. Okay, let me get to what Vladimir wants from you. There is a group of young students from Washington, D.C. here in Guatemala doing a school project, some sort of historical dig at a place called La Antigua. The group is small, a teacher and his six students. We are only interested in one of them, Dorothy Cassell. She is the daughter of Larry Cassell, a man that Vladimir holds responsible for killing his father. He wants the girl taken alive and brought to a safe house, preferably in Key West. He wants the rest of the group butchered like pigs. He wants their throats slit so deep their heads dangle. When the girl is taken he wants her raped often by your men, but not killed. She needs to be alive for Vladimir to use to lure her father into a trap, and ultimately dispose of him in an equally violent manner," Khovasov quietly took a drink of water from the sink counter and then stared at the Ambassador. Cohen stared into a wall mirror, seemingly in disbelief about the arrangement the Bratva thug had presented.

"You okay, Ambassador, you look like you just saw a fucking ghost," laughed Khovasov.

"'I'm okay. I'm just contemplating what type of men I need to do this. I'm also thinking what personal relationships I will need in our Justice Department to help distance us from any connection to the crime. There will be an obvious crime scene investigation that will capture the attention of the country's president, and frankly the world. We will need a plan to suppress this news as quickly as possible, and give me plausible deniability, don't you think," asked Cohen.

"Of course, it will appear to be a violent robbery; an ugly, vicious, brutal scene, but with a typical Guatemalan signature," Khovasov smirked. "These people love to cut necks."

"Not sure it will be that easy, but yes, it can be done," Cohen replied, attempting not to betray his larger concern. The idea of slaughtering innocents, who did not deserve the wrath of a global criminal enterprise, caused him angst. "I will put together a team to do this for Vladimir," Cohen said. "I will need tomorrow to arrange it, and of course, I will need more information.

"Please make sure we have a comfortable van for transporting the girl. Your men should travel in style while they have their way with the little bitch," Khovasov chuckled. "Now, let's go to dinner."

CHAPTER 36

"VLADIMIR, WE KNOW where Cassell lives, where his children go to school, and we have a couple of ideas for you to consider on how to grab them," advised his aide-de-camp, Boris Markov.

"Where did the information come from?" asked Vladimir.

"Vadim visited the cyber kid and had him develop intelligence from multiple social media sources. This Cassell family is on media steroids, with the old man listed in Wikipedia like he is some sort of security rock star."

"Okay, so what are you initial thoughts for attacking these bastards," Belov asked, now eager to know.

"Well, we know the Cassell boy is attending the U.S. Naval Academy. We've got multiple contacts inside the school who tell us he is just finishing the orientation part of it. Soon the upperclass midshipmen will begin to show up at the Academy. We know the daughter attends a university in Washington, D.C., George Washington University. We also learned that she is about to travel to Guatemala for a fucking archeological dig. We can develop abduction plans for both locations. We can have Vadim Kostenko manage the Academy abduction and Yuriy Khovasov manage the Guatemala action. Yuriy personally knows Ambassador Cohen in Guatemala. He can use his own people to pull it off," Markov advised. "And the Ambassador owes us."

"Okay, Boris develop these ideas further with Yuriy and Vadim and get back to me with solid plans in the next few days. Also, I want Cassell's kids to pay first, then we can get to Cassell as the final blow. Killing his wife will be icing on the cake. By the way, where does he live, did Max learn that?" Belov asked.

"He lives in a small town in New Jersey, Cranford, I think he said, with his wife. He works in the city," Markov ad-libbed. "He's a big shot security director."

"Great, close to us, we can make his little town, 'Cranfart,' newsworthy soon," Belov grinned. "But I want it done to him after I destroy his family."

CHAPTER 37

"LA CIUDAD DE Santiago de los Caballeros de Guatemala," is known today as Antigua Guatemala (or simply Antigua). Sitting on top of three tectonic plates, the old Guatemala City is spread out in a valley with the Agua volcano reigning on its horizon. The current Guatemala City was founded in 1776, after a devastating earthquake destroyed the former Spanish capital of Central America."

On October 3, at 4:45 pm, the Guatemalan State Police operations center's phone alerted. The dispatcher, receiving the message, quickly understood the urgency and patched the call from the regional La Antigua police office to its afternoon duty officer. The operations center was located midway between the new capital and the ancient capital.

"This is Captain Otero; how can I help you?"

"Sir, this is Sergeant Pedro Martinez. I am afraid I have some bad news. We have a terrible crime scene here in La Antigua, it's a massacre of some young people, believed to be foreigners. Sir, it is a mess."

"This is going to be a big problem for the President," said Captain Luis Otero of the Guatemalan State Police. He was referring to the nation's new President, a former comedian, who had been sworn into office in the aftermath of the country's latest corruption scandal.

Captain Otero thought, "How he explains this without disrupting the country's new uptick in tourism, particularly in La Antigua area, will be difficult chore for him," but he didn't share that with the Sergeant."

"I've seen a lot of death, but this is the most gruesome scene for me, Captain," observed Martinez. "I have a half-dozen uniformed officers here with me."

"Have your men form a security perimeter around the scene. Don't let anyone trample over it; this will be an international event soon, and I don't think the Justice Ministry will be happy if it's bungled," Otero said with a seasoned tone. "I will be there in thirty minutes."

Littered about the archeological site lay six terribly disfigured and bloodied corpses.

"Captain, the dead's frozen appearance indicates a state of rigor mortis, probably within the past hour. The weather has been in the low seventies, so the bodies haven't degraded much," suggested Martinez.

"Yes Sergeant, we may not be too distant from those that did this. But each hour that has passed since the murders occurred makes it more difficult to resolve. We need our forensics guys up here as soon as possible in order to develop as many investigative leads for us before they disappear or get contaminated," Otero responded. Martinez hurriedly walked away but came back to the captain within minutes.

Each victim suffered deep, broad slashes to the neck. The sole girl's head dangled awkwardly from her shoulders, in silent stillness, connected only by visible strands of tendons. The older man had been completely decapitated, and his head was located a few feet from the body. His eyes remained open, glaring into the night, frozen in time. Dried blood saturated the ground. Some of the blood commingled and pooled, creating within the circle of mutilated corpses a thicker, communal blood deposit, not yet dry.

"Captain, if we could see through those eyeballs, we could capture the images of the attackers. From the look on their faces, it must have been horrifying," Martinez blurted.

"When the forensic team arrives, it will have a hell of time differentiating whose blood is whose," Otero said to those in earshot. "Let's be careful not to disturb the scene but go ahead and see if they all have identification. My God, this is terribly sad." A tear slowly dripped from his eye onto his cheek, followed by several more. Even for a veteran cop like Otero this crime scene was difficult to digest.

"Captain, this is what we have so far - most of the victims appear to be young adults: four males and a female, but there's an older male victim too, looks to be about forty years old," reported Martinez within minutes. "We have not disturbed any of the bodies but have checked for identification. They appear to be American, or possibly Canadian. They're wearing typical college attire from George Washington University. Judging from the scene it appears that they were all involved in some sort of excavation project."

"That's right, Sergeant. I am sure they are part of a university project. Whatever they may have been doing, they certainly didn't deserve this. Their families will be forever changed." Otero closed his eyes as he recited a short prayer to the Blessed Mother.

The grisly scene was less than an hour's ride from Guatemala City. Otero and Martinez stood in La Antigua, Guatemala's most important venue for antiquities. The location, once the capital before its near destruction from a long-ago earthquake, was now a Guatemala tourist mecca. Several highway routes - 7, 10 and 14, intersected the old city, and anyone fleeing could do so in a variety of directions.

"Whoever is responsible for this massacre has probably distanced themselves in one of three directions," said Martinez. "That will be difficult to determine unless we develop directional clues rather quickly."

The captain's cell phone rang. It delivered a cascading cacophony that begged to be answered; its irritating pitch would continue to elevate until the captain hit the answer button. "Otero."

"Captain Otero, this is Ambassador Peter Cohen. I understand you are on the scene of a terrible incident which may involve some American university students. Have you made progress in your investigation? Have you identified any of the victims? In particular, is one named Dorothy Cassell?"

"Ambassador Cohen, we have only begun our investigation. The crime scene is not pleasant, rather macabre, and difficult for us to digest. Once we complete the processing of the scene, we will have a better understanding of the victims' identities. I am sorry to inform you that my protocol is to first notify the Justice Minister, who will then brief our President. This is a most sensitive situation. How is it you knew we were here? And why is it you need to know, Mr. Ambassador?

Otero knew Ambassador Cohen's reputation, and it wasn't a good one, but it was well earned. Otero wasn't intimidated.

"Captain, you know who I am, and who I represent. I don't think you want to embarrass yourself, or shorten your career, by insulting me with your interrogatories. I will expect an update as soon as you establish the identities."

Otero heard the phone go dead and cleared his own phone of the connection. "What an asshole," he muttered to himself.

"Okay Sergeant, we've got a high-level interest in this case. I knew it was to be big, but didn't expect the call I just got. Looks like the Russian mob has an interest in this matter. Ambassador Cohen called me about this scene, and there's only one reason for it."

"Sir, I have found identification for all six victims."

"Is one of them named Dorothy Cassell?"

"No, sir. The female's name is Stephanie Zirgulis."

"Good, then perhaps I can let the Ambassador know and relieve his concern. I don't need him interfering with our investigation."

"But sir, I must tell you, I think there may have been another victim. When the forensic team gets here, they will surely see the evidence of a blood stain pattern that may indicate missing items, and perhaps a body."

"Sergeant, they must be teaching you younger guys some good observation skills at the state police academy for you to come up with that notion so quickly."

"Thanks sir, but it really is a basic observation, considering all the blood that must have flown around. In fact, one pattern suggests something the size of an upper torso and extended arm of someone who may have been on the ground. It almost resembles a chalk outline made out of blood spatter. It is slightly separated from the hacked bodies," Martinez continued. "This is one gruesome site. The splattered blood leaves its own signature. We just need the professionals to confirm it."

"Okay, let's leave the immediate area for the crime scene technicians and let them work their magic," Otero cautioned. "In the meantime, let's get some high intensity lighting up here. Darkness is approaching and I want the forensic guys to benefit from the illumination."

"Already on the way, Captain," Martinez acknowledged.

CHAPTER 38

"VADIM, THE GUATEMALA event has begun. It appears we got the Cassell girl in Guatemala and she's on her way north. So far, a success. Cohen's men are have transporting the girl in a van from La Antigua to a power boat in Puerto Barrios located on the east coast of Guatemala. It will head north toward Cancun to refuel. Then it will hug the Cuban coastline where it may refuel again before transferring the girl in open water to one of our other boats, and finally to Key West. Any delay will be dependent on what interference they may get from the U.S. authorities, if any. Most of their travel will occur during the night, arriving at the transfer point late morning. I heard the scene at the La Antigua dig site could not have been gorier. All the students have been decapitated as I requested. Yuriy told me that Ambassador Cohen grew squeamish about slaughtering the kids, but that's not the little pussy's concern. I asked Yuriy to make sure Cohen's boys take some photos and send them to me while the bitch is in transit to Key West," Belov gleefully expressed. "I am eager to hear of your success later tonight at the Naval Academy. With good luck we should have the girl and the boy in one bucket ready for a gruesome delivery to their father. I want him to suffer our Bratva response before we do him and his wife," Belov concluded.

"Great news, boss. We are ready to deploy around 3:00 am and will have the kid in place at our Eastport safe house well before dawn," Kostenko advised. "The boat show has been great cover for us."

"Vadim, it is certain that our operation so far has not been detected, so your efforts after midnight will not have been compromised. If what you said is accurate, the girl should be close to Key West by the time you take the little Navy bitch," a gleeful Vladimir chirped. "Although I wish we could have had the two abductions executed somewhat closer together, what's happened so far should work. I told Yuriy I wanted the Cassell girl screwed while on the boat to Cuba. I want her to experience the pain I've known, to pay for what her father did to my father. If I were there myself, I'd be putting it up the little puta's butt," Vladimir's scaling rhetoric rising to a higher pitch, which was not lost on Kostenko.

"They know. They know," Vadim responded gratuitously. I heard from Yuriy yesterday. He instructed Cohen's men to do it in the van and continue until they got to Key West. It should make for a quick ride to the east coast of Guatemala and onto the States," Kostenko chuckled. "They get all the fun,"

"Vadim, you are as sick as me; I like it." Vladimir placed the phone down on the armrest, staring out his Brighton Beach living room window. He pursed his lips, knowing his plan for revenge was now in motion.

CHAPTER 39

"WE BELIEVE THE boat departed Puerto Barrios about 2000 hours, sir," reported a young Coastie. "We've been tracking it for the past hour and it appears to be hugging the coast of Belize just south of Mexico's border.

"Roger that," responded Captain Strain. "Keep me posted every fifteen minutes, or immediately if there is a deviation from the coastline toward Cuba. I can't imagine it heading to the open waters this soon."

"Wilco," responded the operator.

The Coast Guard's direction of interest was a powerful cigarette boat, a high-speed vessel that is typically the boat of choice for drug smugglers, and other nefarious bad guys. The Bratva routinely used similar boats up and down the United States' east coast. Today, the Coast Guard believed Cassell's daughter was aboard.

"Please get me Assistant Commandant Keegan," Strain politely requested, "No need for secure." Strain referred to the process that allowed for encrypted conversation between him and Keegan. Time was critical; he could produce a live, continuous non-encrypted connection to update Keegan if desired.

The operator knew what he meant. The call would go through faster that way, and the captain would be able to communicate without using the classified equipment. "This is urgent," the operator thought.

"Yes, sir," replied the duty officer. Within a moment Strain and Keegan were connected on a secure line.

"Keegan," said the Assistant Commandant into the phone.

"Sir, the cigarette is about two hours from Cancun, where it should begin to veer off toward Cuba's southwestern tip, but still in international waters. I suspect they will refuel in Cancun. We've got several assets in non-territorial waters north of the boat at this time. We are trying to determine how, and when, to take it down before it becomes problematic internationally," Strain advised. "Now, it looks like it will hug the Mexican coast up to Cancun, and then head east toward Cuba's territorial waters."

"My sense is we will have to assume that the Cuban authorities are in bed with Bratva and are awaiting the boat's arrival," Keegan surmised. "Or, at least, they're tolerating the boat hugging its coastline before it veers north to Key West."

"Yes, sir, no doubt about it. Once inside Cuban territorial waters, the chances of rescuing the girl become slimmer," Strain advised.

"What are they using?" Keegan asked.

Strain was amused, but it quickly dawned on him that Keegan was a cop who became a Coast Guard intelligence guy. He responded respectfully, "they're using a 2019 Cigarette Racing fifty-nine-footer powered by six Mercury Racing outboard engines. The boat provides 2,400 horsepower and allows the vessel to travel at 72 mph. "Sir, it's a fast boat," he added. The Cigarette has been described as 'go-fast' vessel, that is, 'a super-fast boat designed with a long narrow platform and a *planed* hull that enables it to reach high speeds.' The Bratva have fancied using these high-performance boats regularly in the past, unconcerned with their cost. It owned scores of them, most purchased with drug money. They didn't buy them to sell them; they bought them to gain an advantage over the Coast Guard. And, more often than not, it worked.

"Alright smartass, I get it," Keegan mused tartly. "Keep me updated, please."

CHAPTER 40

"CAPTAIN, ADMIRAL DONALD Merz, the new Director of National Intelligence, called and is making the other sixteen intelligence directorates, and their respective assets, available to us. DNI Merz desires that the Coast Guard Intelligence maintain the lead on this matter. The FBI objected, but were told to stand down, so I am not sure how supportive they will be to your effort. Interestingly, I posited to the Admiral that notwithstanding Cuba's penchant for illicit money, the Cubans may be anxious to develop a healthier relationship with the United States and seize this moment to advance that objective. That is because of your good work in the short time you've been assigned to the Southeast Sector. We will just have to see."

Strain's Cuban counterparts took an immediate liking to him. Aware of the Captain's intelligence role, they believed that he could help serve Cuba's thirst for improved travel relaxations with the United States. As a result, Captain Strain could enter Havana with the ease of one telephone call.

"Should the cigarette head into a Cuban port, your newly established contacts might be of value," Keegan stated.

"Yes sir," Strain responded. "Our ability to communicate directly with their government could make a difference."

"Do we know how many others are on board with the girl, and what other assets they may have?"

"There are at least four Bratva operatives on board, probably all Guatemalans, and Belov's man, Yuriy Khovasov. We are sure that they have long guns along with their side arms. I wouldn't doubt that the fast boat is wired in such a way that, if challenged, it could be remotely destroyed," said Strain. "Having said that, I can't imagine the Guatemalans wanting to give up their lives for the Bratva in the same way the Russian members would."

"I understand Will. If the fast boat reaches Cuba's territorial limits without an interdiction, what is plan B?"

"If the fast boat gets to Cuba unfettered, she'll closely hug the Cuban coastline. We will then have no choice but to stand down and keep it under surveillance. I don't see that the boat has another option other than Cuba in order to re-fuel. The difficult proposition will be whether a decision to interdict once it leaves Mexico's territorial waters, because we will have about ninety miles to work with. Nicaragua, the only other nation that would support Bratva's criminal behavior, is out of range, so we are confident Cuba will be their choice. We will have to await them deciding when to leave Cuba for Key West. Among the tools we would rely heavily upon is the intelligence community's ability to pick up electronic chatter inside Cuba to get that information," answered Strain.

"Will, would it make sense to have you enter Cuba now to nurture assets within Cuba in the event the boat makes it?" Keegan asked.

"Sir, since I've been back from Kuwait, I have made several trips to our Key West Sector. I am working with the Drug Enforcement Administration and the Central Intelligence Agency to enhance our offshore electronic eavesdropping capability within Cuba, as well as working to develop new human intelligence assets inside Cuba. We will have some significant listening tools. I am also confident that our sister agencies, to include the NSA, will be able to muster adequate support for us to know what's going on if the boat makes it to Cuba. I don't believe

I have yet developed the type of human assets within Cuba that could actually help us operationally. The hard part would be to get a fix on their location if they keep moving around on the island of Cuba," Strain added. "Our Israeli friends in Cuba may be able to help."

"Will, the Israeli support is interesting. Regardless, what really scares me is that the Bratva may no interest in exchanging Dorothy Cassell for anything or anybody. It's Larry Cassell the Bratva wants, and his daughter is just one of several poker chips they're attempting use to get him. If the boat gets to Cuba and docks in a Cuban port for refuel, that's one thing, a good thing. But if they elect to keep her in Cuba, our options to rescue her are severely limited, no matter how many assets we have there," Keegan shared.

"That is true, sir," commented Strain. "We will prepare for the worst."

"Okay, but also thinking outside the box, wouldn't the Bratva relish having her back in the United States to make a continued statement. I would recommend that we be prepared for her transfer to another boat in order to make a dash for the Florida Keys," Keegan proffered. "I know I am all over the map, but I feel responsible for getting Larry Cassell involved in this in the first place. He doesn't deserve this."

"Sir, that is part of our contingency planning. We are in communication with U.S. Special Operations Command for additional assets, particularly Navy SEAL support, if and when needed. Further, my understanding is several elements of the Command are preparing for relocation to Guantanamo Bay as a staging area, should Cuba become a larger factor in this scenario," Strain reported.

Keegan noted that "the Bratva operates with abandon inside Cuba. They pay the Cuban intelligence community money that the Cuban government can't possibly match. The Castros knew this and benefitted from an eager Russian mob ready to pay big for illicit favors. Now with the Castros dead, the existing Cuban government's penchant for easy cash persists, and they're always paid in United States $100 bills."

"Yes sir," replied Strain. "Cuba is as corrupt as ever."

"It won't be long before we know whether the Cigarette made it to Cuba. Talk to you soon," Keegan added before terminating the call.

CHAPTER 41

"SIR, WE HAVE another local resource. The Florida Civil Air Patrol are willing to help in the surveillance of the Cigarette. They have a strong presence in open air space between Southwest Florida and the open waters off the northern Cuba border. The Patrol operates under the radar most of the time, not attracting much interest. They fly small propeller aircraft."

"Okay, right now, the more eyes for the surveillance, the better."

"Sir, I will get back in fifteen minutes with an update on the Cigarette. Right now, we are still uncertain as to its directional intent," Strain offered.

"Okay, Will, thanks." Keegan hung up.

Strain then dialed up Colonel James "Holt" Bishop, Florida Civil Air Patrol, out of Naples, Florida.

"Captain Strain, we can be up in the air in twenty minutes. I can muster two Cessnas from the Key West Sector, and two Cessnas from the Naples Sector, and have them surveil the Gulf," advised Colonel Bishop.

"Holt, I can't thank you and the Civil Air Patrol enough. I believe the target boat is about to enter either Cuba's territorial waters or may veer toward the Florida Keys," advised Strain.

"Roger that, our planes' dedicated mission radio operators will be on the common frequency and report periodically as to any sighting," responded Holt.

"Maritime limits and boundaries for the United States are measured from the official U.S. baseline, recognized as the low-water line along the coast as marked on the NOAA nautical charts in accordance with the articles of the Law of the Sea. The Office of Coast Survey depicts on its nautical charts the territorial sea (12 nautical miles), contiguous zone (24nm), and exclusive economic zone (200nm, plus maritime boundaries with adjacent/opposite countries). The Coast Guard has determined that controlling entry of U.S. vessels, and vessels without nationality, into Cuban waters and controlling the departure of U.S. vessels, and vessels without nationality, bound for Cuba is necessary to protect the safety of United States citizens and residents, to improve enforcement of the economic sanctions against the Government of Cuba, and to prevent threatened disturbance of the international relations of the United States."

The Florida Civil Air Patrol (CAP) activated two Cessna 182s. Each plane has a top speed of one-hundred-forty-three knots, or for the layman, one hundred sixty-four miles per hour. Each plane is described as a four-seat, single-engine light plane. In addition to the mission pilot, the other seats are filled by a mission observer and a mission scanner. The scanner, sitting in one of two rear seats, is responsible for looking for the target, in this case looking for the fast-moving Bratva Cigarette vessel. All four planes are supported by a dedicated mission radio operator who remains ground based and dedicated to ensuring the observer's messages are captured and passed to the Coast Guard in a timely manner.

"Holt, that is most generous of the Air Patrol to support us in this effort, particularly on short notice," Strain said. "What I like about your aircraft is they are propeller driven and not planes that would necessarily alert the bad guys that they are associated with the military or police."

"There's no doubt that our guys will love to support your mission." Bishop said.

When talking to local community groups about the CAP, Colonel Bishop usually mentions, "Our support efforts are a way for our pilots to hone their skills. Exciting missions, like aerial reconnaissance to look for missing boats and aircraft or other support missions, like transporting medical technicians or lifesaving medicines, are profoundly satisfying. When asked if they would support the military or police about a corrupt vessel conveying contraband, Bishop responded, "A mission like that only heightens our desire to assist. There's something about playing cops and robbers in the sky. It raises the adrenaline, and we love being part of the party."

"How many aircraft and members does the CAP have," asked an audience member.

"The Civil Air Patrol is an all-volunteer U.S. Air Force auxiliary. It operates a fleet of over 500 aircraft and performs most of its support in continental U.S. inland search and rescue missions. Nationwide, we have about 58,000 members. We perform homeland security, disaster relief, and drug interdiction missions at the request of federal, state and local agencies. Here in Florida, we help with surveillance and rescue missions as needed. This is the one time we take routes over water, usually within our territorial limits," Bishop further explained.

CHAPTER 42

"MAX, THIS IS Will Strain calling, how are you?" Captain Strain asked.

"Mr. Strain, I mean sir, I am so happy to hear from you. I've been thinking of you and your wife. Please, what is it I can do for you?" an exuberant Max responded.

"Max, tell me, what have you been doing these past months? Are you still fighting? How is your friend, Shorty, and your dog, Torre?"

"Yikes, sir, I can't believe you remember all that. No, I haven't fought since the Madison Square Garden bout. Shorty is still short and remains my loyal friend. Torre is getting older, but still feisty."

Shorty, or "коротышка" in Russian, was born Vitaly Rubin, the son of a Russian émigré whose father knew Max's dad back in Moscow, and then in the United States when his dad was an NHL player. Max always had the sense that Mr. Rubin, Shorty's dad, wanted to share with him something about Max's father, but held back. Something haunted him. It was a secret soon revealed to him by Will Strain.

"Great stuff, Max. I am sorry for getting serious too quickly, but I need your help. I am asking you if you would be comfortable giving me Vladimir Belov's location and, if possible, provide it on a daily basis. As you know with your fine-tuned computer skills, Vladimir and his people know how to obscure his electronic signature," Will asked.

"Sir, I can do that, and much more, if you need it from me. I have no love for the son of the man who murdered my parents. I can take him and place him on the Brighton Beach boardwalk if that's something you need," Max growing more excited as he spoke. "I can wipe him off the face of the Earth."

"Captain Strain, I wanted to update you a few weeks ago about the continued interest Belov had in Mr. Cassell. But I didn't have specific threat information, so I didn't make the call, but clearly the Bratva had a direction of interest in him. They asked me to do a deep dive on the Internet about the Cassell family. I did, and gave them back a vanilla report, that is, nothing more than they themselves could have extracted from the Internet," Max added.

"Thank you, Max. Yes, Belov and his Bratva thugs have been aggressively operational in recent days, which is why I am calling you. I need your help with his current location, but I don't want to get you too involved. You are still a young man with a bright future. It is our fight with Belov. You have my cell number. It is encrypted, so send me what you can, when you can. I will make it my business to come see you in the not-too-distant future," Will added.

"Yes, sir, I will get to work on it now."

Will remembered the day he met Max. He was respectful then, and remains that way now, Strain thought.

Strain learned that Max, the multi-talented Russian kid from the tough Brighton Beach enclave, had the discipline, if harnessed, to be a valuable intelligence asset.

Max was a cyber-genius who easily grew bored with the ease of exfiltrating large amounts of money from poorly protected bank servers. He didn't seek to destroy their servers; he only exerted that effort on an occasional Al Qaida inspired propaganda site, which he had no qualms destroying. Max told his sidekick, Shorty, "I hate these asshole hackers who screw with the United States. It's one thing to go after the money, but some of these Islamic groups use the Internet as a tool to attack the United States. They suck." Max was only ten when the World Trade Center was attacked, and the daily flow of broken families and heartbreak affected him even as a young person. It was then that he most missed the parents he never knew.

In cherished, pensive moments, Max thought of the father he never knew, Ivan Valdimirovich Dostoevsky, the young hockey protégé from the former Soviet Union. As a child he had watched videos of his dad playing professionally at the famous Madison Square Garden. There were the old VHS tapes, highlights his mother had saved and put away for him to view as he grew older. In daydreams he enhanced his dad's special memory, often placing himself in proximity of his father.

"Your dad was an honorable man," his maternal grandfather had told him. "From what I have been told from his family in Russia, your dad had an amazing work ethic, an ethic that made him a national Russian hockey star. His destiny was realized when his hard work resulted with a larger prize. He became a National Hockey League player."

Max's dad met his mother, Ekaterina Petrov, after he immigrated to Brighton Beach, where she was called Kate. Max relished the meaning of her maiden name, translated as "rock." In 1990, Kate gave birth to Maksim Valdimirovich Dostoevsky, a towhead, with a full head of blond hair. His young parents called the handsome little boy Max. "The only U.S. citizen in the family," joked Kate.

Belov's request to Ivan to throw NHL games was serious and planned. Belov knew his relationship with Ivan would undergo a permanent change once the proposal was made. It was not a simple request that Ivan had the option to refuse. The Bratva did not like "no." That "no" would have consequences. Ivan said "no."

While in Kazakhstan helping to barter with the Bratva to exchange their super hacker for the American hostages, Commander Strain arranged to meet with Max. It was at this meeting that Max was to learn the truth about his murdered parents. Both Max and Commander Strain were tall and blond with blue eyes. Both were warriors. Though trained differently, they were equally deadly. Sitting directly across from each other, the Coast Guard Intelligence Officer said, "Mr. Dostoevsky, we don't have a lot of time to talk, but let me share with you what I know about your parents. I'll be as straightforward as I can. The United States had a real problem with your history of attempts to defraud U.S. banking systems. However, our knowledge of you as an aggressive anti-terror activist, taking down Al-Qaeda websites, significantly tempers our perception of you. The U.S. intelligence community recognizes that you possess extraordinary computer skills. You may not find that compelling or comforting, but frankly, the U.S. seeks your help. We are aware, obviously, of your connection with the Bratva, and specifically, of your relationship with Mr. Belov. The U.S. is willing to work with you to extract you from his talons, if you're interested." Max sat upright when he heard Strain's mention of Belov.

"Max, Mr. Belov had your parents murdered. This is indisputable. Your dad was an honorable man who refused to forsake the dream he had worked so hard to achieve. He would not compromise his integrity and throw NHL games to give the Bratva the opportunity to win large sums of money on wagers. He had too much love for the game and the team he worked hard to represent. He appreciated the opportunity he was given to live in the USA, and he was determined not to yield to Belov's overture and subvert the game he loved. For this, your dad paid with his life. In addition, he did not know your mom was in danger for simply being his wife. He would have protected her above all else, given the opportunity, but Belov did not give him that opportunity. You have an opportunity to realign yourself with what is good in America and renounce your allegiance to the Bratva. It is up to you. I want to leave you with a way to redemption if you desire to do so. We know you can restore your honor. I think you have it in you to become a silent warrior for our nation. Max, you are still an American."

Max's eyes never diverted from Strain's. "I have always suspected that Belov was something other than what he pretended. I have held a deep internal unease throughout my life, beginning with his visits to my grandparents' home. Belov never touched me, but it was his stare that caught my attention. It triggered a grim emptiness in my soul. I have no love for him, though he treated my grandparents, and me, quite well financially. He was a provider and never asked for anything in return. Apparently, my family had given much more than I was aware. I will take your information to heart and begin to figure out my destiny. On a personal note, I wish good luck to you and your wife. Please tell her I appreciate her not hurting my dog, Torre, when she arrested me. I could tell she had an animal lover's concern for Torre when she and her fellow agents took me into custody. Your wife is a good person."

Strain concludes the Kazakhstan meeting by saying, "Max, here's my personal cell number. You can call me whenever you wish."

CHAPTER 43

"THE 1970 DEBUT *of the United States Sailboat Show in Annapolis, Maryland marked a new concept – the first in-water sailboat show in the country. Today the Annapolis Boat Shows have an unsurpassed reputation for offering the most comprehensive boating exhibitions in the industry. Each of our boat shows gives boaters the unique opportunity to board and inspect virtually every new model on the market, make side-by-side comparisons, and talk to industry leaders about all aspects of buying and owning a boat. Exhibitors are highly motivated to put you in the boat of your dreams at the best possible price. In addition, one can shop from a vast display of boating products and services – everything from financing and insurance to electronics and foul weather gear. It's always a fun and informative day exploring boats and boat supplies."*

"With all these fuckers in town we ought to go out and have some fun tonight," Anton Abdulov suggested.

"Kostenko would not like that we did that so soon before we take down the little bitch," Pavel Agapov quickly retorted. The second day of October was crisp and cool, almost sweater weather in Annapolis, Maryland, and two of Kostenko's henchmen were feeling the need for lusty behavior. The ongoing annual power boat show was set to re-open in the morning. Kostenko's mission to abduct the Cassell boy was then two days away.

"Pavel, we've been in place for almost a fuckin' month and we haven't done shit. I am bored shitless. I need to get laid, and with all these drunk boaters in town, it shouldn't be too difficult," Abdulov hastened to say.

"What about Leonid," Pavel asked. "He's about as horny as you are."

"No way, he talks too much, and when he drinks, he starts to piss people off. He has bad breath, too. I don't need him to create a scene."

"Anton how are you thinking of getting out of the house without anyone making some shit about it," Pavel asked.

"You know they drink and fall asleep by 10:00 pm. You and I will just say we are going for a walk; we get back by midnight," Anton schemed.

"Well, we can try, but if Kostenko gets wind of us doing this, he'll want to kick our ass. He'll expect us to be disciplined," Pavel warned. "I'm game, but only until midnight."

Pavel, Anton, and Leonid all hailed from Brighton Beach, the Russian enclave of immigrants and first-generation offspring. The three immigrated as young boys and had little memory of the Russia motherland. It didn't matter. Brighton Beach offered a microcosm, that is, enough of their heritage to allow them to be members of the Bratva. Pavel and Anton were both imposing figures, dark haired, muscular, and they carried themselves confidently. Leonid was short and stout, and his attire made him look more like a hobbit than a tough thug. Nevertheless, his appearance was deceptive. He was strong as a bull, and his propensity for violence was unequaled.

"Leonid could be a bigger problem for us than Kostenko, if we get caught," Pavel said.

"Stop being a pussy. Just make sure you take a shower without giving Kostenko a clue about our trip into town," Anton chuckled.

CHAPTER 44

"CAPTAIN STRAIN, THIS is Max."

"Max, how are you? Again, please call me Will."

"Yes, sir, I mean Will. Belov has plans to abduct Mr. Cassell's son from the Naval Academy in Maryland. Belov has someone inside, possibly attending the Academy, and this source has provided him with specific stuff about the kid's activities. He has sent a small group of Bratva operatives to set up a safe house in a place called Eastport, supposed to be across the water from the Academy," Max relayed. "Right now, that's all I know."

"Do you have any names of those operatives?" asked Strain.

"Yes, the small group will be led by Belov's favorite man, Kostenko, Vadim Kostenko. His men are Anton Abdulov, Pavel Agapov and a guy named Lenoid Baranov. They are all from the Brighton Beach area. I know them, but they usually walk on the other side of the street when they see me coming. The three of them think they are quite the lady's men. They're assholes who represent Belov and only derive their muscle power from him," Max detailed.

"Thanks Max, I appreciate this, of course. I will be talking with you soon," Strain expressed.

"Watch your back, sir. He wants you, too."

CHAPTER 45

"*THE UNITED STATES Sailboat Show, formerly known as the 'Annapolis Sailboat Show,' attracts more than 50,000 boating enthusiasts from around the world every year to the waterfront of historic Annapolis, Maryland. Home of the U.S. Naval Academy, the Chesapeake Bay town is recognized worldwide as the premier sailing showcase. This is the place to sell, buy, or dream about owning a sailboat. The show showcases and displays all makes and models of sailboats including catamarans, international racing sailboats, family cruising boats and sailing yachts, plus sailing equipment, cruising and charter information, sailing accessories, and daily educational seminars.*"

Kostenko cooked a ten-ounce filet on the outside grill, as he savored the aroma and marveled at the clear view of the Naval Academy. The rental home's front yard view featured a direct line-of-sight from Sycamore Point and over the Spa Creek to the intended point of ingress onto the Academy's eastern perimeter wall at Turner Joy Road. Kostenko's group would breach the same wall in less than two days. Kostenko couldn't resist, his mind drifting toward the execution of his plan to abduct Cassell's son. His boss, Belov, believed that Cassell's father was responsible for the death of his own father. As he flipped the thick filet over for the final time, he took a gulp of the single malt whiskey he held in his left hand. "I'm multi-tasking," he chuckled to himself. I'm cooking, I'm drinking, and I'm planning, not a bad act. He smiled to himself, then thought about the need for him and the other Bratva operatives to remain disciplined, "No drinking tomorrow, don't want to jeopardize the plan." He proudly placed the medium rare filet on a plate and headed inside. "Shut off the grill, stupid," he realized before leaving the surveillance point.

"Looks like you cooked the perfect filet, Vadim," Pavel said to Kostenko as entered the kitchen.

"It is and take your thieving eyes off it. You ain't getting any," Kostenko responded with a slight slur, a sure sign that the alcohol was kicking in. Pavel knew the nightly ritual was probably a forgone conclusion, "Another three drinks and he'd be out cold on the couch by nine o'clock."

Kostenko made himself another drink before placing the meat on the plate he had prepared with a lettuce and tomato salad. He threw some potato chips on the plate, and headed for the TV room.

"I don't want any of your meat. I'm going to get a chicken sandwich up the road later with Anton," Pavel said.

"What about Lenoid?" Kostenko groused.

"He says he's tired and not interested,' Pavel advised.

"I hope he doesn't come in here thinking he's going to watch my TV. Tell him to stay in his room, or better yet, go into the basement and watch TV," Kostenko muttered without looking at Pavel.

Anton walked into the room and heard the direction. "No worries, boss, Lenoid is already three sheets to the wind in his room, watching TV from his recliner."

"Good, let the motherfucker sleep," Kostenko ordered. "You guys can get out of here, too."

With anxious thoughts of getting lustfully lucky, Pavel and Anton hustled out of the residence. "What did you give Lenoid that made him fall asleep so quickly?" Pavel asked.

"Well, he already downed a half-dozen vodka tonics. I made him his last one and added a crushed Ambien," Anton reported. "He gulped half of it down and put the remainder on the table next to the recliner before falling asleep."

"Ha, he has become glued to that recliner," Pavel joked. "That's where we will find him in the morning. Let's go," Anton whispered.

The pair exited through the rear door and walked south onto Severn Avenue. Their first stop was the *Boatyard Bar and Grill*, a short two blocks away. The bar was overly crowded, leaving no options for the Bratva thugs to establish themselves, they thought. Boaters need no excuse for a drink, especially those who are involved in the competitive sales of high-end boat models. There were too many of them.

"These boaters are like Kostenko, they go down too much, too fast," Pavel said. "Let's head into town and find a place. We can stop here on our way back."

"Where you are thinking of going," Anton asked.

"I think the best place to go is *McGarvey's*; at least they've had the best-looking girls," Pavel answered. He turned to the door and moved rapidly out of the *Boatyard*. Now, less than a ten-minute walk over the drawbridge and up past the city dock, they closed in on *McGarvey's*. Anton kept up with Pavel's brisk pace. "Man," he thought, "Pavel is like a dog in heat."

"I told you it would be packed with babes," Pavel stated gleefully. They stood in line behind a hefty, tattooed bouncer and waited to access the tavern's-controlled entrance.

"It'll be a five-dollar cover if you guys want to get in," said the doorman. A young couple exited at the same time; Pavel and Anton were waived in. "Use your heads inside, gentlemen. We don't need any problems." Pavel and Anton looked at each other and nodded in agreement with the bouncer's words of caution. They entered smiling.

Anton was immediately set upon by a tall, thirty plus looking brunette, "Hey boyfriend, buy me and my friends a drink!" She and her two friends occupied the bar stools a few feet beyond the entrance, a prized position for checking out patrons coming and going.

Anton complied, saying, "Of course, what are you guys drinking?"

"A single malt scotch, a Glenlivet, an eighteen-year-old, double shot with one large cube. The bartender knows. Can you handle that?"

"I can if you tell us your names," Anton replied.

"I'm Sara Parker, and this is Thelma and Louise," she replied with a slight slur in her voice.

"What do Thelma and Louise want?" Anton replied, oblivious to the fictional names.

"We are all drinking the same thing. Hey Billy, our new friend is buying us another round," Sara yelled to the busy bartender.

"Got it," Billy yelled back over his shoulder as he juggled three drinks for other bar patrons.

"Make that five, Billy. These guys will drink what we're drinking," she chirped. She grabbed Anton's arm and pulled him closer. Pavel shook his head in disbelief, thinking, "I've seen quick pick-up bars, but this is a first."

"Anton, use cash, no cards," Pavel whispered. Last thing we need is for Kostenko to know we left a footprint here."

The historic Annapolis seaport was home to an unusually large number of active bar scenes for a city of its size. If one bar doesn't work out, patrons cascade up and down Main Street until a suitable one is found. Downtown Annapolis is festive most of the year, but during the boat shows it escalates exponentially, taking on a "spring break" culture of booze influenced bad behavior.

"You didn't tell us your names. Are you Butch and Sundance," she asked. You two look like actors right out of the movies, a taller version of Robert Retford, and your buddy, Paul Newman."

"Who the hell are they?" responded Anton.

"Never mind," she said, "what are your names?"

"My name is Pavel, and his is Anton," he said.

"Pavel means turkey," Anton chipped in.

"Yeah, and yours means asshole," Pavel offered, a bit chagrined.

"They sound European, maybe even Eastern European," Sara said. "Are you guys from overseas?"

"We are, we work for a German boat company, RaJo Boote. We sell small powerboats, and our company is eager to get into the U.S. domestic market." Pavel said with a prepared response for the question. The boat show gave them easy cover for their names and their East European appearances.

Billy brought the five scotches over to the bar. Sara passed one each to Pavel and Anton while Thelma and Louise, seated at the bar, chugged their previous glasses and grabbed the newly poured Glenlivet.

"Thanks for the drinks, boys. Cheers," she raised her glass to clink first with Anton, then Pavel.

Pavel felt a slight touch to his zipper area and glanced at Sara, who winked at him. He knew he was about to get lucky.

CHAPTER 46

THE NAVAL CRIMINAL Investigative Service, (NCIS) had been alerted by Assistant Commandant Keegan's office about a serious threat directed toward the U.S. Naval Academy by the Bratva, set sometime for the early hours of October 3rd. NCIS established an immediate surveillance of the Bratva's Eastport location. Three of the selected surveillance operatives were Charlie Gergich, Josephine "Jo" Smith, and Harper Rose, managed by the senior team member, Shane Ryan. The surveillance team went operational October 1 from land and water. A thirty- foot cabin cruiser was used to observe the Bratva group from Spa Creek. The vessel was white and rather non-descript except for the black decal registration number on its starboard side. It blended seamlessly with the other boat show participants moored at Sycamore point, yards from the target house.

"We've got some activity from the rear door. Looks like two males exiting onto Severn Avenue," Gergich transmitted from his vehicle parked on Severn Court, a position he took after dusk.

Rose and Ryan exited their government vehicle parked along 1st Street, a block away. They walked together as though they were a young couple out for a nightly stroll.

"Charlie, stay with your current position, Rose and I will tail the two," Ryan said over his radio. "Smith, hustle up a block or two on Severn Avenue and I will feed you their location as they walk."

Anton and Pavel departed the property briskly, then slowed to a normal pace, glancing back periodically to see if Kostenko or Lenoid were following. Pavel wore blue jeans and a solid dark blue crew neck sweater; Anton wore a pair of light blue shorts, a multi-colored rugby shirt and sandals.

"It appears they're heading to the *Boatyard Bar and Grill*," radioed Ryan. Rose and I will maintain an eyeball here and let you know." Ryan reported. "Stand by, the bar is packed, and it appears they may back out and head elsewhere. Yup, they're exiting and heading south toward the drawbridge, I'm guessing."

"Roger that, I'll move up to the bridge," Smith said.

"If they make the turn toward town, my guess is they'll check out *Pusser's*," Ryan stated. It's the next logical location for these bar hoppers." *Pusser's* is another hot spot during the boat week and predictably the next most active bar on Pavel's and Anton's walk toward town. Smith leapfrogged from her advanced location to position herself in the lobby area between the *Marriott's Pusser's Caribbean Grill and Hotel* lobby. "I'm in *Pusser's* lobby," Smith reported to the team."

"Roger that, but it does not appear they're heading inside," radioed Ryan. "They're passing *The Choptank* restaurant too, so hustle on up to *McGarvey's*. I'll wager a hundred bucks they're heading there."

"No bet, that's the best place in town to pick up girls," said Rose.

"I wouldn't know," replied Ryan as he glanced at the position she now had taken across the street. Rose smirked back to him and didn't respond on the air.

"I'll take the back sidewalk along the water and get to McGarvey's faster than them," Smith said, "I know the bouncer."

"Okay. Rose and I will stay back and try to determine where these two horn dogs go."

"Gergich from Ryan."

"Ryan, this is Gergich, go ahead."

"Shane, for now just remain in position on Severen Court, but we may need you up here once we determine where these two fellows end up," Ryan stated.

"Understood, sir."

Smith arrived at *McGarvey's* entrance, moving past a dozen patrons who were themselves looking to get inside when she encountered the bouncer, Jimmy. He winked upon seeing her approach. She got closer to him and whispered, "Jimmy, I'm on the job now and need to get inside." He knew what she meant, understanding that *McGarvey's* attracts a lot of young midshipmen and graduates, who from time to time, garner the attention of the NCIS. "Go ahead, love."

"I'm at the far end of the bar with a decent eyeball of the entrance," Smith whispered through a small microphone pinned to her collar.

"Josephine, you are more than prescient. Both subjects are in line to gain entrance. Nicely done. Rose and I will standby outside. Once they get in, let us know if you need more eyeballs," Ryan advised.

"The boys are inside and have already hit pay dirt. They are engaged in conversation with three females who appear to own the corner of the bar," Smith reported. "Looks like we will be here for a bit."

"Roger," Ryan responded. "Enjoy your virgin Bloody Mary."

"Gergich from Ryan. Charlie, break off on the residence. Come up here for Harper and take her back to 1st Street so she can retrieve our 'G-car.' I have a funny feeling we will need it if the party duo goes somewhere else upon leaving here."

"Be there in two minutes," Gergich responded.

CHAPTER 47

"I THINK ONE of the targets is about to leave with one of the girls he has met. She's putting on a waist coat and won't let go of his arm," Smith reported to the team. It was nearly midnight.

"Okay, and the second subject is doing what?" asked Ryan.

"He remains engrossed in discussion with the other four ladies," Smith said. "Doing a lot of shots."

"Okay, team, once the playboy comes out, Rose and I will tail. Charlie, based on where he takes us, be prepared to come up to Josephine to help her keep a tail on the other target," Ryan directed.

Signaling Rose who was positioned across from *McGarvey's* at the *Market House,* Ryan indicated to get the car ready. Rose picked up on the signal and moved to the G-car.

"The playboy in jeans and his gal pal in a short skirt and waist coat are departing," reported Smith.

"Got them, looks like they are walking toward Randall Street. I'll follow. Harper, stand by with the car until we see where they're headed. I hope they're not driving because they appear to be smashed," Ryan deftly whispered, walking behind them twenty paces. The sidewalks were plenty busy with boat show patrons. It was an easy surveillance.

"The couple have turned up Prince George Street," Ryan said.

"I'm in place by *McGarvey's*," Gergich advised the team.

"Thanks, Charlie," Smith acknowledged.

"Harper, just remain with your vehicle. I'm not sure they are driving anywhere," Ryan radioed.

"Gergich from Smith."

"Go ahead, Jo Jo."

"Looks like the party here is breaking up. I will trail the target on foot if you want to tail us with the car," Smith suggested.

"Which one do we have, the guy with the shorts or the one with the blue jeans?" Gergich asked.

"We have the shorts," responded Smith. "He'll be surrounded by four ladies. They are all leaving."

"Rose from Ryan."

"Go ahead."

"Blue jeans and his date have just entered the corner residence at Prince George Street and East Street. Bring the car to this location. We may be here for a bit waiting for the playboy," Ryan chuckled.

"Gergich, Smith, they're walking out," Smith said. "I'll give them some space and then exit to trail them. Just let me know when you spot them outside." Smith left her bar seat while making eye contact with Billy, "I will come back Billy to settle up," Smith told him.

"No worries, Jo Jo, it's on me. Just come back soon when you're off-duty," offered the bartender.

CHAPTER 48

"NICE PLACE," PAVEL observed as he and Sara Parker walked into the Prince George Street apartment.

Sara took off a waist jacket, threw it on a couch, and then turned to Pavel. Looking him straight into the eyes, she began to undo her blouse slowly, button by button. "Are you ready to fuck the shit out of me?"

Pavel looked back intently. "As soon as that skirt come off, you'll find out how quick my cock will be inside you."

Sara was wearing a pink bra, revealing an ample cleavage. She continued to unzip her skirt, surprising Pavel as it dropped to the apartment floor. She wore no panties.

"This will be easier than I thought," he said. Pavel dropped his own pants, his erection displayed in full view to Sara. The only barrier left was his undershorts.

"My, my, Pavel, you look big. Hurry, please," she said with a drunken slur.

Pavel ripped off his shirt and dropped his shorts, approaching the girl with an aggressive embrace, threw her onto the adjacent coach.

"Put your cock in me now. Fuck me, now!"

Pavel couldn't believe his good fortune, thinking this girl is too much fun. As he thrust his pelvis forward, she grabbed his erect cock and inserted it into her wet pussy. She screamed in excitement, wrapping her legs tighter around his hips.

He made it back to the Eastport safe house before sunrise. Kostenko never suspected a thing as Pavel slipped into his bed for a few hours' sleep.

Awake, Anton heard Pavel enter the house. "How did he get so lucky, and me having to walk back here alone. This place sucks," Anton lamented. "I need some sleep."

CHAPTER 49

PETTY OFFICER SECOND Class Raymond Schwartz volunteered to replace Bobby Cassell as the Bratva Target. Ray was Chief Warrant Officer Sergio Lopez's favorite team member. Schwartz hailed from Cranford, New Jersey. He had SEAL blood in his veins from the time he was in grammar school. Every neighbor on South Union Avenue knew Raymond, admiring his commitment to jog twice daily. Yet it was early in high school that Schwartz morphed differently. Wrestling and swimming became his athletic passion. Any legacy of baby fat was gone, and with a chiseled, proportional physique developed by his junior year, the neighbors knew the kid was special. He was a natural swimmer, but that didn't excite him as much as wrestling. The New Jersey State championship, in his weight class, was, in his mind, preordained. The moment he won it, his mother knew he was no longer to be just hers. Out of high school, and eighteen years old, he expressed his interest in the Navy. He didn't tell his parents when he signed up that day; he waited to let them know at dinner, when he broke the news.

"I've enlisted in the Navy," he blurted out. His mother started to cry.

"Raymond, you are too young for that," his father said.

"I am eighteen. I don't want to go to college after high school. I want to be someone special. I want to be a Navy SEAL, and this is the only way I can do that," Raymond responded. "I have to earn it."

"Raymond, I respect your choice, but I just want to make sure you know what this involves. You haven't even gone to your prom yet. Can't you consider waiting a year?" His dad asked as his mom continued to whimper.

"Too late, dad. I will be headed to training by the end of June. The sooner I get going, the better. Don't get me wrong, dad. I will still get my college education, but it'll be on my terms. And guess what, I'll pay for it," Raymond said.

"I get it, Raymond. One of my great regrets is not having served my country in the military. When do you have to report," he asked his son.

"Next Monday," he responded. His mother started to sob once again, this time visibly shaking. Raymond looked over at his mother. "Mom, you don't have to worry about me. It's a win, win situation." He got up from the table and hugged her.

"You're my baby; just give me time to grieve for your future absence. I am so proud of you, and how you are so mature. You have never, ever given us a day of difficulty. Of course, I will support you and your goals. I just have never experienced the notion of not having you here. I will miss you so," his mom added, then placed her face in the tissues that aggregated in her hand.

Raymond looked at his father and saw the tears slowly dripping down toward his mouth. "I am so proud of you, Raymond," said his dad. "Like your mom, I am saddened to lose my boy, but I know the Navy will serve you and us well. This will be our journey, too, as we revel in your future accomplishments. I love you son, too much."

"I love you guys too much, too."

"Why do you want to do this, Ray," asked Lopez. "You know they're going to hurt you when they take you down on the Yard."

"Well, first of all, I'm the only one that's good looking and young enough to make it happen. And it can't be any worse than the shithole assignment we just had in Afghan," Schwartz said. "Besides, I'm the same height and weight as the kid. I also heard that his parents live in my hometown, Cranford, New Jersey. How cool is that?"

"Alright, tough guy. You get to wear his plebe uniform. The collar has been fitted with a transponder to track your sorry ass. Here's a stainless-steel folding knife for your asshole," Lopez proffered.

"Boss, did you want to insert the knife?" chuckled Schwartz.

"No way your butt is probably too big for that knife."

Schwartz unfolded the blade to look at the serrated edge. For a two-inch blade, it looked menacing. He folded the knife back into a secure position and went into the bathroom to tape it to his butt. It would be his only weapon to defend himself should the Bratva operatives seek to terminate him. He used a small piece of duct tape to do the job.

"Hey Sergio, do you know the worst part of sticking a knife near your crack?"

"Yeah, removing all the tape glue from your butt after you remove the knife, right."

"Yup, you got it. Fortunately, I don't have a hairy ass."

"Okay, you may be a little premature with the placement of the knife. We still have another six hours before the intended abduction, but I leave the housekeeping up to you, Ray," said Lopez.

"Funny, sir, but you're right, I'll wait until just before we go operational. Does that raise your comfort level, boss," retorted a smirking Ray.

"It's your call, mister," Lopez conceded. "I'll be in the operations room. It is you who will have to endure the object near your butt."

CHAPTER 50

EARLIER IN THE day, SEAL team members, and four Night Stalker pilots from the famed U.S. Army 160th, mustered in a makeshift operations room located on the Academy's grounds, the officer's club, equally distant from the practice football fields to the south of the Yard and from the north side of the Yard by the Route 450 Severn Bridge. They were there to engage in a multi-agency briefing and be introduced to state and local authorities. NCIS and Coast Guard Intelligence felt it appropriate to brief state and local police about the plan to thwart the abduction. The civilian agencies would work the Academy's perimeter in the event the Bratva thugs managed to evade capture and take their abducted prize outside the city limits of Annapolis. Both the state and local police were already deployed to manage security issues at the ongoing boat show. Their duties have now expanded.

"This is not a normal security operation's briefing," thought Major Dallas Pope, the assigned state police executive invited to attend the brief. "It's definitely over my pay grade, but I love being here with these talented folks."

The Navy SEAL team leader, Sergio Lopez, looked around at the assembly in the room: his Navy SEAL team, NCIS agents, a Maryland State Police Supervisor, an Annapolis P.D. Captain, and a rather distinguished looking man in a business suit who had just walked into the room unabated.

"Good evening, sir, can I ask you to identify yourself to the room," asked Lopez.

"Absolutely, my name is James F. Keegan. I am the Assistant Commandant for Intelligence and Investigations for the U.S. Coast Guard. I am sorry if I am late." The SEALS, the Night Stalkers, and the other uniformed Navy personnel stood up at attention. "At ease, folks," Keegan urged. "Please take your seats."

"Sir, you are not late. I am Sergio Lopez, team leader for the SEAL participation in this effort, in partnership with the NCIS. We realize that this is a Coast Guard lead matter, and although tonight we won't involve Coast Guard assets, we understand that the results of our tactical operation will be of the utmost importance to the Coast Guard, and our law enforcement friends. We appreciate your being here, sir.

"I appreciate that support from your community," Keegan replied.

"Let me introduce Special Agent in Charge Rip Cleary from the NCIS; Captain Jim Brown, Annapolis Police Department; and Major Dallas Pope, Maryland State Police." Lopez looked around the room full of SEALs and noticed Bill Golden and Mike Durant entering the briefing room and seized the opportunity. "Commandant Keegan, let me introduce you to our favorite Night Stalkers." Golden and Durant stood by the room entrance in anticipation of an introduction. This brought the Night Stalkers' participation to six.

"I know them both, Sergio. Hello, gentlemen," responded Keegan. "The 160th is no stranger to us at the Coast Guard. Some of our best have been fortunate to train with them."

"Well, everyone, as Commandant Keegan said, please be seated and we will begin the briefing," Lopez announced.

"Later tonight, well after midnight, we expect that operatives from the Bratva criminal syndicate will initiate a planned activity from Eastport, specifically, a residence located at the end of Severn Avenue.

We know from our intelligence partners that there are four operatives residing there who have been surveilling the Naval Academy for the past month. Their goal is to abduct an Academy plebe off the Yard in the middle of the night. The purpose of their efforts is to use the abducted plebe to both inflict emotional harm on the family of the victim, and then to lure the family into an environment where they can be exterminated in an act of vengeance for a prior law enforcement event. Fortunately, we're in a position to intercept and disrupt the Bratva's plans. The Bratva is known to be a badass, take no prisoner group, throughout the globe. Now they will meet the best of the best gathered in this room. The intended victim just got a pass from having to do his twenty-four-hour post detail. After midnight he will be serendipitously replaced by a SEAL who volunteered to walk post in his stead in the proximity of the Commodore Levy Center and Jewish Chapel. This is located east of the Mitscher Hall, the interfaith Chapel. The SEALs here today scoped out the location earlier today to orient themselves. This may be the first time many of them have been in proximity to a gentile college setting. Just kidding. Anyway, the substitute can expect to be forcibly kidnapped, taken to an inflatable boat and transported back to their Eastport safe house for a period of time. The target has nothing to offer them other than his person, so we don't expect him to be interrogated. We do expect him to be roughed up. So, in anticipation of that, the NCIS will be installing listening devices and cameras inside their safe house while they are engaged in the abduction. We don't know if they expect to relocate the abductee during the night from the Eastport safe house or wait until the next morning. If we determine that their intent is to keep him in the safe house until morning to transport him, then the Maryland State Police and Annapolis Police will work jointly to interdict them. If NCIS picks up information that our SEAL is in mortal danger inside the house, the SEALs will breach the residence. We will call an audible on that.

During this operation, we will monitor their actions with the 160th MH-6Ms, affectionately referred by the special operations community as "Little Birds." ferrying SEALs, prepared to respond tactically. We will also use 'close proximity drones' over Spa Creek. We will not allow the Bratva to do harm to our 'rabbit' SEAL. Having said that, our goal is to work with the police authorities to have the Bratva operatives successfully taken into civilian custody. Any questions?" asked Lopez.

Major Pope raised his hand.

Lopez pointed, "Yes, Major."

"Why don't you just take them down on the Academy grounds, or better yet, now?"

"Sir, what I am about to say I hope will not be construed to be disrespectful to local civilian operations, but this is part of a larger jurisdictional issue that involves multiple agencies, some of which are chagrined they're not operationally involved, and frankly, not here. Obviously, the Academy is federal property, and thus the NCIS lead. The SEALs are here at the invitation of the NCIS, the Navy's law enforcement component. The SEALs, and the Night Stalkers, are here to support them. The Bratva is looking to hurt one of our own. We want to ensure that these thugs regret the day they took a Plebe, much less a SEAL. By the time we finish with them, they will be more than happy to cooperate with the police. They will not be physically or emotionally abused, but they will want to talk with you, trust me. That's all I can intimate," Lopez countered.

"Also, if they decide to do something stupid as they depart the Yard with their captive, the 160th will swoop down on them with the SEAL operators on the side boards, who will do what they are trained to do."

"Got it," responded Major Pope. "I guess my final observation is this. The intelligence community, and federal agencies here present, have overwhelming capability. Should we, as local and state law enforcement, be bringing in our special operations units to assist with any vehicle stop?"

"Major Pope, I don't expect this to go beyond the safe house. I think if the state and local police have a tactical presence that serves their operational plan once off campus, then yes. But I defer to the NCIS as we support them in their law enforcement capacity. I suspect, though, that the federal authorities will take custody of the Bratva operatives and whisk them away in short order. The Boat Show will not be disrupted, nor will the show's participants even know that this has happened," Lopez stated. "We will only intervene if our SEAL is in distress; otherwise, it's up to law enforcement once the Bratva returns to the safe house."

"Understood," Pope, now turning to his Annapolis police colleague. "Captain Johnson, are you okay with this?"

"Yes, Major, I believe we can take second seat on this one, but if the safe house is raided at some point during the night, who will conduct that?"

"The NCIS," Agent Cleary stated.

"Thank you," Captain Johnson responded. "We are here to support you."

CHAPTER 51

"THE EARLY MORNING fall air will provide an energetic boost to my groggy operatives," thought Kostenko. He had set his alarm for 2:00 am to gather his thoughts before waking his Bratva thugs thirty minutes later. He noticed immediately that the overcast sky couldn't have been more suitable for their planned abduction of the Cassell boy. Their reconnaissance indicated that the Naval Academy campus offered an excellent opportunity to traverse the grounds unimpeded and get to the Levy Center's Jewish Chapel, where their mole advised that Bobby Cassel would be performing his duties. He would be situated in an open area on the Yard, not far from King Hall's Mitscher Barracks. Kostenko hoped to find the Cassell boy shouldering an unloaded M1 carbine. The M1 is a lightweight .30 caliber semi-automatic carbine produced during WWII and out of service by the end of the Vietnam War in 1973. As a matter of protocol, the M1 had no firing pin, but it continued to serve a purpose at the Naval Academy, albeit ceremoniously.

At 3:00 am, Kostenko and his four operatives lowered the Bris 12.5 black inflatable into the water at the end of Severn Avenue, in Eastport, across from the Naval Academy. The inflatable, purchased from a Walmart store in Middleton, Delaware, arrived a week earlier and was placed upended alongside the rental house. No one in the community would give the craft a second thought, particularly during a boat show. During the preceding week the operatives ran numerous back and forth trials with the inflatable. In the busy Spa Creek, the dinghy sized boat garnered little attention. It was common practice for boaters to use smaller craft to transit from their anchored boats in Spa Creek into Ego Alley, as the downtown Annapolis canal is affectionately called. Kostenko's inflatable was made with a heavy duty fabric and was known by the commando fraternity to deploy quickly "with proven performance for infiltration and assault." As soon as the special ops community successfully battle tested the craft under a variety of tactical conditions, it became their definitive insertion boat. Kostenko was happy with it. It weighed only two hundred sixty-five pounds and held up to six passengers. One slot was to be reserved for a blindfolded Bobby Cassell, to take him back to the safe house and await the next phase of their mission. Kostenko teased his team that picking out the appropriate paddle lengths presented more of a challenge to him because of their various heights.

Kostenko obtained five plastic adjustable Cabela paddles. He told his guys, "We will just throw them away once we have completed the mission unless we fail; then Vladimir will want to use them to beat the shit out of us," he chuckled nervously. "It's good that they're plastic. It won't hurt as much." No one laughed. Belov didn't accept failure, and they all knew what the consequences could be.

There was little to no moonlight to illuminate the Bratva mission. The streetlight above the bench at the water's edge had been extinguished a few days prior with a sling shot. Kostenko's boys, drinking their beer, used it as an opportunity for target practice. No one in the immediate neighborhood noticed it no longer illuminating for the last few days. The torn American flag remained hoisted in front of the rental house, but on this night, with no wind, it remained motionless. The pole light normally shining on the red, white and blue had burnt out months before the Bratva rented the home. The light had not been repaired, and the Bratva group didn't complain.

Kostenko continued to brief, "with all four of us paddling and our adrenaline kicking in, our cross time will be less than five minutes. Let's go," he ordered.

The four of them took the inflatable from the side of the house, placed it in the water, and hopped in. As practiced, they paddled in unison. All labored with their breathing trying to overcompensate for the effort. "Everyone, slow down a bit, catch your breath, or else this won't go well for us," Kostenko admonished. When the inflatable reached the large rock formation that defined the outer perimeter along the Academy's southern perimeter, one of Kostenko's operatives quietly jumped from the craft and onto the rocks. He secured a line to a bollard just above the rock line along Turner Joy Road. At that hour, there were dozens of midshipmen vehicles parked overnight silently lining both sides of the road, unintentionally providing the pseudo commandos with effective cover. The dark black inflatable was secreted along the bevy of boulders, and benefitted from the calm water. "No waves, no noise," Kostenko thought. "Great."

The remaining operatives followed Kostenko out of the inflatable and onto the rocks. They stood in place until Kostenko signaled for them to jump onto the roadway. Each wore a Motorola portable radio on their waist belt, a wire secured along their back up to an ear, and a wrist microphone clamped to their individual wristwatch bands. Kostenko nodded to them as they gathered in sync on road's edge, kneeling below the height of vehicle roof line. He waved to them to keep low. Then Kostenko signaled to one of his operatives to break off and head east along Turner Joy Road toward the Triton Light located at the most eastern end of the road. Halfway there, or about tenth of a mile, the operative observed a Department of Defense police officer napping in his blue and white federal police vehicle. Based on their Eastport surveillance, Kostenko and his men knew it to be a nightly occurrence.

The officer would have just completed his perimeter patrol work, and now, for the next hour or so, could expect to get some shut eye.

Kostenko had briefed Belov earlier in the day, "Grabbing the midshipman without raising an alarm will be an easy job, boss. We gag him, secure his wrists, and force him to run back with us to the raft. It'll only take minutes. If he gets stupid, we'll knock him out and carry his little ass to the raft. It might take a little longer, but my guys can do it. We should be able to get back to the safe house in less than ten minutes. Once we get things settled and secured, we will get in our van and depart.

Each of the Bratva operatives was dressed in black battle fatigues, or BDUs, and carried a Glock forty caliber, model 35, on his hip. Kostenko loved the weapon.

"Do not fire your weapon unless it is necessary. What we don't need is five thousand fucking midshipmen rushing out here to see what the hell is happening," Kostenko said at the early morning brief before departing from their safe house on the other side of Spa Creek.

"If the fucking kid needs to be put out, then knock him out, hit him across the head, or better yet, choke him out. Just do it quickly and quietly but try and keep him alive for Belov."

CHAPTER 52

"MIKE, THERE'S ADEQUATE ambient lighting for night vision. The low cloud cover is not a problem. We've got the entire practice field along Turner Joy Road in focus," Chief Warrant Officer Bill Golden reported.

"Roger that, we've got the field and most of area in front of Levy Center in view, too," answered Chief Warrant Officer Mike Durant.

Golden's Bird hovered silently over the Severn River north of the practice field while Durant's bird hovered above Eastport. Golden and Durant were each piloting separate MH-6Ms. Neither Bird was heard by the Bratva operatives. They kept their distance, allowing a single unmanned drone, in silent surveillance, to get closer to the Bratva operatives.

The SEALs established a control room within the officer's club, located in the middle of the Yard. "The unmanned aerial vehicle is transmitting good visuals back to us," reported the SEAL's control room, managing the drone's ability to fly in closer proximity.

"Is that the same as a drone," quipped Golden, joking with the SEAL radio man.

"Ha, it may not be able to do what you boys are doing with the Little Birds, but our little drone is directly overhead and making little or no noise," replied the control room.

"Understood sir, just having a little fun with you Navy guys," Golden replied, knowing full well that the latest generation of drones, flying without a human operator, were worth their weight in gold. "They save lives, get into places other aircraft can't. Got to love having them in our toolbox," thought Golden. "The only angst I have with the unmanned aerial vehicle," he once told his colleague, "They fly unmanned. I can't think of anything duller than to fly one of these toys from some remote location. Boring!!!"

Sergio Lopez asked. "Do you we have an eyeball on the 'rabbit,' as well, or just the targets?" Lopez was operating from an improvised command center, not far from the Yard's famous Octagon. In addition to video from the drone, and the Little Birds, the control room received video feeds from numerous static cameras in position around the Yard, integrated in the Academy's existing security system.

Durant and Golden were present in support of the SEAL mission. Their briefing was straightforward: observation, and possible tactical insertion of SEAL Team members, if warranted. The early morning mission was to be a surveillance event, not a fight," Golden and Durant were told by the NCIS at the operational briefing held hours earlier. The SEALs were prepared for a fight nonetheless, and if one of their own was to be used as a 'rabbit' and taken off the Yard, they wanted to make sure he made it back in one piece. Two SEALs were perched on bench seats located on each side of the small aircraft. The Little Birds and their pilots were provided by the 160th Night Stalkers, Special Operations Aviation Regiment (SOAR) for the mission.

"The Flir Pod is picking up the targets exiting the raft. Looks like one is heading north toward the DOD vehicle. The other three are crossing the practice field now," Golden relayed. The Little Birds, equipped with forward-looking infrared (Flir) technology, allowed the pilots to see the thermal images of the Bratva operatives as they approached their target.

"The drone is maintaining a good eyeball as well," reported the SEAL's control room.

"Roger that," replied Lopez. "We have an eyeball on the 'rabbit' and all the targets" Lopez advised. "Terrific coverage," Lopez thought.

"Roger. The 'rabbit' is standing post in front of the Seabees Monument, directly across from the Levy Center and Jewish Chapel in the middle of the Octagon," Golden advised. Earlier in the day, Golden ensured the tennis courts nets were lowered in anticipation that the Birds may need a landing zone near the assumed abduction site.

Kostenko's team stopped paddling in tandem, as he leaned in toward the rip rap grabbing onto a large boulder with an extendable hook. He grinned when he realized the rocks provided him, and his crew, with what looked like natural steps to the roadway. Kostenko tethered the raft using an improvised weighted anchor he threw onto the rock formation.

"Let's go. Head across the field and gather by the Bronson Road entrance," Kostenko relayed over the radio, using it for the first time. The three operatives nodded in agreement. Leonid headed toward the Triton Light north up Turner Joy Road to monitor the DOD officer and, if necessary, kill him before he could respond. Anton and Pavel followed Kostenko, hustling toward the Rip Miller practice field's opening, and then dashing to the opposite side of the field to Bronson Road. There, they took positions behind Kostenko.

"Move now!" he radioed. Anton and Pavel knew where to go. They often practiced their movements back in Eastport. The Bronson Road provided more than ample cover for the group. Moving past the tennis courts, the trio again stopped behind cover to assess the situation. Kostenko took binoculars and peered toward the Seabees Monument. "The boy is there standing tall," he radioed. Anton and Pavel gave him a thumbs up. The lone sentinel had been on a post designed to test the midshipman's stamina and resolve. The solitary figure standing resolute between the Jewish Chapel and Seabee Monument, soon would turn and begin a short fifty-yard march to the opposite side of the octagon, where he would momentarily halt and repeat the march back. Kostenko ordered, "Once the boy makes his about-face to walk the fifty yards east, we will take him down." Anton and Pavel gave him a thumbs up.

The trio got to him before his turn about. Pavel hit him hard across the side of his head with an open hand and the sentinel dropped to the ground. While Kostenko maintained vigilance, Anton and Pavel secured the boy's wrists with plastic handcuffs and placed tape over his mouth. In a moment, the sentinel boy regained awareness, now looking at his abductors with ostensible fear. His ceremonial rifle lay on the ground, pinpointing the spot where he was abducted.

Anton and Pavel each grabbed an arm, began to walk the sentinel back toward the inflatable. The dazed victim complied, but didn't make it easy, making his body limp forcing them to lift him along the way.

The lone Bratva operative on Turner Joy Road had taken up a position to observe the DOD vehicle. The officer showed no signs of movement. The headlights were off, and the vehicle was running, its exhaust easily discernible in the early morning chilled air. The motionless driver was a mannequin. It was a decoy. It worked. Lenoid never suspected, patiently waiting to hear Kostenko's radio instructions. Once he heard the target was in custody, he would retreat, but only then.

"Lenoid, we got the boy, hustle back to the raft," Kostenko radioed.

"Got it. I will be right there, boss."

"Just make sure the dinghy is ready to go," a huffing Kostenko said.

Kostenko knew they were not yet out of harm's way, but he was beginning to feel more confident as they crossed the open Rip Miller practice field. "The boy didn't put up a fight, how lucky was that?"

"I am at the raft," Lenoid radioed.

"Great," Kostenko responded. "You may be able to see us on the field."

It took less than two minutes to traverse the open gate onto Rip Turner Field, and dart across the field toward the inflatable. Kostenko, a heavy smoker, felt nothing. He wasn't out of breath, and he wasn't even sweating, operating on pure adrenaline.

The Night Stalkers observed Kostenko's retreat to the dinghy.

"They've secured the 'rabbit' and are moving him toward their dinghy, we've got an eyeball on it," advised Golden.

"Roger that, the drone is directly above and documenting everything. The 'rabbit' looks to be unharmed," responded the SEAL control room. Then radio silence prevailed for what seemed an eternity, but was only seconds, as the control room processed what they were observing.

"The 'rabbit' has been placed on the floorboard" radioed the control room.

"We have them visually, as well. They are paddling feverishly toward the Eastport residence. It should take them less than four minutes," Golden advised.

As they reached the boulder rocks, they carefully guided the sentinel onto each rock. "Lay him down on the deck of the raft, and let's get the fuck out of here," Kostenko muttered over his radio, with an almost giddy effect. "Sit on him if he tries to move."

Once inside the raft, Kostenko looked about to see if they had been compromised. Not a soul around or responding. "No time for cheering yet," he thought.

"The boy is probably scared," Kostenko assumed. He peered into the boy's eyes and saw calm. "Strange," he thought to himself, "you'd think the kid would be shitting in his pants."

It took less than five minutes to paddle back to the safe house in Eastport. "When we arrive out the dock, let's get the boy into the car and head to New York. No time to go into the house, Kostenko ordered." He took out his cell phone and hit a dedicated button for Belov.

Keegan, observing the video feed, was thinking about options, too.

"Boss, the mop is in the bucket," Kostenko told Belov. "We are about to arrive the Eastport dock."

"I love you, brother, you have made me so proud," Belov responded. "I suspect you will need to get the boy into a car and get away sooner than later. The place could be overrun with police and feds in the morning. They'll first have to get over the fact that he just didn't walk off. That will give you some time, but not much. Get back up here as soon as you can," Belov advised. "Is the boy alert," asked Belov.

"He's alert, but unusually calm. We haven't yet removed his mouth tape or plastic restraints," Kostenko replied. "He just routinely moves his eyes about trying to figure out what happened to him, and who we are."

"Different people react differently to stressful situations. Once in the car, take the tape off, give him some water, but don't ask him any questions, I want first crack at him when he gets up here. He will know pain when he meets me," Belov boasted. "Then his eyes will really begin to dart around."

"Let me know when you make it to the Jersey Turnpike. We can send some relief if your guys are exhausted."

"Thanks, boss. We will be okay. We have already sanitized the Eastport location; they won't find shit," Kostenko said.

"Good, I was getting the feeling you bastards were starting to get too comfortable in that Annapolis area. See you soon."

CHAPTER 53

ASSISTANT COMMANDANT KEEGAN had kept a low radio presence, allowing the SEALs and Night Stalkers to perform their tasks. But now Keegan's decision to take down the Bratva depended on their next move. Once Kostenko arrived at the Eastport dock Keegan believed it best to intervene. The SEALs would execute a hostage rescue and take the Bratva thugs into custody. Keegan, as one of the country's seventeen intelligence directorates, invoked primacy in directing the operation. No one questioned his authority.

As the raft approached the Eastport safe house dock, Keegan came over the multi-jurisdictional radio and ordered, "Take them down."

Upon that order, four land-based SEALs positioned around the perimeter of the residence moved swiftly and silently toward the raft. One of the Little Birds moved in tandem to allow for airborne SEAL teammates to cover their advance.

Kostenko, sitting in the raft's stern, looked up as the darkened figures approached. He stood up in the raft and drew his sidearm. Before he could take aim, the closest SEAL took him out with two shots to the upper torso. He fell overboard into the chilly Spa Creek waters. The other paddlers looked over, then back to the invading team who now had a commanding presence over the raft. Their arms went quickly over their heads.

"Don't shoot," yelled Pavel. "Don't shoot."

The lead SEAL ordered them out of the raft and onto the deck where they were forced to lay face down; they were secured with plastic ties and searched for additional weapons.

One of the SEALS jumped into the raft and raised the abducted SEAL to a seated position. When the SEAL ripped the tape off his mouth, the newly released SEAL spoke up, "What took you guys so fucking long," he grinned. Can you get these ties off my wrist?"

"I'll think about it, smartass," as his SEAL team member sliced off the plastic ties with his 9 inch Dive knife. Then both SEALS reached into the water to snag Kostenko's lifeless body to pull it aboard.

"Lopez, from team one, the 'rabbit' is safe and secure, we have one fatal and three in custody," the team leader reported.

"Roger that," Lopez responded. "Be advised that the responding authorities will arrive momentarily to maintain the crime scene."

No sooner did Lopez finish responding did Eastport's Severn Avenue light up like a Christmas tree, as local, state and federal agencies flooded the roadway. The Night Stalkers with their SEAL appendages returned to the Academy landing zone. It was not yet 0330 hours.

"Well done, everyone," Keegan radioed. He then looked over at Strain and winked. Strain gave him a thumbs up. Regardless, the Bratva threat still lingered.

Keegan had earlier notified Larry Cassell that his son was no longer in harm's way.

"Larry, your son is safe. We have assets here in Annapolis about to resolve the Bratva's attempt to kidnap your son. I will brief you later on the outcome," Keegan reported to the anxious dad.

"Thank you. Jim. Thank you for everything you're doing for my family," Cassell followed, barely able to disguise his emotion.

CHAPTER 54

BALTIMORE CRIME SCENE investigator, Bill Davies, had arrived in Guatemala City as part of the U.S. State Department's initiative to extend technical advice to various Latin American governments not equipped to afford or provide electronic crimes training. Each trainee who successfully completed the course of instruction would leave with twenty-five thousand dollars' worth of computer equipment to complement the newly acquired skills.

"The public's perception of crime scene investigations are usually based on television shows they watched. The shows provide instant answers to establish corpus delicti, that is, to prove a crime has been committed. Sure, TV can provide instantaneous answers to fuel the public's misconception that crimes are easily solved. However, when you have jurors who digest it, then it can be quite difficult for the prosecutor to get them to understand, and appreciate, that collecting and evaluating the evidence of a real crime takes a lot more time and effort," Davies told his Guatemalan class of local and state police.

"What my colleagues and I will present this morning is a broad discussion involving the extraction of useful data from individual computer systems embedded in a vehicle, and which the vehicle relies upon to operate efficiently," Davies stated slowly so that the Guatemalan interpreter could have time to translate. "For example, the systems support devices such as smart phones connected to a vehicle by way of Wi-Fi, Bluetooth, or some other device connected via a USB port. Needless to say, today's cars possess a plethora of small electronic control units worthy of examination."

The interpreter stopped and looked at Davies with a frown. "Plethora?" she asked.

"Many," he replied. "Sorry."

"Thank you, sir, it's me that is sorry. That's a new word for me. I should've known." Davies winked and continued with his comments. "Tomorrow we will concentrate on more traditional crime scene issues like gunshot residue collection, firearms and tool marks, DNA, and much more."

Davies proceeded to remove some equipment from several large, sturdy black leather cases. "Let me share with you some of the latest tools for data collection, or I should say extraction".

Solarski positioned himself in the rear of the classroom he had managed to arrange within the U.S. Embassy complex for the presentations. The State Department brought Davies, and several other criminal investigators, and crime scene personnel from the States to provide the Guatemalan police group with updated forensic techniques and equipment.

The young Guatemala Justice Minister, Juan Villacorta, arrived shortly thereafter, and took a seat in the back of the room. Minister Villacorta told Solarski, "The goodwill we get from their participation goes a long way with building trust between our two countries. I am personally grateful to you and the Embassy for inviting us."

"Wait until you see what's being served for lunch," Solarski grinned in response. Your guys will not want to leave."

"Jim, listening to Mr. Davies talk about the evolution of forensics over the years has been enlightening to say the least, but I had no idea how much vehicle digital information is available for downloading.

In addition, the sheer number of computer systems in each vehicle is stunning," Villacorta said.

"Minister, what is interesting to me is the idea that we sent men to the Moon with a computer whose potency was no greater than a common calculator we give our children. Davies' comments are surely an indication that the world, though seemingly simpler, is a complicated set of 1's and 0's," Solarski pointed out. "I wish I knew more."

"The digital age has us all trying to keep up, Jim. It has my head spinning at times," replied Villacorta.

"Minister, that's what a glass of wine is supposed to do, and a glass of wine, I think, is more enjoyable, and easier to digest than some of this technical stuff. Which leads me to my surprise for you. I've arranged for some California Cabernet Sauvignon to be served with lunch today. I know how much you like our California Napa wines. It's our treat."

"Mr. Solarski, you never fail to impress me. This forensic stuff gets more interesting each day."

CHAPTER 55

"BILL, THE VAN has been located. It's in Puerto Barrios, about a twenty-minute flight from here," Solarski informed Davies. "Let me inform Minister Villacorta."

"How did we learn its location," Davies asked.

"Bill, you won't believe this, but Dorothy Cassell had a tracking device on her person. Apparently, she agreed to have it on her person to give her dad a small measure of comfort. He insisted on her possessing it. Guess what? It is sending out signals now."

"What?" Davies asked with a look of surprise.

"Her dad informed Captain Will Strain of the Coast Guard that her daughter may have a small, watch-sized tracking device on her person, a high-end device from a company called *AirTag*. Her device has a battery with a five-year life, so it should be sending out strong GPS signals," Solarski said.

"That's sweet," responded Davies.

"There is a glitch, however, that must be factored into the surveillance. The device can send out a buzz when activated by an external source, kind of like locating an iPhone. Some devices can emit an alert sound. Obviously, if activated, it alerts the abductors, and that is not good. There must still be one of them in her pocket," Solarski advised. "I hope they didn't try to activate the alarm function."

"I would be inclined to think her father had the device linked to his smartphone. He would then have had the ability to always monitor her location, from anywhere in the world. At least that's what the manufacturer would have promoted," suggested Davies. "Whatever he paid for the device, it may prove to be worth its weight in gold, if she is recovered alive."

"I pray that is the outcome," Solarski replied.

"So that's how we got the information about the present location of the van," asked Davies.

"Yes, it's an incredible development. Just wish we had known it a bit sooner; we may have been able to head them off," Solarski added. "I learned it from our Washington intelligence folks just moments ago. The device last alerted in Puerto Barrios. Washington requested the local authorities to respond to the area, and they located an abandoned van fitting the description. I want to let the Minister and Captain Otero know.

Before Solarski had the opportunity to brief Villacorta, the Minister spoke up. "Jim, our people in Puerto Barrios have located the suspect van, apparently on a lead from your Washington people. I don't know exactly from whom."

"Yes, Minister, I also received information that the victim had a tracking device on her person, and it last pinged at a Puerto Barrios location," Solarski advised. "It is good that the information coming from different sources points in the same direction."

Villacorta and the two Americans moved toward Captain Otero to brief him about the van. They talked briefly with Otero, who acknowledged the importance of the revelation. Then, in unison, they all hustled toward the government helicopter, leaving the La Antigua crime scene to the local investigators.

"My friends, the local authorities have secured the van for us. The sooner we get there the better, as I suspect the mob will soon try to interfere with this investigation, and the van may be compromised.

Right now, the locals don't know why they are securing the van. If the mob entices them with money, the van may go missing, sad to say," Villacorta speculated. "I will brief you more on the Puerto Barrios dynamics once on board."

"Hey, Jim, I am not saying I am afraid of helicopters, but is this one safe for us to get on," asked Davies.

"No worries, my friend, the Guatemalans have recently purchased a half dozen of these from Sikorsky, largely with United States funds, to help the Ministry of Justice with the country's drug problem. Right now, the pilots are American contract employees," Solarski shared. "I know them all, and they are professional special operators, mostly retired from the U.S. Army's 160th Night Stalkers."

"Are they the same guys who flew us up here?" Davies asked.

"Yup, they are the best of the best, and I trust them," Solarski replied with a wink.

"Thanks, that makes me feel better," Davies said.

Solarski and Davies took two seats across from Villacorta and Otero and fastened their seat belts. A crewman with a headset walked through the cabin to ensure everyone was secured in their seats.

"Bill, when we flew up here from Guatemala City, why didn't you seem as nervous as you are now?" asked Solarski.

"That's because you interrupted my dinner, and I already had a glass of wine in me. I was sufficiently mellow. Besides, the information you provided about the event occupied my mind. The difference now is the damn wine has worn off, my friend. I have always been fearful of flying, and that was with planes. You are now putting me on a helicopter for the first time in my life. As a scientist, I know the physics about flying, though I still don't appreciate how these fuckers fly," chuckled Davies. "When we get back to my hotel, you'll be buying me a few glasses of vino."

"With all the mayhem you see on a daily basis, I am surprised to hear you say that," Solarski joked.

"I have learned how to block out a lot of the stuff; I am still human, Jim, and by the way, that is why God invented booze," Davies retorted.

The chopper's blades began to rotate. Davies felt the vessel begin to slightly gyrate before wheels up. He closed his eyes and took a deep breath. Villacorta looked at Solarski and winked, giving Solarski a thumbs up. Otero was on his cell phone. The UH-60 Blackhawk, a familiar machine to United States law enforcement and military community, lifted off the ground. A medium range search and rescue aircraft, it easily converted to serve the Guatemala's interdiction needs and, if necessary, to provide the Justice Ministry with capable transportation to crime scenes around the country. The chopper would have the quartet to the van in less than a half hour. The Sikorsky chopper eased up to hover above the concrete landing zone and quickly dashed effortlessly into the night air. The occupants felt a slight tug on their seatbelts, but no more than they would have experienced rounding a highway curve at sixty miles an hour. Davies chilled out.

Captain Otero placed his headphones over his ears once on board the helicopter, as did the Minister. In Spanish, Otero was handing out further instructions. It was obvious to the Americans that he was in charge. He removed the small microphone from his lips and leaned over to Davies.

"Senor Davies, I have received word that the van remains exactly where our people were told it would be, within walking distance of a large marina. It is secured; there is no one in it; and no one will inspect its interior until we arrive," Captain Otero advised.

"What is our ETA to the landing zone?" asked Davies.

"We are within five minutes, or as Mr. Solarski would say, a Bravo," responded Minister Villacorta. "I am told we will be within walking distance of the van."

"Minister Villacorta and Captain Otero, I know we have talked about the electronic data intelligence this vehicle may yield once we have extracted the data from the vehicle's ECU's, but respectfully, let me reiterate the importance of us gathering the traditional forensics like photographs, fingerprinting, DNA, and other trace evidence from the scene. So, once we get there if there are colleagues around the van that really don't belong there, can we ask them to keep a respectful distance? Not sure of the local professional competence. I am here to serve and guide, not criticize, but it will help tremendously if you set the tone from the start," Davies petitioned.

"Of course, Senor Davies, I get it, and will certainly ensure you have a clean scene," the Minister responded. "I appreciate the fact that you are levelheaded enough to know the importance of the digital versus traditional evidence, particularly after having just witnessed the previous. How you guys hold all that inside, day after day, is mind boggling."

"Thank you, Minister, got to say that we, as forensic operators, ask the same questions regardless of whether the evidence is flesh and blood, tool and die marks, or digital evidence - the who, what, when, and where interrogatories remain the same."

CHAPTER 56

"VEHICLE SYSTEMS STORE a vast amount of data such as recent destinations, favorite locations, call logs, contact lists, SMS messages, emails, pictures, videos, social media feeds, and the navigation history of everywhere the vehicle has been. Many systems record events such as when and where a vehicle's lights are turned on, and which doors are opened and closed at specific locations. Analysis of vehicle data will answer key questions for investigators and may change the course of an investigation."

Solarski gave Davies a wide berth at the La Antigua crime scene before approaching him for what the Americans could do next. The RSO had received information that the suspect vehicle transporting Dorothy Cassell had been discovered "hot" in proximity to the point of departure from the coast of Guatemala via boat. It was ripe for a crime scene review.

"Will you be able to access the vehicle's data, Bill?" asked Solarski.

Depending on the age of the vehicle we may be able to extract where the vehicle was prior to the crime scene, and establish that it was at the crime scene, and if they used Bluetooth to connect their devices. All of it could yield a treasure trove of incriminating data," Davies informed the RSO.

"You have the tools to do that," Solarski inquired.

"Yes," Davies looked at the RSO and replied, "The sooner we get there, the better. I'm done here."

"The technical data that can be derived from a late model vehicle is enormous, Jim," said Davies when he learned the van had been recovered. "It'll pay huge dividends."

"Bill, the Guatemalans have dedicated their helicopter to us. Solarski had been in contact with Minister Villacorta, who authorized a government helicopter to transit the two of them, along with Captain Otero, to the vehicle's location.

"We can be there in thirty minutes, Bill," reported Solarski. "Minister Villacorta is approaching now. Perhaps you can share some insight into what the vehicle's value will be," Solarski responded.

"Hola, Jim," Villacorta greeted on the outer perimeter of the grisly crime scene.

"Hola, Minister Villacorta, and of course you remember Bill Davies, crime scene investigator from the Baltimore City Police Department."

"It is an honor, Mr. Davies, to have you assist us with this tragic situation. My country is humbled and grateful to have your expertise here," Villacorta said. "You may see one or two of the students who attended your seminar here."

"Well, Minister Villacorta, please call me Bill," Davies quickly offered. "I've got to tell you that this is one of the most gruesome scenes I have ever encountered. I've witnessed numerous knifing deaths, but never of this many victims at once. Those responsible certainly have no regard for the sanctity of human life."

"Jim, it may be a game changer to have the van physically and digitally searched," Villacorta commented.

"I don't know shit about vehicle data extraction other than what I heard Bill present to the class. Once Mr. Davies has had a chance to examine the van, I think we will get a greater understanding as to who may be responsible for the massacre at the La Antigua site, and it probably won't be a good thing for some of the Guatemala elites," responded Solarski.

Solarski and Davies headed to the same landing zone where they had been dropped earlier, in proximity of the grisly crime scene at La Antigua. This time the chopper would take them to a more benign crime scene in order to capture the forensic data embedded on the van used by the Bratva operatives, specifically the minutia embedded in the several electronic control units.

"How did the Guatemalans learn about the van and its location," Davies asked Solarski. "And do we have its make and model?"

"It's my understanding that the United States Office of the Director of National Intelligence may have intercepted some signaling after learning about the massacre and notified the Ministry of Justice about a potential vehicle and location We may have gotten lucky," said Solarski. "The van has been described as a late model white Toyota Sienna LE, eight-passenger. That's a lot of room for a group of thugs to take an innocent girl for a ride," replied Solarski.

"That's pretty good detail, Jim. I know I am a small city operative, but if I had access to half of what you federal guys have, I would be a rock star," joked Davies. "The satellite probably was able to home in on the vehicle's GPS signal before it was shut down. Brilliant."

"Trust me, Bill, in the eyes of the Guatemalan government, you are already a rock star. If this van gives up one-fourth of what you think it can, they may make you an honorary minister of justice. On a personal note, I feel fortunate that you are here during this event," Solarski told Davies with a serious tone. "Even the discussions you presented yesterday to their officers on general forensic investigations will pay dividends for the United States from this day forward."

"My pleasure, Jim. Just as a refresher, when and if we have access to the van, it will be necessary to get the vehicle's circuit boards back to a lab. I am not sure what the locals have, but I do have basic readers with me that may yield some data."

"What kind of data does it yield?" asked Solarski.

"Typically, the systems collect performance metrics, and does it constantly. There are dozens of vehicular Electronic Computer Units (ECU) associated with the circuit board that have defined chores. We don't need to know all those available, but the vehicle may give us its previous locations, perhaps even locations that the vehicle deployed from sites prior to the crime scene. Doesn't provide a lot of comfort for the current tragedy, but surely, it'll provide investigative leads and evidence to tie suspects to the horrific crime," Davies provided.

"And you brought equipment with you to examine the data these ECUs collect," asked Solarski.

"I have an oscilloscope that allows me to develop and look at some graphs. These graphs help us understand a vehicle's status quo. But to do it right, like I said, will require a lab, and I'm not sure what the Guatemalans have. It'll be something Captain Otero can advise us on," Davies said. "I also brought what's called an iVe forensic tool that will help acquire, identify, and analyze some of the critical information stored within the vehicle systems. The data obtained are considered *silent witnesses* in my professional community. This tool is commercially available by a company named Berla, and it's what I shared with the Guatemalans at the seminar just yesterday. Perhaps the State Department should arrange for me to leave it here for them if they don't currently possess one," Davies advised.

"Absolutely, Bill, I like that idea. It is just amazing how technology has advanced with cars. What I find interesting is the notion that even as it has advanced, investigators still have to answer the same interrogatories: who, what, where, when, and how," Solarski noted. "What do you think is the most important thing the van will provide." he added.

"Like I said, we may be able to recover the van's previous locations, and other navigation information, like the point of origin. Much of it will be probative for any future Guatemalan case. It certainly can support the efforts of any United States intelligence agencies involved in this matter," Davies informed.

"It's incredible how forensics has changed. It used to be blood and residue," Solarski quipped.

"Still is, but with eighty percent of crimes involving vehicles, these valuable digital components can't be ignored. There's data available now that didn't exist just a few years ago, that can be extracted from devices connected via an USB port or Bluetooth, all hugely helpful. That's one of the major points I tried to make at your State Department sponsored training session."

"Brother, I am so glad you are here," Solarski said.

"Well, Jim, once we get the van's circuit boards, we will be able to put the extracted data in an understandable packet for those that need it. I just hope we can learn from an immediate review some relevant information to help find the girl," Davies said earnestly.

CHAPTER 57

"THE LAB CAN tell us more, but this is what I have so far, based on the tools we have here. The electronic log indicates the van arrived here about the same hour the American authorities reported it. That means they have an hour and a half lead time on us. There are finger and palm prints all over the vehicle and the Guatemalans can obtain latent prints for comparison purposes. There is also DNA that was collected from semen and blood stains; and they, too, will be obtained and processed in the lab. Within the van the blood stains don't suggest anything consistent with a violent episode. However, we did find several long knives, each bore blood residue. Of course, that blood will be compared to the blood samples obtained at the La Antigua scene. The two middle captain's chairs have been removed from the center of the van which left an open area. That's where most of the forensics has been located. When we get the circuit boards back to Guatemala City, we will be able to look for previous travel points. The circuit boards will give us good historical data about the van's movements. Some of the other circuitry will help with the communications," Davies reported to Captain Otero, Minister Villacorta and RSO Solarski.

"So, Bill, listening to what you just reported, there doesn't seem to have been violent, bloody event per se, though she may have been sexually assaulted?" asked Villacorta.

"Yes, that's what I would venture to say, but it is really presumptive, and no way near conclusive," Davies replied. "The van's gas tank is three-quarters full, which may mean they stopped for a fill-up since leaving La Antigua. We should be able to estimate the mileage and then track down the gas station. Not sure if your stations have closed circuit cameras, but it is worth the effort to determine that. Photos of them getting out of the van would be probative, too."

"Thank you for that, Bill. Please update us on additional data that emerges when you complete your analysis," Villacorta said.

"Absolutely," Davies said.

"Jim, it's obvious that these thugs transitioned to a boat here. I will have Captain Otero dispatch some of his men to the marina to begin questioning prospective witnesses. Not sure of the direction of travel, but it might be a good idea to let the U.S. Coast Guard know what's going on and be in position to interdict any suspicious vessel they may come across," Villacorta suggested.

"Agree, I can't imagine they would remain in this area. Common sense does suggest a boat. Then the question becomes where: Cuba? The Keys? Another Central American country?" Solarski mused. "I will update the Embassy now and have it notified the U.S. Coast Guard, as well. Can't hurt to have them on standby."

CHAPTER 58

"JIM, HERE'S SOME of the data that's been extracted from the van and analyzed. We've been able to obtain phone numbers used previously through the vehicle's Bluetooth. Listen to this, the vehicle's previous locations, prior to its arrival at the massacre site, are retrievable. The tracking log provides the history of GPS locations, and it doesn't look good for Ambassador Cohen. His residence appears to be the origination point from which the vehicle drove prior to La Antigua. The tracking history shows it to be a direct drive, based on mileage and time. The event log has been sequestered for evidentiary purposes. The phone logs also have the Ambassador's cell number listed as an incoming call. The date and time have been recorded, and the log event is sequestered. Other documented numbers have New York area codes. We ran a few through an open source site and found that some of them are from the Brighton Beach area in Brooklyn, NY," Davies reported to Solarski.

"Are Captain Otero and the Minister aware of this information?" asked Solarski

"Absolutely. Captain Otero was in the lab just about the whole time the electronic circuit boards were being analyzed. He's becoming an instant expert on data extraction," Davies advised. "He briefed the Minister on the data found so far."

"Bill, I can't thank you enough for all you are doing," Solarski said.

"No problem, Jim. Just let my boss know why I am staying a few extra days, so he doesn't think it's a boondoggle," Davies chuckled.

"Bill, seeing a half-dozen decapitated bodies can't ever be a boondoggle. The State Department will pick up the cost of your additional stay here, no worries."

CHAPTER 59

"THE DISTANCE FROM Cancun to Key West is less than four hundred miles. I will make the call to either divert to the Cuban mainland or go direct to Key West. But I won't do that until the boat reaches the southwest tip of Cuba," Yuriy Khovasov advised Markov, Belov's Brighton Beach aide-de-camp, via phone."

"Vladimir suggests that your boat hug the Cuban coastline until you reach Havana, and then be prepared to divert to Key West if it looks like no authorities are tracking you," Markov advised. "You'll probably need to refuel somewhere along the Cuban border."

"Yes, that would be our plan," Khovasov answered, privately thinking Markov was useless. "We hope to transfer the girl to another boat about sixty miles out from Key West. That boat will have counterfeit passports for me and the girl, if needed. It may not matter, but if we do get challenged before the transfer, it may make more sense to just weight her down and throw her ass overboard, then hustle back to the Cuban border without her."

"That's not what the boss wants. You need to come up with a better contingency plan. The boss wants her ass in the States so he can plant her corpse on her father's doorstep," Markov insisted. "He doesn't want to have gone through the Guatemala bullshit only to come up empty with that plan."

"I understand, Boris. I'll get it done, and she has been screwed by everyone aboard at least twice," Khovasov boasted. "She's wasted."

"Yuriy, the boss will love hearing that, but just save some of that for the guys in the transfer boat. They may want a piece of the action."

CHAPTER 60

"SIR, CAN YOU explain what eGuardian is?" asked the State Department analyst.

"The eGuardian site is an unclassified information-sharing platform hosted by the FBI. It pretty much serves citizens as an on-line mechanism to report suspicious activity by terrorist elements. The info is usually forwarded to the FBI Joint Terrorism Task Force members as FYI," reported the supervisor. "Why, do you have something?"

"Yes, sir."

"What did the alert state?"

"It stated that a group of American university students numbering about a half-dozen, and their professor, will be targeted while on school sanctioned travel, and slaughtered. The communique does not give a motive; does not cite a specific group; nor does it provide the name of the school. The alert was displayed on a public facing complaint site yesterday, but we are only now getting it," reported the analyst.

An FBI analyst forwarded it to our State Department's Overseas Security Advisory Council (OSAC), believing it had a better means to distribute it to universities around the country, specifically, to alert university security directors of an impending threat.

"Okay, just to be clear, the FBI sent a 10/2 threat notification to the State Department's Overseas Security Advisory Council today, 10/3, for us to distribute to our university security director constituents," asked the supervisor.

"Yes. The notification sat with the FBI for the past day before they felt the need to alert us," the analyst added.

"My God, I pray nothing happened today," replied the supervisor.

"Yes, but in all fairness to the FBI, it is vague. It is not specific as to a college, or Central American country," responded the analyst.

"So, I am guessing that this university threat case didn't rise to the level which would require the FBI to forward it on with urgency?" commented the supervisor.

"That's what I'm thinking, too. Like you, I just pray that there is not more to it."

"Okay, then, just to be prudent, let's blast the threat to all of our OSAC university constituents globally to ensure they know. Since we can't narrow it down to a specific country, at least all responsible university security directors who may have kids on a semester travel will be made aware," directed the supervisor.

"Will do," said the analyst.

"Then pass it directly to the DNI's Situation Room," replied the supervisor.

"Will do."

"Situation Room," answered the duty officer.

"Hello, this is the State Department's Overseas Security Advisory Council," replied the analyst. "I just forwarded an FYI alert we received from the FBI describing the contents of a vague threat directed toward unknown college students on a program abroad for the semester," reported the OSAC analyst.

"Thanks, we received that alert today, as well. Pretty porous if you ask me, but appreciate the heads-up."

"Okay, thank you, have a great day."

CHAPTER 61

"DOGCATCHER, THIS IS Brotherhood, come in please."

Yuriy responded, "Come in, Brotherhood."

"Dogcatcher, we are approximately fifteen minutes from the transfer point."

"Copy that, Brotherhood, over," Yuriy replied.

The cigarette he commanded continued to race effortlessly through the Gulf waters. "I'm going to miss piloting this boat," he thought. "Soon I will have the girl brought up top," Yuriy instructed Cohen's men on board. "We should be transferring her ass onto the other boat in about fifteen to twenty minutes. Thanks for working with me on this job. I hope you boys enjoyed yourselves with the little bitch. She doesn't look very appreciative," Yuriy added while holding onto a set of binoculars, periodically inspecting the horizon for the rendezvous boat. Above he heard the distinctive hum of an airplane's engine and trained his sights on it.

"Senor Yuriy is that something we should be worried about?" asked one of Cohen's men.

"I am not worried about it. It is only a small Cessna, probably on a solo flight," Yuriy responded. "What we need to worry about is anything that says United States Coast Guard." He then trained his sights ahead and saw the Brotherhood approaching. "Soon you boys will be able to return to Guatemala. Here comes our transition boat."

Approaching the cigarette was a fifty-foot Sea Ray cruiser operated by two Bratva thugs out of Key West, Florida. "Senor, what type of boat is that?" asked one of Cohen's men.

"It's one big boat, friend, not quite as fast as this one, but a real beauty. It's got about half the horsepower as ours, but we don't need speed returning to Key West at this point. We just need to get back to port without making a big ruckus. As soon as the girl and I board the vessel, you guys can hustle back to Guatemala."

"Si, senor, but we may have to get fueled up in Cuba," Cohen's thug blurted.

"You should have enough gas to make it back to Cancun," Yuriy replied. "This boat has a huge tank, but that's your call."

The Cigarette, with its fifty-two-foot slim length, came to an idle on the relatively calm, smooth gulf waters. Slowly approaching was the Brotherhood, an equally lengthy vessel with its own fifty-foot length, but with a broader beam. Its port side bore toward the Dogcatcher's port side, slow enough for Cohen's thugs to grab its gunnels, and bring the two vessels together as one. One of the Brotherhood mates used a mooring grab hook to secure the Cigarette in tandem with his boat. Both vessels were in neutral for the exchange.

Dorothy Cassell had awakened from a drug induced sleep while lying listless below the fast-boat's deck. Though physically abused she did not feel any physical pain at the moment. When she alerted to someone coming her way, her instinct was to feign unconsciousness. It worked. The thug opened the small fridge, took something, and climbed up the steps to the deck.

"I have no idea where I am, but I need to keep my composure. Dad always taught me to take three full breaths to stay calm. Okay, there's the breaths. Now where the hell am I?" Dorothy asked herself. "Keep calm; don't move," she continued to think as she surveyed the environment she found herself in. A small LED night light slightly illuminated the area, but not sufficiently for her to recognize where she was. "I feel like I'm in a boat," she thought. While time and location were not known to her, she did hear a commotion above. "Sounds like voices greeting one another," she thought.

"Bring the girl to me now," Yuriy shouted back to a Cohen thug.

Seconds later Dorothy squinted as she observed two men coming toward her. "Agarra su brazo izqueirdo," she heard one of them say, "Grab her left arm". She continued to feign unconsciousness as one man grabbed her left arm. The men carried dead weight up the steps and laid her upon the deck. With their engines continuing to idle, the two boats moved in tandem, propelled only by a brisk wind in the vast Gulf water. The Dogcatcher's starboard gunnel married up to the Brotherhood's port side gunnel, now secured together by several lines, was an obvious sign that Yuriy did not want to display much longer. "Should the Coast Guard see this it would raise suspicion," he thought.

Dorothy was brought to the stern of the deck and dropped. She appeared to be in a catatonic state: and it was one of her own making. Her hair contained the dry, caked blood of one of her George Washington University coeds. Her blouse was a wrinkled mess and its buttons misaligned. The thugs made no attempt to put her bra back on, nor did they care about buttoning up her blouse. She sat silently, oblivious to her surroundings.

"Try giving her a sip of water, it's the least you bastards can do for her," Yuriy ordered. "And then move her to the Brotherhood, we need to separate quickly and move on to Key West," barked Yuriy.

"Go help him bring her to me," Yuriy told one of the other thugs holding onto the boat's gunnel. Yuriy placed Dorothy in front of him and began to hoist her up to the Brotherhood, "grab her by each arm," he ordered. The Brotherhood mates lifted her onto the deck and laid her down. Her drooping eyes and limp body was now an act designed to convince the thugs that her continued lethargy was due to the drugs they gave her hours earlier. It was not; it was now her survival mode.

Yuriy vaulted onto the Brotherhood deck, turned back to the Guatemalan crew and said, "Hermanos, muchas gracias por todo, particularmente por violando la puta," he said in broken Spanish, "thank you for screwing her." Tell Ambassador Cohen how much we appreciate his support to Bratva. He'll be rewarded soon."

Yuriy extended his arm to help push the Brotherhood away from the Dogcatcher.

"Put the girl down below. We don't want her on deck should there be a flyover by the Coast Guard. Make sure you secure her wrist to the bed. She may soon regain consciousness."

Yuriy took command at the helm of the Brotherhood. "Hang on, we're heading home to Key West."

Yuriy took a glance as the Cigarette moved south at a brisk pace. Soon, both boats were out of site. "At thirty knots, heading northeast, with the remarkably calm waters, in the early days of October, the boat would arrive in less than two to three hours," Yuriy thought to himself. "I'm exhausted. These last twenty-four hours, I've witnessed a bloody massacre, driven three hours in a van, and rode the last twelve hours in a high-speed boat, but man, do I love this job." Then, anticipating the Brotherhood's approach to the Key West marina, he felt a bit ill-at-ease.

One of the Brotherhood mates came up to the bridge and advised Yuriy, "We have arranged to dock the Brotherhood overnight at a slip closer to the Galleon Marina Motel site. The marina may have a lot of activity this week, but our room, G31, is facing the adjacent roadway. and getting the girl into the room should be not a problem."

"It may be best to just to keep her on the boat for the night and then move her to the safe room later," he reasoned to himself. "We can make that decision upon arrival."

The sighting of the Cessna fly-over hours before began to bother Yuriy more than he let on to Cohen's thugs. "Have you seen any Coast Guard assets flying around?" Yuriy calmly asked the Brotherhood mates.

"There's been little activity today, but this is a Coast Guard hub, so it would not be unusual. We've seen a lot of these little Cessnas flying back and forth, but we just assumed they may have been looking for lost sailors. They don't come from the Coast Guard. The Coast Guard doesn't rely on little planes to do their job," replied the mate. "They send out large helicopters and oversized prop jobs."

"I get it. I will be advising the boss shortly as to our success in getting the girl here," Yuriy replied, still thinking of the little Cessna. He felt anxious.

CHAPTER 62

"COAST GUARD, KEY West, this Civil Air Patrol, N143DC, over."

"Go ahead 143, this is Coast Guard, Key West," the operator answered.

"Coast Guard, Key West, we have two fifty footers about to rendezvous approximately eighty kilometers southwest from your location," advised the civil air patrol pilot. "It appears the two boats are spooning and exchanging personnel."

"Roger that, 143, Coast Guard will dispatch assets to that area and conduct a welfare check," the Coast Guard operator acknowledged, using code for "we are on our way to check out the suspicious activity."

Then the Coast Guard operator stated, "Coast Guard respectfully requests you terminate your surveillance and vacate the area."

Roger that, will comply," answered the Civil Air Patrol pilot.

CHAPTER 63

YURIY INSTRUCTED HIS Bratva operators on board the Brotherhood to put Dorothy below deck and let her sleep on the queen bed in the cruiser's master bedroom.

"Guys, she been violated enough, let her sleep. We need her to be able to walk when we get to Key West," Yuriy told them, not sympathetic as to her health, but rather as a practical display of faux compassion to preserve her as a trophy for his boss. "She needs to be preserved for Belov," he thought. He dialed Belov in Brighton Beach.

The phone stopped ringing, and an eerie silence occupied the line. Without a prompt he began to verbalize his message. "Boss, I was told to call you and give you an update on what's going on," Yuriy blurted, hoping Belov was on the line.

"Hello Yuriy, how are you, and how is the little bitch today?"

"We have successfully transferred her to the Brotherhood and are en route to Key West.

We should be there in an hour, and depending on the cover of darkness, we will either remain on the boat or move to a room at the marina. So far, it appears that we are good to go without any obvious sign that authorities are tracking us," Yuriy informed his boss.

"This is good news, Yuriy. You have done well and must be ready for a good night's sleep. You have been through a lot and have seen a lot. I hope it will not prevent you from getting a good night's sleep.

Most men would suffer from the traumatic effects witnessing the brutal decapitation of so many people, but not Bratva. Yuriy, it is important to send signals to our adversaries; this will be a good one. It may be seen as evil by some, but for us, the Bratva, it serves our interests. In the future, those who hear of this incident will not want to fuck with us. You understand that Yuriy, right? Am I stating the obvious," Belov asked.

"Boss that is not a problem with me. It doesn't bother me; it's all business," Yuriy replied.

"That's why you are our go-to guy," Belov said. "So call me when you get her off the boat and into the safe room. By then, I will be better able to tell you what I next plan to do with her. I can tell you though, it won't be pretty for her father."

Belov hung up.

CHAPTER 64

"THIS IS CAPTAIN Strain."

"Sir, this is the Key West duty desk. The Florida Civil Air Patrol N143DC advises that the two target vessels have conjoined briefly. Air Patrol diverted north without a second pass, but before they did, they observed the separation of our two target vessels. The cigarette headed southwest, while a large cruiser headed toward the tip of Key West.

"Thank you. I advised the officer on deck that we will not be doing a welfare inspection of the cruiser. We will continue to surveil from a distance and monitor the cruiser's arrival at the Key West marina. Keep me advised," Strain ordered.

"Roger that, sir, will comply," the Coast Guard duty desk responded.

CHAPTER 65

"THIS IS KEEGAN."

"Sir, thanks for taking my call," the captain respectfully replied.

"Of course, Will, I would never not take a call from my favorite Captain," Keegan replied. "How are things developing in the Gulf?"

"Well, we dodged a bullet when the Bratva's Cigarette boat diverted north, averting a stay in Cuba," Strain advised. "There has been a transfer of persons from the Cigarette to a fifty-foot cruiser, and we are now monitoring its transit to Key West. We believe that Dorothy Cassell and a Bratva operator are now on board that cruiser and about one hour away from a Key West marina. We have decided for the safety of Miss Cassell not to attempt an open water interdiction. We feel it best to surveil it from afar and take tactical action once she is on land, or at least, once the vessel is secured at the marina. Our belief is that Bratva will probably want to keep her on board until dusk, and then move her to a safe location. Once we confirm that, our assets will initiate an operation to liberate her. We are fortunate to have the Florida Department of Public Safety Highway Patrol and the local Key West police here to assist us. We work with them frequently, and they are family to us," Strain explained. "They have been fully briefed."

"I agree, and their decision to avoid Cuba and head to Key West is a blessing. I pray for her safety and can only imagine what these bastards have already done to her. Will, I won't burden you now with an update from the State Department on the Bratva's actions in La Antigua massacre, but I can assure you it will upset you." Keegan advised. "I wish you and your local task force tremendous, good wishes as you continue to manage this operation. We can brief you further after the Dorothy Cassell event is resolved."

"Thank you, sir. As far as the local law enforcement community knows, this is nothing more than a drug bust. I will soon advise headquarters what our next steps are in order to conclude this operation. Please let Larry Cassell know he and his family are with us in spirit on this operation, too."

"Get her, Will, we need to get her. I don't want to fail the Cassell family. They have been through so much in the service of this nation," Keegan ended the call.

Captain Strain detected a slight faltering in his voice, suggesting a bit of regret, if not guilt, for involving the former Secret Service Director in the affairs of the ongoing Bratva attack on the United States government.

CHAPTER 66

"BOSS, WE'VE GOT a problem with Ambassador Cohen. He called a few minutes ago, distraught. He's scared shitless that he will soon face the wrath of the Guatemala Justice Ministry for the abduction of the Cassell girl and the massacre of the college kids. He has suggested that if it happens, he will not hang alone; he will bail on Bratva," Markov relayed to Belov.

"Yeah, I just read about the massacre in the New York Post this morning. The article indicated that the U.S. Embassy is actively engaged in the investigation, and letting the media know of its progress. Apparently, there is some whiz kid, a forensic guy, from the Baltimore Police Department there, coincidentally providing forensic training. The article indicated that some of the investigative leads involve the successful analysis of electronic digital information from the van that was used. What it didn't indicate, and that I found interesting, was how they located the van in the first place, so quickly," Belov calmly noted.

"I don't have that information, but the Ambassador may, particularly if the Post is reporting it. He just needs to calm down before he gets himself in trouble, and I don't mean with the Guatemalan Justice Ministry," Markov said. "I mean with us."

"That van must be a treasure trove of information. Not that I am an expert on electronic data, but why would Yuriy elect to use a late model vehicle and then abandon it, for the police and U.S. authorities to scour?

When we send our best people, like you, out to perform our work, we need to make sure they are more sophisticated in modern day electronics. Yuriy screwed up, and I will deal with him later. Get the Ambassador on the phone," Belov demanded. Markov sat down in front of Belov's desk and dialed the Ambassador's phone. When it began to ring, he handed the cell phone over to Belov.

"Ambassador, this is Vladimir Belov, how are you?"

"Vladimir, I am not good; I am sure Markov told you. Since the massacre, the judicial heat on me and my people here in Guatemala City has become oppressive. What happened at La Antigua is all people are talking about here in Guatemala. The government authorities, backed by the U.S. Embassy, are aggressively investigating the murders. It is obvious that the media are aware of the abduction of one of the students from the massacre site. How they figured that out so quickly is a mystery to me. Your man Yuriy, and my boys, departed the scene quickly and left no trace of which I am aware that would have allowed the Guatemala police to pursue them," Cohen said as his voice began to pitch up. "This young American kid working through the Embassy with the police is something we couldn't have anticipated. Apparently, he came up with the notion that one of the students was missing."

"How did he do that?" asked Belov.

"How the fuck do I know? I am not a forensic examiner," Cohen replied. "Normally, we control the police. We could have silenced the reporting in the news, made up cover stories, but this investigation took on an urgency I've never seen before. I called the police commander once I heard they were responding to the murder site, but he wouldn't give me any information. My concern is that this matter got out of hand because of your man, Yuriy. The assault on the kids didn't have to go down this bloody in the first place. You people put too much pressure on us to assist you. You people wanted it to be bloody. Now it is a global event, reported everywhere. You people are to blame, not us."

"Whoa, Ambassador, take a deep breath. Don't panic; we can fix any matter. It may take money, or it may take some violence, but you need to keep your powder dry and not overreact. From what I hear and read, the van that was used gave the investigators some information that could lead back to you and us. That is our Achilles heel right now. That's a big lesson for us to understand for future events. We will look at the embassy and media reporting to see what can be done to suppress any focus on you," Belov assured the Ambassador. "It would also be helpful if you could destroy that damn van."

"I need it to be done sooner than later," Cohen interjected, "or I will have to develop my own plan."

"Ambassador Cohen, you do not have your own plan; there will only be a Bratva plan," Belov said sternly.

"Where is the girl now," asked Cohen.

"You don't need to know," Belov reported. "Someone will get back to you." Belov hung up.

CHAPTER 67

"BORIS, GET YURIY on the phone and let's coordinate what to do with the girl today. We may need to jettison her sooner than I wanted. It might be time to insulate ourselves," Belov said, in a pensive mood as he stared out his home office window toward the Brighton Beach boardwalk. He was sitting not far from where his father's brain matter splattered and caked on the sidewalk. "Poppy's last breath," he thought, "will be avenged."

"Will do, boss," Markov responded.

"Poppy," he petitioned his father's memory, "what should I do with the Ambassador? I know what to do, Poppy, it is what you would do if the Ambassador got weak-kneed. Kill him and make it gruesome to send a needed message to his own people. I will, Poppy."

"Boss, Yuriy is on the phone," Markov handed over the phone once again.

"Yuriy, what do you know?"

"Boss, we have just entered a Key West marina and will be docking soon. Once we get tied up to the dock, we will take the girl to a safe house nearby. It doesn't appear we are being tailed. We did find a small token-like device, about the size of a half-dollar, when we left the van for the boat at Puerto Barrios. I am not sure what it was, but I threw it some distance from the van. It may have been a tracking device, and if so, would explain how quickly the authorities found the vehicle." Yuriy stated.

"Yes, Yuriy, like I told the Ambassador, this has been a technical learning experience for us. It appears their tracking of the girl ended at the port. It may be that no one knows that your group successfully left Guatemala. Nevertheless, the Ambassador is not happy with your using the late model van. Apparently, the Guatemalan investigators have developed the ability to analyze the vehicle's electronics and retrieve historical information contained on those chips to identify movements. Older vehicles don't have that, but late model ones do, like the van you used. The Ambassador thinks the sophistication of their investigation is due, in large measure, to the U.S. Embassy involvement. He fears it could lead to his doorstep. We can worry about him later," Belov advised.

"Boss, the girl is out of it, a combination of the drugs we've pumped into her, and her being screwed so often by the Guatemalans who feasted on her. When we transitioned boats they were not happy to head back home. They are a strange, sadistic bunch who work for the Ambassador. In addition, the Guatemalans need desperately to shower," Yuriy chuckled. "I am happy to have our own boys with me here in Key West," advised Yuriy. "At least they shower."

"Okay, good luck getting to the safe house," Belov replied. "Give me a call when you get settled and we can discuss our next move with the girl and her asshole father."

"Okay," Yuriy said before shutting down his phone.

CHAPTER 68

THE BROTHERHOOD ENTERED the Key West waters at Buoy Number One, red-right-return, each red buoy located on the cruiser's starboard side to indicate a boat's proper way back to return to the marina. The cruiser slowed as it approached Buoy Number Four, and the boat's captain turned into the Key West Bight Marina located on the northwest end of the island. Once docked, Yuriy's intent was to bring Dorothy to a safe house near the main thoroughfare, Duval Street. As he stood up on the cruiser's deck, he appeared relieved as he observed a calm, late afternoon dock arrival. "Soon, I can let the boys secure the girl, so I can shower and head to Sloppy Joe's Bar for dinner," Yuriy sighed.

"How's the boat's gas level?" Yuriy shouted to the cruiser's captain.

"Got at least a half tank, but tomorrow morning I'll take the boat over to the Chevron fuel dock," responded the captain. "A full tank can take us to either Florida coast."

"That's good information. I will know soon what our next destination will be," Yuriy said. "Once you've fully secured the boat to the dock, we'll move the girl off to the safe house." Yuriy directed several of the Bratva crew to take up surveillance positions off the boat and closer to the marina's entrance in anticipation of the girl's removal to a waiting black SUV with tinted windows. The marina featured thirty-three transient slips used by boats like the Brotherhood. This day, most of those transient slips were void of any overnighters. There was only a thirty-foot cabin cruiser secured to an adjacent pier, and a forty-foot sail boat secured to a pier on the opposite side, as though the two boats had to be mutually exclusive from one another: one a motor, and the other, a sail.

"I will remain on board for another half-hour to power down some of the systems on the cruiser," the captain advised Yuriy. "I will catch up with you guys soon to go out for something to eat, if you want."

"Okay," Yuriy replied as he and another thug brought Dorothy off the cruiser's deck and onto the pier. She was weak-kneed. Yuriy spotted his waiting SUV, and the three moved slowly toward the vehicle. Yuriy glanced right and left to observe where his thugs took up tactical positions.

"Hustle ahead and open the rear door. I can manage the girl without you," Yuriy ordered.

As the thug opened the SUV door, Captain Strain exited with a drawn nine-millimeter Sig Sauer, semi-automatic pistol aimed directly at Yuriy's center chest. Yuriy stopped ten feet from the vehicle where the pier's decking ended, and the parking lot's macadam began. His two forward observers, as yet unaware of Strain's interdiction, remained intent on looking away for outer perimeter threats.

"Let her go, and drop to the ground," ordered Strain, as a separate agent swiftly circled around the SUV from the opposite side to assist in the Strain challenge. Yuriy stopped the girl, but he did not release his grip on her arm. His thugs heard the verbal challenge and drew their weapons, actions that did not end well, as both were terminated by Strain's Coast Guard teams perched nearby. The covering thugs were taken down with single shots fired simultaneously to the head of each. Yuriy stood steadfast. He did not reach for his weapon, but his close-in protection thug did. Strain adjusted his aim and hit the thug in the head with one round, from less than six feet. He was dead before his corpse hit the macadam. Strain visually tracked the thug's weapon. It fell to the ground a split second sooner than the thug's head did. Strain's colleague moved to the corpse and kicked the weapon away, continuing to train his duty weapon at Yuriy.

Finally, Yuriy released his grip on the girl and held his hands slightly above his head. The sound of gunfire was sufficient for him to comply. He dropped to his knees, as additional Coast Guard agents hustled to the SUV to further assist.

Strain holstered his weapon and reached out to support Dorothy, carefully placing her in the rear of the SUV.

"Dorothy, you are with friends," Strain told her. Dorothy looked up at Strain and nodded in appreciation. "My God, this young lady has the ability to respond this way after all she has been through. What an amazing person," thought Strain. "She will need a lot of help to overcome the ensuing PTSD." Strain hopped into the SUV with his colleague to take Dorothy to a nearby Coast Guard clinic for an initial physical examination.

Within moments of the gunshots, additional units from the Florida Highway Patrol and Coast Guard Investigative Service arrived at the scene to secure a larger perimeter and establish a crime scene to document the condition of the three thugs taken out by the agents.

Once the SUV departed the area, Strain called the local Coast Guard duty desk, "This is Captain Strain, please get me Assistant Commandant Keegan."

"Roger that, Sir. Stand by," responded the local operations center's operator.

"This is Keegan."

"Sir, we have Dorothy Cassell. We are on our way to Key West's Trumbo Point where we have a helicopter asset standing by to transport her to a Miami hospital for further medical evaluation. Fortunately, all the action here took place near Coast Guard properties. There were three fatalities, all Bratva operatives who drew their weapons. We have Yuriy Khovasov and the cruiser's captain in custody. They are being transported to the local state police barracks for processing. Our investigators will be present for the interrogation. The state and local police have been terrific," Strain reported.

"This is good news, Will. When I hang up I will contact Director Cassell and let him know she's recovered. I assume that once she is physically able, we will have her transported via a Coast Guard asset to Miami Sector where she can be repatriated with her family," Keegan asked.

"Sir, as soon as she gets medically cleared here, she'll be in the air."

"Will, I suspect she has suffered. Her family will be disturbed when they learn to what degree, but the poignant fact remains, unlike her fellow students, she is alive. I want to thank you for your efforts to get her out of harm's way. This will deal a critical blow to the Bratva organization once it is revealed to the general public," Keegan said.

"Yes sir, but we should all be on high alert, and prepare to defend against future Bratva retaliation. When Belov learns we have once again foiled his effort to retaliate for father's death, he will be like a wounded bear," Strain replied. "He'll be blind with rage."

"Amen, Will. That threat is real. Stay safe and keep me informed."

CHAPTER 69

FLOATING SILENTLY IN the air space above the Gulf of Mexico flies the untethered "Angel of Death." The aircraft was known to inflict deadly firepower on targets in the Afghanistan and Iraq war and feared by the Taliban. It's an array of side-fixed 40 mm Bofons cannons and 25 mm Gatling guns had the capability of annihilating the enemy, and on more than one occasion, did. Today, it approached its prey, a Bratva chartered Guatemalan speed boat, or Cigarette, with a call sign, the Dogcatcher. The C-130 soundlessly approached its target, spotting the Cigarette from an altitude of 7,000 feet. It descended, now closing the gap to confront the Bratva boat.

After casting Dorothy Cassell off to the Brotherhood, the Dogcatcher traveled swiftly back toward the Mexican territorial border resort of Cancun, en route to Guatemala. The Bratva thugs believed the Cigarette had ample fuel to reach Mexican waters, and at sixty knots per hour, had estimated an arrival in three hours' time. Taking turns at the helm, the thugs were able to alternate rest as they continued homeward bound, encountering only small Gulf swells. The transit seemed effortless. The sunset was not far away, and the expected panorama would be a welcome vista.

Suddenly, the three crew members alerted to a dull, ominous sound, an aircraft approaching overhead. Even the cigarette engines could not muffle the oncoming presence of the AC-130 as it flew closer.

"Mire arriba, un avion," said one of the thugs. "Parece ser un avion militar," said another.

As the gunship encircled the boat, the Guatemalans grew nervous. The boat's captain hastened to a full throttle toward the southwest, and the Mexican border. He tried to zigzag the boat's course to prevent the plane from accurately targeting it, but in the open Gulf waters, the cigarette remained vulnerable.

"Whose plane is it," asked one thug.

"There are no markings on the plane," responded a crew mate. The three thugs grew more anxious as they digested what the plane's presence meant to them. They surmised it wasn't going to be a friendly encounter. "Mas rapido," said the first thug. "Vamonos, este no es bueno."

"Call Ambassador Cohen and advise him we need help. Tell him we don't know who these people are, but they are threatening," demanded the helm operator.

"I will," responded the thug standing next to him.

"Sir, we are locked, loaded, and ready to fire on the target upon your order," the AC-130 gunner advised the aircraft's captain.

"Stand by gunner, I want to make another close pass before we initiate "Operation Revenge," replied the captain.

"Roger that, sir, standing by," replied the gunner. The fixed wing aircraft did need to use all of its deadly weaponry; the Gatling gun alone would make the encounter stunningly deadly. The Cigarette was a sitting duck, and the Guatemalan thugs knew it.

"Gunner, stand by, we will descend down to two hundred feet before commencing fire," advised the captain. Normally, the modified AC-130 was used as a transport plane to ferry military equipment and manpower, even Presidential vehicles with Secret Service agents, but this day, the modified air fortress equipped with fire power that sent chills down the spines of enemies, possessed more than enough destructive power to incinerate the fifty-two-foot boat.

Ambassador Cohen picked up his iPhone and answered. "Hola….. hola……hola." Before the thug could answer, the connection went dead. Ambassador Cohen looked down at his iPhone. "Something happened to the boat," he thought. He began to shake.

"Gunner, we will do one more pylon turn around the target before commencing warning shots at its bow. If the vessel does not comply then we will make another turn. Then, the option to directly target the vessel will be authorized. Stand by."

The gunner knew what to do and laid down a conventional strafing forward of the Cigarette's bow. The Cigarette did not comply.

"Gunner, commence direct fire at the target, fire at will," the captain ordered.

"Roger that sir, these are for Dorothy." The gunner aimed the C-130's two 25 mm cannons directly at the Cigarette's helm and fired repetitive bursts, a tease, before the guns decimated the fiberglass hull. The gunner's reservoir of ammunition would assure its destruction. As the thugs threw up their arms in surrender, the successive rounds were already on their way. Too late. The thugs were obliterated, the Cigarette's hull fractured.

"Gunner, we will make two additional circles to ensure the target is no longer seaworthy. Standby for the turns," the captain reported.

The Cigarette appeared decimated as it moved in small concentric rotations. The crew was no longer visible at the helm, in fact, there was no sign of life.

"Take out the remaining threat, gunner," the captain ordered.

"Roger that, sir."

The gunner fired additional strafes, sinking the Guatemalan boat as it took on water. It rapidly sank to the Gulf's bottom, in international waters, no longer to be of service to Ambassador Cohen. In seconds, not minutes, the boat was gone, and the crew was gone. The generosity of the Gulf waters would determine whether the Guatemalan's bloated bodies would rise to the surface for sea life to feed upon or be found later and identified.

The Angel of Death ascended to an altitude of twenty-one thousand feet, its port side doors secured by the gunner, and then headed north, toward an unknown, unnamed air strip.

"Good job, gunner," the captain said.

"Thank you, sir."

CHAPTER 70

"JIM, SO YOU know, we have successfully recovered Larry Cassell's daughter. She's in a bad way, physically and mentally. These Bratva bastards, and the Guatemalan operators that Bratva employed, apparently did a lot of physical and emotional damage," Strain conveyed.

"Where exactly was she recovered?" Solarski asked.

"In Key West, Florida. We had assets following the suspects from their Mexican east coast departure point, through open waters in the Gulf, and ultimately into United States territorial waters. The thugs have been dealt with, and when I see you in person, I can advise you of the rest of the story. The Ambassador's men who abducted her have also paid a price." Strain added. "That's all I can say, right now."

"I understand, Captain," Solarski replied.

CHAPTER 71

LARRY CASSELL, AND his wife, Rosemary, stood on the tarmac at the Coast Guard's Miami Sector awaiting a Coast Guard helicopter transporting their daughter, Dorothy. It was midnight. They hadn't seen their daughter since early September when she left New Jersey for her second year of school at George Washington University, in Washington, D.C.

Cassell and his wife had been flown to the sector on a Coast Guard Gulfstream, arriving a short time earlier than the helicopter carrying their daughter. It was a perfectly timed event. In deference to the former Secret Service Director, the local office sent two vehicles and four agents to support the family. "The Secret Service will provide security for the Cassells until further notice," current Secret Service Director James Murray ordered the local agent-in-charge, Carly Strain.

"Roger that, sir," Carly replied.

"It is our honor to do so. Always family, even when you leave the agency," Murray said.

"Yes, sir, always," responded Strain.

The Cassells watched the Coast Guard helicopter arrive and maneuver into its dedicated tarmac slot, all deployed wheels hitting their designated mark perfectly. Coast Guard helicopter pilots learn to nail wheels-down early on during training. A tarmac versus the stern of a Coast Guard vessel in at high seas is a relatively easy landing. The

Cassells waited patiently for the rotor blades to come to a stop. Rosemary was anxious. As the chopper's port side door was guided down to the tarmac leaving a staircase, the Cassells moved forward to greet their daughter.

Captain Strain alighted first, and then turned to offer his hand to Dorothy as she alighted from the chopper. Two Coast Guard personnel stood at attention at the base of the steps. Dorothy grabbed Strain's hand and right arm as he began to take her to her parents.

"Oh, honey, I am so happy to have you home," Rosemary tearfully expressed, as she embraced her daughter. Larry Cassell allowed a momentary embrace by his wife to settle in before he moved forward to embrace both of them, a family reunion. Tears flowed from all of them.

Strain respectfully backed up a few feet to allow the reunion to unfold.

The Cassell family had experienced two major events in one day. Bobby escaped a Bratva attack earlier in the day, which was a testament to Captain Strain's relationship with Max. Strain thought, "Too bad Max didn't have the La Antigua attack information. We could have prevented both."

Larry Cassell disengaged from the ladies and approached Strain.

"I know, we as a family have a lot to be thankful for, but I want to thank you for helping to keep my family safe. You and Assistant Commandant Keegan will always be in our thoughts and in our prayers," Cassell said softly.

Strain, never circumspect, responded. "Sir, you and I both know the Bratva will not end with this episode. If anything, we have only re-awakened a wounded animal. They will continue to target us and our people. I am concerned. We need to develop a proactive plan to take their corrupt enterprise down. I am sure we will be talking with you soon. For the time being, enjoy your family and I pray that all of you, especially Dorothy, heals," Strain said.

"Thanks, Will."

The Cassells moved their daughter to a waiting Secret Service vehicle. Agents stood at the ready on each side of the vehicle. For them, this was more than protecting an elected official or head of state. This was family.

CHAPTER 72

"THIS IS THE Office of the Assistant Commandant for Intelligence, United States Coast Guard," advised Sector Washington duty desk. May I have Captain Strain, please?"

"Who's calling," asked the young Coast Guard operator.

"As I just stated, I am calling on behalf of the Assistant Commandant."

"Stand by, please."

"This is Captain Strain."

"Sir, stand by for AC Keegan."

"Will, the cigarette boat that transported Dorothy Cassell to Key West was intercepted by intelligence assets in open waters on its way south to the Mexican coast. It failed to comply with instructions to halt. The vessel was determined to pose a real and present danger and was terminated by an agency with access to a modified C-130 gunship. It sank, and there were no survivors," Keegan stoically relayed.

"Well, sir, when you don't comply in the wake of being suspected in a serial abduction episode, I'd say that your continued existence is going to be problematic," replied Strain. "Can't say I have much sympathy for the thugs, but I can say they will have to answer their Maker. We have received intelligence reporting that Ambassador Cohen is up to his neck in the conspiracy to abduct Dorothy Cassell. The State Department is working with the Guatemalan Ministry of Justice to bring him into the

Embassy for a discussion. The evidence down there totally implicates him. He may find it necessary to start talking to us sooner than later. If we could get his cooperation, he may be able to reduce his exposure to a long jail sentence. It will be his choice to continue to partner with the Bratva or deal with the Ministry."

"Yes sir, my contact in Guatemala, Eli, knows him well, and has described him as someone who thinks he's beyond ever admitting guilt or failure. But Eli says, if he feels he is surrounded by disloyal members of his inner group, he may be willing to fold quickly and offer testimony to whomever the highest international bidder may be."

"Will, we own him in Guatemala, forensically. We must weigh the value he may present to us in our battle with the Bratva," Keegan advised. "Please tell your friend Eli we are thankful for his support. Coast Guard Intelligence and Investigations values him as a great partner. His reporting has been spot on."

"Sir, he can be crude, but he's always credible," Strain replied.

"How are the Cassells holding up?" asked Keegan.

"Director Cassell is all business. He and his wife will remain in Miami until Dorothy is released," Strain responded. "Secret Service Director Murray assigned some of the Miami agents to escort the Cassells while they're here in Florida. The Secret Service met the family at the airport and transported them to the Miami International Medical Center for further observation and continued assessment," Strain relayed to Keegan.

"I am sure that will help the parents to work with Dorothy to begin a process of healing," Keegan replied. I applaud Director Murray."

"Seriously, boss, these Secret Service guys are phenomenal. Carly is lucky to have such outstanding folks in her new office. She and I treat them as our family, and as you know, for a Coast Guardsman to feel that way about another agency means they are special," Strain offered.

"Will, whatever these folks need, we are here to help them," Keegan stated.

"Understood, sir. I will make sure that message gets passed onto the Cassell family and the Secret Service guys," Strain added. "Carly and I are heading over to the hospital now to offer our support."

CHAPTER 73

VLADIMIR BELOV LAID on his bed, alone, sweating, grasping for answers as to why his attacks on the Cassells had failed. "I want fucking revenge for the death of my father, and I can't get it," he thought. His thoughts went dark, envisioning further retribution on Cassell and Strain. "I want to send a message to the Coast Guard. I will do it with directed energy weapons, the same we used in Cuba; then I will abduct the Strains and kill them; then I will suck Cassell into a space that I control and personally kill him. That's my plan. Now, I need the right people to plan it and execute it with me. I am tired of failing. I have lost some of my best people. This kid, Max, I need to bring him inside and see what he can do."

Belov reached to the night table and took a final sip from his glass of Chevas to help him sleep. He would develop his plans in the morning.

CHAPTER 74

"JIM, THE JUSTICE Ministry is available to help in any way to repatriate the remains of the university students and the professor back to the United States," Minister Villacorta advised Solarski.

"Minister, thank you for that offer. I will need your office's assistance to escort the remains to the airport and ensure they get boarded onto a United States Air Force C-141. The U.S. Embassy's Consular office is working with the George Washington University to work out the families' needs. The students are from different parts of the country, but it appears that the remains will go to a central point, possibly to Joint Base Andrews outside Washington, D.C., and from there sent to their hometowns," Solarski reported.

"Jim, my heart aches for their families. We are here for you and the Embassy," Villacorta added.

"Minister, Ambassador Fitzpatrick told me this morning that she is most appreciative of the assistance the Ministry has provided us, and I second that," Solarski said.

CHAPTER 75

"DAD, I FEEL compelled to attend the funerals of my fellow students. I feel so guilty, being the only one to survive this horrific ordeal. Although I have no memory of what happened to me during the abduction process, I know my fellow students, and my professor suffered a horrific demise. Why? I have no idea why God spared me, and not them. Their families now pay a price that my family doesn't have to," Dorothy cried.

"Honey, I know you ache. Your mother and I don't have all the answers. What we do know is that we feel blessed that our daughter is home safe with us. We have much to be grateful for, and thank God that you were spared from death. We also pray that your friends and the professor rest in peace. Our desire today is to ensure you receive the help you need to heal. Your brother will be getting some emergency leave from the Navy for a few days. Together, we can take a trip to the Jersey shore and have some quiet time. As far as attending funeral services for your classmates, I heard there will be a memorial, a *Celebration of Life*, in the future at the university for them. That may be an appropriate day for you to pay tribute to them collectively," Cassell told his daughter.

"Thank you, dad; you have always been there for me. I love you and mom too much," Dorothy said softly. "I need to rest now."

CHAPTER 76

CAPTAIN STRAIN'S PHONE alerted him to an incoming call. He knew the number immediately.

"Hello, Eli," he answered. "Don't tell me you have updated information," Strain asked. "Your intelligence sources are good!" Strain's phone alerted again, with another incoming call. He ignored it.

"Mano, I fear that I do, and it involves the safety of you, and your wife. You both are in serious jeopardy. I believe your community refers to it as a "clear and present danger." Our Mossad picked up chatter that the Bratva wants her targeted as leverage to get to you. Bratva believes it can force you into their web of destruction, eventually seeing you dead. They have plans to abduct her," said a hurried Eli Polack.

Mossad, the Israeli's premier intelligence agency, is also known as the Institute for Intelligence and Special Operations. Once an Israeli, like Polack, is attached to the Israeli network, he never detaches. Polack remained a connected and trusted extension of the organization.

"The Brits are online with the chatter the Mossad confirmed. Bratva is on the move to attack your wife and get to you. Be careful, mano!"

"Eli, I just hung up with her. She is on her way to a salon to get her hair done. She left the Miami Field Office only moments ago. Let me get back on the phone with her," replied a steady, calm voice. "I appreciate the heads-up."

His cell phone alerted again. "Call Keegan ASAP," it read.

CHAPTER 77

DAYS AFTER THE Naval Academy and La Antigua events concluded, the Keegans arrived in Farnham, England to attend the wedding of a friend's daughter. Pam and Chris O'Toole hailed from England, but had been living as Keegan's neighbors in Annapolis, Maryland for the past twenty years. The O'Toole's affection for their adopted Annapolis would now be challenged with their daughter Emma's wedding, and potentially raising grandchildren in England. The Keegans planned the trip with an idea of spending additional days touring Spain. The trip came perilously close to being cancelled when the Cassell attacks occurred. Keegan felt it his duty to remain in the States to monitor future Bratva challenges to Cassell, but the Coast Guard Commandant strongly encouraged him and his wife, Cindy, to make the trip. "Jim, you need and deserve a break, go, go, go…." the Commandant urged. "We can manage the intelligence desk while you are away."

Keegan acquiesced. "Roger that, sir. Thank you. We will go."

At their Annapolis home, the Keegans packed for a two-week stay.

"The likelihood of the O'Toole's remaining in the United States looks grim," Jim told Cindy. "No kidding, grandparents need to be near their grandchildren. I guarantee you that once the young couple gets pregnant, an O'Toole for-sale sign will go up on their Annapolis home."

An hour's drive from London, the quaint Farnham community is one of many similar towns that dot London's outer perimeter. In

America, that's an acceptable commute to the big city. During mid-to-late October, Farnham begins an aesthetic transition involving an array of boutique shops, adorned with Christmas excitement, along a matrix of quaint cobbled streets. Farnham's bustling town center, already adorned in the upcoming Christmas season, features the coming of Ole Saint Nick, charming to any American visitor. The town's Christmas spirit provided a festive backdrop for the anticipated O'Toole wedding services at the 12th century castle turned Saint Andrews Parish Church.

Having departed the night before, the Keegans arrived Thursday morning on a direct flight from Baltimore/Washington International Airport. They hoped to get a full day of rest before the weekend wedding, knowing the anticipated social events would blossom soon after vows were exchanged. Their Virgin Atlantic flight offered coach seats providing limited room to wiggle back and forth over the six-hour flight; neither could get comfortable enough to sleep. An hour limo ride from Heathrow airport to Farnham offered them little reprieve. The limo driver's incessant chatter prevented either from nodding off. Upon arrival at the Mercure Bush Hotel, the driver hustled out of the vehicle to open Cindy's door. The chilly air provided a refreshing antidote to the last twelve hours of travel. Keegan came around to grab Cindy's hand as the driver removed their luggage from the trunk and delivered it to the hotel entrance. There was no bell hop. Keegan nodded his head in appreciation and took custody of the luggage. "Cindy, I have your bags; just go ahead inside and begin the check-in process," Keegan suggested. "I'll settle up with our driver."

After completing the transaction, Keegan waved the driver good-bye and entered the small lobby area of the boutique hotel. There he read his wife's face. "This is not good," he thought. She timidly advised him, "The room is not ready, honey. We can check our bags and go for a short walk-through Farnham. The clerk said the room should be available in an hour." Keegan didn't allow his facial countenance to betray what he really felt.

"Okay, perhaps we could walk through town and see what it looks like," Keegan answered. "How do you feel?

"I feel pretty good now. Guess I have my second wind," Cindy responded.

"Look at this brochure, honey. 'The Surrey Hills offers paths and walkways that lead through the woodland alongside attractive rivers and the historical Abbey ruins and gardens'. We can cover a lot ground here in Farnham in an hour."

"What are you, a tour guide," asked Keegan.

"No, I'm reading the hotel's pamphlets," Cindy replied.

"Okay, let's go for an hour, then get back to the hotel. When the room's ready, I'll be ready for a nap," Keegan yawned.

"Me too," whispered Cindy, "But after our nap, we'll have time to check out the town at night, right?"

"O'Toole told me that some of the local pubs get great reviews," Keegan offered, but he said *The Hog's Back Brewery* was one of the better ones," Keegan cited.

"I'm game; let's go walking," Cindy prompted.

"Saint Andrews Church is beautiful," Keegan commented as they strolled past. "It's too bad the O'Tooles couldn't convince Emma to have her wedding here."

"Jim, there's a small problem. Emma and her fiancé, Matthew, are not Episcopalian. The Saint Joan of Arc Catholic Church, not far from here, will do fine," responded Cindy. "By the way, Jim, having a young couple even consider getting married in a church these days is a welcomed event, and you can't have a better role model than Saint Joan of Arc."

"Wasn't she French?" asked a quizzical husband.

"Farnham has about a thousand years on Annapolis," Keegan noted. "And the English influence on Annapolis is pretty evident. There's not much difference between the two distant towns. Even today, the township inhabitants could easily be interchangeable."

Both town centers shared heavy vehicular traffic chugging through their cobbled roads, which were lined with salons, bars, restaurants, and churches seemingly on each corner. Farnham's pattern of embedded cobble stone streets appears to have been reproduced in Annapolis.

"I think I understand why the O'Tooles chose the Mercure Bush Hotel. It's literally in the middle of the town. It could be in the center of Annapolis and the hotel's bar is large enough to fit all the drunks the wedding reception produces," Jim chuckled to Cindy.

"Okay, turn here and we will find ourselves in front of the hotel," Cindy advised. "Let's get checked in and get to our room. The clerk arranged for our luggage to be brought to the room once it became available. That is a good thing, since there are no elevators."

The desk clerk presented two keys to Cindy and directed the Keegans to their second-floor room via the stairs. Upon entering the room, Keegan did what he was always trained to do. "Okay, where are the exits, where is the fire extinguisher," he quizzed himself.

"Cindy, I absolutely love these English towns and their history, but when I see an electric shave socket dangling loose from the bathroom wall, I get somewhat nervous about hotel safety," Keegan said.

"You're the consummate worry wart," Cindy quickly shot back. Once you get ensconced in the room's fluffy bed, you'll not worry more about it. I'll take a quick walk to the pharmacy across the street and get you some melatonin. It'll take the edge off so we can get some meaningful sleep over the next few days. Be right back," Cindy suggested. Jim didn't argue.

Cindy carefully closed the door. Then she began the walk down the narrow hallway to the stairs she had just walked up to get to the room. "There's no elevator, nor would I want to use one," she thought. Every step she took seemed to prompt the noisy floorboards to talk to her. She grinned to herself, but cautiously noted the creaking noise wasn't exactly comforting. The hotel desk clerk told her it would cut the walk to the pharmacy in half if she were to take boutique hotel's side door through the courtyard. As she bolted out to the courtyard, she marveled at how quaint the hotel's two-story ivy encrusted brick and mortar looked, so similar to the Annapolis structures back home. "We'll have to have our morning breakfast out here," she thought. "These wooden tables with their wide-spanned umbrellas are perfect, no matter the weather."

It took no longer than ten minutes to purchase the melatonin and return to the room. She hoped the creaking floorboard would not awaken Jim. "The walls are paper thin," she worried. She withdrew the room key from her left rear pocket and carefully manipulated the key's large brass plate to insert the key. "God, if this key makes any more noise, Jim will be opening the door for me."

That was not to be, nor did it seem that melatonin would be needed. Jim was in a deep sleep. She took one pill and placed the bottle next to Jim's water glass. She thought, "I hope he finds it if he awakes too soon." Then, she disrobed, put on a t-shirt and slid carefully into bed next to him. Her mind continued to race, thinking how smart it was that she selected the hotel's classic double room versus the classic twin room. The double room allowed for a small chair and an ottoman. "What the heck am I thinking about? I need to count sheep or something else," she thought. Then the melatonin she swallowed kicked in.

CHAPTER 78

FOR THE NEXT three hours the Keegans lay comfortably asleep, until the Assistant Commandant's personal phone rang.

"Keegan," he answered rubbing his eyes. He thought Cindy had put in a wakeup call so the two of them would not miss an opportunity for dinner.

"Hello, Jim, this is Paul Swallow." Swallow was Scotland Yard's authority for Global Intelligence and known by most of the United States Intelligence Directorates as a helpful, can-do person.

"I am sorry to bother you, particularly on your personal time. I suspect you just took a nap to make up for the five-hour time gap between our countries," Swallow said politely.

"Hello, Paul, not a problem," responded Keegan as he looked over at his wife, who was still sound asleep. "We need to get up anyway to get on track with the local time. How can I help?"

"No, Jim, it is how Scotland Yard can help you. We have picked up some troubling intelligence from Israeli Mossad, specifically concerning Bratva's future intentions toward some American folks. I need to share it with you soon, like now. It is pretty serious information, and affects one of your senior operatives, and potentially his wife, a Secret Service agent. I live not far from your hotel and can be there in ten minutes. It won't take long to brief you. We can meet in the hotel's pub, perhaps over a pint of beer."

"Wow, Paul, I like the way you brief. I'll see you in the pub in fifteen minutes."

The hotel pub featured a half-dozen tables, a small bar, and had an aggressive burning hearth, providing some welcome heat and ambiance. The two intelligence operatives were alone in a room adjacent to the bar area, void of any other hotel guests.

"How did you find me in Farnham? It's not like my team lets the world know when I travel to attend a private wedding.

"Wasn't hard, Jim, we've always had a good relationship with the U.S. Coast Guard, as well as with your former agency, the Secret Service. Now, who do you think let me know where you were? How about your brother, Tommy, my favorite Secret Service agent, now that you're gone!"

"You don't get any better than my brother, always loyal, even to you Scotland Yard guys," Keegan joked.

"Oh, come now, Jim. Scotland Yard has always supported the Secret Service," Swallow chirped.

"Tommy knows that well, and he remains appreciative of when Scotland Yard raised the Tower Bridge, splitting a presidential motorcade in half," smirked Keegan. "To this day, it provides him with one of his favorite memories of Scotland Yard's operational capabilities. He talks about it at every family event."

"Oh, we were just having some fun, Jim. Besides it gave your President some special time with our then new Prime Minister."

"The President didn't think it was too funny, but Tommy did, and looked at it as an event for which one day he'd have fun returning the favor. Payback is sweet," Keegan joked.

"Well, Jim, let me make it up now. I am afraid I have some pretty potent information for you to pass on to your Coast Guard. We've been working with the Mossad on a pervasive global Bratva problem. As you know better than me, the Bratva recently committed a heinous massacre of young, innocent college kids and their professor in Guatemala. They abducted a girl, and even attempted to abduct her brother from the Naval Academy. You guys did a solid job in foiling the attacks. Bravo to you and your intelligence community. Now we are picking up more dire chatter, along with the Israelis, that the Bratva is still focused on your Captain, Will Strain, and his wife, Carly. We don't know their operational plans, but something is in the works. Your man Strain and his wife are in jeopardy."

"Understood, Paul. Let me make a quick call right now to confirm his location." Keegan took a separate cell phone out of his shirt pocket and dialed a dedicated Coast Guard Intelligence communications line provided by FirstNet, a private-public dedicated communications service, giving first responders, and the intelligence community a dedicated, prioritized global network access.

"Duty desk, may I help you?"

"Assistant Commandant Keegan here. I need to know Captain Strain's location and current contact information," stated Keegan.

"Roger, sir, can you please advise the color and doll/toy of the week?" requested the operator. Though the call was encrypted, the request just added a human dimension to the authentication process.

"Blue and cabbage patch doll," responded Keegan.

"Thank you, sir, we show Captain Strain at his home in Ocean Reef, Florida. It appears he's currently on the phone with someone in Guatemala."

"Roger, continue to ring him and have him call me directly ASAP, understood?"

"Yes, sir, I'm on it," the operator replied. "I will text his phone as well."

Swallow slowly sipped from the beer the hotel bartender delivered, his gaze never deviating from Keegan. Keegan's beer sat undisturbed on the bar, as he worked his phone to connect with Strain. Swallow sensed the intelligence he delivered may be playing out real-time somewhere in Florida. He said a private prayer as he watched the seasoned Keegan do his job, albeit while on vacation.

"This is Keegan."

"Sir, we have not been able to get through to Captain Strain. It appears he is still actively using his phone and does not answer our pinging," advised the duty desk operative.

"Connect me with the Miami Sector Operations ASAP. I will hang on the phone," Keegan directed. "And, let them know you have verified me."

"This is Miami Sector operations sir. How can we help you?" asked the duty officer.

"This is Assistant Commandant Keegan; we have an emergency brewing in the Key Largo area. It is potentially a life and death situation affecting one of our senior personnel. I need two MH-65C's loaded for bear and vectoring toward Key Largo, Florida now. I will provide additional information shortly. Have the on-duty commander for flight operations contact me as soon as possible," Keegan ordered.

"Roger that, sir, I will get the choppers in the air."

Just as Keegan hung up, his phone rang.

"Sir, this Will Strain. I don't have the time to give you a full brief, but Israeli intelligence provided me information that my wife, Carly, is in immediate jeopardy from the Bratva. I am headed to her office in Miami. My next call is to the Secret Service Field Office, but I saw a text that you were attempting to contact me," Strain calmly related.

"Yes, Will, I just got a heads up from a Scotland Yard colleague here in England. He, too, had similar threat information. I won't keep you from doing what you need to do. Just so you know, I have just directed two choppers to be in the air to support you in the event they are needed to relocate either of you. Keep in touch with the Miami Sector Operations desk. The desk will keep me updated, so no need to burden you with calling me back," Keegan said.

"Roger that, sir, thank you!" Strain hung up and called the Secret Service's Miami Field Office.

CHAPTER 79

CARLY HAD PULLED her government vehicle into the strip mall and headed toward the Lili Salon, located in the middle of the lot where there was ample parking. She took a parking space directly in front of the Salon where she could see Rosa, her hair stylist, through the Salon's front window reading a paper. As she opened her door and stepped onto the macadam, she noticed a large white van pulling in behind her car. It was the same van that only a few moments earlier stopped in front of her at a traffic light. Though not suspicious then, she did think it odd it was a commercial Enterprise van bearing New Jersey plates. "Must be a one-way rental. Long-ass trip for someone to drive a rental all the way down here," she thought. "But then again, there are a lot of people relocating here."

On duty, Carly was accustomed to wearing a pant suit, but today she elected to wear a Sonoma dress purchased from a Kohl's department store the week prior. It would be appropriate attire for the DEA retirement event later that day. Her husband, Will, liked it too. It featured a bold print, crew neckline, and short dolman sleeves. She liked how it fit, and it had a small pocket big enough for her iPhone. Forget the duty gun that would be secured in the trunk.

"Hey, Will, how do I look in this dress. I got it for twenty-five bucks," she asked as she prepared to leave their Ocean Reef home earlier that morning.

"You could wear anything and make it look great, honey, but I do like the dollar amount. You should have bought two," Will responded with a devilish grin.

"I did," Carly responded.

Carly usually wore her Secret Service issued Sig Sauer weapon and a Secret Service badge on her belt around the hip, but with today's apparel she kept both items in a specially designed concealed-carry purse.

The Enterprise van quickly veered toward the government car and stopped at a forty-five-degree angle to her car. Carly tightly held her purse in her right hand while grabbing the top of the driver's side door to close when the encroaching van's side door slid open to the rear. Three men exited toward her. The fourth, the driver, remained inside the van. In a flash, her mind consumed the developing action. She knew who they were, not by name, but she had seen the garb many times in Brighton Beach, New York. They were Russian mobsters. She was trapped in a vortex formed by the two vehicles. The thugs were on her as she began to fend them off with swift kicks to their groins and stiff finger thrusts to their throats. She threw her purse back into the government car before she collapsed to the ground as one of the brutes got the better of her, and an unlucky punch to her right temple caused her to lose consciousness. They picked her limp body up and threw her into the van. It took less than seven seconds. As the Enterprise van sped away, Carly's hairdresser, Rosa, ran to the parking lot, watching the van's sliding door close. She grew frightened. "Calm down, Rosa," she said to herself and mentally noted the license plate. She repeated, "431GMS; a yellow-colored plate, the state of New Jersey." She stood silent in the parking lot for a moment, which seemed like an eternity. She then turned to a colleague standing at the Salon's front door and yelled, "Call the police, Miss Carly has just been kidnapped."

CHAPTER 80

WILL WAS CATCHING up on Coast Guard Sector business from his bedroom desk, transmitting his notes from previously held telephonic meetings to the Miami and Key West Sectors when his phone rang. Carly had left the Ocean Reef home for the Miami field office an hour earlier. "This is paradise," Carly had said as she embraced Will before she departed earlier that morning.

Strain's iPhone alerted. "Strain."

"Hello mano, this is Eli. I have just learned from sources that your wife is in imminent danger. I don't have any specifics, but it would be wise for her to remain static and defended," Eli blurted.

"She left this morning for her office," Strain responded. "I am in the process of contacting her now, and then I'll head to her office," Strain advised. "She's very well defended there by virtue of her agents," Strain responded gratefully. "Thanks Eli." Strain knew he had to quickly go operational.

Strain exited his Ocean Reef residence in his Coast Guard assigned vehicle onto Gatehouse Road heading to a shortcut exit, Card Sound Road. It cut twelve miles off a Miami commute, winding through the Crocodile Lake Wildlife Reserve and onto Route One north. He and Carly bought their soon-to-be retirement home on a cul-de-sac at the end of the private community's Sunrise Cay Drive. Three quarters of the home's exterior faced the Atlantic Ocean.

As Strain drove toward Gatehouse Road, he grabbed his phone. With a single hand he toggled up Carly's cell phone number. It rang and rang, until finally a recording was initiated. "This is Special Agent in Charge Carly Strain. I am not at liberty to take your call currently. If this is an emergency, please contact the Secret Service Field Office at 305…" It was a sixth sense moment. Will disconnected before the number was given. He knew it by heart and dialed it. A short distance south of the Ocean Reef exit gate, the captain decided to pull his car over in order to contact the Secret Service's Miami Field Office. He spotted a McDonalds' parking lot just beyond the Route One merge and decided it was the best place to make the call. The lot was active with coffee and *Egg McMuffin* aficionados. He weaved between cars and took a spot on the east side overlooking an aged Travelodge motel.

Strain dialed up the Miami Field Office.

"Secret Service," said the receptionist.

"Hello Gina, this is Captain Strain. I would like to speak with my wife, please."

"Good morning, Captain. SAIC Strain left the office about fifteen minutes ago. She had a hair appointment. She joked that she needed to look her best before she attends a DEA retirement party tonight. Truth be told, sir, she never looks bad!" Gina had no idea that her answer would cause Will's mind to go into synaptic overload. Only his training and experience prevented a meltdown. He remained disciplined and focused.

"Gina, give me the address of the salon, and then let me talk to the duty desk ASAP." Strain uttered back with authority. Gina snapped to attention, sensing the captain's concern.

"It's the Lili Salon, located at 3552 W7th Street, Hialeah, Florida. It's only about ten minutes from the office," Gina reported. "I am passing you to the duty desk."

Strain had his earphones in place during the conversation, and now engaged his vehicle's shift into drive, pressed on the accelerator in a controlled, but swift exit out of the McDonald's lot.

"Agent Deschak," answered the Miami field office duty agent.

"Agent Deschak, this is Carly Strain's husband, Will Strain. I have reason to believe that my wife may be in harm's way. She departed the field office a short time ago for the Lili Salon located at 3552 West 76th Street. Please hang up on me and contact the local authorities and request that they respond to that location to do a welfare check on your boss. Give them a description of her and her vehicle. Not sure it will pan out, but I am concerned that Bratva operatives may be on site and will attempt to abduct her at that location, if I am right, having the local police on site will help gather any on site witness testimony that might help us track suspects. I'm guessing the office may have agents in the field that can respond as well. I suggest you put that out over the Miami frequency. I'm on my way, but it'll take me thirty minutes to be in the area. Please keep me posted."

"Roger that, sir," Deschak responded. He pushed a dedicated button for the Florida State Highway Patrol multi-agency frequency and reported a possible abduction scenario at the Lili location. He calmly provided descriptive information for the responding units. The Dade County Sheriff's office arrived within minutes, followed by the highway patrol, and several agents from the field office.

A Dade County Deputy Sheriff officer was first to arrive. He observed several salon employees standing outside crying hysterically. "Did you see any activity in the parking lot in the last few minutes," asked the young deputy. One girl, Rosa, spoke up, "I saw Miss Carly being abducted."

The deputy scanned the lot and observed Carly's federal government vehicle parked in a space directly in front of the salon. The driver's door was ajar. Her purse, containing her gun and badge, were found on the front seat undisturbed. There was no sign of forced entry or violence, and no blood.

"The perps have her. She's been abducted," the deputy reported on the multi-frequency. "Standby for suspect vehicle description." He turned to Rosa, "Okay, ma'am tell me please what you saw," the deputy sheriff asked in a calm tone.

"Yes, it was an Enterprise rental vehicle, a large white van. I jotted down a license plate number. It is 431GMS, with a yellow New Jersey license plate. I hope that helps."

"It does, more than I can tell you right now," responded the deputy. Before taking additional pedigree information from the employee, he turned his head left and spoke into a shoulder microphone. He calmly proceeded to put the description of the vehicle over the multi-agency frequency. Dozens of police vehicles from local, state and federal agencies were alerted at the same time. Secret Service agents working in the district were now aware that their SAIC was in distress, in harm's way. Agents in the office began to bolt toward their government vehicles. Other agents, already in the field, dropped what they were doing and headed toward the area.

Their SAIC was missing.

CHAPTER 81

WILL STRAIN SWITCHED to the Florida State agency-wide radio system and heard the deputy sheriff's radio traffic. As he pulled back onto the road from the McDonald's parking lot, he activated his government vehicle's emergency lights and accelerated. Normally, Route One Highway was an active roadway, and today would be no different. His emergency lights would ensure his travel north went unabated, and his Coast Guard vehicle now had the appearance of any highway patrol vehicle engaged in an emergency response.

"Captain Strain, this is Agent Deschak. The police have put out an alert advising that your wife, according to witnesses, had been abducted and forcibly placed in a white Enterprise van, with a New Jersey registration, 431GMS. Her purse, gun, and badge were found left on the driver's seat inside her G-car, but her iPhone remained on her person, perhaps in a pocket. We were able to trace the cell phone's GPS location and provided it to the Florida Highway Patrol."

"I got the alert, Richie, the GPS information is great. What is the last direction of travel?" asked Strain.

"Sir, before we lost the signal, the iPhone signal had it on Route 997 moving south about five miles north of the Route One merge," Deschak reported.

Strain couldn't believe his good fortune and quickly calculated that if he made it back to the merge, he could be well positioned to spot the van. It had only been twenty minutes since Carly was abducted.

"Thanks, Richie. Please continue to keep me informed of any new developments."

Will made a U-turn at the intersection of East Palm Drive and Route One. He elected to go south on Route One rather than West to 997. It was a shorter distance. In this situation cutting off a quarter mile meant being able to observe, which was an advantage. He calculated the time of the abduction and the direction of travel and took the gamble. As soon as he got back to the merge, he turned off his emergency lights and moved with the traffic southbound on Route One. As he passed the Card Sound Road exit, he theorized, "These guys are heading to Key West. They don't change their playbook; it's the same one they used for Dorothy Cassell, but in reverse." He didn't have time to pray. His thoughts had to remain disciplined. He could pray later.

"They must be getting ready to ditch the van. Soon the area will be saturated with cops," Strain processed the thought. "They're moving to either another vehicle or to a boat." Strain's logical thinking, even under stress, was an innate talent. "There's no way it is a boat. It must be a vehicle first, then perhaps a boat, from Islamorada," he factored.

"I've got to intercept them before they make it that far." Strain thought of his wife as she left home earlier that morning and how beautiful she looked in her new dress. "I'm going to get you, Carly."

CHAPTER 82

CINDY KEEGAN AWOKE from her nap and noticed that her husband was gone. She sensed that he was going downstairs for a cup of coffee. She freshened up and headed for the lobby.

"Hey, you, you came here for a wedding, not to work," she blurted to Keegan as she observed him at a table with two beers. "Oh, I see the brew, never mind. Hello, I am Cindy Keegan," she said as she extended her hand to Swallow. "I don't mean to interrupt a private moment, but I think I could handle a beer, as well."

"Honey, have a seat. This is my friend, Paul Swallow, from Scotland Yard. Paul was updating me on some intelligence affecting the Coast Guard. Paul is a good friend of our agency and for that matter, the United States."

"Pleasure to meet you, Paul. I hope it is good intelligence. We could use some! Anyway, we love this small town," Cindy replied.

Swallow waved the bartender over to order Cindy a beer. "Cindy, I hope you don't mind the way beer is served here in England. We tend to feature warm beer."

"No problem, Paul. I am sure it will be fine."

Keegan's phone alerted, and he saw it was the duty desk. "Keegan."

"Sir, this is the duty desk at USCG DC. We don't have a lot of information, but what we do know is Captain Strain's wife has been abducted and it is an active, ongoing event. We know Captain Strain is aware of it and is working with the Secret Service, and state and county police, to resolve the abduction. The duty desk will notify you of any additional information."

"Roger that, make sure that the Miami Sector is aware of the event and providing aerial support as I have already requested," Keegan ordered.

"They are on it, sir," the duty desk came back.

"What was that all about, Jim," asked Cindy.

"Captain Strain's wife has been abducted. It is an ongoing event. We don't have any resolution yet," Keegan told his wife.

Swallow sat stoically as he heard Keegan describe what he knew thus far.

"Paul, hang tight. I am sure more information will be forthcoming in the next half-hour. Sounds like a dynamic event. It will unfold in a good way, I pray. It appears that your intelligence reporting is spot on," Keegan advised. "I can't tell you how much we appreciate Scotland Yard reaching out to us."

"I can only say a prayer, my friend," Swallow replied.

CHAPTER 83

IN THE REAR of the van, the Bratva thugs had placed a mattress, its manufacturer's thin plastic protective film still in place. The width of the mattress fits snuggly between the van's interior walls, set back toward the rear doors in an area of about five by seven over a metallic floor. Carly was thrown through the open sliding door and onto the mattress. The driver had maneuvered the rear-view mirror to help gauge what was happening. Upon hearing the sliding glass door open he glanced toward the mirror. Carly's limp body had to be lifted further toward the rear of the van and the plastic made it easier to slide her from the center. Two of the thugs managed to maneuver her while the third thug, injured by Carly's thrusting jab to the throat, went to the van's right front seat to recover. He was bent over, coughing and hacking.

"Take off her underwear as soon as you get her inside," said one thug. The second thug pushed the first thug toward Carly. Once on the mattress they managed to shut the sliding door.

"Let's go, move the fuckin' van," said a thug. "Pull her dress up and get those panties off. Fuck her or get out of the way and I'll do it. The boss wants her screwed, if she comes around all the better."

"Boss we've got the Secret Service bitch in the back, and the boys are lubing it up now to have their way with her," relayed the injured thug, letting him know that Carly had been successfully taken.

"That's great news," responded the Bratva chieftain. "Now, enjoy her. Let me know when you transfer her to the other vehicle."

"Will do, boss."

The van driver sped onto Hialeah Gardens Boulevard and headed toward the Florida Turnpike to turn south toward the Florida Keys. A determined Bratva thug tried to slide his penis into Carly but failed. Embarrassed, he feigned success as she began to stir from unconsciousness. He couldn't get an erection."

She glanced scornfully at her attacker. She didn't fight back. She couldn't; his weight kept her down. But she knew she hadn't been penetrated. The second thug with his pants down to his ankles, took over and slid his erect penis inside and came quickly.

"Hey jerk, you blew your load in less than thirty seconds. The boss won't be happy when he hears that," the first thug admonished.

"Oh, like you were a fucking stud, jerkoff," came the reply. "Wait until the boss hears you have only a four-inch dick."

"Hey, do you want a piece of this bitch while her pussy is still warm. She's nothing but a cum-sponge now." The front seat passenger was in no condition to move, his throat still hurting from Carly's earlier thrust.

"No, but Vladimir said to give her a good finger fucking when we are done. He said he wants her pussy to be as bloodied as we can make it."

"Great. Hand me that empty beer bottle. I'll let her know what it feels like to be screwed by a Corona."

"Ha, ha, ha, that's a great one. We need to tell that one to Belov."

Carly lay still, her head to the side, doing her best to ignore the pain, while her dress now covered her face. She was numb and didn't visibly react to the vulgar thrusting. She concentrated on breathing, and on not reacting to their violations. Though numb, she remained aware. She wanted to be as unattractive to them as she could. "Be limp," she advised herself. The beer bottle thrusting continued for a few miserable moments. She was an unwilling participant in a violent orgy. Finally, the thugs disengaged. They shoved a rag into her mouth and tied her wrists with nylon rope.

The van was a half hour from Florida City, where the driver intended to veer onto Route One with a clear path to a safe parking area to switch vehicles.

Carly was now alone on a mattress, no longer being violated, but feeling the unwanted vaginal pulsation, the pain growing by the second. Tears began to flow from her eyes.

"Will," she prayed, "please find me."

CHAPTER 84

"GINA, GIVE ME the duty desk," Will Strain requested with a commanding, but calm and confident voice.

"Yes, sir," Gina responded, herself aware of the gravity of the situation.

"Duty desk," answered Agent Deschak.

"Richie, this is Captain Strain again. Keep me on the phone as you do your best to get the office agents and the Highway Patrol notified via radio. I am on Route One, heading southbound toward the Route One/905 merge. I have an eyeball on the suspect vehicle. It has just pulled into the *Big Chill Restaurant* parking lot, adjacent to the Key Largo Bayside Marina. I am about to take up a position of opportunity to observe what's going down. When you get the responding units by radio, advise them to arrive in a stealth mode, if possible, that is without lights and sirens. Stay online with me, if you can. Okay?"

"Yes sir, we have additional guys on the duty desk to assist me with your needs. You are on speaker so we can put your instructions over the multi-agency frequency real time."

"Thanks, guys." Strain plugged in his earpiece to his iPhone. It was not a tactical piece of equipment he would have chosen, but he had to work with what he had.

"Sir, our agents and the Highway Patrol have been advised of your location and the location of the suspect's vehicle; the multi-agency frequency is clear for you," Richie advised.

"OK, thanks, Richie."

The Enterprise van moved slowly through the parking lot and proceeded to the southernmost end of the Marina's parking lot. It pulled headfirst into an empty space, next to an unoccupied Toyota Tundra truck. The van and truck were separated by a thin line of newly planted palm trees and parked no more than two spaces away from a blue self-contained recreational vehicle (RV). The RV had been running for some time. Condensation dripped from its underside, forming a small pool of water underneath its frame. The condensation was generated by the vehicle's air conditioner, which had been placed on full mode earlier. The Bratva thugs had prepositioned it, left alone, and unlocked, and in place for the transfer of their female hostage. Other than the RV, the Enterprise van and truck, there were no other vehicles in the parking lot.

From Route One, Strain observed the van park near the other vehicles. "It has to be a vehicle transfer, probably to the RV," Strain thought. He bypassed the *Big Chill* entrance and pulled into the adjacent marina lot, about one hundred paces from the RV. It permitted him to maintain eye contact with the van while providing him cover for an anticipated dash to interdict the thugs.

"Richie, let the responding units know that the suspects look to be making a transfer to another vehicle, an RV. There's a Toyota truck in the mix, parked next to the van. All vehicles are along a tree line between the *Big Chill* and Bayside marina," advised Strain.

"Roger that, sir, all responding units are aware," Deschak answered.

"Read the body language," Strain cautioned himself. "That'll dictate my move." His thoughts were not part of the multi-agency radio traffic.

He heard Richie's voice from the open phone. "Sir, this is Richie, responding units are two minutes out from your location."

"Thanks, Richie. Let them know I have an eyeball on the suspect vehicles and am standing by. I will keep you posted." Will didn't want to spend any more time explaining his further observations to Deschak. He knew he had to go operational, moving swiftly forward to eliminate the thugs and get his wife back. "Two minutes is too long to wait," he thought. He didn't let Richie know.

One Bratva thug exited the van and walked briskly to the RV. The Toyota truck appeared empty. He remotely unlocked the RV's driver's door and hopped inside. Another thug left the van and approached the RV waving to the driver to hit the open button, and a look of disappointment flashed over his face when there was a momentary pause. He waved again and yelled something in Russian. Finally, the door opened. Strain exited his vehicle to move closer. The delay gave Strain time to close his distance. He had his issued Sig Sauer drawn and at the ready. Its magazine possessed thirteen rounds, a single round chambered, more than enough to take out the thugs. He padded his left pocket to feel for additional magazines. Strain gripped the Sig Sauer firmly, stiffed his arm and pointed it at the RV.

"Go, go," Strain ordered himself to move toward the Toyota truck for cover. He verified it was empty. Now within fifteen feet of the van and adjacent to the RV, he crouched slightly behind the truck's cargo bay. He now had a clear visual of the two thugs.

In a whisper he engaged his phone to transmit his new position, "Ritchie, can you copy me?"

"Yes sir, we can all hear you here," Ritchie responded.

"It looks like they are about to transfer my wife from their van to an RV, prepare to copy - Florida registration, HPBG85. Pass that along to responding units, I'm going to affect a takedown now," Strain advised.

"Roger that," Ritchie responded in awe of the captain's intended action. "Damn, I wish him the best. What a ballsy guy," Deschak thought.

The van's sliding door opened. Strain observed that Carly could not stand up on her own. "They've drugged her," he observed.

The thug who opened the RV returned to the van to assist in removing Carly from the van's side door, now fully ajar. Neither one had a weapon in hand. Strain, aware of his advantage, reacted. The Bratva thugs were too occupied carrying her to notice him; he was within feet of them. Meanwhile, the thug in the RV prepared for Carly's insertion, unaware of his predator.

"I can't let them get Carly into the RV," he reasoned as he closed the distance, now less than ten feet. "I wish I had a silencer on this gun," he thought. "Too bad, get focused," he counseled himself. Strain decided to take out the RV thugs, relying on the two carrying his wife as being too occupied, he raised his Sig Sauer to the RV driver's head who had left the driver's seat to assist the two in removing Carly. Strain observed that the driver's stare was concentrated on the RV's interior and not on Strain's approach. The van driver did not see his death coming. A single shot to the side of his head killed him. There was little destruction as the bullet entered the head, but the exit wound was more destructive: blood, brain tissue, and small bone fragments spread throughout the van's interior. The gun's loud report stunned the other two thugs carrying Carly and stifled them long enough for Strain to fire one round into each one of their heads. The head shots were efficient and deadly, as that of the van's driver. As they collapsed, Carly fell on top of one of them, breaking her fall. Strain recognized that she was not injured by the fall and he elected not to respond to her. He sought out the fourth Bratva operative, scanning the length of the vehicle looking for a sign, a movement, to betray the thug's location within the RV.

At that moment, two Secret Service vehicles, followed by two Florida Highway Patrol vehicles, entered the parking lot, taking tactical positions in proximity to the scene. They exited their vehicles with their weapons drawn and pointed in a purposeful direction at the RV. The Secret Service guys recognized Captain Strain and prepared to move closer to support him.

"Highway Patrol, we are moving forward to assist a friendly" yelled one of the agents. The troopers knew what that meant, appreciated the heads-up, and covered the advancing Secret Service agents.

Strain saw the agents advance and shouted to them, "there's one inside the RV. Come up and attend to Carly."

The agents established a defensive perimeter around their SAIC. One of them, a former SEAL medic, directly tended to her, lifting her up in his arms, and retreating in the direction of the Highway Patrol vehicles. Two troopers, weapons drawn, came forward to assist, embracing the agent holding Carly in a protective cocoon. One of the troopers observed that Carly's wrists were secured with plastic restrainers. Her hands appeared to the trooper to be in distress, as she took out her tactical knife and cut the offensive plastic from her wrists.

"Lay her down behind the troop vehicle, and let's assess her condition," the agent said. Carly remained lethargic.

The trooper popped open her vehicle's trunk and grabbed a first aid/trauma kit, and blanket. She placed the blanket beneath Carly's head, careful not to raise her head too much, as her face appeared pale. She placed her Troop hat under Carly's legs to keep them elevated.

The remaining agent stayed with Captain Strain, both moving in tandem toward the RV's sliding door. At that time, they heard a single gunshot from within the vehicle. They instinctively retreated toward the truck, their weapons remaining directed at the RV. Additional troopers arrived, taking up tactical positions in the bar and marina parking lots, as they are trained to do. They established a secure perimeter. Within minutes a Florida State Police tactical team converged on the site and developed a plan to breach the RV's side door. Captain Strain and the Secret Service agent backed off from the RV to allow the troopers to execute the breach. The troopers opened the side door and found that a lone thug had shot himself in the head. "He's dead," a trooper shouted.

"Carly is alive," Strain prayed. He could not have cared less about the Bratva operative's suicide. "Saved us the trouble of killing him," he thought. Will hustled to be next to his wife, but not too close, not wanting to disrupt the assessment process the agent and trooper continued to conduct. He was relieved to see her vitals were okay.

"How bad did they violate her," he asked himself.

A female trooper, standing in proximity observed Strain's facial expression. It conveyed a silent emotion, not anger, but something more powerful and forceful – an internal strength to fight the emotion to respond to the terrible physical attack on his wife's body without all the facts. "Being angry takes up too much brain power," he believed. He wasn't angry when he shot dead three of the four Bratva thugs. It was tactical, methodical, and necessary. "Limit useless emotion," he was trained. His bride, the love of his life, now lying on the ground in front of him, and attended to by arriving paramedics, had been violated because of the perception he had something to do with the assassination of Belov's father. The Bratva thugs who abducted Carly hoped to get to the captain when they tried to coerce him to come to them. It didn't happen as they planned. Fate was on Strain's side. They had no idea their abduction would be thwarted by the very target they failed to get. He caused their demise. "Now, I want Belov," he thought, but he was careful not to say it. "I will seek a Bratva revenge, but on my terms."

Overhead, two MH-65C's hovered. Strain looked up and marveled at the support he was receiving from his Coast Guard family.

"Captain, we are getting a request from the choppers for permission to land on Route One," advised a Florida Trooper.

"Yes, please. One of them will be able to transport my wife to a Miami hospital for treatment," advised Strain.

"Understood, sir. We will create a landing zone on the highway," the trooper responded.

The Florida Highway Patrol anticipated the need for emergency medical services and requested the ambulance based on the facts previously broadcast over the interagency radio network. What they didn't anticipate was the extent of Bratva's brutality toward the female Secret Service boss. Those responsible for it didn't need an ambulance. They were dead. The paramedics who responded observed what the Bratva thugs had done to her. It appeared to them they brutally penetrated her vagina. The medics applied heavy gauze to the bloodied area.

"These bastards really did a number on her," whispered one of the paramedics as he applied the clean compress. Will heard the comment but didn't react.

The paramedics prepared Carly for transport to the Homestead Hospital, located on Baptist Way, normally a half-hour's drive from the deadly crime scene. With the Coast Guard helicopters in proximity, the dynamic changed. "The Coast Guard has two assets in the air," Will thought. He assumed a seat in the rear of the ambulance, next to his wife, who was now fully sedated by the paramedics. "Using one would cut the travel time in half." He held her hand securely, his thoughts darting in numerous directions, while his gaze trained upon Carly's angelic face.

As the ambulance turned onto Route One northbound, the two Coast Guard MH-65C's flew overhead. One of the helicopters landed while the other remained in a defensive posture. The ambulance driver drove up to the ad hoc landing zone and stopped. Without any radio directions everyone on the scene knew instinctively that the helicopter was there to transport Carly to the hospital. Instead of a thirty-minute drive, the Coast Guard helicopter would have her at the hospital in less than fifteen minutes.

As the MH-65C helicopter landed on the LZ created by the Florida Highway Patrol Strain took a deep breath and nodded in appreciation. These were his people, and now the Highway Patrol were part of his extended professional family.

With the Carly transfer complete, Will and one of the local field office Secret Service agents boarded. Will's mind was racing. "There will time for payback later. Let's just get Carly the help she needs. Find out the damage these brutes did to her and let her begin to heal."

CHAPTER 85

THE OVERSIZED COAST Guard chopper arrived at the hospital parking lot's landing zone, where two Secret Service agents were in place to secure its arrival. Additional agents arrived in the moments after wheels-down; several more were deployed to remain vigilant outside Carly's hospital room. For them, this was personal. She was not a politician, nor one of the international potentates they protected. This was Carly, their boss, and they were devoted to her. Each agent had a Sig Sauer P229, a nine-millimeter handgun, strapped securely to the waist belt. Additional ammunition is available on their belts at the ready for a protracted gun fight.

"If there's one thing the Secret Service teaches its personnel it's how to shoot a gun," preached the instructors at the Beltsville, Maryland, Rowley Training Center. "What we can't teach you, however, is how you will eventually respond. That inner strength is in your gut. We hire people who tend to have that strength." The agents saw that quality in Will Strain and adopted him as one of their own. They gave him a respectful distance, granting him a great deal more personal space than he probably needed. After all, they reasoned, he was a far greater asset to protect her, his wife, than they could be. They were to be there for him, his outer perimeter. They had his back!

"She'll remain sedated for a couple of hours, Captain," advised the hospital's floor nurse. As the tending nurse left Carly's room, she glanced over at Will. She noticed a moist streak rolling down his cheek. She had seen countless similar scenes. "The compassionate tear emanating from a trained, tough man," she thought, "He needs to heal, too."

"Captain, I will return soon." The nurse winked at the agents outside the room as she worked her way to the floor's centralized nursing station.

"Captain Strain," whispered agent John Seybold. "I am going to grab a cup of coffee. Would you like a cup?"

Will looked Seybold in the eye and said, "Thanks, John. I am afraid I've had my quota of coffee already today." His last cup had been with Carly earlier that day while at their Ocean Reef home. He closed his eye lids and took a soothing gasp of air. Seybold observed his response and deferentially backed out of the doorway.

"Dude, this Captain Strain is an impressive guy," Seybold said to his fellow agents. "I'll be back with our coffee."

CHAPTER 86

WITH CARLY SEDATED and stabilized, Strain knew it was time to brief the command at Coast Guard Headquarters.

"Duty Desk, Lieutenant Savannah Riera."

"Lieutenant Riera, this is Captain Will Strain, Intelligence Miami Sector. I need the duty desk to patch me through to Assistant Commandant Keegan."

"Roger, wilco. Can you provide me with the color/doll of the day?" asked Riera.

"Yes ma'am, Blue/Cabbage Patch," responded Strain.

"Thank you. Stand by, Captain." Riera then used an encrypted connection.

"Sir, are you aware the Assistant Commandant is currently in England?"

"I am. Thank you, Lieutenant."

"This is Keegan."

"Sir, this is Will Strain. I am calling to update you on today's events. My wife, as you are aware, was abducted by Bratva operatives. Unfortunately, she was violently abused by them. We successfully recovered her with support from the Secret Service and Florida Highway Patrol. She is now recuperating in a Miami area hospital. Thanks to your foresight, she was transported to the hospital by one of our Coast Guard assets. I am appreciative of your thoughtfulness to have the Coast Guard choppers in the air. Sir, the Bratva attacked my wife today, and she paid a physical, and no doubt, future psychological price. Three Bratva operatives were killed, and one killed himself as agents and troopers approached his vehicle. The Bratva leadership needs to be decapitated and the corrupt organization dismantled. How, and when, will be determined soon. I hope we can assist in this effort," Strain advised.

"Will, first, my heartfelt condolences and wishes that Carly heals. You are in my prayers. Let me just tell you that the Brits and the Israelis certainly rose to the occasion with their intelligence reporting. The Miami Sector Operations Desk kept me updated on how the events developed. Unfortunately, the distribution of the intelligence missed perhaps by minutes. It was that close. A few minutes may have prevented your wife from getting abducted. Still, the response by you and the law enforcement community was stellar," Keegan proffered. "You being in the right place at the right time is the single factor that saved your wife from further violence, and perhaps death. You are to be commended for that. My wife and I will return Sunday from England. I will be in the office first thing Monday morning to discuss this further. God bless you and Carly. We pray for her speedy recovery."

"Thank you, sir."

CHAPTER 87

HER EYELIDS FLUTTERED rapidly for a moment, then returned to a restive state. Sitting vigil next to her, Will missed the eyelid transition. His phone was held gingerly in his right hand and dangled precariously close to slipping out of his grasp and onto the floor. As he slipped into a light nap, the device fell to the floor, creating a noise sufficient to keep him from devolving deeper into sleep. He awoke to observe Carly opening her eyes. As he reached to retrieve his phone he caught her stare and soothing smile. It was an omen to Will. She was to be okay. "I am sorry for waking you," he said softly. The sedatives had done their job, temporarily mitigating the consequences of her brutal ordeal.

The man she loved sat as her silent sentry to protect her. "He's there for me, always," she thought.

"Where have you been, honey," Will asked tongue-in-cheek.

"How long have I been sleeping, and where are we?" Carly asked.

"You've been here for twelve hours," Will responded as he stroked her hair.

You've been out for most of the day, sedated since we found you. The county paramedics administered a sedative to you while in an ambulance, before transporting you to the Homestead Hospital on Baptist Way. The nurses kept you sedated for a few more hours to allow you to heal.

CHAPTER 88

THE OCEAN REEF home took on the appearance of a VIP residence. It wasn't, of course, but now under the de facto protection of the Secret Service, the home belonging to Carly and Will Strain was well defended by the best. The Miami Field Office's Deputy Special Agent in Charge, James Thrift, made sure of it. He deployed half the Miami office to secure the site, prepared to ward off any Bratva retaliation in the wake of her abduction. The threat against the Strains was not an event that intimidated Thrift. He agreed with Captain Strain, "That was not going to happen." Regardless, the threat level against the Strains was presumed to remain high. The Secret Service had never before entertained a direct threat against one of their own, as it did with the threat levied by Bratva against the Strains. Through several social media platforms, the Bratva was known to want them dead.

Thrift knew what had to be done. His whole career prepared him for this mission. He had cut his teeth as a young Washington, D.C. Metropolitan Police Officer. After a two-year stint, he sought a higher calling and transferred to the Secret Service Uniformed Division. There he excelled as a counter-sniper before becoming an instructor at the Secret Service Training facility. Thrift's superiors encouraged him to apply to be a special agent. He didn't think it necessary to satisfy his love of his job, but when it dawned on him that his family might one day end up in Florida on the government's "dime," it was a no-brainer.

"Sir, my name is James Thrift, from the Miami Field Office," Thrift said as he introduced himself to Captain Strain. We haven't had the opportunity to meet each other, but I am a big fan of yours."

"James, it is indeed a pleasure to meet you, and all of your personnel that have responded to our home to help protect my wife," Strain responded. "I will come back to you shortly. I want to check on Carly now."

"What can I get you to drink?" asked Will, as he assisted her to gently slip into the living room's tan leather recliner. Carly herself positioned the living room recliner there only days earlier, as it provided a vast visual of the Atlantic Ocean's blue water. The residence, situated at the corner of Exuma and Andros Roads, would not normally be within the price range of most government employees, but Will and Carly were able to accrue a combined government salary. Having no children and two incomes made the difference. Recognizing that ownership was within their grasp, they took the opportunity to invest in their future. Ocean Reef was to become their intended retirement home for many years. It was a gated community, but not an impenetrable one. Their new neighbors welcomed them, almost as celebrities.

"Honey, the view is what I need right now," whispered a tired lady. "But I will take a lemonade."

"Great, I made a gallon of it yesterday. Be right back." Will hustled out to the kitchen.

As Will went to the kitchen to fetch the drink, Carly stared at the ocean waves, the rhythm allowing her mind to travel to a distant peaceful place, and the view to somewhere less dangerous. The smart TV above the gas fueled fireplace was rarely used during the day. For Carly, the ocean view, and a good book, took primacy.

"Here you go, sweetie." Will placed the glass on a side table, and then took a blanket draped over his arm to place over Carly's legs. "I am going to check on the Secret Service guys and see if they want some of this lemonade," Will said. Carly closed her eyelids and responded with a slight smile to acknowledge Will's hospitality toward her colleagues. "I love that man," she thought.

"Will, you need to relax. You've been through some difficult times, too," Carly cautioned.

"I'm fine, Carly. I need to keep moving, 'stability in motion,' as Einstein would say. Like riding a bicycle. I guess it's how I am wired." Privately, he thought, "Killing the bastards that harmed you is more than an elixir for me. I am not done."

The Secret Service agents established a secure perimeter around the Strain's home. They used the garage as a security room for communications and operational deployment. It helped that there was a bathroom and a small refrigerator in the corner of the garage. The Secret Service relied heavily on both.

Will entered the garage, where he encountered Thrift. "Hey James, I made tons of lemonade. You guys interested?" I'll bring it out and put it in the fridge."

"Will, thanks, but I am afraid we took up too much of your fridge space with water and juices. I am sure space will become available soon."

"I also have a ton of fruit I'll bring out later. There are chips and pretzels in the cabinets on the wall. Help yourself."

"Thank you, sir."

"James, Carly and I are grateful beyond any expression we could muster to thank you and your agents here to provide us with a secure, calm environment. It will allow her to heal faster. I am confident of that."

"Will," Thrift responded, his voice noticeably halting, "we are here because we have great regard for your wife, our agent-in-charge. She means more to us than just a boss. She and you are part of our Secret

Service family. I can speak for everyone; we are here for as long as you need us. Frankly, sir, I have been inundated by an overwhelming number of New York Field Office and Washington, D.C. based personnel who have offered to come here on their own "dime" to help. I am sure it is the same in the Coast Guard."

Strain stood in silent awe as tears welled up in appreciation for what he had just heard. Thrift, observing Strain's demeanor, reached out to pull the captain into a soft bear hug. "We love you guys," Thrift said, and then backed off.

Will wiped the tears from his cheek with the back of his wrist. "Thank you, James. I guess I needed that. I thought my Coast Guard mates were family, and they are, but you guys are giving them a run for the money. Again, I thank you more than you can know."

Will walked back to the kitchen door as Thrift spoke. "Sir, I assume you have heard that Director Murray, along with former Director Cassell, will be visiting Carly tomorrow. They are due to arrive late in the morning after a brief visit to the Miami office. Then they travel here to spend some time with Carly."

"I am not sure she's aware of the visit, but I'll tell her about it now. I better go out and get some bacon and eggs," Will chuckled. Strain knew that Larry Cassell probably harbored a strong desire to talk with him. They now shared so much; both having lived through terrible personal attacks on family members.

From the kitchen Will saw that Carly ignored her lemonade, falling into a deep sleep. "Good for her; the melatonin is kicking in."

CHAPTER 89

"THIS IS THRIFT," as he responded to an incoming call.

"James, this is Jim Murray, how are you?"

"Director, if I was any better, I'd be in heaven."

"Ha, that's a good one. I am sorry that we missed you at the office meeting this morning. It went well. Although you had many of your guys posted in Key Largo. It was a sufficient quorum for an office meeting. In fact, there were a dozen agents in the office from New York and D.C. who came down on their own for "working vacation" as they called it. I guess you may know what that means."

"Good to hear, sir. I had a tough time keeping some of the agents back in the office. They all wanted to be here to support their SAIC," Thrift offered.

"Yes, and that's how it should be. I love the respect they have for her. James, I have former Director Cassell with me. We should arrive at Ocean Reef at about 1100 hours. We don't want to arrive too early, and certainly don't want to place a burden on the Strains. Can you advise us on protocol?"

"Sir, they know you are coming. In fact, Captain Strain joked he intends to have bacon and eggs for you both. I wouldn't be surprised if he meant it," Thrift said tongue-in-cheek.

"No doubt. He really is a great guy. Perfect for Carly," Murray responded.

"I will let him know when you are on your way," Thrift inserted.

"Thanks, tell him that Director Cassell requests a toasted poppy seed bagel. See you soon."

CHAPTER 90

CASSELL PLANNED TO meet Director Murray at the Secret Service Miami Field Office. From the Miami airport, he thought of using an Uber ride to take him from the airport to the field office. Director Murray had a different idea and texted Cassell he would be there to pick him up. The field office assigned Joe Savage, a newly minted Secret Service agent, to drive Director Murray and his aide to the airport, where they would personally meet Cassell. A nervous Savage chose to use an armored Chevy SUV from the underground parking lot. He and his important passengers arrived at the Miami airport terminal a half hour early and waited for the former director to exit. The vehicle's air conditioning was on full blast while Murray worked on his phone. Savage perspired, though it was mid-October, and the weather was comfortable in the eighties, a typical representation of South Florida for that time of year.

"There he is," Director Murray said as he exited the SUV to greet Cassell.

"Jim, thank you for letting me hitch a ride to the Strain's residence," Cassell stated as he hopped into the SUV. "It's nice and cool in this car." Savage swallowed nervously. The field office driver carefully looked over to his right shoulder without moving his head to steal a glance of the former director. Director Murray sat in the right front seat, while Cassell and Murray's aide sat in the rear.

"Larry, our driver is Joe Savage. He is fresh out of the Secret Service Academy," advised Murray.

"Joe, how long have you been on the job?" asked Cassell.

"Sir, I have been on nine months. I graduated just last month."

"Well, I applaud you for coming on board. These are difficult times for law enforcement," said Cassell. "We need people like you more than ever, and I hope you have a wonderful career."

"Thank you, sir." Savage enjoyed the greeting, but worried about what he might hear inside the vehicle. The conversation would not be edited, and the young office agent thought he was in unchartered waters. He gripped the wheel tightly and focused on his directions to the Strain residence. "God, I hope I don't screw this up," he fretted internally.

"Larry, I am so happy that we can make this visit together," Murray responded, "I know that the captain has such great respect for you from previous work you both did on behalf of the U.S. government. I've been briefed by the Director of National Intelligence on your efforts to support the intelligence community from your private sector position, specifically to counter the Bratva. Knowing you were the Director a generation ago speaks volumes to all of us, the current Secret Service, that you are still ready and able to help out the government when asked. I guess our role never ends, even in retirement."

"Jim, I never wanted to be involved in this global Bratva drama. Lord knows it has taken a toll on my family. I think what the Bratva did to my family in Guatemala, and what it tried to do to my son at the Naval Academy came way too close to exterminate the dreams I have for my family's future. I pray every day for the families of the George Washington University students and their professor whose lives were terminated by such evil. I hope and pray those families find a way forward."

The young field office agent driving them didn't know what to think about the conversation; what Cassell said puzzled him. It was an earful, and his left leg began to shake slightly in a nervous response to the high-profile assignment, and to what he was hearing. He had heard rumors of Bratva brutality, but until now, didn't realize it affected such persons in high places, and so close to home.

"Larry, Bratva's multiple attacks on the Coast Guard and the Secret Service are about to be answered. Like your daughter, Captain Strain's wife, Carly, was horribly violated while in Bratva custody. The van became a torture chamber," Director Murray relayed. "Joe," Director Murray addressed the young agent driver. "What you hear, stays here, and is not for public consumption, or even discussion with other colleagues." Savage acknowledged with a deferential acknowledgement and a "Yes, Sir."

"I was afraid of that. I hope she is doing well," Cassell replied. "I can imagine what Captain Strain is contemplating. I share the same thoughts."

As Agent Savage neared the Ocean Reef gate, he knew that he had heard too much. He also knew it had to remain an untold story, at least while he was an agent.

CHAPTER 91

"THEY VIOLATED MY wife. They have no idea what trouble they have made for themselves," Will Strain made the rare acknowledgement to the Assistant Commandant for Intelligence for the United States Coast Guard.

"Captain, I can advise you this. As a friend I would advise you not to make statements to any of us that could come back to haunt you. What happens to the Bratva thugs that orchestrated the recent killings and abductions will be the responsibility of several cooperating agencies. You are not authorized to conduct any solo intervention. Is that clear, Will?" Keegan admonished. The Assistant Commandant had great respect for the captain and did not want him doing something outside the scope of his authority that would place him in criminal jeopardy. It was a strong paternal admonishment.

Strain responded, "Yes, sir, I will not take any action, but I wish to be advised as to what actions may be considered."

"Will, my concern is, you're too deeply involved emotionally, which is understandable. The temptation to take unilateral action against some of the Bratva elements can be compelling. Your previous actions, heroic I may add, to terminate those who abducted your wife, was necessary, and it was fortunate that you were able to respond. Faced with the information you had in Key Largo, you pieced together a fantastic tactical response, and in partnership with the Secret Service and Florida

Highway Patrol, you all reacted professionally. We know that those thugs responsible for your wife's abduction received their marching orders from a higher source, who we know to be Vladimir Belov. Please consider that pursuing him is something that belongs not to you, but to those responsible for his apprehension. It cannot be revenge, and it must be justice. So, I am asking that you pledge to me, you will let us handle it," Keegan requested.

"I will, sir," Strain responded in compliance.

CHAPTER 92

A KNOCK AT the front door alerted Carly. She overheard the Secret Service radio traffic on her personal hand-held radio housed in a power charger, alerting the outer perimeter agents that the Director was in proximity. She expected the knock.

"Yes, hello, come in."

"Boss, the Director and former Director Cassell are about five minutes out," Thrift advised Carly.

"Thank you, James. Bring them in once they arrive. I am ready for them," Carly directed.

"You bet, boss."

"James, you are the number two in the office, I think you can call me by my first name, don't you?" admonished Carly with a grin.

"Yes, ma'am," he teased back as he exited the home.

She heard a soft knock. Carly slowly opened the door.

"Director Murray and Director Cassell, I am honored that you made the trip to see me."

"Carly, I have an entire agency that wants to be here with you. We represent them all. You have been in our collective thoughts and prayers," Murray replied as he gave her a slight, respectful embrace.

"Carly, my wife, Rosemary, and I are grateful that you have made it home. Our daughter, Dorothy, told me last night that she sends her love to you," Cassell offered as he tightly embraced Carly for a moment.

Tears welled up in his eyes as he disengaged. Carly observed this and pulled him back into an embrace.

Thrift excused himself for the remainder of the visit to give them private time.

CHAPTER 93

SEVERAL DAYS LATER Carly received a telephone call that caught her by surprise.

"Carly, this is Mary Logue."

"Oh, my goodness," gushed Carly. "I am so glad to hear your voice. And what's with the Mary Logue bullshit, so formal, how are you?"

"Carly, I am fine, but I have been worried about you. I have heard through Secret Service contacts that you have been through a most traumatic time. From what I have been told, you have suffered greatly. I am calling to invite you to get out of your current situation and sample a change of scenery. I want you to consider coming to my home in Eastport, Maine for some quiet time to heal. Eastport will give you an opportunity to have space to relax. The vista outside the living room window provides a view of the water between the U.S. and Canada that is unequalled. I know you live in Key Largo and have the ocean, and it is certainly warmer, but this is Maine. The weather is spot on this time of year, albeit sweater weather. I also need you here so I can help you. You are my sister, and I need you, sister!"

"Mary, even in Secret Service School we could tell what type of person you were. Our class, the class you managed and administered throughout the six-month training program, respected and loved you. If fact, some of the guys in the class were so enamored with you they fantasized dating you. Of course, that evaporated when they saw your husband, Jim, a former NFL football player."

"You are too funny. Jim is doing well, holding down the fort in our California home. My time here, at my parents' home which we inherited, is slightly problematic in that I don't have him here with me. I miss him. The good news is, I know how to fix things and there's a lot of room. So, I look forward to getting you up here to share some wine and stories. Former agents live off stories that we can't share with the public, or even family, so it'll be so much fun to have you spend some time here," Mary suggested.

"Mary, I can't thank you enough for the kind offer. I accept! I think you could be just the company I need. My husband is incredibly supportive, but for the next few weeks he's going to be extremely busy working with the Secret Service, FBI, and other agencies to track down additional suspects who attacked me and the Cassell family.

"You have a great man, Carly," responded Mary.

"You bet I do, Mary. Let me work on the logistics with my office in the morning. My people here in the Miami Field Office have been overwhelmingly supportive of me and Will. Since my coming back to our Ocean Reef home from the hospital, the office established a security perimeter around our home and have not left. Visiting you will relieve them of protecting me. Director Murray and former Director Larry Cassell both visited me. What's amazing to me is that Director Cassell, who has had his own personal experience with Bratva, took the time to visit. I can share that with you when I see you in person in Maine. I am so excited."

"Tell Will you'll be safe in Eastport, Maine. I will see to that," promised Mary. "All you have to do is arrange to get to Portland, Maine. I will handle the rest of the logistics. Once up here, Carly, we will hike, go out on elk sightings, and visit the local pubs and the few bistros we have here. I will provide you with ample opportunity for downtime so you can recover from all that has happened. There will be plenty of wine. You can sit back and enjoy the awesome view of the Canadian border, a short distance across the water. Like I mentioned, the cooler weather this time of year provides an unequaled contrast to the Florida ambiance. Both are equally calm, but Maine is the icing on the cake. I can't wait for you to get here."

"Thanks Mary, but I am still going to bring my duty weapon," Carly chuckled.

"I don't blame you, but just so you know, I have a Remington 870 shotgun up here that you know all too well how to use," Mary responded. "I hated shooting that damn weapon, but it sure feels comforting to have it here. Love you, girl, see you soon."

"I will be there," Carly responded.

CHAPTER 94

"I WANT TO talk to Vladimir," Ambassador Cohen demanded on the phone to Markov.

"You want??? Calm down Ambassador, no one demands to talk to the boss that way," replied Markov. "You don't manage him; he owns you and everything you possess. Don't ever forget that."

"Fuck you, moron, I own Guatemala, not your boss! You asses up there came down here, asked me for help in abducting the Cassell girl, and now it's a global incident. You can't come here to use my people to slaughter a half-dozen Americans with my people and expect it to go away without red flags raised all over the hemisphere," Cohen grew more agitated as he spoke. "Thanks to your Belov's incompetence, the Justice Ministry is asking questions I don't want to answer. Because if I have to, there will be others dancing to the music with me. Now, connect me with Vladimir."

"I must laugh at that, Ambassador. Like you have never engaged in slaughtering your own citizens. Like I said, calm down! The boss will not want to hear about you having to dance to any fucking music that'll indict him. I will have him call you soon, but I will say this once more - your tone needs to change before you talk to him, before you talk too much bullshit. You are saying all the wrong things, sounding distraught and nervous. It will only make your situation worse, trust me. He will not be happy with you," Markov advised.

"Fine, have him call me," Cohen demanded.

Markov hung up in disgust.

CHAPTER 95

"WHERE ARE MY guys, and where is my boat," asked an agitated Ambassador Cohen. "Why haven't you returned my call?"

"Whoa, Ambassador, calm down. What the hell are you asking?" responded Belov. "And how did you get this cell number?"

"I have my contacts. The boat that transported the girl from Guatemala up to Key West has not been seen, or heard from, since the transfer point. It was supposed to have refueled in Cancun and should have been back here in Guatemala yesterday," Cohen sternly advised. "This whole endeavor to kidnap the girl, murder the group of her friends, and ferry her up to the States has been nothing less than a total cluster fuck. It was all done to satisfy your egotistical need to revenge your father's death. Now you've gotten the Guatemalan government and the U.S. Embassy focused on me as complicit in this. I resent it, and you better do something about it," Cohen added. Cohen waited for a response. All he heard was a dial tone. The connection went dead.

CHAPTER 96

"THIS IS SOLARSKI."

"Hello Mr. Solarski, this is Ambassador Cohen. I am not sure if we've ever met, but by way of introduction, I am the Guatemalan Ambassador to Israel. I have been told that you are someone I may talk to freely, and confidentially, about a recent event involving U.S. citizens who were unfortunately murdered at the La Antigua a week ago."

"Ambassador, I would be happy to discuss anything with you about the incident. Not sure that you have to offer, but my first question would be this, have you had the opportunity to discuss this matter with the Guatemala Justice Ministry?" asked Solarski.

"What I must discuss is too risky to bring to their attention at this time. It is the Americans that will benefit from what I have to offer. I know who killed the kids," Cohen provided.

"Okaaay," Solarski responded in a slow cadence. "I am available anytime. Do you want to come to the Embassy?"

"No. There is a small boutique hotel with a small bar and restaurant adjacent to the Embassy, I can meet you there this afternoon," Cohen offered.

"Yes, I am familiar with the location, Ambassador. I will see you there at three o'clock, by the bar," Solarski suggested.

"Thank you, Mr. Solarski."

CHAPTER 97

Statement from William Peters,
President, George Washington University,
Washington, D.C.

THE GEORGE WASHINGTON University expresses its sincere condolences to the families of the students and their professor who tragically and senselessly lost their lives while in the performance of a university research program conducted at La Antigua, Guatemala. It is a sad time for the George Washington University family as it seeks to understand the loss of members of our family. We also offer our best wishes to the Cassell family as it seeks to heal from the tragic ordeal suffered by one of the students, Dorothy Cassell. The university has scheduled a celebration of life memorial to be held at the Charles E. Smith Center on November 17th to remember Professor Michael Bligh, and the following students, Sid Rosenberg, Thomas McCarthy, Bernard McGovern, William Berthrong, and Stephanie Zirgulis.

CHAPTER 98

"I THINK I better wire up for this meeting," Solarski told his colleagues inside the U.S. Embassy. "I would bet my next paycheck that the Ambassador will either 'fess up to knowing about the massacre or want to provide some damning information about the Russian mob, generally."

Bob Cozzolina, the likeable Drug Enforcement Administration's Legal Attaché to the Embassy, happened to be walking by Solarski's office and observed him placing a wire behind his back and clipping a microphone discreetly under his T-shirt. "Going out on a date?" He asked.

Solarski looked up and grinned. "Not unless you think Ambassador Cohen is a hot date," Solarski chuckled.

"You're meeting with Cohen today wearing a wire?" Cozzolina perked up. "Damn, life is getting rich around here."

"Yup, at his request. Anything you need me to ask?" Solarski offered.

"Well, you know we've been tailing him for some time now. He's one of the most prolific money launderers in this region. His reach extends to Russia, Israel, and most of Europe," Cozzolina added. "You need help covering the meeting? He usually travels with a band of Guatemalans and former Shin Bet types."

"We know the hotel pretty well, Bob. Much of it is already wired, as you well know. We should be able to monitor the discussions from here and keep an eyeball on his entourage with the embassy video equipment.

I wouldn't be surprised if he were to come inside the Reforma without anyone," Solarski advised.

"Well, if he starts talking about illegal money transfer stuff, you know I'll be all ears," Cozzolina said.

The Hotel Residencial Reforma is the same boutique hotel, located next door to the U.S. Embassy along the Avenida de la Reforma that offered a quiet and discreet seating to Solarski when Eli met Captain Strain. It was an ideal location for a confidential conversation.

"I'm going to head over there in a few minutes and wait for him in the bar area. I'll find a seat closest to the embassy compound for better reception. If you observe his boys coming inside, feel free to come over for lunch on me," Solarski joked before leaving his office and heading to the outer checkpoint. He walked through the revolving security door to exit onto the sidewalk. As was his usual custom, he halted briefly to look both ways, not for vehicles, but for suspicious individuals who may surveil him. He performed a check of his own person, instinctively patting his pocket for his commission book and his side for a weapon. Both his credentials and his issued Glock 19 were where they were supposed to be. One of the perks of working inside Guatemala was the authority the country's Justice Ministry granted to the Americans. "I can carry a gun anywhere in this country," Solarski frequently mused, "What a soothing benefit."

Cozzolina remained inside Solarski's office to monitor the meeting with the RSO's local security asset. The mic was live and Cozzolina visualized Solarski's location as he greeted the hotel staff. Prior to entering, Solarski scanned the parking lot in front of the hotel, a large parcel of land for parking. At best, the lot was half-full of rental cars on any given day, mostly American visitors to the Embassy. Today, there were no vehicles in the lot during late afternoon. With the lunch hour completed, the next wave of bar and restaurant patrons wouldn't occur until after happy hour, around four. It was three o'clock when Solarski walked into the registration office.

"Como esta amigo?" (How are you friend?) Solarski asked the manager. "Estoy aqui para encontrar con un amigo negocio, el llegara aqui pronto. Yo va esperar a el en el bar" (I am here to meet a business acquaintance. He will be here soon. I am going to wait for him in the bar).

"Senor Solarski, me gustaria introducirle a mi hijo, Ricardo. El va trabajar aqui conmigo para aprender las responsibilidades del hotel por el mes que viene," (Mr. Solarski, I would like to introduce my son, Ricardo. He is going to be working here with me in order to learn the responsibilities of the hotel for the next month), said the manager, proudly introducing his son.

"Ah, tengo mucho gusto en conocerle, Ricardo," (It is a pleasure to meet you, Ricardo), Solarski shook the boy's hand, nodded with a smile and said, "Espero que usted obtiene muchos creditos de la Universidad por la experiencia." (I hope you obtained many University credits for the experience). He then moved past the small registration through a small back door and into the bar.

Cozzolina observed the video camera feed as Solarski entered the hotel. He smiled to himself as he listened to the banter. "Solarski should run for mayor of Guatemala City," he said to the local embassy security aide. "He speaks Spanish better than you, and you were born here."

"I know," said the aide, "For someone born of Polish ancestry, he sure has a lot of Latino in him. We like it!"

CHAPTER 99

AFTER PICKING UP Carly at the Bangor International Airport, Carly and Mary Logue had a seventy-five-mile ride to Eastport, Maine. "Carly, sorry for the long drive, but Bangor is the closest airport to my home. Some friends and relatives fly into Portland, but that is double the distance."

"Mary, I can't thank you enough for sharing your home with me. This is what I needed, and your friendship, too," Carly voiced. "Your family raised you well."

"Carly, my hope for you is that your stay here gives some time to heal," Logue replied.

"Mary, I remember much of what happened to me in the van. I am sickened by the thought that human beings can inflict such evil upon other human beings. I know none of it is my fault; it was a vengeful response to Secret Service investigative work. I know there is information that suggests our intelligence community eliminated the former Bratva chieftain, but I have not been briefed on it. I don't know who did it. What I can share with you is this, while I don't feel guilt, I can't help but feel ashamed I didn't prevent it from happening. My situational awareness on the day the bastards abducted me, sucked."

"Whoa, girl. First, you are lucky to have someone like Will who is one man who completely understands such malevolence and how to tactically respond to it. What happened to you was evil. Will is equipped to defeat this type of evil. He did it when he took out three out of the four attackers. All of them are now in hell where they deserve to be. Will does not look at you in a manner for you to be ashamed. His love for you is deeper than anything else you have ever known. My God, girl, you could not be loved more," Mary cautioned, almost as a reprimand, calculated to snap Carly out of her depressive state.

"Mary, I love him so much," Carly invoked. "I pray he doesn't view me differently now that this has happened."

"Carly, do you remember *water rescue* during your Secret Service training? I told the class that the more swimming you do, the more confident you become as a swimmer. In a marriage, you learn to stroke. Every day with more strokes, your marriage improves. With Will you've learned to swim in Olympic pool proportions. Carly, your man, Will, like my guy, Jim, are the type of men our moms prayed we would marry one day. You got lucky; you got a cute guy. Just kidding, don't tell my husband I said that. Seriously, Will knows he is lucky to have found you. You will go home, back to him, back to your office, and you will find two families that support you unconditionally, love you and continue to protect you," said Logue.

As she pulled the car onto her driveway she said to Carly, "Do believe how close we are to the Canadian border? I love the fact that Jim and I were able to keep this home. My parents loved it here; and so, do we. Once you get settled down, we will be able to make several short trips where I can show you some local places of interest. One is in nearby Pembroke which features a rare phenomenon known here as 'reversing falls.' It attracts a lot of seals, eagles, and is a great spot for whale watching."

"Yes, that sounds fantastic. I look forward to the trips."

Mary grabbed Carly's suitcase out of the trunk and led her inside the home.

"Wow, Mary, you live here part of the year. How do you and Jim manage to keep it in such great shape, especially with the varied climate changes."

"Carly, I am one of four daughters. My dad never had a son and I believe he wanted one, but since I was a tomboy, I think he looked at me as the closest he'd ever get. Dad taught all of us things most girls never learn. He had us working on cars, appliances, and sheetrock. I'm not talking about re-wiring appliances; I'm talking about tearing the whole appliance apart to learn how it worked and then putting it back together again. My dad even taught us how to fight and defend ourselves. Together with mom, they could not have been better postured to raise a family like ours, particularly me. They were always, always there for my siblings and me. And now, as I get older, but still active, I am there for them. I love them dearly, and you're right, they did teach me well. They taught me to be a good friend," Mary related. "Now, let's pop open a bottle of wine!" she pleasantly chirped. "Then I'll start the grill for dinner."

CHAPTER 100

SOLARSKI SAT AT a small table in the corner of the bar, his back to the wall. The front parking lot was clearly visible through the window on the opposite side of the room. The bartender was out of sight when the Ambassador slipped into the room. Solarski quickly stood up and moved forward to greet the lone guest.

"Hello, Ambassador, you arrived without a car. I hope you didn't have to walk too far," Solarski ad-libbed.

Cozzolina observed the Ambassador being dropped off less than a block away from the hotel. Two SUVs took up positions on the other side of the Embassy compound along the avenue. "Solarski may not have seen him arrive," Cozzolina thought. "The Ambassador intentionally walked the outside perimeter of the parking area to avoid detection." Cozzolina spotted four of Cohen's Guatemalan thugs in a small group outside their parked vehicles, smoking and chatting amongst themselves.

"James, may I call you by your first name?" Cohen asked politely.

"Of course, Mr. Ambassador," Solarski responded, but he quickly thought, "Only my dad referred to me as James, and that was when I was in trouble."

"James, I thank you for taking the time to meet with me. I walked a bit to get here; I needed the exercise," Cohen joked.

Solarski gestured to Cohen to sit with him at the private table.

As the waiter walked into the dining area carrying a box of wine to replenish the bar's stock, he caught Solarski's wave. The bartender acknowledged with a head tilt and left the box on top of the bar. He hustled to the table. "Yes, Senor Solarski, what can I get the two of you?"

"Ambassador, are you interested in a cup of coffee or a glass of wine," Solarski asked.

"A glass of wine would be fine. Will you have one?"

"I am afraid I will have to hold off on a glass of wine until dinner time," Solarski responded, then addressed the bartender, "May we have a glass of your Quilt Cabernet Sauvignon, and a cup of coffee with cream and sugar. "Mr. Ambassador, the Quilt I just ordered for you is a California red cabernet; it's pretty balanced and food friendly. Do you want something to eat?"

"That sounds good, James, I am not sure this bar has the type of wines one would find in my wine cellar, but if I like this Quilt, I may have to add it. Indeed, I will have to invite you back to my home one day soon and offer you the best that I have."

"That'll be fine, Mr. Ambassador." Solarski responded as non-committedly as he could fashion.

"Seriously, I recently ordered four cases of a rather complex Cabernet Sauvignon from an up-and-coming Napa Valley vineyard, the brand name, *Melanson*. When I heard about the vineyard, I immediately studied its production. One of its best features is that its plantings are all located on the side of a hill with maximum sun exposure. That's a good thing in Napa Valley. The *Melanson Vineyard* has such a disposition. Perhaps that's a bit too much data right now," Cohen grinned.

"Not a worry, Ambassador. When I think back to my college days, not having the smallest desire to drink wine, I now marvel how much a good red lends to my daily dinner enjoyment," replied Solarski.

The bartender delivered a hefty glass of the Quilt and a large mug of coffee. He then retreated behind the bar to stock the shelves with the bottles he had just brought to the bar, and more importantly, to mind his business.

Solarski raised his mug to the Ambassador, "Here is to Guatemala and its people. It is a joy to be stationed at this Embassy." They clinked and sipped.

"So, Mr. Ambassador, how can I be of assistance?"

"James, I am not sure you know exactly who I am, or how I represent this beautiful country. I am here to serve her, and I have devoted my life to her," Cohen offered. "It means the world to me to be in service to my country."

"Sir, I always thought you were from Nicaragua," Solarski chirped.

"Yes, I am impressed that you know that, but I probably shouldn't be surprised, knowing your position within your embassy," Cohen diplomatically countered. "My ambassadorship actually is conferred upon me by the Nicaraguan government. While I serve Nicaragua as its de juris ambassador, I am also serving Guatemala as its de facto ambassador. I represent both countries to Israel. It helps tremendously with my money transfer business to be so well rooted in Latin America."

Cozzolina, listening on the wire, couldn't help but gag at the conversation's false pretense. He knew Solarski was playing it cool. "Cohen," Cozzolina whispered under his breath, "is as corrupt as they come. His position as an ambassador was nothing more than a smoke screen. He paid people off in every country in which he operated his money transfer business. He had skeletons in each of those countries, some of which he helped bury. The DEA knew how he operated, using thousands of mules and human traffickers to launder money in other countries with reckless abandon."

"James," I need your advice."

Solarski took a sip of his coffee and placed the cup on the table before looking Cohen directly in the eyes. "What is it you need, Mr. Ambassador?"

"James, I know things about the Russian mob that your country needs to know, and soon. Things that could perhaps get me killed. I will need a level of assurance for me and my family, to keep us safe from the mob, the Bratva. I know who is responsible for the La Antigua murders and can incriminate the architect at the highest level of the Bratva organization," Cohen looked at Solarski, who didn't flinch. For the first time in his life, Cohen was scared shit.

"Mr. Ambassador, if I may be candid, I've had many opportunities in my career to entertain requests like yours. But admittedly, you are the most important person to ever make such an offer to me. There is no way I can accept your help unless you give me something more substantial about what you know about the massacre. For example, if you were culpable in any way, it will take more than my assurance to safeguard you from any judicial action to which you may be exposed. I know you previously asked Captain Otero several probing questions shortly after the mass murder. That raised eyebrow. I'm not sure what your concern was, or what level of knowledge you had at that time. Then, there was silence on your part. You withdrew from the matter without asking any additional questions. That doesn't bode well for you. Frankly, prior knowledge of the Bratva threat in order to prevent the atrocity is the information we needed. You apparently had it and didn't provide it," Solarski replied bluntly, not deviating from his steady glare at Cohen. "James, the Bratva directed some of my people to participate in the murders. I knew they were using my people to help intimidate the group, but I didn't know that they would be involved in murder. I learned recently that our people who assisted Bratva are missing. I don't know what happened to them. They have not returned to Guatemala.

What I fear is that Vladimir Belov, Bratva's leader, did something to them, and will do something to me to stop me from talking about his dastardly deed. So, I am asking you to connect me with the right people. However, I need assurance that I will not face judicial action," Cohen petitioned.

"Well, I wasn't expecting this conversation, Ambassador Cohen. Do you have any documentation, recordings, physical evidence or digital evidence that would support your contention that Belov is responsible?" Solarski petitioned. "As you know, this incident has garnered international attention. Identifying the people who orchestrated the atrocity will be front page news."

"James, I know. It is precisely why I think I need to provide the Embassy with the information it needs to bring the Bratva to justice, before the Bratva attempts to extinguish those of us who know the truth. I need your help," Cohen pleaded. "I can give you Belov."

"Mr. Ambassador, let me return to the Embassy and work on it. I'll get back to you very soon. We can meet again, perhaps at the Embassy in a secure room." Solarski finished his cup of coffee, left a fifty-dollar bill on the bar, winked at the bartender, and walked with the Ambassador to the restaurant parking lot. Within seconds, Cohen's two SUVs pulled into the restaurant parking lot. His bodyguards jumped out of the rear SUV to form a perimeter around the Ambassador. "Well, that was pretty well executed, Mr. Ambassador," observed Solarski. "Whoever trained your people should be congratulated."

Cozzolina observed the entire rendezvous play out on the Embassy's video surveillance system. "Man, these guys are efficient for Guatemalans. Must be Israeli trained."

Before leaving, Ambassador Cohen made a final request. "James, please don't delay this. I am willing to come back to you as soon as you are available to see me."

"Mr. Ambassador, it may well be later this evening. Like I said, I will get back to you soon. You have given me a lot to work on."

The Ambassador nodded before entering the open rear door of his SUV. His security detail secured the door before hustling back to their follow-up vehicle. The two vehicles sped off in tandem. Cozzolina, watching the departure, grinned.

CHAPTER 101

"WILL, I WAS on the phone this morning with the DNI, Admiral Merz. He has worked out an agreement with the other Directorates that gives the Coast Guard Intelligence and Coast Guard Investigative Service the authority to continue its work targeting the Bratva for crimes against our organization, and the U.S. Secret Service. The DNI has instructed us to rely on the FBI, and other agencies that may have statutory authority, to investigate the Bratva threats. We are obligated to coordinate any and all intelligence and investigative leads, and to the extent necessary, partner with them on any operational actions. As an agency, we will respond to the Bratva threat whenever its violent animus is directed toward our people. The DNI appreciates that the Bratva attacks on the Coast Guard is ours to defend against. Simply put, other agencies may not be as aggressive as us to extinguish the immediate threat." Keegan advised. "When and where necessary, we will be proactive."

Strain responded, "Sir, I am on board with that."

"Will, I had previously ordered you to back off and let others follow up on actionable intelligence. I did that because I was concerned that your emotions, at the time, would not serve you well. That directive is rescinded. I want you to be part of the coordination for any future multi-agency response, and to be intimately involved in its planning. I think your relationship with the super hacker kid, Max, may be useful to hunt down all the remaining Bratva personalities involved in the mayhem."

"Sir, when I spoke to Director Cassell last week about Max, he was surprised to learn that it was Max who provided us with the timely information that Belov's Bratva planned to abduct his boy from the Naval Academy. It was lamentable that Max had not been privy to the Bratva's plans to abduct the Cassell daughter at La Antigua," Strain said. "Twenty-four hours would have made a world of difference."

"We ought to bring Max down to D.C. and get him fully debriefed. We'll determine how to best use his insider position to bring this Bratva monster down," Keegan replied.

"I will get that done," Strain assured him.

CHAPTER 102

"BORIS, GET DOWN to Guatemala and dispose of this fucking idiot," Belov barked to Markov. "If we don't shut him up, he'll betray us. We never should have relied on him, or his flotilla of incompetents, to take care of our business."

"What about Yuriy?" Markov replied.

"We haven't heard from him in the last twelve hours. That's not good. We have to assume he's been compromised, and hopefully dead," said Belov.

"Vladimir, with Yuriy unavailable, and Cohen's people who assisted us in the abduction unavailable, who am I going to rely on to get rid of the Ambassador?" asked Markov.

"You will get it done with cash; cash is king. Explore using the Israelis. They are the best, and they don't talk," Belov urged frantically. "Just get on a damn plane and take care of business down there."

Markov was on a plane out of John F. Kennedy International airport later that day en route Miami. From there, he took a direct flight to Guatemala City. He secreted cash into his checked bag. He wasn't concerned about the Guatemalans; he could pay them off. He just didn't need the Americans catching him transporting cash without declaring it.

CHAPTER 103

STRAIN'S COAST GUARD secure office phone alerted.

"This is Captain Strain."

"Captain, this is Jim Solarski. I am calling to update you on the massacre investigation. Today, I had a meeting with Ambassador Cohen. He appears fearful and seeks to ensure his own safety. He wants to convey some damaging intelligence about the Bratva and its participation in the La Antigua murders. I put him off for a few hours to get directions from the intelligence directorates about accepting his information. He is anxious to come back later today and give his version. I think he's up to his neck in complicity and he's nervous about the Bratva hanging him out to dry," Solarski advised via a secure Embassy phone.

"Jim, we believe that he was deeply involved in the planning of the event. Not sure to what degree he knew how gruesome it would be. Of course, he is scared that the Bratva will want to eliminate him so he can't talk to us. Get him back to the Embassy as soon as you can to get his information, however skewed it may be. We need to get him before the Bratva does. Time is of the essence," Strain advised.

"Understood, Captain, I will contact him as soon as we hang up. I will update you later tonight," Solarski replied.

"Thanks, Jim. Be careful not to stand too close to him anywhere outside the Embassy grounds," Strain half-joked.

CHAPTER 104

"MR. AMBASSADOR, WE can receive you here at the Embassy at 5pm. Is that acceptable?" Solarski asked.

"I will be there," Cohen responded. Solarski detected a nervous quiver.

"Sir, we can only allow one vehicle inside the Embassy compound, your second vehicle will have to remain outside on the boulevard," Solarski advised.

"Fine, that's not a problem. See you at 5."

Solarski turned to his DEA counterpart, Cozzolina, and shrugged. "This is going to be one interesting evening, Bob."

Cozzolina responded, "Jimmy, Cohen better have a lot to say if he expects us to help him. He is on the short end of the Russian mob's patience, and of the DEA's patience, for completely opposite reasons. With us, he lives, with them, he dies. This guy sees his local empire crumbling. He has been too comfortable and grew too greedy. The Bratva figured out how to use him for their own purposes. It watched him devolve into a depravity that has clouded his thinking. The Ambassador is suspected of much criminal activity: drug trafficking, human trafficking, money laundering, and corruption of a generation of politicians throughout Central America. It's welcome news that he perceives himself cornered. Can't wait to hear what he's about to say to you. I'll be recording it."

Solarski notified the exterior post, "Ambassador Cohen's limo will be arriving at 1700 hours. Once it arrives, we will allow the Ambassador to exit his vehicle and enter the Embassy. I will be there to meet and greet him. Once he's inside, use the K-9 to scour his vehicle for any contraband." The exterior post knew what he meant, drugs and guns. "Make his driver and body man feel the pressure."

"Yes, sir. Understood," replied a dutiful Marine.

CHAPTER 105

"WELCOME MR. AMBASSADOR," Solarski said upon Cohen's exit from his SUV. "Twice in one day, who would've thought?" Solarski noted Cohen's pale appearance as he grabbed the door frame to exit his car.

"James, I look forward to sharing with you some highly sensitive information. The sooner we get on with the meeting, the quicker I can regain a sense of calm in my rather chaotic business life. You are someone I trust. You will be helping me and my family from what I fear could be our doom," Cohen confessed, slightly choking on his words.

Solarski wondered, "What does he know, that he didn't know just hours earlier. I can't get over the change in his appearance, like he's been through an exorcism."

"Here, James, I've brought you a bottle of the *Melanson* Red Cabernet from my wine cellar. I spoke about its high quality to you earlier today."

Solarski reflexively raised his hand to his head as blood and bone fragmentation splattered onto his face, as the Ambassador's body fell to the ground. The bottle of *Melanson* gripped in his right hand splintered when it hit the pavement. His body man, the Ambassador's trusted security guard, placed a Glock 19, nine-millimeter, inside his own mouth, and pulled the trigger. The bullet entered the rear of the guard's throat leaving a hole the size of a dime; the exit hole was the size of a half-dollar.

The guard's body dropped quickly, falling onto the Ambassador's body, ironically the same person he would otherwise be shielding. It happened in a second. The experienced Solarski kicked the Glock away from the two bodies and dashed toward the Ambassador's driver. An on-duty Marine sentinel pulled out a Remington 870 shotgun from a small closet inside the guard booth and aimed it in the direction of the front gate, covering Solarski's movement to the vehicle.

"Get out of the fucking car now," Solarski drew his own weapon and barked at the driver. Solarski grabbed the driver by the neck and pulled him down to the ground. "Don't move." He frisked the driver for weapons. He found none. "That's odd," he thought. Then he checked the driver's ankle and found a small Smith and Wesson, .38, Model 60, stainless steel, five shot. "The Chief," he thought. He took custody of it.

Another Marine hustled up to Solarski's position and over his radio ordered the front gate secured, "Lock us down." Several other Marines rolled out of their security down room, brandishing fully loaded M-16s, and took up pre-ordained defensive positions.

"Keep your focus on the Ambassador's security follow-up car outside the embassy gate," Solarski ordered. No sooner did Solarski state the order, then the SUV sped away.

Cozzolina sprinted out from the Embassy entrance and headed toward Solarski's position. "Jimmy, are you okay," he yelled.

"I am okay." Then he yelled, "Marine, come over here and cuff this guy," Solarski walked over to assess the fate of the Ambassador and his turncoat guard. "They're both dead," he said to Cozzolina.

"I see the Ambassador's security vehicle departed, Jimmy, I'll work my way to the front gate. I'm sure the locals will be responding," Cozzolina said.

"Keep them out of this facility, Bob, and if they give you shit tell them, this is an American investigation, on American property. I'll contact Minister Villacorta to advise him what's just occurred, and request that he respond."

"So much for the anticipated intelligence coup," Cozzolina yelled to Solarski as he hustled to the front gate post. "This looks like Bratva's revenge." Solarski nodded in agreement.

The Doppler effect of the police sirens indicated the responding police vehicles were closing the distance to the Embassy from various directions.

The Marines took up outer perimeter positions on Solarski's orders. The RSO at the embassy manages the Marine detachment, and they reacted as trained. They liked Solarski and knew him as a cool-headed performer under stress. They also liked him because he made the Marine detachment feel useful in their role, far beyond the square-badge reputation that exists in some embassies around the globe.

"Sergeant, have two of your Marines take this driver into the interview room. Give him another pat down and secure him to the wall," Solarski requested of the on-duty sergeant of the guard. "Sergeant, do you have an iPhone on you?" Solarski asked.

"Yes, sir."

"Take some photos of the crime scene from all angles, as well as the bodies and a close-up of the weapon lying over there. Be careful not to disturb the body positions," He added. "We may let the locals come into the compound to assist at some point, but I want our own photos. Also, alert your duty desk to ensure that the video coverage of the courtyard is preserved."

"Minister Villacorta, please," Solarski requested from his cell phone within visual feet of the carnage. The police sirens now were at fever pitch.

"Hola, esto es Minister Villacorta."

"Minister, this is Solarski at the American Embassy. I regret to inform you that we have just experienced the horrific murder of Ambassador Cohen by his personal bodyguard here on embassy property. The

Ambassador's bodyguard then committed suicide with his own gun. The local police are about to arrive. I don't want to allow them inside until you, or Captain Otero, are present. We are documenting the crime scene now. We have the Ambassador's driver in custody for questioning. The Ambassador's security detail fled after the shooting. They had been located in a separate vehicle outside the Embassy grounds."

"Amigo, I am so sorry this had to occur on Embassy property. It doesn't surprise me that Cohen is dead. With his involvement in a variety of illegal endeavors, it was a matter of time. Why was he there?" Villacorta asked.

"He was here to provide information about the student massacre and Bratva's involvement," Solarski advised. "Now we won't know, but I think we have a pretty good idea who set this up. Can you get here soon?"

"I am heading to my car now. I can be there in fifteen minutes. I will alert Captain Otero," Villacorta replied.

"Thank you." Solarski walked over to the front gate.

"Bob, I just spoke to the Minister. He's on his way," Solarski advised Cozzolina.

"What do want to do with the locals when they arrive," Cozzolina asked.

"We will tell them the Minister is on his way with Captain Otero. Once they arrive, the police will be allowed onto the Embassy compound to access the crime scene. The Marines have already begun to secure the video tapes of the incident, and they'll photograph the entire scene," Solarski advised.

"What a lost opportunity to learn what Cohen knew." Cozzolina added. "I'll head over to the Marine security room and begin to interview the driver."

"Thanks, Bob. That'll be a big help. And Bob, the bottle of *Melanson* was supposed to be for you." Solarski grinned.

"Man, you are a cold dude, Solarski," Cozzolina replied with a wink.

CHAPTER 106

"CAPTAIN, THANKS FOR showing up. We have the Ambassador's driver in a secure room. My colleague, DEA agent Bob Cozzolina, has already begun interrogating him. He seems as surprised as the rest of us about the way the Ambassador was killed, specifically, by his own bodyguard. He did say that the bodyguard had met yesterday with someone he recognized as a Bratva person, an operative. He's given a detailed description. The description was that of a Russian. I'll bring you to him," Solarski advised Otero in the presence of Minister Villacorta, who had just entered the Embassy courtyard.

"Thanks, Jim. I will have a couple of my men to hustle over to the bodyguard's residence. They can be there in ten minutes," Otero said. "Thanks for letting us onto the Embassy grounds to be part of the investigation. I know, diplomatically, it can sometimes cause friction. We appreciate your partnership."

Solarski led the two officials toward the Embassy's security room, where the driver was being questioned. Outside the room they encountered Cozzolina.

"Bob, this is Captain Otero and Minister Villacorta," Solarski said, introducing the two Guatemala Justice officials. "They are friends, Bob."

"It is a pleasure to finally meet you, Bob, I have heard good things about you. I hope your recent move to Guatemala has gone well," Villacorta said.

"Minister, I love your country and I am sorry that this is how we must meet. I would have hoped it could have been over a nice dinner," Cozzolina said. "Perhaps when this matter concludes, I can make amends."

"I love this country, too, and I appreciate you saying that," Villacorta replied as he and Captain Otero walked into the security room to interview the driver.

The driver's facial expression, upon seeing Captain Otero, wasn't lost on Cozzolina.

"You're shaking, Manuel. Is there something you need to tell me?" Otero asked the driver, looking him directly in the eyes. It wasn't the first time they looked eye to eye. In another time, a decade earlier, a younger Sergeant Otero encountered a young Manuel, who was being interviewed for passing counterfeit U.S. currency. "I remembered this mutt from a counterfeiting case years ago. We identified him as a suspect," Otero blurted. At that decade old interview, Otero learned the suspect was in an adjoining room being questioned for passing counterfeit notes, Otero breached the interview room door, swiftly walked past the detective conducting the interview, raised his hand like a tennis player about to serve a ball, and smacked Manuel on the right side of his head. The suspect drifted awkwardly across the room and landed against a wall. The detective deferred to the sergeant, closed his folder, and retreated to the hallway, his interview portion of the obviously completed. Sergeant Otero picked the young thug up off the floor and placed him on a chair for further interrogation. It didn't go well for Manuel. He served five years in a Guatemala jail. His salvation was an invitation by Cohen to become one of his local thugs.

"You remember me, Manuel," Otero continued.

"Si senor, yo recuerdo usted muy bien."

"I know you remember me well. You need to tell me what caused the Ambassador to be killed in the Embassy courtyard by his man, and you better start talking now," Otero said, demonstrably agitated.

"I was not part of it. All I know is, I was told to drive him here. I am one of several drivers he trusted. I was told not to leave my driver's seat once inside. I thought that was something the Embassy demanded. I grew suspicious when I saw the Ambassador's bodyguard arguing with a stranger earlier today. The man was from the United States, a Russian from the New York City Brighton Beach area. We always hated to see these guys arrive in Guatemala to deal with the Ambassador, because it never ended well. People always died. I've never seen a grow man cry like the bodyguard did after this guy talked to him," Manuel said.

Otero didn't expect to hear the explanation. His mind raced down an additional line of questioning. "Who told you to remain in the driver's seat?"

"The bodyguard."

"Can you describe the person the bodyguard spoke with, and is he still in the area?" Otero countered.

"He's a short Russian looking guy, close cropped haircut, well balding. He was in a blue sport jacket, no tie, khaki pants, and wore white Nike running shoes. He talked to the bodyguard for at least two hours outside the Ambassador's residence, on the sidewalk. He's probably at the airport now trying to depart the country."

"Do you know his name?" Otero asked.

"I think he goes by Boris, but I am not sure," the driver replied. "Whatever he told the bodyguard was enough to cause him to kill the boss," he said. "That's all I know, Captain. I've grown up since you first met me. I don't want to go back to prison. I will work with you, I promise. I have a family now; I don't want to fail them."

"Okay, fine, the Americans will have additional questions for you," Otero replied. "I will reach out for you later. Don't tell anyone you talked with me." Otero briskly left the interview room to get to the courtyard and use his phone. He had to get his people to the airport to look for the Russian.

Solarski and Villacorta trailed the pre-occupied Otero into the courtyard. The experienced Cozzolina remained with the driver. His DEA background prepared him as an excellent interrogator. He would nurture the opportunity with the driver to develop him as a future source.

Both bodies remained in the courtyard with tarps draped over them. The Ambassador's blood seeped under the non-porous tarp to memorialize the exact position of the body, a bloody outline.

While standing in proximity to the bodies, Otero took the time to make his call. He had stood by many similar crime scenes, but never one with an ambassador who may be part of a conspiracy to heinously murder innocent college kids. Indeed, these bodies were not going anywhere fast. Experienced investigators all think alike. "Jim, I suspect that Captain Otero is notifying the airport security group to be on the lookout for this Russian guy," whispered Villacorta.

Solarski replied, "Yes, and if he determines that the Russian got on a plane to the United States, I will ensure he gets picked up on arrival. Let's hope he is found here first. That would save us a lot of time."

"This is Captain Otero, Guatemala State Police, I need to talk to a supervisor immediately," Otero authoritatively expressed to the dispatcher.

"Captain, this is Lieutenant Gomez, how can I help you," answered the supervisor.

"Lieutenant Gomez, thank you for receiving my call," Otero responded. "We have had a recent murder/suicide at the United States

Embassy and believe a suspect is currently at the airport, ready to board a plane to Miami." explained Otero. "We need to interdict him." He then provided the airport police supervisor with the description he received from Manuel.

"Sir, we will fan out and scan the passengers heading to Miami. There is only one flight departing from the airport at this time for the United States and it is Miami," advised the Gomez. "It hasn't departed yet, so it shouldn't be difficult to locate the suspect."

"Thank you. Please contact me as soon as possible with any result." Otero said.

"I have airport security looking for the Russian," Otero told Solarski and Villacorta.

Within seconds, his phone rang.

"Captain Otero," he responded.

"Sir, this is Lieutenant Gomez; we have your man. It was an easy find. He sticks out like a Russian. We have him in an interview room should your investigators want to talk to him now. He doesn't know why we interdicted him, at least nothing we have said. His plane is not scheduled to leave for another two hours," Gomez relayed.

"Good work. We will have someone there in fifteen minutes," Otero advised. Otero himself intended to conduct the interview.

CHAPTER 107

"BOSS, WE HAVE taken care of Cohen. He won't be sharing any information with the Embassy," Markov advised Belov by telephone while waiting for his plane to Miami.

"Did you have to use the Israelis?"

"No, I was able to convince the Ambassador's bodyguard to do it. I told him if he didn't comply, his family would be killed. It worked. He muttered something about not surviving, that he would take his own life. I gave him a lot of cash, but I guess if he puts a bullet in his head, he saves face."

"Good work, Boris, and quick too. I'm impressed. I am sure we can send the family a bonus either way, his imprisonment or suicide," Belov said. "Now get your ass back to Brighton Beach. It'll probably get intense for us up here, and we will need your help."

"I'm about to board a flight to Miami in two hours. I will let you know when I get there. I should be back in New York by late tonight and home before 2:00 am," Boris replied. "I will text you when I get back to Miami." Boris hung up with Vladimir.

"Excuse me sir, but may I see you boarding pass," an American Airline employee asked Markov.

"Sure, is there a problem?" Boris asked.

"These two gentlemen behind you have a few questions for you."

Markov looked back and realized that his stay in Guatemala might be extended. "How can I help you?"

"Drop your bag and put your hands behind your back," said Lieutenant Gomez. "You are wanted for questioning."

"You going to handcuff me, for what? I have done nothing wrong," Markov protested.

"Well, there's a State Police investigator here who thinks differently," Gomez replied as he escorted him to an airport holding room for questioning.

CHAPTER 108

MARKOV KNEW THAT his call to Belov just gave the investigators valuable time, a window of opportunity, to pursue his mob boss, Belov. Belov would not expect an update until he arrived in Miami, leaving Belov in the dark for the next four to five hours. "If he doesn't hear from me, he will grow concerned, but that won't be for at least six hours. Shit," he thought to himself. "I am not talking to these assholes."

Captain Otero entered the airport interview room and found Markov handcuffed to a wall bar. "Is this the Russian?" asked Otero.

"It is, Captain. We've only been in the room for fifteen minutes. Mr. Markov hasn't spoken; he just shakes his head," replied the airport security agent.

"Thank you. Please leave us. I have a few questions for Mr. Markov that you don't need to hear," Otero said to the agent.

"Understood, sir. I will be outside in the hallway, should you need me."

Markov looked up at Otero and grinned.

A moment later, Markov sat on the floor, his left arm dangling above his head, awkwardly secured to the bar. His chair lay next to him, violently thrusted to the side from the force of Otero's left hook to the side of the Russian's head. Markov was dazed, but remained sufficiently aware, not daring to test the captain with an insolent stare.

"You do not stare, and grin, at the State Police," Otero warned. "Get your ass back on the chair." Markov slowly complied. The strike drew no blood, but a welt on Markov's temple area grew large.

"You got sloppy on this one, Mr. Markov. Your boss will not be happy when he learns your efforts to assassinate the Ambassador have been documented in a suicide note his bodyguard left behind. I know I don't have to advise you to remain silent. I know your loyalty to Belov will not permit you to talk but let me say that devotion is ill-advised. You will never leave Guatemala. You will spend the remainder of your life in our prison," Otero warned. "And that is not a good life for a Russian, that's my message to you." Otero stood tall over Markov. "I have two options," Markov quickly reasoned, "life in a Guatemalan prison, or cooperate, and hope the United States works with me to target Belov. I'll choose life in prison." The thought of Bratva's revenge upon their own was a powerful tool. Markov knew "the Bratva would target my entire family back in Brighton Beach if I talk, and that will not end well. I'm fucked."

Looking at the floor, Markov said, "I have nothing to say."

"A popular ambassador's chief of security left a suicide note to his family that implicates you in his murder earlier today. The note indicates you were here in Guatemala for the sole purpose of orchestrating that murder. You left him a lot of money for his family. I'd say you are in a bit of trouble," Otero told him. "Good luck explaining that one to your Mr. Belov."

When he heard Otero invoke Belov by name, he looked up and stared at the captain for a moment. His head then drooped, and he began to tremble. Captain Otero left the room.

CHAPTER 109

"BOSS, I HAVE become aware through social media that Markov has been detained at the Guatemalan airport and taken to a local police station for interrogation," advised Max.

"I spoke to him only four hours ago. How did this happen?" replied a puzzled Belov.

"An airline passenger waiting to board filmed the police event and put it on social media. My artificial intelligence app picked up on the facial recognition to alert me," Max said.

"Well, if that is true, then Markov is dead to me if he starts talking. It means he will have screwed up the entire Guatemalan event. I've lost Yuriy, Vadim, and their operators. And now, I have lost Markov." Belov said to his new confidant, Max, The Secret Service knew him as Max, the super hacker. Strain knew him as a trusted confidant.

"Vladimir, what will you do now that the government has foiled your attempts to eradicate Cassell and his two children. The Guatemalan massacre has been all over the global news, and the Bratva is seen as the culprit. You have lost most of your trusted people to either arrest or death. Your only option is to lay low and avoid their tentacles," Max cautioned.

"Max, I am not wired that way. I will buy off any politician I need to in order to stifle any federal effort to attack the Bratva. We already own the New York United States Senators, both morons, and

I will kill those who keep coming at me. I am safe here in Brighton Beach. The authorities are deathly afraid of trying to breach this compound. You should know this strategy better than anyone as an ultimate fighter champion. I am grateful you have accepted the offer to join my inner circle. Together, we will destroy the bastards who killed my father. You must remember it was my father who rescued you from the Secret Service's grasp. You would have spent a generation in prison for your hacking crimes, if it wasn't for my dad. Remember that!"

"I am appreciative beyond your imagination for your father's efforts to rid me of the hacking charges the government leveled against me. I am here for you," Max feigned. Internally, Max thought, "Your father killed my parents. I know what I must do. Your existence on this earth is measured in days, not years."

"Max, do you know anything about *directed-energy weapons?*"

"Not sure about how they are constructed, but I know they exist and have been used by different governments, and most recently by some Antifa groups around the country to wreak havoc at protests," Max responded. "In fact, the small lasers that the Antifa crowd bring to their pseudo protests are used to blind the cops. Smaller version, but similar technology, I think."

"I am not thinking of small lasers. There is a new generation of developed weaponry that has, as a unique feature, the ability to target individuals with a highly focused energy source, a laser-like weapon, but with more sophisticated capability. The military has been using larger applications to destroy military equipment. Our Cuban friends have been using smaller versions of the weapon to target U.S. embassy personnel in Cuba and screw around with U.S. diplomats' brains. From what I've read the injury is called the *Havana Syndrome*." Belov said. "That's what I want to explore."

"I am aware of the news reports in Cuba. It seems that use of directed microwaves can screw up the way a person thinks, make them crazy, suicidal even. It is serious shit," responded Max.

Belov replied, "Yes, before Markov screwed up, I had him communicate with our Cuban brothers to see what, if anything, they can help us deploy. It was the last successful mission Markov accomplished before he headed back to Guatemala. I want to use the technology discreetly against Strain's people at the Staten Island Coast Guard complex. I want to send a message that Bratva can still muster an attack. I like the idea that I can cause them a slow, mentally challenged life, and perhaps hasten their death, sending Strain a message that he cannot escape Bratva. I admit they have, so far, defeated my attempts to kill them. I am not satisfied that we only harmed their family members. I want to begin to plan an attack setting up an orchestrated scenario first against Cassell, then against Strain. I will get back to you with my additional thoughts on this soon. I will have our Cuban friends work on the directed energy weapon. You do not have to be part of that."

Max departed Belov's apartment and headed home. "This guy is losing it," he thought. "*Directed Energy* as a weapon, really? Wouldn't it be easier to just blow them up, shoot them, or even poison them? Like crazy Putin does to his foes!"

CHAPTER 110

"CAPTAIN STRAIN, THIS is Max, I need an opportunity to talk with you about Belov's next move. It is crazy and dangerous. Sir, it might be best if we met in person."

"Max, how are you? Of course, I can meet with you," Strain assured him. "I am currently in Washington, D.C. at Coast Guard Headquarters."

"Sir, as you know Belov lost a dozen of his loyalists in recent failed events: Annapolis, Florida Keys, and Guatemala. With the lack of trusted lackeys, he has chosen me to be his new aide-de-camp. It was more out of desperation than any allegiance to me. He trusts me and wants to use my cyber skills to serve his needs. I have accepted his request so I can be of value to the memory of my mom and dad. Truth be told, I want to get him in a proverbial "arm lock." I want to use my proximity to put him in a place where he will have to capitulate. I can do that with your help, Captain Strain," Max stated. "I only wish I had been privy earlier to Belov's attempts to abduct Mr. Cassell's daughter and your wife, so that I could have helped prevent the incidents. It was fortunate that I happened to learn of the Annapolis event in time to prevent that from happening in a bad way."

"Don't blame yourself for anything. We appreciate what you were able to provide, Max. Without his former trusted aides to do his bidding, I suspect he will now operate the Bratva organization through a periscope. It'll limit his operational ability and will cause him to make mistakes.

He needs someone like you to enhance his perspective, and become his eyes and ears," Strain replied.

"Thank you, Captain. I can drive down there and be there in five hours," responded Max.

"No, Max. I will get on a plane and meet you at the JFK Airport later today if that works for you," Strain advised.

"Wow, sir, that really makes it easy for me," Max replied, "Belov needs to be countered and soon. I have some of Belov's future plans I can share with you at JFK."

"Having someone like you supporting the intelligence community is a godsend, Max, I will see you soon. Let me double check the logistics, and then I will send you my arrival time and location."

CHAPTER 111

"CAPTAIN STRAIN, I have Assistant Commandant Keegan and Director Cassell on the call," Lt. Riera reported.

"Thank you, Savannah," Strain replied.

"Gentlemen, thank you for taking my call. I just got off the phone with Max, our super-hacker savant. I will be heading up to JFK in a few minutes to debrief him. He has somehow managed to land a position serving Belov as a trusted aide. He is offering to share with us Belov's current intimate thinking," Strain stated.

"For something like this to come full circle is just short of spooky," Cassell interjected, referring to how Max had once been a federal defendant in a global hacking case, and was now morphing into a patriot.

"Larry and Will, you guys have suffered too much with this corrupt Bratva organization. It is time to take Belov and his remaining thugs down. Having Max on board is great news. I look forward to being briefed after Will has had the opportunity to meet with him. Will, remind me again what is Max's beef with young Belov," asked Keegan.

"The bastard's father killed Max's parents over a generation ago. The kid was raised by his grandparents, albeit with the financial support of the Bratva. He now knows that the Bratva was responsible for the deaths of his parents," Strain added. "The money used to support his upbringing was Bratva blood money. He hates the Bratva."

"Roger that. I guess that's more than enough motivation for him to work with us. Wish you a safe trip," Keegan added.

"Yes, I look forward to getting his help. His assistance to bring down this asshole excites me more than you can imagine. Or second thoght, you can imagine! Good luck!" Cassell added.

CHAPTER 112

"JFK, THIS IS N143CJ," relayed the Coast Guard Commander, flying an approach into the airport."

"We have you, Coast Guard 143, and you are clear to land on runway 31L," the JFK Tower;" acknowledged. "Upon wheels-down, proceed to PA Building 269 at will."

"This is 143, understood, JFK Tower," the pilot responded.

With wheels-down, the Coast Guard executive jet pulled off the runway and taxied to the rear lot of the Port Authority Police building. Strain sat in the jump seat behind the two pilots for the entire flight. Strain observed Max standing next to a Port Authority Police uniformed officer as the aircraft maneuvered to the rear of Building 269. As the jet came to a halt, the ground crew chalked the wheels, and the co-pilot left his seat. He moved to open the door and lowered the steps to the tarmac. Strain briskly disembarked.

Normally, such an arrival was the province of an international potentate. Today, the honor of such a private arrival was to support Captain Will Strain, United States Coast Guard. "Sir, parking our plane here is quite convenient," the co-pilot said to Strain.

"Yes, the Port Authority Police have always treated the Coast Guard as a sister agency," Strain replied. "I don't envision my meeting this afternoon will take more than an hour. So, we could have a wheels-up rather soon. I will keep you guys informed." Strain released his seat belt and followed the co-pilot to the exit door. The ground crew stood by to offer a hand, but none was necessary. Strain had no baggage. Strain eyed Max and acknowledged him with a wave.

"Max, great to see you again," Strain said. Max was standing next to a uniformed Port Authority Officer.

"Captain Strain, it is great to see you as well," Max replied.

Then the officer spoke up. "Sir, I am Officer Phil Lamonaco. I will be escorting you both to an interview room inside our building."

"Hello Phil, great to meet you," Strain reached for his hand to shake.

"You're not related to the New Jersey State Trooper, Phil Lamonaco, are you?" asked Strain.

"Yes Captain, he was my uncle. His son, my cousin, is now with the State Police. It's been over forty years since he was murdered," Lamonaco advised. "He remains a legend within the agency."

"I've read about him. He was one brave trooper. I appreciate your assistance today, and your service as well," Strain replied.

"Our pleasure, Captain, I have several relatives in the Coast Guard. They would never forgive me if I didn't do the right thing for you guys. Follow me and I will get you situated in our building." Lamonaco led the two men to a private office. As Strain looked about, he thought, "I am sure this space could speak volumes about suspects who saw the JFK Airport as a place to break the law and later confessed to their deeds.".

"It still does, Captain," Lamonaco winked and then left the two alone in the room.

"So, Max, I am eager to know what it is that brought us together."

"Captain Strain, Belov has asked me to research Mr. Cassell's daily routine. I believe he is interested in orchestrating a confrontation to personally kill him. Belov is a wounded animal. He knows each previously planned attack against the Cassell family and yours has failed. He laments the fact that he has lost so many inner circle loyalists, and he is looking for some way to save face within the Bratva organization. There is much talk about him being a failed leader, and he senses it. He sees the answer to those questioning his leadership is a quick success," Max related. "First with Mr. Cassell and then you."

"Max, I am grateful for your trust and confidence. This information will no doubt save lives. We can feed you information about Director Cassell's future routine activities that you can pass to Belov for him to prepare an attack, but it'll be in our backyard, and it will be designed to draw him out of his fortified compound. With your help, Max, we will create a scenario that allows us to take him down before he wreaks havoc on more innocent people," Strain suggested. "I agree with you, he's a wounded animal."

"Yes, sir, I can weave any information you provide into my reporting that will look legit to him. I will send you what I develop on Mr. Cassell prior to sharing it with Belov. This may give you an opportunity to have it redacted or modified. Trust me, when I do a deep dive, it is a wide search of the Internet," Max responded.

"Man, I am so glad you are assisting us. That would be outstanding. I believe this will be an opportunity for us to encounter Belov on our terms. I look forward to what you prepare. My wife, by the way, continues to send her best regards to you," Strain said.

"Captain Strain, I am aware what the Belov's men did to your wife. Belov brags about it. I am sorry for that and please express to your wife my sentiments. Those involved met their demise, and I suspect you were involved in that success. "I wish I had known his plans to attack your wife so that I could have warned you sooner. I did not know what his grand plan was. Now, Captain, I am in a better position. When I get his plans, I will make sure you get them."

"Thank you, Max," Strain replied, appreciating the young man's comments.

"Captain, there is something else. I've been hacking into Belov's email accounts. He uses several accounts, mostly for command-and-control purposes, to direct his Bratva operatives. There's one topic with which I am not knowledgeable. He refers to something he has researched and may have financially supported as a *directed-energy* weapon. When I talked to him recently, he mentioned that he was going to target a Staten Island location. He seems to express glee at having the weapon to use. He has tasked some Bratva operatives who have used them in the past, I believe in Cuba. Again, if I develop any more about it, I will get it to you," Max added.

"Yes Max, I would be very interested in that information. I will investigate the matter. *Directed-energy* weapons can be quite devastating," Strain replied.

Strain alerted Officer Lamonaco that the meeting was over.

"Sir, I can escort you to the tarmac if are ready. The pilots have not left the cockpit and are ready to depart," Lamonaco advised.

"Yes, I am ready," Strain replied, then turned to Max. "Max, I look forward to hearing from you soon. Please let me know if you need anything. We are here to support you."

"Thank you, Captain, and please give your wife my best regards," Max replied as he welled up.

The Coast Guard jet received a priority JFK wheels-up. Strain was back at Joint Base Andrews within the hour. Assistant Commandant Keegan sent Garcia to pick him up.

The U.S. Coast Guard jet glided to a smooth arrival at the airbase.

"Welcome back, sir. Do you have any bags," asked Garcia. The boss told me to advise you he will meet you in his office upon your return to HQ. He's been in meetings with the Commandant all morning and early afternoon on budget requirements to support the new acquisition of a second generation of its National Security Cutter."

"I know the cutter well, Garcia. The white-hull patrol cutter represents the most technologically sophisticated vessel in the Coast Guard. In our operational role this vessel will be an invaluable asset for the Coast Guard Intelligence Directorate. Thanks for the ride," Strain replied. "I have a lot to tell the boss."

CHAPTER 113

STRAIN'S PERSONAL PHONE alerted as he sat in his Coast Guard Headquarters office. "Hello," he answered.

"Hi honey, how are you?" Carly asked.

"Hey princess, I'm fine. Great to hear your voice. I am back at Headquarters waiting to meet with the Assistant Commandant. How is everything going up in Maine?" Strain asked.

"Will, Mary Logue has been terrific. Her place up here is spectacular. A bit chillier than Ocean Reef, I might add, sweater weather," chuckled Carly. "But for me emotionally, it's been a win-win opportunity. I should be returning home in two days. Will you be in D.C. or Miami?"

"I will be wherever you are," Strain answered quickly. "We've been busy with some recent intelligence received from a variety of sources about Bratva's next moves. If you could meet me in D.C., I could then accompany you back to Miami. By the way, Max has been a wealth of information for us. I remember you telling me when we returned from the Kuwaiti presidential trip that Max may turn out to be an honorable guy once all this Bratva bullshit plays out. Turns out your instincts proved correct."

"That's great to hear, Will. I really like him."

"Carly, when I met the kid at the Atkau airport in anticipation of the transfer of the abducted C-5 hostages, I knew he was someone different than the person that you had arrested as a super-hacker. There was something that indicated a personal disdain for the Bratva. Now, we know. The mob brutally killed his parents while he was only an infant, then arrogantly raised him through his grandparents. The Bratva betrayed him his entire life. Fortunately, he grew up to be a strong, smart man, and harbored a suspicion toward the mob. That suspicion has turned out to be a charm for us," said Will. Carly knew the story.

"How have you been staying in touch with him?" Carly asked.

"I've been texting with him regularly since the day we left him at the Buzzard Point landing zone. You remember, you made a comment about how happy Max was to have his buddy, Shorty, and his dog, Torre, there to meet him. You marveled at how cute it appeared that Shorty and Torre were competing for Max's attention," Will recounted. "Remember?"

"Yes, it's been about nine months since that day," Carly recollected. "So, Max has been an insider all this time? Unfortunately, he wasn't privy to all that Belov planned in the recent past, or else he would have given you a heads-up, I'm thinking," Carly said.

"Carly, I am being called in to see the boss, I will call you back soon."

CHAPTER 114

"WILL, I HAVE some time available now. Why don't you brief me about your meeting with Max before you leave for the day? I can update you on the latest developments to our National Security Cutter program, too," Keegan offered.

"Roger that, sir," Strain replied. "I will be there in five."

From his headquarters' office kitchenette, Keegan made himself a cup of coffee as Strain walked in. "Hello, Will, would you like a cup of coffee?"

"No thank you, sir, I am 'coffeed' out today, had multiple cups on my way up and back from seeing Max at JFK," replied Strain.

"Tell me about Max."

"Sir, we had a great meeting. As I told you, he's been tapped by Belov to be his new aide-de-camp. Belov has apparently run out of confidants. Max reports that he's working to supply Belov with an information package, providing him with misleading, but seemingly relevant data on Director Cassell's daily routine. With the information Max reports, Belov will hatch a plan to attack Director Cassell, another one of Belov's moves to retaliate and seek revenge. I briefed Director Cassell while en route back here, and he is eager to participate in any plan to interdict Belov. I will remain in close contact with Max as he learns more of Belov's intentions," Strain added.

"We are lucky to have Max in place," said Keegan.

"There is another interesting facet of the Max debriefing, sir. Max relayed that Belov is also thinking about using *directed energy weapons* against the Coast Guard. He mentioned Belov wanted to target a Staten Island location which, of course, means Sector New York. Max said that Belov would use his operatives who are familiar with what has been reported to have occurred at the U.S. Embassy in Cuba."

"Did he note any timeline for something like that to occur?" Keegan asked.

"He had no other notion about it and admitted that he didn't know a lot about that type of weaponry," Strain advised. "He's just a super hacker and mixed martial artist champion. I guess we can't expect him to know it all," Strain chuckled.

Keegan's secure phone alerted to an incoming call from the duty desk.

"Excuse me, Will. This is Keegan" he answered. "Stand by, I have Captain Strain here in my office. I will be putting you on speaker. Go again with your notification Lieutenant."

"Sir, we have received a report about suspected d*irected-energy* attacks involving Coast Guard personnel at Sector New York," Lt. Riera reported. "The exact number of victims is still being assessed, but at least a dozen of our people has been receiving medical attention. They have developed flu-like symptoms, and it isn't Covid. There is no further information currently, sir."

"Thank you, Lieutenant. Captain Strain and I will follow up on it with the Office of the Commandant. Please keep us updated."

"Yes, sir."

"Will, I suspect you'll be working the phones. Let me know what's going on as the day progresses. Any information you develop I will relay to the DNI later tonight," Keegan added. "I will have to brief you later on the National Security Cutters."

CHAPTER 115

"WE DON'T KNOW exactly where the weapon's platform is located, but our guys are engaged in a wide area perimeter search," Strain added.

"It's one thing to have this reported as attacks in the Middle East Theater, or in Cuba against an American embassy, but against us by a Russian sponsored criminal organization obviously raises serious issues," Keegan offered. "Will, has this specific information been reported to the Pentagon, and to the Office of the Director of National Intelligence?"

"Yes sir. Directorate's duty desk officer transmitted the details to the Pentagon's *Office of Special Operations and Low-intensity Conflict Section*," Strain declared. "They've been advised."

"Because it is a domestic threat, I will work with the DNI's office to ensure Coast Guard Intelligence takes the lead to coordinate the New York investigation. And that means for you to drop whatever you have going on and handle this. I trust you more than anyone in this organization. If it leads to the Bratva using these weapons domestically as your Max confirms, then Belov is going to have a much shorter tenure at the Bratva helm than he planned."

"Got it, sir, I will get working on staffing immediately. Our representative to the FBI's Joint Terrorism Task Force (JTTF) in New York is reporting the attack. The task force offers a plethora of assets from participating agencies, particularly the NYPD," Strain admitted.

I know the CIA has its own task force for d*irected- energy* weapons, but its focus is international. Notifying the JTTF will ensure that everyone gets the information."

"Okay, Will, just please keep me advised at any hour of the day."

"Roger that, sir!"

CHAPTER 116

TWO HOURS LATER, Strain received a call.

"This is Captain Strain."

"Sir, this is Lieutenant Savannah Riera. I have an update on Sector New York. We have more information regarding the attack on our guys in New York. Unfortunately, additional symptoms are being reported and are more egregious than first known. The number of those affected are reported to be two dozen. They are experiencing ringing in the ears, loss of balance, and headaches, some severe. They are all receiving medical treatment at this time," advised the duty desk lieutenant.

"Thank you, Savannah. Please notify the Office of the Assistant Commandant with this update."

Within a short moment Strain's phone alerted again.

"This is Strain."

"Will, this is Keegan. I just received the duty desk update from Lieutenant Riera. This is more serious than we originally learned. Do you have any information on what type and size of weapon being used?"

"Sir, I've been working the phones and just learned that all affected persons worked in proximity to the Anchor Place Boat Yard, where we maintain the Sector's vessels. "We have removed all of our people from the location and secured the perimeter."

"Do the experts think the weapons are operated from a static position in a building, or are they mobile, that is, contained in a large vehicle like a van that moves about?" Keegan asked.

"The initial forensics suggests that threat emanates from a vehicle parked in proximity to Anchor Place and equipped with an interior weapon. We know that even a small weapon can deliver highly concentrated electromagnetic energy toward a target to cause harm. It appears the weapon used is sufficient to cause severe pain, possibly permanent injury," Strain explained. "So, if that is the case, and unlike the *Havana Syndrome* event where the Cubans, and possibly the Russians, targeted our embassy from a static location, the initial indication is that it appears to be a vehicular attack. In the past hour we have requested surveillance video be retrieved from our Sector's digital cameras and reviewed. We are also seeking to obtain video that may have been captured from the contiguous community within a quarter-mile radius. Should we be able to identify a suspect vehicle, as well as its license plate, we may be able to trace the vehicle's prior movement. That may be possible because the NYPD maintains a robust license plate reader surveillance program. Once an image of the suspect license plate is captured, the NYPD can determine if the vehicle transited through any one of the city's tunnels or bridges," Strain replied.

"That's impressive, Will, I know you're busy so I will let you continue to develop the investigation. I look forward to hearing more as we move forward," Keegan commented. "By the way, with all that is going on, I haven't forgotten to update you on the latest with the National Security Cutters. I will do that when this current crisis subsides."

Later that night Keegan was home reviewing the USCG intelligence draft report to be sent to the DNI. It was almost midnight. The original discussion was to describe the upgrades to the *National Security Cutters*. He added the latest information he had on the *directed-energy weapons* threat. As one of the seventeen intelligence Directorates that contribute to a daily presidential brief, Keegan's words were concise and accurate. Keegan knew the d*irected-energy* weapon's assault would dwarf most of the other agency reporting. "I wish I had better information for him," Keegan thought, "or something more conclusive."

The secure phone at his residence alerted. "This is Keegan."

"Sir, Captain Strain here. We have identified a suspicious Enterprise rental van and provided the NYPD, through the Joint Terrorism Task Force, with the license plate number. We have video that shows the van in proximity to the Anchor Place Boat Yard on numerous occasions. Other community videos reviewed depict the van's travel as it approached our Sector, establishing important time and date information. Cameras supporting the Verrazano Bridge have been most useful. The NYPD has tracked the van traveling to and from Staten Island and have even managed to determine that it exited the Belt Parkway into Brighton Beach. They are currently exploring video from cameras located in that area that may reveal a specific location. We should know more by tomorrow morning.

"Will that is great news, great, great news. If nothing else, it allows us to prevent this vehicle from entering our New York Sector. Having said that, our Sector is so porous we may have to consider a recommendation to extend the secure perimeter. I know that is not something the local community will want, but like other venues, the threat supports added features to reduce vulnerabilities. We can add that to the after-action report. Thanks, Will, and any update on our personnel?"

"Sir, their conditions range from those released after being treated, to those admitted to the local hospital for observation," Strain advised.

"Thank you, Will," Keegan said quietly. "Talk in the morning."

Keegan re-tooled his report for the Presidential brief and sent it off.

CHAPTER 117

MAX DIALED CAPTAIN Strain's private cell phone. "Captain Strain, this is Max, do you have a few minutes?"

"Hello, Max. Of course, I do," Strain responded.

"Sir, recently Belov gave me a tour of the extensive fortifications he and his father have developed, or should I say, implemented within, around, and below his residence over the years, and they're impressive. The Bratva owns most of the condos and apartments adjacent to Belov's primary residence. Many are connected with hidden passageways to be used as escape modules in the event the location is raided by law enforcement," Max related.

"Max, that is extremely helpful information. One day soon, Belov will expect such an event," Strain replied.

"I have prepared computer assisted drawings of the layout. They demonstrate all the ingress and egress points that support Belov's residence. I emailed them to you just now," Max informed Strain. "Sir, the location would leave a Mexican Cartel reeling in envy. The extensive tunneling Belov and his father established as escape routes are sophisticated and well equipped. The escape routes feature multiple options. For example, if you enter the tunnel in one direction, another tunnel egress point becomes available within twenty feet leading ninety degrees into another tunnel. All ingress and egress points are cleverly disguised. Belov can enter his maze and escape into his neighborhood blocks away from numerous points," Max promoted. "It's beyond impressive."

"Max, these drawings are invaluable. I will print them out," Strain observed. "This labyrinth has had to have taken years to complete, and the idea that it has remained secret is most impressive," Strain commented. "I am surprised that local and federal law enforcement are not aware of its existence. On second thought, perhaps they are."

"Max, does Belov have the tunnel system laced with weapons or explosives?"

"Yes sir, Belov's father was paranoid about being caught inside the residence. It was not so much law enforcement that he feared, but his own people. He was almost Stalin-like in his distrust of some of the Bratva elite around the globe. He was insistent that the residence allow for him and his closest associates to re-locate undetected several city blocks from the residence," Max advised. "As far as weapons availability within the maze, the elder Belov always fancied the Israeli nine-millimeter UZI sub machine gun, which he has pre-positioned throughout the escape routes. As a Jew, Belov felt an allegiance to the weapon. It's a legacy weapon that helped the Israeli military and police defend the country. The UZI was battle tested. It survived every physical abuse it encountered. He joked that the UZI was an ugly weapon but became pretty when it was needed in battle to kill the enemy, as the younger Belov explained to me. So, the entire underground complex has UZIs deployed discreetly, hidden every fifty feet throughout the tunnel complex, usually in storage closets not much bigger than a home medicine cabinet. Each UZI is ready to use; and several additional magazines containing thirty rounds each were also stored. I don't know of any explosives," explained Max.

"How is it you came privy to the tunnel?" Strain asked.

"Belov took me for a tour yesterday. I created the drawing from memory, and then developed computer assisted diagrams on my laptop.

To answer your question, he explained that it was time for me to know. I had just provided him with the background data I developed on Larry Cassell, the same information that your people screened. He reviewed it in front of me, and his mind immediately came up with a plan to kill Mr. Cassell. He saw that Mr. Cassell's daily routine involves a daily jog in a New Jersey suburb, not far from the Garden State Parkway. He told me he would get back to me with a plan to encounter him," Max relayed. "I think his trust in me has accelerated since I am his only confidant these days."

"Max, this is great intelligence. I look forward to learning his final plan. It's interesting he is thinking of taking out Mr. Cassell in his hometown. Please stay in touch. We need you, Max."

CHAPTER 118

"SIR, WE HAVE located the van not far from Belov's Brighton Beach residence, or for a better description, his personal secure enclave. It was just sitting there on a side street. Pretty sloppy for Belov and his operators, if you ask me. Our investigators obtained a warrant to seize the van and transport it to JFK where the Joint Terrorism Task Force has a multi-purpose hangar. It'll be forensically examined there. It has generated much interest within the Intelligence Directorate community," Strain reported to Keegan. "Somehow, the New York Post got wind of the story. They agreed to keep the story quiet until the investigation concluded."

"Will, that's interesting, just today the New York Times reported similar stories against our diplomats, and even some military, who have suffered brain damage and other injuries as a result of suspected *directed-energy* attacks," Keegan advised. "The reporting didn't mention us. The reporting suggests, however, that an intelligence official may have wet their whistle. As we noted prior, up until now these attacks have occurred solely in China and Cuba. Whoever shared the information with the media is not helpful."

"Sir, a forensic review of the van should yield some good clues, but what we already know is the van had been physically altered. For example, the van's sliding door had been replaced with a replica door composed of fiberglass. This will allow the weapon's wave propagation a more conducive path to propel its concentrated energy toward targets, in this case, our people," Strain reported. "There is no doubt who provided the Bratva with this technology."

"Captain, I agree. The Bratva is just an extension of the Putin regime, and the Russians have elected to attack us in our homeland using the Bratva thugs. That's a big leap from Cuba," Keegan assessed. "Let me know if the van yields additional investigative leads."

"Will do, and Max reported that he has developed a Cassell social media profile for Belov that includes Cassell's daily workout routine. He allowed us to edit it before he presented it to Belov. Belov will use it to figure out where he can target Cassell. We have been working in tandem with the Secret Service on this, too," Strain advised.

"Is Director Cassell still considering the idea that he be used as the bait to suck Belov into a snare?

"Yes, he's determined to do so. He wants to help bring the mastermind behind his daughter's horrible abduction to justice. He wants to be there in person when it happens."

"I can understand that, Will, but he may be a bit old to be part of the scenario. Reaction time is critical to a special operative; you should know that," Keegan suggested.

"Sir, respectfully I don't think it is my place to tell him. What I do know is getting Belov out in public to engage him is better than confronting him in his fortress."

CHAPTER 119

"BASED ON MAX'S reporting we have learned that Belov intends to travel to Cranford, New Jersey's varsity baseball field, located on the south side of town, next to the town's football field, tomorrow morning. He is aware that former Secret Service Director Cassell jogs there each morning at 0630," Strain relayed to Keegan. "Max has provided us with Belov's intention to be armed with a four-inch folding knife, and a small Sig Sauer 365 strapped to his left ankle. Belov told Max he wants to kill Cassell with the knife to make a Bratva statement, and to cause him as much pain as possible before gouging out his eyeballs. Max said that Belov will be dropped off on the Garden State Parkway southbound at a location less than fifty yards from the baseball field where Director Cassell jogs."

"Will, I know Director Cassell is still healthy, and in good physical condition, but again, is he really the right person, or should we use a decoy?" asked Keegan.

"Director Cassell insists on being involved as a live target for Belov. He feels that to be present on the baseball field will add to Belov's heightened emotion. The circumference around the baseball field is a quarter of a mile. Cassell's customary practice is to jog around it for three miles. After his jog, his practice is to head over to the pull-up bars to do his age defying fifteen pull-ups, an exercise that dwarfs his forty push-ups. We have come up with a tactical plan to observe and respond, using three Secret Service counter-sniper teams," Strain added.

"How did you pull that off?" Keegan asked.

"Not hard. The Secret Service has a vested interest," Strain said.

"No, I mean, how is it you're able to use Secret Service counter-sniper teams? Seems to me that they are only deployed for protective events," Keegan said.

"Realistically, they are among the best shooters in the Nation. One of them is a female, Frances Larkin, Frank Larkin's kid sister," Strain advised.

"She works for the Secret Service?" asked Keegan.

"Yes, she has been a counter-sniper for the past two years. If you recall, Belov killed her brother in Saudi Arabia."

CHAPTER 120

A SMALL CADRE of serious law enforcement officials gathered at the Cranford, New Jersey, municipal building, occupying the room normally reserved for courtroom proceedings. The court was not in session.

"Let's have everyone's attention," Chief Ryan Greco bellowed out. "We will begin the briefing for tomorrow's tactical event. Present in the room along with members of the Cranford, N.J. Police Department, are representatives from the New Jersey State Police, U.S. Secret Service, and U.S. Coast Guard Intelligence and Investigations agents. The FBI sent a Joint Terrorism Task Force Member, DEA agent, Mike Cavalla, another local boy from Cranford who knew the area. Larry Cassell stood in the back of the room with Captain Strain.

"Everyone I would like to introduce Captain William Strain, United States Coast Guard. He will explain in detail the morning event and how it is expected to unfold. Captain?" Chief Greco backed off the microphone, deferring to Strain. Strain approached the podium.

"Good evening, everyone, and thank you for being here in support of a law enforcement effort to take an extremely dangerous person off the street. As a matter of background, we are targeting the current chieftain of the Russian mob, also known as the Bratva, an international criminal enterprise, whose global leadership operates out of Brighton Beach, New York. They have a presence in most of Latin and South America, as well as Eastern Europe. They are involved in almost all aspects of criminality: drugs, human trafficking, gambling, extortion and cybercrime, to mention a few. Tomorrow's operation is to intercept the leader of the Bratva. Information we have indicates the mob leader plans to kill several people he believes are responsible for the death of his father, the previous Bratva leader. Our target's name is Vladimir Belov. Early tomorrow morning, before dawn, we will deploy various tactical units to the Cranford varsity baseball field, adjacent to the town's football/track field. Our intelligence indicates that Belov will be dropped off on the southbound side of the Garden State Parkway in proximity to the sports fields I just cited. He is expected to move to the varsity baseball field to observe his intended victim jogging around the baseball field. Belov will be armed, and his intent will be to kill. We will not let that happen. We will have three sniper teams deployed in and around the varsity baseball field. Jogging on the synthetic turf field is a normal routine Belov knows the target to perform daily. The Secret Service snipers will assume triangulated positions: the announcer's tower at the varsity field, on top of the roof of the indoor swimming pool, and on top of the Concession structure. Additionally, we will have at the ready representatives from Cranford Police and members from all the agencies present here. Representatives will be located, and respond from, the dugout under the announcing booth behind a curtain, the pool facility building, and the adjacent baseball field's dugout. We will operate on one frequency. The Secret Service will distribute handheld radio units to all participants. The victim will be wired up for communication and will have his own personal weapon. For those of you who do not yet know who the intended victim is, allow me to introduce him. He is the recently retired Director of the Secret Service, Larry Cassell. Director Cassell is in the back of the room, and I would encourage all of you to say hello to him as we break from the briefing. Our intelligence indicates Belov will arrive sometime between 0630-0700 hours. We will have advance notice of his departure from Brighton Beach. As I indicated, he intends to exit a vehicle from the Garden State Parkway southbound less than fifty yards from the varsity field and work his way toward an ostensibly unsuspecting victim in order to slaughter him with his knife. That won't happen. We will do what we have to do to take him into custody, but should he become violent our folks will prevent him from doing harm to anyone. I thank you for your participation and look forward to seeing you at the field in the morning. Chief Greco, I turn it back to you."

"Thank you, Captain, and thank you, Director Cassell, for your participation."

CHAPTER 121

AT 0500 HOURS, the Cranford response group deployed as planned. Secret Service Uniformed Division Sniper Technician Frances Larkin established her position on top of the announcer's tower along the field's third base line. Her position allowed her and her spotter to neutralize any threat within one hundred yards. She was certified up to a thousand yards. At 0630 hours, her position would not be detectable. Her fellow teammates, another sniper, and his dedicated spotter, deployed to the indoor swimming pool roof, and a third team on top of the concession stand located equidistant between the other two positions. From the three vantage points, the entire field was covered.

The Secret Service provided a common radio link, issuing the Cranford Police, the Coast Guard operatives, and the State Police individual portable radios and earpieces, operating on Charlie frequency. The Secret Service New York Field Office monitored the transmissions and was the designated operations command post. The Cranford Police Department dispatch was provided with an encrypted radio to monitor the event, as was the Cranford Fire Department's ambulance crew, positioned at a nearby school lot to respond to the field if necessary.

At 6:10 am, Strain's phone alerted him to an incoming call. "Captain Strain, this is Max. Belov has exited his residence. We should be there in half an hour. I will call when he exits the car on the parkway."

"Thank you, Max." Strain advised all on the Secret Service network of the departure.

Larry Cassell arrived, as he did every day, at 6:30am for his daily jog. The early November weather had him wearing a light-colored sweatshirt and pants suit. It served to cover a radio and sidearm, both of which he wore on his belt. Bluetooth allowed him to rely on a wireless earpiece for communication. The frequency used was encrypted, but the field office could still record all transmissions.

Now they waited.

At 6:40 am, Strain's phone alerted to an incoming call. "Captain Strain, this is Max again. Belov just exited the car on the Parkway. He is approaching the baseball field."

"Thank you, Max, I will meet you later at the Cranford Police Department," Strain replied.

"I will be there; good luck."

"Be advised Belov is en route the field," Strain radioed to all participating personnel.

"I have an eyeball on him," responded Cassell, discreetly ignoring the point of Belov's penetration.

As Belov approached the field, he realized that he didn't have to breach the fence. There was an opening. He stopped to gaze across the field. He saw a lone jogger on the baseball field slowly rounding first base. "I've got to time this, so I don't spook him; I want to get within striking distance," Belov thought. "As he rounds the field again, I will enter through the fence from a thirty-foot distance and take him from behind."

"Cassell from Strain, it appears he has stopped to observe your activity. Looks like he is gauging his opportunity to encounter you."

"I've got him," Cassell responded. "Looks I will be passing him, and he will try to attack from behind."

"Here he comes, about to enter through the fence," Strain radioed. Each baseball field had live camera coverage. The Cranford Police disabled the live streaming normally available to the public. However, live coverage remained available for Strain to observe from a monitor placed in the camouflaged dugout.

Belov saw his opportunity. He calculated his move to encounter Cassell as he came around left field, heading home. Belov remained concealed, finally coming out to the outfield's synthetic turf field less than thirty feet behind his target. Cassell stopped and turned as Belov closed the distance. Cassell observed a large knife being snapped into position and recognizing the threat, he slowly walked backwards. He did not reach for his weapon but kept his gaze as Belov's approach shortened the distance between them.

Belov screamed manically at Cassell. "Now you are mine, you piece of shit. You killed my father, and now I am going to cut you up. I will leave your head on the ground for the Turkey Buzzards to feast upon."

Cassell held his ground and showed no fear. As long as Belov was more than twenty feet away, he felt confident he could draw his weapon and stop him. As much as he wanted to inflict pain upon the Bratva chieftain, he knew he had to control his emotions. He thought about Dorothy, and what Belov's order to violate her meant. He grew angry, but cautioned himself, "Take a deep breath." He knew the Secret Service snipers were in place and were prepared to take action if Belov accelerated his approach with the knife. Belov shortened the distance, now within twenty feet of Cassell, still holding his knife over his head. Cassell stopped his retreat and reached for his sidearm. As he removed the weapon from its holster, he heard a single report from Frances Larkin's JAR, (*just another rifle*). Cassell observed Belov drop to the ground. The JAR's round entered Belov's chest exactly where Larkin aimed. Larkin exhaled and prepared for another shot. It wasn't necessary. "Point of aim, point of impact. That was for my brother, asshole" Larkin said to herself.

Belov dropped to the turf; his knife once tightly gripped in his hand, fell to the ground. Belov was no longer a threat. Cassell secured his weapon as he bent down to check Belov's pulse. The dugout emptied out, as Strain and the others hustled out to left field. They slowed as they neared. No need for attempted resuscitation. The Bratva thug was dead. No one had an appetite to revive him.

"Revenge is achieved. This man was responsible for a lot of evil, and now he is no longer able to hurt more," Cassell said to Strain.

"He's responsible for hurting your daughter, my wife, and those GW students and their professor in Guatemala. His death is justice. I believe the shot came from the Secret Service counter sniper, Frances Larkin. How symbolic. God bless her, and her brother's memory. I can't thank the Secret Service enough for providing the support," Strain said.

"I will have my officers secure the scene and wait for the Union County Medical Examiner's Office to respond to take custody of the body," Chief Greco said.

"Chief, your department responded on short notice to assist us today. What a testament to the Cranford Police Department. Thank you," Strain replied. "The Coast Guard will always be there for you."

"Headquarters from car one, advise the Fire Department's ambulance that the subject is dead at the scene, no need to respond," Greco radioed. "Also, contact Union County Prosecutor's Office and let them know we have a fatality here on the baseball field; request that the Medical Examiner's office to respond to the scene."

"10-4, Chief," responded Sergeant Tommy Fenney. "Nice job out there, Chief." That's one way for the good guys, revenge is sweet," he thought, not wanting to put his comments over the Cranford radio frequency.

Fenney sat back in his duty desk chair and smiled. He thought, "this is a good time to retire."

ABOUT THE AUTHOR

Mr. Sloan served more than twenty-five years as a special agent with the Secret Service. During his career, he held numerous positions of increasing responsibility as agent-in-charge of the Baltimore Field Office where he oversaw complex financial crimes investigations. Prior to that, he was agent-in-charge of the Major Events Division where he managed security systems for the U.S. government's designated national special security events ("NSSE"). He remains an active member with the Secret Service's NY/NJ Electronic Crimes Task Force. Upon retirement, he served as a senior security manager with the New York Stock Exchange and Western Union International, responsible for implementing company-wide security processes. Mr. Sloan has authored two books: Bratvas Rose Tattoo and Guardians of Democracy.